Fall of Night

THE MORGANVILLE VAMPIRES NOVELS

THE
MORGANVILLE
VAMPIRES

Fall of Night

Rachel Caine

 NEW AMERICAN LIBRARY

New American Library
Published by the Penguin Group
Penguin Group (USA) Inc., 375 Hudson Street,
New York, New York 10014, USA

USA | Canada | UK | Ireland | Australia | New Zealand | India | South Africa | China

Penguin Books Ltd., Registered Offices: 80 Strand, London WC2R 0RL, England
For more information about the Penguin Group visit penguin.com.

First published by New American Library,
a division of Penguin Group (USA) Inc.

First Printing, May 2013
10 9 8 7 6 5 4 3 2

REGISTERED TRADEMARK—MARCA REGISTRADA

LIBRARY OF CONGRESS CATALOGING-IN-PUBLICATION DATA

Caine, Rachel.
    Fall of night: the Morganville vampires/Rachel Caine.
        p. cm
    ISBN 978-0-451-41425-0
    1. Women graduate students—Fiction. 2. Vampires—Fiction. I. Title.
    PS3603.O557F35 2013
    813'.6—dc23   2013000648

Set in Centaur MT

Printed in the United States of America

ALWAYS LEARNING   PEARSON

With all my best to my MIT alumni contacts, especially the lovely Sarah Vega, who introduced me to Jack Florey and helped me capture some of the unique flavor of the school. Errors are all hers. No, that's wrong. I mean all mine.

This book couldn't have been possible without the love, support, and encouragement of many people, but especially Sarah Weiss, Janet Cadsawan, and NiNi Burkart. Thanks, ladies. You rock. Always.

Fall of Night

ONE

The billboard at the border of Morganville hadn't changed since Claire had first driven past it on the way into town at the tender age of sixteen. It seemed a lifetime ago, but here was the same old sign, faded and creaking in the dry desert wind. It had a 1950s-era couple (white, of course) next to a finned car as big as a boat, looking into the sunset. WELCOME TO MORGANVILLE. YOU'LL NEVER WANT TO LEAVE.

Yet here she was. Leaving. Actually *leaving*.

The weight of it felt suddenly unbearable, and the billboard dissolved into impressionistic swirls as tears formed hotly in her eyes. She was finding it hard to catch her breath. *I don't have to go*, she thought. *I can turn around, go home, go back where it's safe* . . . because as crazy and dangerous as Morganville was, at least she'd learned how to live in it. How to adapt, and survive, and even thrive. It had become, well, home. Comfortable.

Out there . . . she wasn't sure what she'd be anymore.

It's time to find out, the more adult part of her said. *You have to see the world before you can give it up to be here.* She supposed that was right. Didn't the Amish send their kids on *rumspringa* to find out what life was like outside so they could make a real decision on whether to stay in their community? So maybe she was on a kind of vampire *rumspringa.*

Because that was what she was leaving, even though she definitely was not one of the plasma-challenged: a vampire community, with almost everything in some way related to them—to protecting them, making them money, giving them blood. In turn, at least theoretically, the vampires protected the town and the people in it. That didn't always work, of course. But the surprising thing was that it *did* work more often than not. And, she thought, from the way things were settling down now, it might work lots better this time around, now that the town's Founder, Amelie, was back in charge. And sane. Sane was a plus.

"Troubled?"

The voice made Claire gasp and turn, blinking away tears, because she'd actually forgotten that he was standing there. Not Shane. She'd left early, before her boyfriend was awake; she'd actually sneaked away before dawn so that she could be off without good-byes she knew would rip her heart into pieces. Here she stood with her suitcases and her stuffed backpack, and *Myrnin.*

Her vampire boss, if you could call being a mad scientist a profession, was standing next to the big black sedan he occasionally— *very* occasionally, thankfully—drove. (He was not a good driver. Understatement.) He wasn't dressed crazily this morning, for a change. He'd left the Hawaiian shirts and floppy hats at home, and instead he looked as if he'd stepped out of an eighteenth-century drama—breeches that tucked into shiny black boots, a gold-colored satin waistcoat, a coat over it that had tails. He'd even tied his normally wild shoulder-length hair back in a sleek black ponytail.

Vampires, unlike humans, could stand perfectly still, and just now he looked like a carved statue . . . alabaster and ebony and gold.

"No, I'm not troubled," she said, aware she'd hesitated way too long before answering him. She shivered a little. Here in the desert, at night, it was icy-cold, though it would warm up nicely by midday. *I won't be here then,* she realized. But Morganville would go on without her. That seemed . . . weird.

"I am surprised you did not bring your friends to say goodbye," Myrnin offered. He sounded cautious, as if he was far from sure what the etiquette of this situation might be. "Surely it's customary that they see you off on such a journey. . . ."

"I don't care if it is," she said. A tumbleweed—a thorny, skeletal ball of nasty scratching branches—rolled toward her and she sidestepped it. It plowed into a tangle of its fellows that had piled up against the base of the billboard. "I don't want them to cry. I don't want to cry, either. I just— Look, it's hard enough, okay? Please don't."

Myrnin's shoulders lifted in a minute shrug. For the first time, as he turned his head away, she saw that he'd secured his ponytail with a big black bow. It fit what he was wearing, and it was weird that it didn't look out of place on him. *He looks like Mozart,* she thought—or at least how Mozart had been dressed in the paintings she'd seen.

"It must have been easier when people dressed like that," she said. "Being a vampire. People made their faces white with powder, didn't they? So you didn't stand out so much."

"Not just their faces," he said. "They powdered their wigs, too. One could choke on the arsenic and talcum. I can't imagine it was good for the lungs of the living, but one does what one must for fashion. At least the women weren't tottering around on five-inch heels, constantly in peril of breaking bones." He paused for a moment, then said, "What made it easier for vampires was that we lived by candlelight, lamplight—it makes everyone look healthier, even the sick. These harsh lights you favor now . . . well. Difficult. I heard that a few vampires have taken to those spray-tanning salons to get the proper skin tones."

She almost laughed at that, at the image of a badass vampire like Oliver—ferocious and fearless—standing around in a Speedo to get himself painted. But Oliver had left Morganville, too . . . now banished from Amelie's side, where he'd been ever since Claire had first come to town. That had probably been the right thing to do, but Claire felt bad for him . . . a little. He'd betrayed the Founder, but he hadn't meant it—and he hadn't had a choice.

If any vampire could survive in the human world, though, it would be Oliver. He was clever, ruthless, and mostly without a conscience. Mostly.

"You can still change your mind," Myrnin said. He was perfectly still, except for the wind ruffling his clothes and the bow on his ponytail; he didn't try to meet her eyes. "You know you don't have to leave. No one wants you to go, truly."

"I know." That was all she'd been thinking about for hours. She hadn't slept, and her whole body ached with nervous tension. "You're not the only one to tell me so." Shane, for instance. Though he'd been quiet about it, and gentle. It wasn't that she was angry with him—God, no—but she needed desperately to make sure that he trusted her as much as she trusted him. She loved him—that was what made it so, so hard to do this. She *needed* him. But he'd screwed up, big-time, in believing a big lie about her told by one of their enemies. He'd actually believed that she'd been sneaking around behind his back with his best friend, Michael.

She needed to think about how she felt about that disappointment on her own, but all she could really think right at this moment was how much she wanted to feel his warm, strong arms wrapped around her, his body shielding her from the cold. How much she wanted one more kiss, one more whisper, one more . . . everything.

"The world out there isn't like it is here," Myrnin said. "I know it hasn't been easy for you here—and I've been a significant part of your challenges, as well. But, Claire, I do know something of the world—I have been in it for hundreds of years, and although technology changes, people are little different, then or now. They are afraid, and they use that fear to excuse their own actions—whether it is theft or hatred, violence or murder. People bond themselves into families and groups for protection, and strangers . . . strangers are always at risk."

He was right. She'd come to Morganville a stranger, and she'd been at risk . . . until she'd found her group, her family, her place.

Claire took in a deep breath. She kicked sand with her sneaker and said, "Then I'll find my group there, where I'm going. You know I can do it. I did it here."

"Here, you are exceptional," he said. "There, who knows? They might not value you as much as we do."

He'd put his finger on her greatest fear—the fear of not being the best. Of being just . . . average, like everybody else. She'd always worked so hard to excel, worked at it with a passion that was close to fear; going to the Massachusetts Institute of Technology was the Holy Grail of that quest, but it also came with a double-edged risk. What if she wasn't good enough? What if everybody else was faster, better, smarter, stronger? She couldn't fail. She *couldn't.* "I'll be fine," she said, and forced a confident smile. "I can do this."

He sighed then, and shrugged. "Yes. Yes, I imagine that you can," he said. "I wish it were otherwise. I'd rather you stayed here, safe."

"Safe!" She burst out laughing, which made him give her a hurt look . . . but really, it was ridiculous. Nothing about Morganville, Texas, was truly *safe*—it took a vampire to even suggest that. "I— Never mind. Maybe being safe isn't the best thing all the time. I need to be sure who I am out there, Myrnin. I need to be *Claire* for a while, and find out who I am deep down. Not part of something else that's so much more . . . confident than I am." Or *someone* else. Because it wasn't just Shane; it was Myrnin, as well.

He looked at her directly with those warm dark eyes that seemed so human and yet, at the same time, were so very not. He'd seen so much—ages, generations, all kinds of horror and death, brilliance and beauty. And it showed. "I will miss you, Claire. You know that."

"I know," she said, and couldn't look away. She wanted to, but Myrnin's gaze held hers like a magnet. "I'll miss you, too."

He flew at her and embraced her, a sudden and awkward kind of thing; he was too strong and too fast, and it drew a startled little squeak from her as her body remembered all too well how it felt to have fangs sinking into her neck . . . but then he was gone again, stepping away, turning toward the horizon, where pink was painting the hills and scrub brush of the desert. The wind was cold and picking up speed.

"You should go," Claire said, and got control of her pounding heart somehow. "My parents are on the way. They'll be here any minute."

"A very poor escort I'd be to leave you out here in the dark, prey for anything," he said. "Highwaymen, and all that."

"Myrnin, there haven't been highwaymen in at least a hundred years. Probably more."

"Robbers, then. Serial killers. The modern bogeyman under the bed, yes? Bad men skulking in the darkness have always been there, and always will." He flashed a smile at her, which was made unsettling by the extra-long eyeteeth, but he was still glancing uneasily at the horizon. Myrnin was old; he wouldn't burst into flames with the rise of the sun, but he'd be uncomfortably scorched. "I'm sure you're familiar with the concept."

"More than a little." She sighed, and caught sight of car headlights speeding over the crest of the far hill. *Mom and Dad.* She felt a little surge of excitement, but it was quickly overwhelmed with a huge wave of sadness and longing. It felt different from what she expected, leaving Morganville . . . leaving her friends behind. Leaving *Shane.* "They're coming. You should go."

"Should I not see you off?"

"In that getup?"

Myrnin looked down at himself, baffled. "It's most elegant!"

"When you were partying down with Beethoven, maybe, but today you look like you're on your way to a fancy dress ball."

"So I ought to have worn the casual shirt with it, then?"

Claire almost smiled at the idea of one of his loud Hawaiian shirts thrown on over breeches and boots. "God, no. You look great. Just not . . . period appropriate. So go on. I'll be fine, okay?"

He looked at the car, coming fast toward them, and finally nodded. "All right," he said. "Professor Anderson will be expecting you. Don't forget, you can use the telephone to call me."

He seemed proud he'd remembered that—modern tech not being his strongest skill—and Claire struggled not to roll her eyes. "I won't forget," she said. "You'd better get in your car. Sun's coming up—I don't want you to get burned."

It was. She could see the hot gold edge of it just cresting the hill to the east, and the sky above had turned a dark indigo blue. In minutes, it'd be full daylight, and Myrnin needed to be under cover.

He nodded to her, and gave her a formal, antique bow, which looked weirdly perfect in that outfit. "Be careful," he said. "Not all dangers have a vampire's fangs. Or a vampire's predictability." He moved fast to the driver's side of his car, opened the door, and then hesitated for one second more to say, "I will miss you very much, Claire."

He slammed the door and turned the engine on before she could say, "I'll miss you, too, Myrnin." And then he was gone, roaring back into Morganville's town limits.

As he did, he rocketed past yet *another* car that was going way too fast out of Morganville. Claire's parents were still a couple of miles away, heading in . . . this car was heading *out*, toward her.

And she knew that car very well.

The big, black hearse skidded to a halt just at the border of the billboard. In fact, it fishtailed sideways as it stopped, and the passenger door flew open so hard Claire was surprised it didn't break off . . . and then her boyfriend, Shane, was hurtling out of it, heading for her at a run.

"No," he blurted, and threw his arms around her. "You don't get to go like that."

She felt stiff for a moment, with shock and fear of the pain that was coming, but then the familiar lines and planes of his body made her relax against him. Two halves, fitting as if they'd been molded that way, despite the fact he towered over her. And then she was kissing him, or he was kissing her, and it was wild and hot and desperate and agonizing and heartbreaking, and when they finally broke with a gasp she rested her forehead against his chest. She could feel him breathing too fast, hear his heartbeat pounding too loudly. *I'm doing this to him,* she thought. *He's hurting and it's my fault.*

But she knew she wasn't wrong about this. She loved Shane, loved him with so much certainty it was like sunrise, but she also knew that he had to see her differently—and she needed to see herself differently, if they were going to last. When he'd met her she'd been helpless, defenseless, and now she needed to prove she was not just his equal, but his independent equal.

Whether he—or she—liked it or not.

Over at the car, Michael had gotten out of the driver's side and was leaning against the fender; he seemed content to wait, but he was also eyeing the horizon, where the sun was rising fast. In minutes, he'd be bathed in light, and at his very young vampire age, that was not good.

Claire put her hand on Shane's cheek, a silent promise, and then dashed over to Michael to throw her arms around him. In the thin dawn light, he looked human again—skin tinted pink, eyes the endless clear blue of a summer sky. He kissed her cheek and hugged her with careful strength. "You didn't really think we'd let you get away with no good-byes, did you?"

"No," she said.

He kissed her forehead, very gently. "Come back safe, and come back soon," he whispered to her. "We love you."

"Love you, too, Michael," she said, and stepped back. "You'd better get inside."

He nodded and retreated to the car's blacked-out back bench seats—vampire tinting was way better than anything on human cars, and it would keep him safe from the fierce Texas day—and then it was Eve's turn.

Michael's wife hadn't taken time to get properly dressed; she looked exactly as if she'd bounced out of bed in her cartoon bat pajama bottoms and tank top, with her dyed-black hair in a messy scraped-together knot at the back of her head. She still had sleep wrinkles on her cheek, and without her Goth makeup, she looked ridiculously young. She was also wearing vampire bunny slippers. Myrnin had given them each a pair for Christmas, since they'd all found his so hilarious, and as Eve marched toward Claire, the rabbit slippers' mouths flapped up and down, their red tongues flashing and plush teeth biting the ground.

Not outdoor wear, but Eve clearly didn't give a crap.

"Hey," she said, stopping a couple of feet away and crossing her arms. "So. There's this, then."

"Yeah," Claire said. "I just—I couldn't—"

"Couldn't woman up and say good-bye? Jesus, Claire Bear, you didn't even leave a *note*! How could you do that?"

There was no defense to that. It was true. She'd figured that the good-nights they'd said were also good-byes, but now . . . now she knew that they weren't. Shane's twisted anguish had told her that, and so did Eve's tears, shining unshed in her eyes.

Claire moved forward, and Eve uncrossed her arms just in time to receive the embrace. "Idiot," Eve said. "Dork. Loser. So, you're just going to run off in the dark and . . . and leave us . . . and . . ." She was crying now, and Claire felt the hot tears on her shoulder soaking through her sweater. "And we might never see you again, and I love you, Claire. You're like my little sister, and—"

"I'm coming back," Claire said. She hung on fiercely, while Eve bawled and let it all out. "I swear, I'm coming back. You can't get rid of me like that."

"I don't *want* to get rid of you!" Eve's balled-up fists hit her back, but softly, lacking any force. "God!"

There was only one thing to do, and that was let her cry it out, and Claire did, fighting back a rising tide of tears herself. This was why she'd tried to sneak away . . . not because she didn't love all of them, but because the good-byes were so, so painful.

Her parents' minivan rolled up to the sign, pulled to the shoulder, and Claire heard the engine shut off. She patted Eve's back a few more times until her best friend gave a shuddering nod and stepped away.

"Hello, pumpkin," Claire's father said, and smiled at her from the driver's side window. He looked tired, she thought, and it shocked her how much more gray there was in his hair. He didn't look well, though her mother had assured her he was doing much better. "Ready to go?"

"Almost," she said. "Couple of minutes?"

"Take your time." He looked as if he understood, but it was definitely the Dad Look that he leveled at Shane—the disapproving, not-good-enough up and down assessment.

Shane didn't notice, and even if he had, he probably wouldn't have much cared at the moment. He closed the distance between them as Claire came back, and although he didn't put his arms around her, the feeling of an embrace settled around her.

Safe. Safe, with him.

"I don't like this," he said. "I don't like knowing you can't forgive me, Claire. Please, I said I was sorry. What do you want me to do? Beg? I will. I'll get on my knees right here if you want, in front of your dad—"

"No!" she blurted. "No, it's— I'm not angry; really, I'm not. But I need this. *I* need it. I don't usually ask for anything for myself, but this is mine, Shane. It won't be for long, but it gives us time to—to see if we're really strong apart, like we are together."

She also needed him to understand that he'd screwed up, and she couldn't be one of those doormat girls . . . ready to forgive him when he did unforgivable things. He hadn't trusted her word. He'd believed—despite what he knew about her—that she'd been sneaking around behind his back, with Michael, which, well, *never*.

And so she couldn't fall for the fast, easy apology. Not even here, on his knees, in front of her father, which was about as extreme as it could get.

Tears clogged her throat again, and when she saw he was serious about it, she reached out and grabbed his hands. Big hands, scarred over the knuckles from fights; gentle hands, too, when it counted. Hands she loved, especially when, like now, they rose up and touched her burning cheeks, cradled them in coolness. His thumbs traced her cheekbones softly, and he bent closer to whisper, "I am so sorry, Claire. Please. Please don't go away."

"I—" She closed her eyes because she felt dizzy, pulled by the force of his wanting, and even a deep breath didn't set that right.

"Shane, I have to go. I *have to*. That doesn't mean I don't love you, or that I won't come back." She opened her eyes and met his fierce, desperate gaze. "I said I'd marry you someday. I still mean it, if you mean it."

That woke an equally fierce grin. "Oh, I mean it. I'd do it tomorrow if—"

"I know," she said. "But I can't. Not yet."

He let go of her, but he didn't step back; he took her hands and raised them to his lips to kiss them, one at a time. She shivered at the heat of his lips, and the longing on his face that he didn't give a voice.

"If you need me . . ." he said, and then stopped himself with a bitter little smile. "But you probably won't."

She silently held up her cell phone. "Speed dial."

"Call me today," he said. "Call me every day."

"I will," she promised. "Shane—"

"I know," he said. "Look, I hate good-byes, too. But sometimes, we need them just to survive."

He meant that, and it left her wordless and stunned, and all she could think to do was kiss him one more time, gently. It was a promise, and she meant it with everything in her heart and soul.

And then she walked over to where her suitcases lay, and helped her dad load them into the back of the minivan. Shane moved to help but she discouraged that with a shake of her head; she needed to do this herself. She was afraid she'd break down and run back home to Morganville, to the house they all shared, if she didn't go *now*, on her own.

It didn't take long to change her life. Ten minutes, maybe. With the morning sun washing golden over the billboard, over Shane standing with his arm around Eve next to the hearse, with

Michael safely behind tinting in the back, she tossed her backpack in, closed the door, and waved. They waved back.

And then somehow she was in the passenger seat, buckled in, though she didn't remember doing it, and the minivan was accelerating north, away from Morganville.

Away from everything she'd left behind.

She twisted in the seat to watch Shane and Eve disappear into the distance. Once she couldn't even see the billboard anymore, she turned face front and took in a deep, trembling breath. *I will not cry*, she told herself. *I will not.*

It finally occurred to her to ask the obvious question of her father. "Where's Mom?"

"She said she'll meet us at the airport. You okay, kiddo?" her dad asked. He kept his eyes on the road, and his voice was neutral, but he held out his right hand, and she took it. "That's my girl. You're okay. I remember driving you here, you know, to school. You seemed so much smaller then, honey, and so much more vulnerable. Look at you now—you're a lovely, confident young woman. I'm very proud of you. And I know that was hard for you."

She didn't feel lovely, or confident, or like a woman. The only thing she felt was young, and right now, very raw with loss. But she smiled anyway, and gulped back the tears, and when her voice was steady she asked him how his job was going, and what the doctor was saying about his heart condition, and a thousand little things that made up love.

They talked all the way to Midland.

It wasn't just Mom waiting at the airport, to Claire's astonishment. It was a *party*. When she came inside with Dad, wheeling her two suitcases, she immediately saw a giant bright pink banner that said CONGRATULATIONS!, with giant clusters of balloons lifting either end. And a *crowd*. A cheering crowd.

She didn't know what she was seeing, honestly . . . and then faces started to come into focus. Her teachers from high school—Mrs. Street, Mrs. East, Mr. Popp, Mr. Shelton . . . her favorites. And then classmates, at least ten of them. Some had been friends, but casual friends; most of them would have just graduated from high school, she guessed, since they were all about her age. She'd been two or three years ahead of them, thanks to testing out of most core subjects.

She hadn't missed them, but it was nice to see them, anyway—and strange, too, like having a dream where everything from the past was suddenly in the present, throwing everything out of whack. It was weird and funny and wonderful, and as she got hugs and backslaps, passed in a dizzying dance from person to person, she felt as if everybody in the airport was staring at her and wondering what the hell was going on.

When she caught her breath, she felt a sudden acute sense of those who were missing: Shane. Eve. Michael. Myrnin. Maybe even Amelie and Oliver and a half dozen others she knew—however unexpectedly—she would regret not being here to see this. Myrnin would have been delighted. He'd have been grabbing a pile of cupcakes from the tray, and punch from the cooler, and remarking on how the red color of the sugary liquid looked remarkably like diluted blood . . . and Shane would have wearily threatened to stake him. Eve would have voted in favor. Michael would have laughed.

It suddenly all seemed both too much, and too little.

The Midland airport was not exactly used to celebrations, but it seemed to put smiles on the faces of the security people, and even the jaded, weary business travelers with their battered, sturdy suitcases. Claire's were new, and polka-dotted, lime green and purple. She wasn't sure if they were too weird or not, but at least she wouldn't lose them.

The party was short—fifteen minutes, and then Claire's dad began to cheerfully remind people that she had a plane to catch. Her mom hugged her tight as the first of the visitors began to leave, and said, "It's so good to see you, sweetie. Even just for this." She pushed Claire back to arm's length and gave her the mom inspection, up and down. "You look a little thin, sweetie. Are you eating?"

"Yes, Mom, I'm eating. Don't worry. Once I get to Boston, it's all snacks and cafeteria food and pizza, so I'll probably gain ten pounds the first week."

"Well, you could do with another ten pounds, anyway." She nervously brushed at Claire's hair, rearranging it around her face. "Oh, dear, you could use a haircut, too. Well. Promise me—do you think you've got everything you'll need? Do you need sheets, or towels, or—"

"I'll be okay, Mom," Claire said, and caught her mother's hands in her own. "I'll be fine."

Mom took a deep, convulsive breath and let it out before she nodded. "I know," she said. "You probably need clothes, though. You always do."

It was an old refrain. Mom had her hair fixed nicely, and she had makeup on, and the sweater and pants she was wearing fit her well. Her mother had always had much more fashion sense than Claire possessed, and it had been something Mom had seen as a social shortcoming. Claire didn't. She figured when she was ready to care about those things, she would. But right now, the comfortable geek-girl tee, loose sweater, and jeans were all she really needed.

"I've got enough clothes," Claire said. Half of them had been given to her by Eve, who'd rolled her eyes at the destitute nature of Claire's closet and donated things that were—by Eve's standards, anyway—conservative enough.

"And money? You've got enough money?"

"Yes." She did. She'd gotten a salary from Morganville as Myrnin's assistant, and she even had a credit card, one that Amelie had assured her would be accepted anywhere in the world. It was very shiny. "Honest, Mom, I'm fine."

"I know you are, you always are." Her mother sighed, and folded her in a suddenly fierce embrace that smelled of powder and perfume. "Are you looking forward to seeing Elizabeth again?"

Claire's friend Elizabeth from high school had moved to Cambridge as well, though she was attending a school other than MIT. But honestly, beyond exchanging e-mail and phone calls, and the flurry of sudden plans in the past few days, she didn't really *know* Elizabeth anymore. Two years apart was a lifetime these days.

She still remembered the rush of excitement and consternation she'd felt opening the first e-mail. *Your parents told me you were moving to town,* Elizabeth had written. *You CANNOT live in a dorm!!!! I'm renting a place. Share? PLEASE PLEASE PLEASE?* That was Elizabeth, all right; she probably had been bouncing up and down, unable to stand still while she wrote the *pleases.* And there was no reason not to accept.

Except now, Claire felt a little sick to her stomach. *Maybe I should have just stayed in the dorm.* But she hadn't had such good luck with that before at Texas Prairie University.

Mom noticed her silence. "Oh, sweetie. I hate you going so far away, but I'm so proud of what you've accomplished. I know it's just the beginning of such great things for you."

That was a very odd thought, suddenly. She'd done so much these past few years in Morganville that the idea there was *more*... well. It just seemed strange.

Like the thought that she was about to get on a plane and fly to Dallas, and then on another flight off to Boston. She'd been in Dallas only once before...with Michael and Eve. With *Shane*. And she remembered every second of that sweet, beautiful, wild weekend, where the two of them had just begun to discover each other in new and personal ways. It was...it was magical, in her memory.

Going back to Dallas without him seemed just the opposite of magical. It seemed like the ominous sign of a curse.

Dad helped her check her suitcases through to Boston, and she got past the nervous excitement of showing her ID for the tickets, and then it was—all of a sudden—time for good-byes again. Hard ones. She threw her arms around her dad's neck and hugged him breathless, and kissed him on both cheeks, which made him surprised and happy; she was usually more reserved than that. Her mom got the same, and they both pretended not to notice how unsteady each other's voices were as they said all the usual things, all the loving things.

And then she was in the security line, and leaving her past behind her with a finality that was more than a little terrifying. *I'm alone.* Funny. She'd faced so much these past few years—life and death and all the stages in between. Loss and love. Heartache and joy. Most of all, danger, constant and unremitting danger...

...Yet, she was shaking all over as she handed the TSA agent her ID card and her ticket, and frantically wondering if she'd scrubbed her backpack clean of all the usual Morganville survival aids—silver nitrate, stakes, blades, the works. What if she'd overlooked something? What if . . .

"Miss? What's this supposed to be?" The uniformed officer frowned at her and held out her ID card.

Oh. Her *Morganville* ID card. She'd grabbed the wrong one, and quickly blushed and fished out the Texas driver's license instead. "Sorry," she said. "Uh . . . library card."

He hadn't read the text, luckily, and he just shrugged, scrutinized her face long enough to make her even more nervous, then waved her through.

Shoes were hard to get off—she hadn't planned for that—and her hoodie had to come off, too. Her backpack passed through scanners without trouble, thankfully, and then she was clutching all her stuff, breathless with relief, on the other side of the barriers. Claire walked barefoot to some seats, donned her hoodie and her Skechers, put her ID back in her wallet (moving the Morganville ID safely to the back to avoid confusion with legit state-issued stuff) and then, finally, took a moment to let the enormity of it hit her.

She was committed. Checked in. Bags headed for the plane. Her dad was shipping the rest of the boxes directly to her new apartment.

She was on her own. Completely, utterly, totally on her own, going into a new world without Shane, without parents. Without enemies, even.

Nobody cared. People walked past her, and ignored her existence.

Claire sat for a moment in silence, taking that in and adjusting herself to the reality that outside of Morganville, she was just some mildly pretty eighteen-year-old girl headed up to college, like ten thousand other girls she'd see along the way. Not someone special at all.

It was, she thought as she picked up her backpack and headed toward her departure gate, the scariest thing she'd ever done, and the most freedom she'd ever had.

Ironic.

TWO

Elizabeth Porter met Claire at the baggage claim, holding a giant sign that said BEST FRIENDS 4EVA and waving excitedly, which was good, because otherwise Claire probably wouldn't have recognized her. The chubby, shy Elizabeth from school was gone, replaced by a sleek, tall girl with short platinum blond hair. Her fashion sense had changed, too, from geeky to sexy—she had on a button-down shirt, pleated schoolgirl miniskirt, knee socks, loafers, even the required Smart Librarian glasses. Guys watched as she jumped up and down, squealed, and threw her arms around Claire with the enthusiasm of a cheerleader at a championship game. A *winning team* cheerleader, at that.

"You're here, oh my God, I'm so excited! Claire!" Elizabeth suddenly pushed her out to arm's length and stared at her. She'd gotten taller, and now topped Claire by at least three inches. "You look . . . different."

"You don't?" Claire said, and laughed. Elizabeth joined in, and it was like they'd never spent a moment apart . . . but only for that second, because then Elizabeth stopped laughing, and something strange flashed over her face. Two years ago, Claire wouldn't have recognized it, but now she knew fear when she saw it. *Well, that's weird.*

It was only a flash, and Elizabeth pasted on the bright smile again. "I just wanted a change," she said. "You know, leaving Texas, becoming a new person—you want that, too, right?"

"Right," Claire said. Her heart wasn't in it; she didn't want to change anymore, really, but she wanted to be more of what she already had become—more *Claire*. Elizabeth, on the other hand, seemed to have bent herself to becoming someone completely different, from the outside in. It hadn't stifled that spark Claire had always liked about her, though. It still showed in the bouncy way Elizabeth helped her drag her luggage off the carousel, and chattered all the way out to the parking lot.

"Why do you do that?" Elizabeth suddenly asked, very seriously, as Claire loaded her suitcase into the trunk of Liz's ancient Ford Taurus.

"Do what? Um . . . doesn't the luggage go in the trunk?" Surely the world hadn't changed *that* much.

"Look over your shoulder," Elizabeth said. "You've done it every few seconds since you came out of the terminal. Are you worried about someone? Did someone follow you?" She looked very serious again, and earnest, and Claire suddenly realized that her friend was right—she'd been checking routinely, automatically, to be sure nothing was sneaking up on her.

Morganville caution.

"Oh," she said, and mustered up an apologetic laugh. "I guess—well, the part of town I've been living in isn't that safe. I got used to looking out for myself."

"Well, you're in civilization now, not Backwardstown," Elizabeth said, and slammed the trunk lid. "Banzai, bitch, we are *moving!*"

Claire climbed in the car, and Elizabeth got in, whooped in excitement, and turned the music up loud and sang along at the top of her lungs as she steered them out of the parking garage and into a weak afternoon sunlight.

The drive was really educational, because Cambridge didn't look anything like Dallas. Dallas had been steel and glass, heat and angles; Cambridge was age-rounded, grassy, still virulently green even though fall chill was thick in the air. The trees were so much taller than she'd expected, and the *colors* . . . Claire gaped like a kid at Christmas, too stunned with the beauty of it to join in the sing-along, even though she liked the song Elizabeth was currently belting out. The houses were small and square and so *neat* and at the same time so . . . old. Everything in Morganville looked old, too, but in a falling-apart way. This looked more like lovingly cared-for history.

"You're going to need a car," Elizabeth said suddenly, turning the radio way down. "I know you walked all the time in Hicksville, but we're not going to be living *that* close. You're going to really love the apartment, it's super cute and yeah, it's kind of small, but cozy, really . . . okay, it's a pit, but we'll have fun, right? So. Tell me about this *boy.*"

The switch of topics was sudden, but that was Liz; she'd always been like that, leapfrogging from one thing to another without much in the way of traffic signals. "The boy's name is Shane," Claire said. Just saying it twisted hard inside her, and for a second she could hardly breathe; it felt like a fist closing over her heart and crushing it flat. Tears suddenly gathered in her eyes, and she had to breathe deeply to get herself under control again. "He's—he's—"

"Super cute?" Elizabeth supplied, when Claire hesitated. "Adorable like a fluffy bunny? A giant dickhead? What, girl, come on! Spill!"

"Perfect," Claire said. No, that wasn't right. He was far from perfect, that was the whole point of why she'd come here to put some space between them. *Perfect for me, though.* "He's taller than me, and has really broad shoulders, and yes he's super cute—and he makes me happy." There. She'd said it. "I love him."

"Love," Elizabeth sighed, and shook her head. "Snap out of it, girlfriend. I don't want you mooning over some Texas loser when you've come to prime dating territory! I thought you said you wanted to get some distance?"

"I did," Claire said. Right now, she was missing Shane with an intensity that made her shaky. And not *just* Shane. She missed Eve and Michael, and the easy way they all fit together as friends. She already felt that Elizabeth, as positive and funny and energetic as she was, intended to push her to be something she wasn't, and that Liz wouldn't take no for an answer. *Eve would have just made me feel comfortable,* she thought. *And welcome. We haven't even made it to the apartment and Liz is already trying to make me speed date.*

"So forget about Cowboy Hottie and let's just start out two fun single girls, ready for anything. Right?"

"Elizabeth—"

"Right?" Elizabeth took her eyes off the road long enough to give her a commanding stare.

"Right," she said. "Just—just drive. You're making me nervous."

"You've gotten all serious, did you know that? What did they do to you out in the sticks?" Liz pouted a little, but she started humming along with the radio in a few seconds, and the clouds cleared. "I hope you like blue. I gave you the blue room."

Elizabeth hadn't been kidding. It was *blue*, this room. The apartment was in a run-down building that had probably once been a big house, but had been sliced into four narrow sections, each with three stories. Claire's room was at the top of a creaky, flaking staircase, and it was really . . . blue.

The walls had been painted an unfortunate, shiny dark color, that made everything look even more cramped than it really was (which was pretty small). There was room for the battered twin bed, a broken-down dresser painted a distressed pale blue, and a mirror old enough to have dull flecks all over it. Vintage would be one word for it.

Claire tested the mattress. Vintage would be a word for that, too.

"It's great, right?" Elizabeth demanded, having wheeled her larger suitcase in behind her. With the two of them and the two suitcases, there wasn't room to walk. "Cheap, too. The rent's only two thousand a month, plus utilities."

That brought Claire bolt upright from the sagging bed. *"Two thousand?"*

"Not *each*," Elizabeth said. "I mean, split, so a thousand for you." She laughed outright at the expression on Claire's face. "What, you didn't think living here would be cheap, did you?

Come on. The reason prices are low in Texas is nobody wants to live there!"

I do, Claire thought, and swallowed hard. She hadn't counted on paying that much in rent, but she could manage it. Eating anything but Ramen noodles and peanut butter was pretty much off the table, though.

Elizabeth was looking worried now. "It's not a problem, is it?"

"No," Claire said. "It's okay. I just—" She swallowed the words, *hate this room,* and said, "just didn't expect it to be quite that much. I should have asked."

"I should have warned you," Elizabeth said. She sat down on the bed next to Claire and bounced up and down, which strained the old springs to their limits. "Sorry, I just thought—I guess I was scared you'd say no. And I couldn't stand it if you said no, Claire. I just—it's so nice to have somebody from the old life, you know? Someone who knows me. Really knows the real me."

"Isn't this the real you now?" Claire gestured at—all of it. The outfit, the hair, everything.

"I guess so. I just—sometimes it feels so strange, and I wish I could go back to being . . . a kid, you know? A kid at home, with nothing to worry about." Elizabeth sighed and stopped bouncing. "I spent so long wanting to be on my own and now it's—it feels weird. And pretty frightening, to be in charge. Right?"

Claire didn't answer this time. She put her arm around her friend, and they sat together in a suddenly comfortable silence for a few long seconds, before Elizabeth—practically a Ritalin kid, with all her energy to burn—wiggled free and grabbed Claire's hand to haul her to her feet. "You have to see my room!" Elizabeth said brightly. "You'll love it, we can fix yours up, too, make it really yours. . . ."

She kept talking as she pulled Claire toward the door, and to be honest Claire wasn't really listening until Elizabeth, midway down the stairs, finished up a sentence with, "and the ghost."

"Wait." Claire pulled her to a full halt. "What did you just say? *Ghost?*"

"Sure! The house is haunted; isn't that the coolest ever?"

Claire waited a second. She had always been able to tell, in Morganville, if something paranormally weird was going on around her, but here it just felt like a drafty, creaking old house. "You're sure?"

"Well, yeah, of course! I've seen her. It's a lady in white, I think, and she drifts around on the stairs sometimes. Cool, right? I think she probably died here. Maybe she was *gruesomely murdered!*"

Maybe it was a Morganville thing, but Claire was reasonably certain she'd never thought of someone being horribly murdered with quite so much enthusiasm. She'd seen too many examples of it in real life. That, she realized, was the real gap between her and Elizabeth now . . . life experience. Elizabeth still lived in a world where the worst that could happen was a stolen wallet or a minor accident. She didn't know how fragile things were, or how hard you had to fight to hold them together when the world spun out of control.

Claire felt ancient, even though she was a full year younger. She said, "Um, can I see your room now?"

"Creepy talk creeping you out?"

"Little bit, yeah." Shane would have had a brilliant comeback, or Eve, but Claire couldn't come up with one, suddenly. It didn't matter. Elizabeth pulled her down the rest of the twisting flight of stairs to the second landing, and opened up the door and flicked on the lights.

"Ta da!" she sang, and did an extravagant sweep of her arm.

The room was as orange as Claire's was blue. To be fair, only one wall was painted that color, but it was the far one, and it practically glowed in the dark. So did the bedspread with its profusions of ruffles, and the piles of pillows. It *was* nice, though, even if it was unsettlingly bright . . . Elizabeth had taped up band posters and some kind of fantasy art featuring winged, half-naked male angels. Her dresser was practically covered with makeup and piles of jewelry. It was the girliest room Claire had ever seen, actually, and that included Eve's. At least Eve's was *dark*.

"It's really . . . cheerful," Claire said. That was true. It also gave her a headache. Maybe that was the incense, which smelled like freshly peeled . . . oranges. That seemed a little bit too much theme for sanity. On the plus side, she was suddenly grateful that Liz had chosen blue for her bedroom. "Well, let me get unpacked, and you can show me the rest of the place, okay?"

"Not much else to see. There's a tiny little living area and a crappy kitchen. No TV; I figured we could stream something if we wanted to watch it, but I'm not really into that stuff anyway."

"What stuff?"

"You know, TV, books, films, all that kind of stuff." Liz dismissed it with a wave of her hand. "I like the real world. Besides, only geeks go all nuts over made-up stories."

That was a shock, because Claire clearly remembered squealing with Liz over the latest Harry Potter book, and excitedly chattering about what Snape would get up to next. This Elizabeth— this platinum blond, carefully made up, fashion-conscious young woman—this one was a stranger. "I still like it," Claire said. Not defensively, because she really didn't feel a need to defend it. She was just stating a fact.

But it seemed like Elizabeth took it as a personal attack. Her face turned pink around the cheeks and at the top of her forehead, and she glared and said, "Well, I *don't*, so let's get some ground rules straight—you don't bring home any geeky weirdos who want to sit around and play games or talk about movies or that stuff. You'll never find a guy that way, and you'll ruin my chances, too!"

"A . . . guy?" Claire felt suddenly at sea, because this conversation was getting weirder and weirder. "Liz, I'm not looking for—"

"Fine, sit around and sulk about your stupid cowboy all day and night, but I'm finding someone worthwhile."

"What's worthwhile for you?" It might have been goading, but Claire honestly wanted to know. Sort of an anthropological experiment.

Elizabeth looked puzzled for a second, then ticked off what she wanted. "Money," she said. "A decent job, something medical or finance or something. And a good car. He's got to have a good car. Also, he should have short hair and wear ties most of the time. Nice silk ties, not those crappy Kmart-special ones."

She had remarkably specific rules, Claire thought. "Found anybody yet?"

"Not yet, but I know what to do. I go to the places that those kind of men show up, like upscale food stores and the opera, and I wait for one to notice me and talk to me. I've gotten loads of conversations. Sooner or later one of them will date me."

That was . . . Well, Claire didn't have any other word for it: bizarre. "Don't you want to—I don't know—meet somebody and fall in love because you're just . . . right for each other?"

Liz shrugged. "Don't really care about that," she said. "Romance is for idiots. I'm done with all that stuff."

"Liz—" Claire didn't know how else to put it. "What the hell happened to you? Because you're just not . . . not the same."

Elizabeth gave her a long, bitter look. "You don't want to know," she said. Claire remembered the flash of fear in Liz's eyes at the airport, and wondered even more. "I'm just telling you, your boyfriend? He may pretend to be Prince Charming, but he'll show his true colors. They all do." She stepped into her room and took hold of the door. "Let me know when you're unpacked; we'll make some dinner."

Then she shut the door, and Claire was left standing on the stairs, feeling very alone. Elizabeth *had* changed, all right—far more than Claire herself had, even with all the pressures of Morganville. She was trying so hard to be adult that she was going to break something—probably herself, Claire thought.

But Liz was right . . . she did need to unpack. Though when she went back upstairs, and surveyed the depressing blue room again, the first thing she wanted to do was take her suitcases and run, run away, run back to . . .

. . . To Shane.

Claire took out her phone and scrolled the address book. All the familiar, aching names. *I can call him,* she thought. *I can call right now.*

Instead, she put down the phone, took a deep, slow breath, and threw the first suitcase open on the low, creaking bed.

Maybe putting things in drawers and in the narrow closet would make her feel less . . . lost.

An hour later, though, the suitcases were empty, and the drawers were full of underwear and T-shirts and clothes, what needed to be on hangers successfully on the closet rod, and her battered assortment of shoes neatly arranged . . . and she put the small number of personal things she'd brought with her around the room. She hadn't bothered with posters, but she had framed photos of Shane, and an album of photos of Michael and Eve and Myrnin and Amelie and everybody else she knew in Morganville who'd stand still for it, or even those who wouldn't, like Oliver, taken on the stealth. A record of what she'd left behind, the good and the bad. Even Myrnin's pet Bob the Spider had his own close-up. He was surprisingly kind of cute.

And Claire still felt lost and alone. Having the familiar around only made all this seem more alien.

She kept arranging things until she realized it was verging on obsessive, and finally hooked up her computer, logged on to the house WiFi (at least that was decent) and found e-mail had exploded like popcorn in the microwave of her in-box. One was from her dad, telling her to call to confirm she was safe in her new place. Ditto from Michael, and from Eve, and even an awkward, formal note from Myrnin that boiled down to the same thing (she was surprised he'd actually figured out how to manage it on his own). It was all really sweet, but she couldn't stand to talk to them right now; the despair of having made the decision loomed all over her, and she knew she'd break down and cry if she heard a familiar voice. So she sent out e-mail instead.

It was all she could do not to beg them to come to get her and take her back home.

No, I won't do that. I didn't quit, she reminded herself. *I didn't quit when I got to Morganville, and people were actually trying to kill me. I'm not going to quit now, just because I don't like my room and my housemate's kind of nuts.*

It suddenly struck her that there was no message from Shane. Not one.

A lump formed hard in her throat, and she involuntarily looked up at the closest picture she'd placed of him. It was her favorite.

She'd caught him relaxed, laughing, and the warmth in his face always made her feel safe and happy.

But what if that light was gone? What if she never saw it in him again—if he'd forget about her while she was gone, or everything changed between them? *It'll be your fault,* something in her said. *Because you walked away.*

Claire reached for her phone and ran her finger lightly over the screen. So easy to call him. It only took a couple of motions, and then the phone would ring, and . . .

. . . And what if he didn't pick up?

Claire dropped her phone and rested her burning forehead against her palms, and just as she was ready to crawl into her crappy, sagging bed and cry, her computer let out a little musical tone to tell her a new message had come in.

She grabbed the mouse and frantically clicked, and a video came up. It was murky at first, and then a light clicked on, and she saw Shane's face gilded by it. He was in his room, she saw . . . it was just as messy as ever, and the sight of it, and him, made her throat close up with frantic longing.

"Hey," Shane's image said. It wasn't Skype, not real time, just a recording, so she controlled the almost crazy impulse to talk back to him, blurt out how much she missed him, loved him, *needed* him. She couldn't stop herself from touching the screen, and tracing the lines of his lips with her fingers. "So, I guess you're there, at your new place. Hope it's awesome. If it's not, you'll make it awesome, because that's what you do. It's your superpower. Also, this is for Claire, so if I hit somebody else in the list by mistake, stop watching now or I'll have to kill you."

That made her laugh, and he must have known it would, because he smiled just a little. It made the skin at the corners of his eyes crinkle a little. "So anyway," he said, "Claire, if you're seeing this, and you're not so pissed at me you just delete the whole thing without watching . . . I miss you. I miss you so bad it hurts. I keep walking around the house and wishing you were here, and that I could—that I could figure out how to fix the screwed-up stuff I did. Until I can do that, though, I guess what I'm saying is that I miss you. That's all. So if you're lonely there, not out partying and meeting fancy Boston guys, maybe we can be lonely together."

He'd been avoiding the camera, but now he made eye contact with it, and she felt like he was staring right into her. And that smile . . . it broke her heart.

"Love you," he said, and logged off, as if he was afraid to be caught at it.

It made her eyes fill up with tears, and she sat for a few more minutes, starting it over, replaying it, watching his lips say the words.

We can be lonely together.

She was reaching for her phone when Elizabeth—without knocking—threw open her bedroom door with such force that it knocked over one of her empty suitcases. "Hey!" she said brightly. The dark mood she'd been in was already gone, and looking at her brilliant smile, Claire wondered if she'd imagined some of it. "Ready for some delicious homemade dinner?" Liz asked. "Because I'm totally starved." She put her hands on her hips and looked around the room, then looked around again. "Um . . . did you unpack?"

"Yes."

"Wow. I really need to show you how to decorate, don't I?"

Not if this paint color is any clue, Claire thought, but she kept it to herself. She'd quietly get a can of something neutral and redo things to the way she wanted them—no confrontation, no drama, no fuss. "So, what's for dinner?"

"How about mac and cheese with some chicken? It's leftover KFC, but it's still good, I swear."

It did sound good. Claire hadn't even realized she was hungry until her stomach started growling, and she slid out of the chair behind her computer and stuck her phone in her pocket on the way out the door.

Dinner wouldn't take *that* long.

. . . Except, it did. Elizabeth was hell to cook with; she wanted everything done just right. Claire stuck the macaroni in boiling water, and Liz got upset and took it off the burner because she wanted to check the temperature of the water first. Claire asked why, and that brought on an insane volume of information about cooking pasta at just the right temperatures, and the physics and chemistry of food, and honestly, even as much of a physics junkie as Claire was, she couldn't really apply it to box pasta with reconstituted cheese substance that sold for a buck a box. She just backed off and let Liz conduct all her temperature observations, mix the sauce, and generally obsess about getting the chicken chunks just the right size to go into the pasta once it was done. All this took about an hour, which was about half an hour more than Claire wanted to spend on mac and cheese, even if Liz added something she said were Chinese herbs and white truffle oil. In the end, it tasted pretty much like she expected, but by then Claire was willing to eat the box, too.

Claire took the cleaning-up role, which seemed to suit Liz, and when that was done, she headed for the stairs.

"Wait," Liz said. "So—you're leaving? Just like that?"

"What do you mean, just like that?"

"It's our first night here! Don't you think we ought to, you know, celebrate? I have a movie we can watch, or we can just catch up and talk—" Liz was practically begging her. "Please? I know it's been a really long time and maybe—maybe you're just really feeling lost, and I want you to like it here. So let me help."

I just want to go upstairs, call Shane, and spend all night talking. But if she said that out loud, it would sound like she was some girl who couldn't exist without a boy, and wasn't that what all this coming-to-MIT had been intended to prove? Pretty ridiculous to fail the first test, on the first day she was apart from him.

"Sure," Claire said, and tried to force some cheer into her voice. She felt horrible, but it wasn't Liz's fault. Her former best friend was trying to fill the void, and the least Claire could do was let her.

Besides . . . she could call Shane later.

Elizabeth was, as it turned out, a movie *fanatic*, and six hours later, Claire finally begged off from the video assault and climbed the stairs, feeling more like a zombie than a survivor of the living-dead attack. Watching gory horror movies on the first night in a creaky old house, with a flaky roommate, was not nearly as much fun as it had been in the Glass House, surrounded by people she loved and trusted. That house had always seemed—and been, on some level—*alive*, and protective of them.

This one felt cold, alien, and utterly indifferent to her life or death, which made imagining the creaks and bangs to be serial killers intent on murder all too easy.

Claire made it up the steep climb, turned on the lights, and climbed in bed with her phone. She thought about shutting the lights off again, but in her sleep-deprived, overstimulated state, every shadow looked like a monster, and she thought she could see things moving at the corners of her eyes.

Better to leave them on.

She dialed Shane's number and snuggled down in the pillows, warm and safe, finally, beneath the covers even if the mattress felt weirdly hard, and the sheets smelled of unfamiliar detergent.

His cell rang, and rang, and rang, and finally it went to voice mail.

That was like an ice dagger to the heart; she felt numbed and destroyed, all at once. *He didn't answer.* She'd called, she'd watched the video, and he wasn't there, wasn't answering. She was too tired to think rationally, so the next thing in her mind was that he'd gotten angry, turned his phone off, maybe even blocked her calls. What if he'd gone out? When she'd moved to Morganville, Shane had been dating other girls, though not seriously . . . maybe he'd already called one of them, gone out to the movies, or . . .

. . . Or worse. Maybe he was already forgetting her, laughing at some other girl's jokes. Someone older and prettier.

Stop it, she told herself angrily, and shut off the phone. *Just stop it.*

Claire shut off the ringer, tucked the phone under her pillow, and tried very, very hard not to cry.

She'd never felt so abandoned, or so lonely, in her life.

THREE

SHANE

)

It hadn't taken me long to pack up most of my crap. Truthfully, I didn't have that much; I wasn't a fashion victim like Eve—hell, even Michael had more clothes than I did—or a collector of stuff. A few well-aged tees, some jeans that had seen the worst of acids and bloodstains and buckshot, and not in that fancy-ass designer way. More the "I survived that" way.

I decided to ditch the stereo—it was a thirdhand ancient thing anyway, and cheap—and that was the biggest thing I owned, besides weapons.

It was the weapons that were going to be tricky. A shotgun weighs a decent amount. Throw in multiple other deadly sharp things, some stakes, a couple of crossbows, and you've got a problem . . . particularly if you're planning on having no fixed address for a while. In other words, I had to pick what I could easily carry in the battered camping backpack my dad had once used for the same purpose. Turned out that minus the clothes, my phone, some basic stuff for not smelling gross, the pack weighed about fifty pounds when I finally got it on to test it.

Doable. Soldiers pack that much plus body armor, and I wasn't exactly humping it through the mountains of Afghanistan.

As I shucked the backpack and leaned it against the wall, I sensed someone watching me . . . and I was right. Michael was leaning in the doorway, arms folded, watching me. "Can't talk you out of this," he said. It was a statement, not a question.

"Nope."

"You're sure this is the right thing to do."

"Yep. You and the missus need some alone time. Last thing you need is me hanging around here like the new house ghost, haunting Claire's room. Besides, man, I don't do emo."

"I never said you had to go."

"Never had to," I said, and checked my phone again. No calls. Every time I checked and I didn't see Claire's name, I felt the dark, jagged ball of anxiety inside get a little bigger, choke me a little more. "You giving me a ride to the border or what?"

"Shane—"

I gave him a long look, and he shut up. "We've been through a lot, Michael, but I'm not going to collapse into your manly arms and cry about it, okay? I already said I don't blame you. I don't. It's not your fault she left us . . . it's mine. I should have trusted her more. I should have believed in *you* more. I got some things to make up for, not just to her but to you. And it's probably better I do that away, so you and Eve can get to feel actually married without me lurking around in the background." That still hurt, the idea I was holding them back; I knew that was part of why Claire had decided to go, too. But he and Eve *did* need alone time. It was just truth, hard as it was.

"I'll give you a ride," Michael said. He walked over to my backpack and picked it up like I'd loaded it with feathers. "You got weapons in here?"

"A few."

"You know that it'll get your ass arrested out there, right?"

"Only if I've got really bad luck, or I decide to hold up a liquor store with 'em."

"You are a cocky bastard, did I ever tell you that, bro?"

I flashed him a grin. "Did you really think you needed to?"

He backslapped me as he passed. "Come on, criminal. Eve will kill me if I don't let her say good-bye."

"Oh man, that means she's gonna cry. Again."

"Like a river," he assured me. "Good thing you wore a black shirt. That mascara never comes out."

I stopped him at the top of the stairs, and for a moment we just looked at each other. Then he set the backpack down, and hugged me hard. No need for words or speeches or anything like that; he just offered me a fist to bump, I bumped, we were good.

And then we went downstairs to where Eve was pacing the floor, chewing on a neon-colored thumbnail. Sometime in the past couple of years girls had started painting their nails weird, so the neon thumb didn't match the other four fingers, which were standard Goth black. She'd tied back her color-streaked hair in a ponytail so tight that I wondered how it didn't give her a migraine, and she looked pale even though she'd gone light on the rice powder today. In fact, she didn't look particularly Gothed-out anymore—dramatic eye shadow and liner, but not a lot else.

Although she was wearing her combat gear—tight black shirt, cargo pants, heavy boots. Everything but bandoliers.

"So you're going after all," she said. She didn't sound particularly surprised about it, and I recognized the dangerously flat tone of her voice. "I'm not sure if you're crazy or just in love."

"Not much difference right now, Eve. I take a couple of weeks, head up to Boston, stay close in case she needs me . . . and if she doesn't, if all's well and she doesn't want to see me, I come home." I was trying really hard to avoid feeling like a stalker, because something inside me was hard-core bent on seeing her, even at a distance. I wanted her to have her freedom—she wanted it, and needed it. But I also couldn't shake the idea that letting trouble-magnet Claire go off across the country without backup was . . . a very bad idea. "I just need to make sure she's okay."

"Me, too," Eve said. She bit her lip, and somehow held back the tears I knew were lurking just under the surface. "At least *you* didn't sneak off in the middle of the night without a word."

"She was trying to make it easier," I said. "It isn't that she doesn't love us. You know that."

"I know. Didn't make it any better to wake up and find her gone, did it?" She nailed me with a dark look, and I had to agree. The feeling came back to me: shock, abandonment, my stomach dropping toward the center of the earth. Before I could deal with that, Eve hugged me, and I hugged her back. She felt as familiar and warm to me as the sister I'd lost so long ago now, and all of a sudden it dawned on me that for any number of reasons, I might not make it back to Morganville once I left. Accidents happened. They could happen anywhere. "You watch your back, Shane. I mean it." Her voice was muffled against my shoulder, and it sounded unsteady. "You come back to us or I swear, I'll find you, dig up your stinky corpse, and kick its ass until it freaking disintegrates."

I patted her on the back and kissed her cheek. She smelled like flowers, but not the sweet and innocent kind . . . more like the night-blooming ones. "You watch Michael's back and don't worry about mine, tough girl. And damn sure watch your own."

She sniffled a little, but the tears didn't quite break free, and she compensated by giving me a hard shot to the shoulder as she stepped back. "Don't I always? What are you going to do when you get there? If you get there, I mean, because knowing you, you'll end up in a bar fight before you're out of Texas."

"Not fair. I never go into bars." I wouldn't be allowed in one at my age, anyway. "My fights are always in the parking lots. Get it right."

"Idiot."

"That's the best you've got, Gothika? Because I expect quality insults from you, and that's not really measuring up."

"Look, Steroid Brain—"

"Okay, that's better, but work on it."

"You are such a *tool!* I love you, you know, right?"

"Right," I said softly. "Scary girl."

She blew me a kiss and turned away so I wouldn't see her cry. I glanced at Mikey, who was waiting near the door with my bag.

One last look around at the Glass House, *my* house . . . at the couch where I'd played countless hours of video games, at the kitchen where we'd yelled at one another over whose turn it was to do dishes and trash duty, at the carpet we always said we'd steam clean one of these days. At the scars on the walls from battles that had almost cost us our lives.

One last look at home.

"I'll be back," I promised them, and myself, and then Michael and I walked out the doorway and into the cold, vast world beyond.

On the way down the steps I checked my phone, again. Nothing from Claire. It was late now. Maybe she hadn't seen my video. Maybe she'd seen it, and hadn't cared. Maybe she was angrier than I'd ever thought.

Maybe she was out having fun and had already forgotten all about me. That was the scariest thought of all. Sure, I might be charming by Morganville standards, but she wasn't locked into the shallow end of the pool now, and there were plenty more to choose from. Genuinely smart college boys.

Thinking about that made me stupid. I knew better than to check my phone and forget my surroundings—we lived in Morganville, after all, and one thing you didn't do was get distracted in public, at night.

And as Michael headed for the car with my backpack, and I fumbled with the phone and tried to see if I'd missed a call, it cost me, because a dark shape rushed at me from the darkness, and I was unprepared.

Not a vampire, as it turned out. I could have handled a vampire. This was a *dog*. A big, scary dog, something like a Rottweiler, maybe, and it wasn't barking; it was intent on biting. I heard the growl coming at me, and next thing I knew jaws had clamped down on my arm, and my phone went flying. I dimly heard the crunch of metal and glass, but that was not the biggest problem I had at the moment. I'd put on my heavy coat, which was helping, but this dog had a seriously painful grip on me, and a lot of weight behind it; he shook his massive head, and I saw a shine of red in his eyes. Not natural.

I surprised him by not trying to pull away, but instead throwing myself into him and over, flipping him clumsily on his side. He let go of me with a surprised yelp, and I rolled up to my feet and spared one glance for my phone.

Destroyed.

No time to mourn; I was in serious shit, because this dog wasn't just a dog; the hellhound glare of its eyes was proof enough of that. I'd never seen anything like it before, not even in Morganville; dogs were pretty predictable, but this one was coming after me like I was a steak and he'd been starved for months. All my weapons were in the pack, which was with Michael, and besides I really didn't like the idea of killing a dog, even one that was trying to kill me.

It launched itself at me in a running leap, growling, showing way-too-sharp teeth, and I fell backward to the grass and put one foot up like a soccer player going for a goal. Good timing. My foot caught the dog underneath and changed the trajectory from down to my throat, to up and headed for a hard landing against Michael's car.

Michael caught it as it bounced off. More accurately, he got it in a headlock and held it there as it snarled and fought and ineffectively clawed the air for purchase. I heaved in thick, fast breaths and got to my feet in a postfight burst of adrenaline. The sleeve of my coat was shredded, and I could feel bruises deep into my arm, but at least I hadn't lost any flesh out of it.

Lucky.

"What the hell?" I said, and Michael shook his head.

"No idea," he said. "It's almost as if it's been turned, but you can't do that. Animals can't become vampire. They don't have enough—will, I guess."

"Tell that to the devil beast, then, because he damn sure looks like he's been turned."

"Whatever he is, we can't leave him running around out here," Michael said. "You mind waiting a bit until this is taken care of?"

"Do I have a choice?"

"Not unless you want to share the seat with him, locked in the car."

"Yeah, I haven't had my shots—better not. Throw me your phone," I said. "Mine's trashed. I'll call it in."

"Let me see your arm."

"I'm fine, man."

"Let me see."

I took off the coat and rolled up the long sleeve of the thermal I was wearing beneath. Red bruises that were going to black-and-blue in a few hours . . . and some distinct dark, welling spots of blood. Funny. I hadn't felt the punctures at all.

I wiped the blood off.

No wounds.

"Shane?" Michael sounded worried. Hell, he was right to be. I shook my head, and he pitched his phone to me. I fielded it neatly, dialed 911, and reported devil dog in a vampire headlock. They didn't sound surprised. That's my hometown for you. He repeated the question after I hung up, with a more urgent edge to it.

"I'm fine!" Well, maybe I wasn't, but I knew how this would go . . . if nobody knew what was going on, I'd get my ass hauled up in front of the Founder, or, worse, Myrnin, who'd siphon blood off of me and hem and haw and make crazy statements and finally say he didn't know what was going on. So I'd prefer to skip the drama and work out my problems on my own. Right now, the idea of letting anybody poke and prod me sounded horrifying. "They're on the way."

They were, too, at high speed. The cop car that wailed toward us screeched around the corner, and the two police inside bailed as the doors flew open. One was a vampire, which was nice, since apparently it was taking vampire strength to subdue angry Fido.

The other was the former mayor, now returned to police chief (which was where she belonged, I thought). Chief Hannah Moses looked at each of us in turn, considered the state of my arm and jacket, and then focused on Michael and the dog. "Hal, if you'd please wrangle the dog . . . ?"

Hal, the other cop, nodded and moved in. He and Michael did a complicated little maneuver transferring control of the snarling, writhing, snapping Fluffy, whose devil-red eyes continued to haunt me. Hal dumped the dog in the trunk of the police car, where it immediately began attacking the metal with a fury that chilled, and then he returned to us. "That's the third one," he told Hannah, who nodded.

"Third one?" I asked. "Mind if I ask . . ."

"You can ask, I'm just not sure I have an answer," Hannah said. She looked strong, tall, competent, perfectly put together . . . she held herself like a woman who wasn't afraid of anything, and that was almost true. She was afraid of failure, and she'd failed at being mayor, because that was a job nobody could win. But give her a weapon, a uniform, and a problem, and I couldn't think of anybody I'd rather get behind. "I can't tell you what they are, Shane, because I don't know. All I know is that we got a report of a wild dog last night that was attacking people, and it looked just like this one. Had to shoot that one, it was going after a kid. Two more tonight. I'm hoping like hell this is the last one."

"Experiment gone wrong out of Myrnin's lab?" Michael wasn't afraid to go there. Well, he was only half a step ahead of me, actually.

"I checked," Hannah said. I'd have paid to hear that conversation. "He says no. He says he wouldn't. He likes dogs."

"Probably true," I said. "And Claire would never put up with him experimenting on helpless animals. He cares what she thinks, even if he doesn't care about anybody else."

The sound of the dog in the trunk was like a demon in a tin can, and it was unnerving me. The whole police cruiser was rocking on its tires. Hannah didn't so much as glance at it. Michael cleared his throat and said, "What are you going to do with it?"

"Find out what's going on, or try to," Hannah said. "So far, nobody's been killed, but I don't like it. Nothing good ever comes of weird things happening in this town." Before I could comment on how true that was, not that she needed my opinion, she focused on me. "How's your arm?"

I showed her. I'd wiped the blood away, and all that showed was bruising. "Nothing broken. Coat's toast, though."

"It makes you look tough," she said, and smiled. "Going somewhere?"

"Yeah. You know. Out."

"Of town."

I was silent. I'd gotten approval from the Founder to bug out of Morganville for a while, but that didn't mean Amelie couldn't change her mind. She did. Often. And I wasn't her favorite person, anyway.

"Well," Hannah said after a few seconds of whistling wind, "I suppose you should be on your way, then. Tell Claire we miss her."

"She's only been gone a day."

"And yet," Hannah said. She was still giving me a professional kind of smile, but now it had a softening of warmth to it. "You'd better do right by that girl, Shane."

"Thanks, Mom." I meant it sarcastically, but you know, if Hannah *had* been my mom, I'd have probably turned out a lot more badass. Not to mention less prone to stupid mistakes. "Michael's giving me a ride out of town."

"Better get going, then." She nodded to me, to Michael, and she and Hal got back into the snarling, rocking police cruiser, shut off the flashers, and headed off to wherever you unloaded insane devil dogs.

My arm was starting to ache. Nothing bad, though. Just hot and abused. I'd had lots worse. *Lots* worse. Michael stuck my bag in the backseat and we went back in the house; he had a nice leather jacket that he let me have for the trip, with the warning that if I got it torn up he'd patch it up with strips of my bleeding flesh, which, hey. Brotherly love.

I'd left Morganville a couple of times before—once with my dad and mom, when we'd fled after our house burned and my sister died. Then again with Michael, Eve, and Claire (and the much-loathed vampire Oliver as our chaperone). Still, approaching the town boundary made my heart speed up and my palms clammy; it was a built-in resident reaction. Despite the chill in the air, I rolled down the window to see where we were, and I shivered when Michael's car sped past the ghostly, creaking billboard where we'd said good-bye to Claire in the predawn light. I let out a slow, shaky breath and rolled the heavily tinted window back up. It was like traveling in space, riding around in vampire cars.

"Feels weird, right?" Michael said. In the dashboard's green light, his pale skin looked alien. So did his eyes—wide and dark, pupils gone huge to take in available light. "No matter how much we tell ourselves it's okay to leave town, our bodies still don't believe it. We're used to liking the cage."

I admit it: I was a little surprised. "You feel it, too?"

"Sure." His smile was bitter around the edges. "Dude, I grew up here, never left here until I was made a vampire. Still got all the instincts. We're born with them, and trained into them, right?"

I nodded silently. I felt itchy and weird, and the ache in my arm had sunk in deeper. Even with the heavy leather jacket, I felt cold. I also became aware of a weird odor coming from the jacket—the scent of a vampire. I'd never really smelled it before. Michael had, since turning vamp, smelled only like whatever body spray Eve had given him; vamps didn't sweat. Strange, that I could smell something else now.

Something buzzed in the pocket. I pulled out the phone and stared at it for a second, then blinked. "Oh. Your phone. Sorry."

"Keep it. Yours is fried. I'll get a new one. That way at least we can keep track of you and know you're safe."

I wasn't sure how I felt about that, suddenly—about the vampires being able to track my phone. But then again, I supposed if they wanted, they could dispatch Michael or any other vamp to find me. Wouldn't be that hard. They knew where I was going, anyway.

"Thanks," I said. "Eve texted you a picture of herself in a nightie."

"What?" He grabbed for the phone, but I held it out of reach.

"Kidding. She just asked when you'd be home. You know, to rip all her clothes off."

"Maybe this giving you my phone thing is a bad idea."

"Depends. What kind of pictures *does* Eve send you?"

"Good thing I'm not the jealous type—" He stopped himself, but too late, and there was an awkward, thick silence for a few long seconds.

Because I *was* the jealous type, and we both knew it. I tried not to be, but the green-eyed monster part of me had roared out on a couple of occasions, and Hulk smashed my trust with Claire the last time.

Hence, me traveling alone.

"I'll ignore any pictures, I swear," I said. "I'm texting Eve now." I pushed buttons and lost myself in the tech world for a few more heartbeats, and when I came out of it, the strangeness between me and my best friend was mostly gone. Mostly. "Done. If she sexts me now, it's her own lookout."

He punched me on the arm, lightly. It was the uninjured one, thankfully, but I still felt echoes through to the other side. Ow. Yeah, definitely going to leave a mark. "You're lucky I love you, man."

"You're lucky I don't stake your undead Dracula wannabe ass."

He just shook his head. "Seriously. You going to be okay out there on your own?"

"Claire's out there," I said. "Alone. So yeah. I have to be, right?"

"She really can take care of herself, you know. She's proved it about a hundred times already."

"I know," I said. This time, my voice came out softer than I intended. "That's kind of what scares me. Because what if she doesn't need me anymore, man?"

That got me a sideways flash of a look before he turned his attention back to the road. "She needs you for more than just protection. It's how it works. You want the strong girl, you understand that she's with you because she wants to be. Not because she has to be. You know that, right?"

"I guess. I mean, yeah, but . . . hard to break the habit." I turned toward the window, but all I saw was my blurry reflection in the darkened glass. Michael was looking at me again, I could feel it. "How long 'til we get to the bus station?"

"Another half hour," he said. "Sleep if you want."

"Yeah," I said. "Yeah, I think I will."

I didn't.

But I pretended.

It didn't occur to me until later, when I was on the bus and headed on a long, exhausting trip across country, that I'd forgotten to text Claire and tell her about my broken phone, and by then . . .

By then it was too late.

FOUR

"Are you nervous?" the girl standing next to Claire whispered. "I'm nervous." She sounded it. They were in a fairly large group of incoming students being led around by an upperclassman at night. It was the end of Claire's first day of orientation, which had been exhausting and full of way too much info to absorb at once; her brain was swimming with maps, people, names, streets, stunningly gorgeous buildings. . . . She still hadn't met her Special Projects instructor, Professor Anderson, who wouldn't be available until the morning, but she'd filled up her day trying to learn more about the MIT campus.

But it had been impossible to resist the little orange slip of paper she'd received, that had given her where to meet for the "special tour." And it hadn't disappointed. An hour of complicated rules, and the Orange Tour had shown them absolutely incredible things . . . tunnels, rooftops, secrets of all kinds. Claire hadn't thought she had a head for heights, but it turned out she did . . . more than a lot of the others on the tour. She'd been able to stand right on the edge of the tallest building, and look straight down. It was exciting. Dizzying, but exciting.

MIT was . . . unique. Like Morganville, it was pretty much a self-regulating system, with its own history, rules, and environment . . . once you were on the campus, it felt as if the MIT universe was the only universe that mattered. She'd met a ton of people, and they were all a blur. There were at least five upperclassmen leading the tour group, but only one wore a T-shirt that said I'M NOT HERE. His name was Jack, and he was the one who talked the most.

Seeing the cool, creative energy of the dorms taught Claire that it had probably been a huge mistake to stay off campus with Elizabeth, but done was done on that score. She was committed, and it would be too much of a drama to try to beg off now. Plus, she'd already prepaid the rent.

"Hey," the girl whispered again. "Are you nervous?"

"No, it's fine," Claire said. She supposed to normal people there was something spooky about the tour—after all, it was after hours, they were trudging around in the dark, and the upperclassmen leading the tour were doing their best to freak them out. But she couldn't get nervous about it. She supposed Morganville had raised the bar way too high on that one. "We're safe. They're not going to let anything happen to us, trust me."

"I don't know where we are," the girl whispered back anxiously. She shuffled maps, frowning; like Claire, she had a ton of materials, but unlike Claire, she hadn't come armed with a backpack to stow it in. "Do you know? Because I thought we were heading for Baker House. Isn't that right?"

"I think so."

"But—we're way off, right? Look, I think we're not even on campus . . . no, wait, we are . . ." The girl's anxiety teetered on the edge of panic, and there wasn't much Claire could do to help. She checked her phone, supposedly to look at the GPS, but quite honestly, she was checking to see if she'd gotten any messages.

She had. Voice mail from Michael. Again. She'd skipped listening to the last three because she was hoping Shane's name would pop up . . . but just as she started to stow the phone away, she saw a text pop up.

It was *still* Michael . . . but it said, *This is Shane hit me back.*

What?

Claire lagged behind a little, texting back—risky to do on unfamiliar ground, in the dark, but this couldn't wait. *Y R U on Michael's phone?*

A few seconds, and the text came back. *Broke mine sry.*

It sounded like an excuse. A bad one. But accidents did happen. *Was waiting,* she texted back. *Saw vid.*

No answer for a long moment, and then he typed back, *I meant it.* That was all. Just that.

And she stopped walking, closed her eyes for a moment, and pulled in a deep, chilly breath. Then she texted, *Miss U.*

He responded, *Luv U.*

Her eyes stung with tears, and she hesitated for a long second before she texted back, *TTYS.* Talk to you soon.

"Hey!"

Claire jerked her head up at the urgent whisper from a few feet away, instincts coming alive and screaming, but it was just the girl, the nervous one, still clutching all her brochures and maps and binders. She looked even more paranoid than before. What was her name, anyway? Started with a V. Vita? No, Viva. "Viva," she said, and the girl nodded. "What's wrong?"

"We're supposed to be going to Baker House," she said. "But it's not on the map!"

"Well, it's supposed to be a secret tour," Claire said. "So maybe it's called something else on the map."

"But——" Viva shifted uneasily. "I just—I just want to go back. Would you share a cab with me? Please? We can get one on the street up there."

The rest of the group was walking briskly on, heading through some trees, and they were being left behind. Well, that didn't seem like a good idea under any circumstances.

Claire put her phone away, shifted the weight of her backpack (which wasn't much, at least not now—a tablet computer, a couple of books she was interested in, and the load of goodies from orientation. She wasn't used to it being so light). "Let's just catch up," she said. "Come on. We can't bug out now, they'll worry about us." And she jogged onward, looking back to be sure Viva was coming. She was, probably only because she didn't want to be left alone.

Claire was definitely *not* interested in going back to the house ahead of schedule. Liz had moped about her going to orientation, had fussed about when she'd be back, and then sulked about the fact Claire expected to be gone until late. The drama had been intense. No reason to add to it by coming home off schedule . . . that would probably lead to a theatrical scene about how Liz's plans had been spoiled because Claire didn't do what she said.

Two days in and I already hate living there, Claire thought. *Probably not a good sign.* But she'd hated Morganville at first, and now . . . now she really missed it.

And Shane. God, she missed Shane so much. She missed Eve and Michael, and (probably stupidly) Myrnin, too. She'd spent the day providing the mental running commentary from her friends and boyfriend, and from Myrnin when she spotted something excessively and geekily cool. It was getting easier and easier to summon up a mental replica of Myrnin in her head. That was probably worrying.

Cambridge was so *busy.* Even this late, there were loads of cars zipping around, planes crossing the starless, light-washed sky, crowds gathering for mysterious and unknown reasons around shops or parks. The Morganville in her wanted to tell them all to go home and be safe, but she knew that was verging on crazy. The world these laughing people lived in was a very different place.

She was in a very different place.

The raggle-taggle group of students that their tour guides were leading came to a sudden halt, because in the clearing ahead there was a big group already gathered. There was no apparent purpose to it—just people gathered, talking, some sitting and reading, some playing games, a few paired-off couples so into each other it didn't matter others existed at all. As Claire caught up (and a breathless Viva caught up with her), the entire group came to a stop halfway inside of the crowd, and their guide held up his hand.

"Hang on," he told them. "We're really close, I just have to check something. Stay here. Oh, and remember what I told you if security shows up. Don't tell them my name, and don't tell them where you're going."

Viva held up her hand, "Um, Jack? I can't find Baker House on my map . . ."

"Just a second," he said, but his words were lost in a sudden chorus of phones buzzing, beeping, and pinging. People around them fumbled for their devices, and Claire checked hers out of habit. Nothing.

But the people around them whooped, cheered, high-fived, and . . . began to dance. All their phones were blaring out a song Claire recognized. Most of them had some kind of glow-in-the-dark things that they pulled from their pockets, and within seconds it was a full-on instant rave.

Their little group was an island of clueless in a sea of moving, jumping bodies . . . and suddenly, she didn't see their tour guides anywhere. They'd just melted into the crowd. Gone.

Viva's eyes were huge, and she was clutching all her official MIT loot to her chest as if someone might want to rip off her maps and binders. She crowded closer to Claire as a guy with huge holes in his ears and a shaved head began kangaroo-jumping around near them. The noise was deafening.

Claire spotted the campus security uniforms approaching, and pointed, and Viva gasped and looked as if she might faint. "Jack!" she yelled, and turned in a circle, staring wildly. "Jack, they're coming! Jack!"

But their tour guide was nowhere to be seen, and now, as more campus security descended, the flash rave broke up and students began scrambling away in a hundred directions . . . leaving their little tour group frozen and stunned.

There was no sign of their guide anywhere.

Claire, whose survival instincts were a lot more finely honed, had been prepared to cut out, but Viva's shaking hand on her arm prevented her from following the upperclassmen, and before she could get Viva to flee with her, it was too late. There were three security guards flanking them, frowning and looking very serious.

"Okay, you know this area's off-limits," one of them said. "Names!"

There was a confused babble of voices, and he cut them off with an impatient gesture and pointed to Claire.

"Claire Danvers," she said. "But we were taking a tour. We didn't know it was off-limits."

"Likely story, Miss Danvers. If you were on a tour, where's your guide?"

"Um . . ." Viva held up her hand. "He left? I'm Viva Adewah."

He made notes. "Uh-huh. Name of the guide, for the records?"

"Um, I don't know. He took off and left us here!"

The three security men exchanged a look, and the center one made another official-looking note in his book. "And where were you headed?"

He got a shifty look and mutters from all of their fellow abandoned group, and Claire sighed. "Baker House," she said. "Which isn't real, right? And Jack Florey's not a real person?"

"Opinions are divided," the cop said, and put his notebook away. "It's the Orange Tour, by the way. Long tradition. Sometimes they let us hassle you. Guess this was your lucky night. You're all from Fifth East?"

"How did you know?" Viva asked.

"Because if you weren't, you'd have a different guide. Head that way. You'll get back on track quickly. Stay together. No wandering off on your own. And congratulations. You're part of the history now—you've survived an Orange Tour. Now, don't let us ever catch you hacking."

A hack, in MIT jargon, meant a real-world mod . . . like the

most recent one, which had been to turn the Earth Sciences building into a giant Tetris game with colored interior lights. Hacks
didn't destroy, they just ... creatively amended. But Jack Florey
had given them the rules of hacks, too—and they sounded remarkably like the rules of surviving Morganville. *No stealing. No destroying property. And never hack alone.*

Odds were, most people on this tour would, at some point, be
involved in a hack, or at least see a really good one.

But probably not her, Claire reflected, with another little burst
of regret. She wasn't here to be a freshman; she was here to study
with Professor Anderson, on a Morganville-approved study course,
and Amelie wasn't likely to be in favor of anything that wasn't
strictly on the curriculum.

Escorted by the watchful eyes of campus security, they trudged
back toward the center of campus, where the dome of the Maclaurin Building dominated the landscape. Viva was still sticking close
to Claire's elbow. She looked small, and lost; the others in the
group were laughing and happy, glowing with adventure and excitement. They seemed born to be here.

Viva didn't. And Claire realized with a jolt that the kid was
young—younger than her and the others in the group. Not *much*
younger, but enough to matter and cripple her with self-
consciousness. "Hey," Claire said to her. "So, where are you from,
Viva?"

"Iowa," she said. "Rockwell City. You probably never heard
of it."

True, she hadn't. "Is it nice?"

"Not like this. I mean, this is—" Viva flapped a hand around
them, helpless to describe it. "Different. It's great, and I thought I
knew what I was getting into, but it's so—"

"Real," Claire said. She knew how it felt. "Bigger than you."

"Yeah." Viva clutched her binders closer, like a magic shield. "It's a lot of pressure, and classes haven't even started. I just feel—"

"Alone?"

Viva nodded, looking ashamed. "They all seem so comfortable already."

"I wish I could help you, but I'm not living in the dorm. Wait— maybe I can help." Claire grabbed Viva's arm and towed her sideways, aiming for a laughing mixed group of girls and boys; they seemed friendly, and she liked the T-shirt one of them was wearing. It meant he had a good sense of humor, at least. "Hey, guys? This is Viva. I've got to take off, but could you make sure she gets back to the dorm okay? I'm Claire, by the way. Claire Danvers."

"Hey," the boy in the T-shirt said. He had messy, curly hair that flopped in his eyes, and a million-dollar smile. "I'm Nick Salazar. This nutcase is Oded, that's Jenny, Amanda, Trent . . ." He reeled off names as if he'd known them all his life, though Claire was pretty sure he'd just met them. "Nice to meet you guys. Viva, right? Cool name."

"Thanks," she said. She looked scared, but determined.

"Hey, you need a bag," Jenny said, and dug in her backpack to come up with a tote with the MIT logo. "Try this. What room are you in?"

"Screw that, the question at hand is what's your major?" Oded said. "Because let me just tell you right now, any answer other than World of Warcraft or Advanced Ninja Studies will not be accepted."

"Fight Club," Viva said. Oded considered, and offered her a fist bump. She took it.

"I stand corrected," he said. "She just leveled up."

Claire wanted to stay with them—wanted it so badly she could taste it. The easy, silly friendship reminded her of what she'd left behind, and she craved it . . . but she really did need to talk to Shane. So she drifted off, and Viva—deep into the conversation now—hardly noticed her departure. Claire jogged off to a trail that led to Stratton Student Center. It was, at this hour, not very busy; she found a quiet table, acquired mocha, and sat down with her phone.

Then she dialed Michael's phone.

"Hey." Shane's voice was dark and warm and deep, and she sank into it as if it were a blanket. "You okay, tough girl?"

"I am now," she said. It wasn't quiet where he was; she heard a rumble, maybe wheels. "Are you driving?"

"I'm mobile, yep. You know me, always moving, like a shark. I'm restless without you."

"I miss you," she said. She leaned against the wall. "I *really* miss you, Shane."

"How much?"

She laughed. "Not enough to tell you in public, especially while you're driving."

"Damn, there goes my chance for some hot sexy talk."

His voice just did things to her, she realized . . . made her feel warm and liquid inside, made her think all kinds of things she probably shouldn't be picturing out here in front of food court staff. "I hate my housemate," she said, to change the subject to something safer.

"Elizabeth? I thought she was your best friend in high school."

"She was. In high school. But—"

"She changed? Yeah, that happens. Look what happened to Michael."

"Shane!"

He laughed again, low in his throat. "Kidding, Claire. I'm just saying people change. If you're not there for it, it's not always easy to adjust to it, right? Which is why I hate this. I hate missing your life. I hate missing those little moments that change you. Because they're going to change *us*."

He was right, but . . . but also, not. "I need to change a little on my own," she said. "Shane, I love you, and I want to be with you, but I need to breathe, too. I need to fly a little and see how far I can go. That's why I took this chance. It's not forever. It's just a while."

"Maybe a short while if your housemate drives you crazy. What's she doing?"

"Let me see . . . she's a drama queen, and not in a fun way; she's controlling; she's OCD; she's passive-aggressive . . ."

"You had me at drama queen. I have got to meet this chick."

"No, you really don't, trust me. She used to be fun and nerdy, but now—now she's so self-consciously *not*, you know? She's working so hard to be cool that she's uncool. I think maybe she had a bad relationship."

"Roger that. Seen too many tragic examples. You know, the ones in the hipster hats who try looking like some unholy love child of Jack White and Ashton Kutcher?"

"I learned a new word today."

"Which is?"

"Fidiot."

"Ah, you're so cute. You didn't know that word? You know what it stands for, right?"

She lowered her voice to a whisper. "Fucking idiot?"

"I love that you have to make that much of an effort to curse.

Like you're worried you might scar somebody. Seriously, it's ador-able. So, been attacked by any vampires yet?"

"Not a one."

"Zombies? Giant spiders? Water monsters?"

"It's been really quiet on the supernatural attack front."

"Too bad, 'cause I got attacked by a devil dog. It was not awe-some."

"A *what?*"

"A big-ass dog with glowing red eyes. Trust me. You do not want to face a pack of these bad boys. Makes wolves look like tea-cup poodles."

"But you're okay, right?"

"Yeah," he said, altogether too lightly. "I'm okay. Nothing but bruises. The cops—and I guess, vampires—are taking care of our devil dog problem. Nothing to worry about, trust me. We'll be okay. Aren't we always?"

"Almost always." She swallowed a lump in her throat, because the confidence in his voice had made her feel unexpectedly fright-ened. "Please, Shane—don't get cocky, okay?"

"Oh, *now* you want to do sexy talk?"

"I'm serious! Please. *Please.*" The image she most remembered right now was of him floating in a tank of murky water, bleed-ing . . . dying, at the hands of enemies of the vampires. And it ter-rified her. "I hate it that I'm safe here, and you're . . ."

"Swimming in an ocean of danger, with sharks? Hey, it's what manly men do. That, and wrestle rabid badgers."

He was being flippant, and it killed her. "Shane!"

He was quiet for a long moment, and then he said, "Are you okay, Claire?"

"Yes—I—I—" She took a deep breath. On the wall across

from her was a poster promoting delicious bagels, and she focused on the colors, the shapes, and tried to clear all the frantic noise from her mind. "I'm okay. Let me know when you get your new phone—can I call you on this one until then?"

"If you want." He seemed pleased about that. "I know you're getting settled and all, but maybe I can call around this time at night? Would that work?"

"Yeah. That works."

"Because I don't want to miss a day with you." She was silent, not because she disagreed, but because she was overcome with a wave of emotion so strong she couldn't get the words out. He mistook it for something else, because he hurried on, tone turning more impersonal. "So, yeah, I've gotta hit it. Talk to you tomorrow, right?"

"Right," she managed to choke out.

"Is it pushing you to tell you I love you?"

"No." It wasn't a wave of emotion, it was a sea, and she was drowning in it. "Love you." That was all she could manage. She hung up the call, and burst into hot, hard tears. She struggled to keep them quiet, but she knew everybody could tell what was going on. Just another sad, homesick, lonely freshman having a breakdown. Great.

It felt good, though, in a weird way. Six coarse food court napkins later, the storm passed, and she was left with a weary, empty ache inside, but an equally empty brain. Her eyes felt swollen, and she knew she looked a mess, but sometimes . . . sometimes the emotions just were too big to hold.

She tossed her trash, avoided the glances of other students, and started the walk home. The row house she shared with Elizabeth wasn't that far—about six blocks, about the same distance she'd walked from Texas Prairie University to her old home at the Glass House. She spotted some students walking, and most had earbuds in, rocking out as they strolled, but she couldn't even think about that . . . Morganville had taught her to pay attention, or else.

So she was aware within the first block that someone was following her.

He started out far back, but no matter how fast her pace, he steadily closed the distance. Claire caught glimpses of him in blurry glass windows, but she couldn't tell much about him, except that he was taller than she was (wasn't everybody?) and broader, too. Not Shane's size, not nearly, but big enough, if he meant her harm.

In Morganville, she'd have readied a weapon, but this wasn't Morganville. Defending herself wasn't quite that clear-cut. What if she staked some totally innocent person?

"Hey!" the man finally called to her, when he'd caught up to about twenty feet. "Hey, Claire?"

She turned, still walking, and saw that it was one of the guys from the campus. Nick. There must have been something warning in her body language, because he slowed down and held up both hands, looking suddenly cautious. "Sorry," he said. "It's me. Nick. I know, it's weird I'm following you because we just met, but . . . I didn't want you walking by yourself, that's all."

"Oh," Claire said. She felt torn between continued suspicion and an intense desire to believe in someone's innocent intentions, for a change. Surely the entire world couldn't be *that* hideous, right? Yes, she'd had bad times; yes, guys she'd trusted had betrayed her. But it wasn't right to assume that everybody was like that. "Oh, well, thanks. What about Viva?"

"She's hanging with my crew, headed for the dorm. Not that I actually have a crew, per se, but more of a horde. Possibly a gaggle. So, you're new, right? First year?"

"Yes," she said.

"Already living off campus, though?"

"Well . . . it was probably a mistake. The dorms seem fun."

"It's epic adventure," Nick agreed soberly. "Maybe you're not up for it."

She almost laughed. "Yeah, that's me. I'm terrified."

He smiled, and fell in step with her. A comfortable distance away, a gentleman's distance, nothing intrusive. "You don't seem like the wallflower type."

It felt so natural and friendly that it came as a shock to her when she suddenly thought, *I think he's flirting with me. Is he? Am I flirting back? I shouldn't be, should I?* It was confusing and strange, and for a perilous second, some rebellious part of her thought, *Why shouldn't I? I came here to stretch my wings. Well, this is stretching.*

"I'm pretty shy," Claire said. "Really, I am."

"I could tell by the way you dragged Viva over and announced her to the world. So, what's your major?"

The inevitable college question. She didn't hesitate. "Physics."

Nick seemed pleased, not daunted—another difference between MIT and, well, everywhere else. "You don't just get to say physics. I mean, what flavor? Chocolate, vanilla, applied, theory . . ."

"A little of both."

"I hate to be the one to break it to you, but I'm pretty sure there's no 'little of both' major. You don't know yet, do you?" When she didn't answer, he shrugged and stuck his hands in his jeans pockets. "It's okay. According to the literature, people change around. Probably good to give it some thought before you commit."

That's why I'm here, she almost said. *To give it some thought.* It was about so much more than her choice of study, but she didn't know how to say that, and she didn't really want to give him the wrong idea. "What's yours?"

"My major? Mechanical engineering, emphasis in robotics. Second year. Haven't flunked me out so far."

"Do you think it's possible to take a human brain and wire it up to control a computer?"

He missed a step, but only one, and said, "Ah, I get it, you're asking me a Classic *Trek* question. 'Spock's Brain,' right? Where the planet of women grabbed Spock, removed his brain, and stuck in a machine to power their systems?"

"I—" She had no idea what he was talking about; she'd watched some *Star Trek* but not the old episodes. Her parents had been kids when those were on. "Uh, I guess so."

"Geek cred points for trying to stump me, but sorry, you'll have to do better than that. Would you like to try anime for a hundred?" When she looked blank, he sighed. "What took it down, anime, or the *Jeopardy!* reference?"

"*Jeopardy!*, I guess. I know a little about anime."

"A *little* about it? Girl, we need to get you on a study program, fast. You're not going to last a week around here if you can't keep up with the pop culture references. How about *Lord of the Rings? Firefly? Doctor Horrible?* No? Clearly we have a lot of work to do."

He chattered on, and it was warm and funny and sweet and for a change, not at all life-and-death drama. She lost track of time and progress, and all of a sudden she realized they'd walked right past the steps to her row house apartment. She turned and backtracked, and gave Nick an apologetic smile.

"Ah. The old homestead, I perceive. Well, I did my Guy Duty—you're okay from here?"

"Yeah, I'm okay," she said. She glanced up. Elizabeth's windows were dark; she'd already gone to bed. "I should probably—"

"Go, yeah, you should. So just . . . see you around, then?"

"I'll see you around, Nick."

"Good night, Claire." She gave him another smile, and he returned it, and took a few steps away before he turned back toward her, pulling out his phone. "Okay, this is probably way out of line, and feel free to Xena Warrior Princess my ass, but can I—?" He waved the phone at her, and he looked so puppy-dog cute that she almost said yes.

"I can't," she said, quietly. "Sorry. I've got a boyfriend."

"Oh. Oh, right, of course you do. What was I thinking? Sorry."

"No, don't be—look, *I'm* sorry. I guess I was just—I shouldn't have let you think that. I was just lonely, you know?"

"I know lonely. Lonely is a good friend of mine. No harm, Claire. I'm not going to go curl up in a fetal ball and cry for more than, you know, six hours, max." He flashed her a ridiculously funny smile, and she laughed in return. "See you around, then."

"See you."

He walked off, hands in his pockets, all loose angles and baggy jeans. The only thing he and Shane had in common, she thought, was the confidence. Shane could sling a casual nerd reference, but Nick probably couldn't string together more than a few sentences without one; Shane knew his way around a fight, and Claire was fairly certain that she could take Nick with one hand tied behind her back. Maybe two.

And yet, there was that traitorous little tingle of interest. Probably just because he represented everything that wasn't Morganville—a normal world, where the biggest thing most people had to worry about was the latest episode of their favorite show, or whether a girl would give up her phone number for a winning smile.

She liked that world. She just wasn't sure that she was part of it . . . or ever would be. That was, Claire realized, what Nick represented to her: a world where a guy could just be amusing and interesting and funny, and not fight for his life every day against overwhelming odds. A life with a home, and kids, and just the usual, mundane worries.

No vampires and monsters. No wonder she felt some tingle of attraction.

Claire unlocked the front door, smiling quietly to herself, feeling oddly relaxed now, off her guard, and when she heard the scrape of footsteps behind her she turned, still smiling, and said, "Nick, I thought—"

It wasn't Nick.

She didn't know this guy. He was tall, broad-shouldered, handsome in a heavy kind of way that was probably going to turn unpleasant on him in a few years. He was Monica Morrell's type, she thought, and all of that went through her head in the same second as her threat assessment. No gun, no knife, but he carried himself as if he was ready to move at her, and alerts flashed red somewhere deep inside her.

She braced, ready to move.

"Hi," he said, and stopped a few steps below her, but blocking the way down. "So, you're Liz's new roommate, right? She said she had an old friend moving in with her. I'm Derrick."

"Derrick," she repeated. Liz hadn't mentioned him, but then, that didn't necessarily spell trouble. Nevertheless, Claire edged one foot into the doorway, and calculated ahead what her body needed to do next in a hurry. *Shift weight, swing right, complete the turn,*

slam the door, lock it. It was a one, maybe one-and-a-half-second movement. Derrick didn't look that fast, but she'd been fooled before.
"If you're looking for Liz, I think she's already asleep."

"No problem," he said. "I'm not coming in. Just wanted to
say hi."

"Hi," Claire said, without any warmth; she still felt weird
about this. She didn't like being doorstepped, especially by someone with that odd look in his eyes. "Look, it's late. Sorry, I don't
mean to be rude, but I—"

He held up his hands, but somehow, she didn't take it as an
apology, or a sign of surrender. "No problem. Just wanted to find
out what your name was."

"Claire," she said. "Good night."

She kept her eyes on him as she stepped inside, closed the door,
and shot the bolts. For the first time, she was grateful for all the
locks. Derrick didn't move, at least until the door closed, but she
felt a weird tension in him, as if every muscle was shaking with
the desire to rush her.

Claire slid aside the small metal flap over the peephole and
looked out.

Derrick's face loomed huge, *right there*, staring as if he'd known
she'd do it. She let out an involuntary gasp, let the flap slip down,
and backed away until she bumped into the stairs. Honestly, she'd
faced down vampires on her doorstep, and they generally weren't
that creepy.

She sat down on the steps, and in the dark next to her, in the
shadowy space between the stairs and the hall table, she heard a
breathy whisper. "It's him, isn't it? Derrick."

Somehow, Claire wasn't surprised it was Liz, huddled there with
her knees drawn up to her chest. She was wearing fuzzy pajamas

that were a pale gray in the dimness, and she looked like a terrified little girl.

Claire got up, sat down in the narrow, dark space with her, and put her arm around her friend. Liz leaned in, and she was shaking, really shaking. Claire stripped off her coat and put it over Liz's shoulders. "You're all right," she said, and hugged her. "Liz, it's okay. He's outside. The door's locked."

"But he's *here*." Even though it was a whisper, it sounded like a wail of despair. "I didn't think he knew where I was, but he's here. He knows."

"Liz—who is he?"

"I met him at my old school. It was a blind date; my friend set us up. I didn't like him, but he—he just kept trying to date me. At first it was just texts and calls and flowers, but then he started following me. I started dating this other guy and he—he—" Liz's voice faltered, and she swallowed hard. "He just disappeared. He finally called me and said he had to move away, because Derrick had shown up and told him if he didn't that he'd be dead. He told me—he told me that Derrick said he'd rather see me dead than with someone else, and to watch my back. So I left. I quit school, moved out of town, changed my hair and how I dressed, made new friends. I didn't think he'd follow me, I really didn't."

"But you were afraid he would," Claire said. "I know because of all the locks on the door."

Liz nodded miserably. "He sent me letters. He was really angry I left. He tracked me down in the last place I was, and sent me pictures of my new haircut telling me how cute I looked. He sent stuff to my mom and dad, too. He knows where all my family lives."

"Did you talk to the police?"

"Sure." Liz sniffled and straightened a little, and her voice gained some strength. "They took it seriously and all, but he never made any threats we could prove. He's being really careful. It's like he's done this before and knows what to do not to get caught. That's what makes it even scarier. I'm sorry. I should have warned you—I should have warned you what you might be getting into. I mean, you're just . . . You've always been so nice and gentle, and I don't want to put you in the middle. . . ."

"I'm not that gentle," Claire said. "Did you know I learned how to fight? And I can use a bow and arrow?"

"You *what?*" Liz sounded incredulous. "You mean, you shoot at targets? Did you get into it because of that movie? And anyway, how does that even help?"

"I mean the town I was living in was someplace where you'd better have good aim," Claire said. "And a strong stomach, and steady nerves. So if Derrick wants to come creeping, he's in for a big, ugly surprise. I'm not going to hesitate to defend my home, myself, or my friend. Get me?"

"You—you're serious. What, you think you're going to shoot him with an *arrow?*"

"Well, not right now, because I didn't carry them in my luggage," Claire said. "The bow's packed in my boxes. Should be here soon, though. Meanwhile, what do you know about using a knife?"

"I—excuse me?"

"Come on," Claire said. She got up and offered her hand. "Let me show you."

"Claire, I can't fight him!"

"Why not?"

Liz seemed to be at a loss for words. She took Claire's hand and pulled herself up to her feet. Claire switched on the light, and Liz seemed about to object; she winced and reached for the switch.

Claire stopped her. "What are you going to do?" she asked. "Are you going to live in the dark, locked in here? Afraid to look out, answer the door, leave? Yes, he's out there, and he's clearly not going to leave you alone until one of three things happens: he hurts you and gets arrested, or he makes a mistake and gets arrested, or you stop him."

"You want me to *kill him*?"

"I didn't say kill. I said stop. That means defend yourself. There's a difference between losing a fight and giving up. If you want to fight, come with me."

"I—" Liz looked at her for a long, uncertain moment. "You're different. I thought that from the beginning when you got off the plane, but it's more than just surface, more than just how you look. You're really different. You got . . . strong."

"In Morganville, you only get strong," Claire said. "Or, I guess, dead. But yes. And I know this isn't Morganville, but we can still act for ourselves. Come on. First lesson is how to defend yourself with what's around you. . . ."

Liz hesitated when Claire pulled her toward the kitchen, and stared toward the door. "Is he still there, do you think?"

"Maybe," Claire said. "I don't really care. Let him get frostbite out there, or get arrested for trying to peep. Don't play his game. Play yours."

"I don't *have* a game."

"You will," Claire promised her, and gave her a smile that was probably every bit as scary as anything Derrick had in him. "You will."

———

Myrnin hadn't given Claire a whole lot of information about her new mentor, only a name (Irene Anderson) and the fact that she had once lived in Morganville, and been Myrnin's assistant. It was fairly impressive that she'd survived the experience, but that hadn't given Claire much context for what Anderson would be like.

Turned out that she was *awesome*.

For one thing, she was a whole lot younger than Claire had expected—mid-thirties, maybe. And when Claire knocked on her office door, she thought she'd arrived in the wrong place, because the petite woman standing there had no desk, and was wearing overalls that had seen better days, and was using some kind of very small handheld blowtorch on a pile of metal.

"Just a sec," she said, without taking her eyes off what was happening. It was more like ten seconds, but then the woman shut off the burner, set it aside, and made a quick note on a pad of paper nearby. "There. Got it. So, you're my ten o'clock, right?"

"I'm Claire Danvers. You're . . . ?"

"Dr. Irene Anderson." The woman shoved goggles back on her head, and they slid to hang hilariously off her blond ponytail, then clattered to the floor. "I know, not what you were expecting, am I? Everybody says that. Including my own family. Hi." She came around the workbench and offered Claire her hand to shake. It was a decisive, firm grip, and she held Claire's gaze long enough for it to be evident she had blue eyes to go with the blond hair. Shane probably would have called her hot, though Claire was never sure exactly what his scale seemed to be . . . it had more to do with attitude than type. "Good to meet you. You're young to have survived a year or two doing what you were doing."

"Are we not supposed to mention . . . ?"

"Morganville? Sure, you can. Sorry. Native caution is very normal. I've always been so careful about not discussing Myrnin that I often forget to use his name even when I'm able. Speaking of the man, I hear he's better now."

"Better than he was when I got there."

"Ah. That's good. I didn't want to leave, but he was just too unstable for his good or mine, and I thought it was better if he had a vampire assistant for a while. Did he?"

"I—don't know. He's never told me much about people he worked with before me. I know that he, um . . ."

"Killed a lot of them? Yes, I know that, too. And, of course, he killed the sainted Ada. He'll never get over *her*." That earned an exasperated eye roll, which stopped when Dr. Anderson noticed Claire wasn't smiling. "What?"

"Ada's—well, dead, I guess. I suppose technically this would be the third and final time. As in, not coming back."

Dr. Anderson covered her mouth with one hand, and closed her eyes for a brief moment. "How'd he take that?"

"Not very well," Claire admitted. "He kind of lost it. But he's better now. I think it helped, letting go. He still has these— episodes, but they're not as bad as they used to be most of the time. More aggravating than terrifying."

"That's quite a change," her new professor said, and looked at Claire with more assessment. "You've done something I was never able to do, then. Congratulations. I was informed Myrnin had cracked the code on the disease—"

"We're calling it Bishop's Plague these days."

"Ah. Bishop's Plague . . . but now I think you had more to do with solving it than he did. Right?"

Claire didn't answer. She looked around the office—though it was more junk room and lab than office—and saw a small, cluttered table stuffed in the corner. It had a duct-taped, sagging office chair, but no visitor accommodations. "Is this where we're going to work?"

"This? No. Definitely not. I was just tinkering while I was waiting for you. Before we go, you'll need ID."

"I have a student ID card—"

"Not that." Dr. Anderson went to her desk, opened and closed drawers, muttered, and finally came up with some kind of black magnetic strip card with a logo on it that looked eerily familiar—the Founder's sign. She typed and moused on the computer, then ran the card through a mag strip device. "Here. Press your thumb in the box where it says." She passed Claire a small tablet device, and Claire did as requested. While she did, the tablet clicked, and she realized it had taken a picture, too. Before she could ask about it, Dr. Anderson took it back and tapped on the screen, then took the mag strip card she'd made and put it into a small white device attached to the computer.

It made some soft whirring sounds, and thirty seconds later it spit out a finished ID card, complete with picture and thumbprint. Dr. Anderson examined it, pronounced it good, and decorated it with an MIT lanyard as she handed it over. "Wear it around your neck," she said. "No tying it on your belt, or backpack, or wearing it as a headband, and trust me, I've seen students try to do all those things. If it's not in the right place, you'll get a visit from security, and you really don't want that. Where we're going, security's very, very serious." Dr. Anderson, Claire saw, was already wearing her own ID. It looked identical, except for the photo. "If you cut your hair or dye it, or your physical profile changes at all, you get new ID. It has all kinds of data encoded in it. Sounds Orwellian, right? It is. Get used to it."

Claire scrambled to follow as Dr. Anderson shucked her lab coat, tossed it on a hook, and led the way out of the office and down the long hallway to a sealed door with an electronic pass reader on it. Anderson buzzed in, but when Claire started to follow her through, the other woman stopped her. "Use your card after me," she said. "If you come through without swiping, alarms will go off. Like I said. Secure."

Claire nodded, and let the door shut before she ran her own badge and got a green light to enter. She slipped the lanyard back over her head and stepped through into a very different world.

This part of the building looked new, shiny, and sterile. It was bustling with activity—grad students, professors, people in suits who looked like official government types, or maybe private industry. It was often groups composed of all of those, huddled together, walking and talking. She caught snatches of conversations about genetics, about drug therapies, about nanotech, and that was all in only a two-minute brisk walk. Dr. Anderson exchanged nods with most of them, but there was no small talk.

Dr. Anderson's lab was marked with a simple white card in the slot that read RESTRICTED. Nothing else on the card . . . but when Claire moved to the side a little to allow Anderson to swipe through, she saw that there *was* something else on the paper, after all. The Founder's logo had been printed on it holographically, so it was only visible from certain angles.

The door made a soft sighing sound as it opened, and a puff of cool air that smelled like metal and chemicals washed over Claire. Dr. Anderson shut it behind her, and Claire badged through. She didn't need to be told twice about the security measures.

Inside it was . . . well, Myrnin's lab, only sane, orderly, and clean. But she recognized a lot of what was going on at each of the worktables, though instead of using Dark Ages alchemical techniques, Dr. Anderson had modern chemistry setups and state-of-the-art instruments and computers. It was like porn, but for science geeks. "Wow," Claire breathed, and ran her fingers tentatively over a brushed-steel worktable, not quite daring to get her fingerprints on any of the blindingly cool equipment yet. "You're—"

"Well funded? Yes. Amelie wanted to establish another, less chaotic method of research to validate and record Myrnin's discoveries. You know him; he's brilliant, and he's the living embodiment of chaos theory. So my job is to find out *why* his discoveries work, document and make them easily reproducible with modern equipment and techniques. And now that's your job, too."

"I was already doing that. Trying to, anyway. When he'd let me."

Dr. Anderson sent her a warm, knowing smile. "Yeah, I know how that goes. Working for Myrnin means being zookeeper, nanny, and best friend. Trouble is, knowing when each of those things is necessary, because making a mistake means you become a Happy Meal. Badge of honor for you to have survived the experience, Claire. And for getting the hell out of Morganville. Bet you think the worst is over, right?"

Claire shuddered, thinking about the draug, and Bishop, about the thousand life-threatening moments she'd made it through since coming to town. "Hopefully," she said.

"You're wrong," Dr. Anderson said. She sounded certain, and sober. "You live there, at that level, it's like living inside a video game. Surviving is a high, an achievement. Then you come out here into the real world, and the PTSD starts to set in . . . because nobody cares what you went through, or that you survived it, and your body's used to a constant adrenaline pump. It's like coming off a drug. If it hasn't hit you yet, it will . . . normal life takes a lot of getting used to, Claire. But if you need to talk to someone, well, I've been through it. What's the biggest thing you're missing so far?"

"Shane," Claire said. Her throat got tight and raw, and for a moment she couldn't go on. "My boyfriend."

"Ah," Anderson said. Nothing else. Her eyebrows went up, but she didn't ask anything, and after she'd waited a moment she got the idea Claire wasn't going to tell, either. "Let me give you the tour, then. I assume you're familiar with Myrnin's dimensional portals? Did he teach you how to operate them?"

From there, the hours passed fast, full of technical discussions and equations, lightning-fast chains of thought as each of them built on the other's ideas and work. By noon, they had a working mathematical expression of how the portals worked, and Claire matched it up against the work she'd done with Myrnin on the same thing.

Dr. Anderson's final version was better, cleaner, and covered more theoretical ground.

The afternoon was spent learning equipment, most of which Claire had never seen, though some of it she'd heard about. Most fascinating was a genetic sequencer hard at work cracking the code of vampire DNA. "It's deceptively human," Dr. Anderson said. "Tough to tell the difference, because there's really very little to find. It's almost as if the DNA was only part of the equation for how vampires change—it's not just a physical process. And I don't have any equipment that can capture something that only happens on the spiritual plane, at least, not yet."

"I might," Claire said. She felt tentative about it, and a little overwhelmed by what Dr. Anderson was doing in this very sparkly lab; who was *she* to pretend to be an inventor? It didn't feel nearly as weird when she was with Myrnin; everything seemed possible.

Here, she felt very . . . young. And inexperienced.

But she had Dr. Anderson's undivided attention. "Go on."

"I . . . I thought that since Myrnin had made machines that interacted with vampire powers, then it might be possible to make another machine to cancel them."

There was a long, strange silence, and Claire felt herself growing hot and uncomfortable under Anderson's steady stare. Then her professor said, very carefully, "Do you have such a device?"

"Maybe? I mean, I know it can amplify vampire *emotions.* I think if I can use it in reverse, it could make them afraid instead of angry, cancel out their aggression and hunger. . . . It's all really just a guess right now."

"But you built it."

"I have a prototype."

"Where?"

Dr. Anderson was taking this way more seriously than Claire had ever expected. Even Myrnin hadn't seemed so impressed. "It's packed, they're delivering it with all my stuff this week."

"You *shipped it*?"

"I thought it might be hard to get it through security at the airport."

"Ah. Excellent point. But you really thought it was safer to trust it to a moving company? Do the vampires know you have this device?"

"Myrnin does."

"And has he told Amelie?"

"I don't know," Claire said. She felt more than a little off balance, as if she had done something bad but she wasn't sure what exactly it was. "Shouldn't he have?"

"If he thinks you're worth keeping alive, he won't," Dr. Anderson said. She had a remote, calculating look in her blue eyes, suddenly, and it was chilling. "The last thing Amelie would want is a device like that, capable of giving humans a way to control vampires. When is this device scheduled to arrive here?"

"Um, tomorrow, I think. They're just supposed to put the boxes in my bedroom if I'm out."

"Don't be out," Anderson said. "Be home. Check the box you put it in before they leave, and then call me as soon as you're alone and I will arrange for an escort. I want this device of yours put in the secured area as soon as possible, just in case it works as you say. Vampires don't like us developing new weapons against them, Claire. I've seen others end up dead for simply talking about one, and you've actually *made* one. This is something that Amelie can't, and won't, ignore. I'm really surprised that Myrnin allowed this at all, and even more surprised that he hasn't told Amelie about it."

Claire thought, with a sudden burst of cold inside, about what had happened to Shane's family when they'd left Morganville. Amelie had been dead set on keeping her secrets, and when Shane's mother had begun remembering too much, talking too much, she'd ended up dead. It was pure luck that Shane and his father hadn't died, too.

What she had done in developing this device—no, this *weapon*—was a whole lot worse than just blabbing about Morganville. It could be a real threat to them. To their very lives.

Dr. Anderson was right. It was something the vampires wouldn't ignore . . . and now that she was out of Morganville, accidents could happen. None of her friends would know the difference.

She was alone.

"Hey," Dr. Anderson said, and gave her a small, careful smile. "Easy. You look a little spooked."

Claire nodded, unable to say much.

"You got used to thinking of yourself as safe from them, didn't you? That they were on your side. It's easy to make that mistake. They will treat you as an asset, or even as a friend, right up until you cross the line and become a threat, Claire; you've already done that, even if they don't know it yet. You've gone from Amelie's subject to Amelie's enemy, even though technically you've never turned against her . . . she won't wait for the actual betrayal. Just the seeds of it are enough." Anderson's eyes were still calculating, still cool. "Are you armed?"

"No. It's the real world. I didn't think I needed to . . . there are laws against it, right?"

"Would you rather be fined for carrying a concealed knife, or dead in an alley?"

"Are those my only options?"

Dr. Anderson's smile warmed up, and the seriousness faded a bit. Just a bit. "Not necessarily, but I believe in planning for the worst-case scenario."

"You'd really like my boyfriend, Shane," Claire said. "Okay. I'm used to carrying a knife—silver, right?"

"We have new processes that allow us to have just a silver layer on the edge. It's more reliable and holds sharpness well." Dr. Anderson walked to a locked cabinet and opened it with a palm print and complicated code punched into the keypad; she reached in and came out with a knife in a leather scabbard. It was dauntingly large, and when she handed it over, it felt heavier than Claire was used to carrying.

"Do you have anything . . ."

"Smaller? No. Sorry. It'll fit in a backpack handily. If you want to carry it on your person, I'd advise you to take up the current trend of carrying gigantic handbags. Watch the edge. It's sharp enough to slice anything but diamond. And for God's sake, *carry it*, Claire. You're no good to me at all if you're dead. Until you start working, I can't even be sure you're any good to me at all, but I'm willing to give you the chance." Anderson patted her on the shoulder in an impersonal, kind sort of way. "What time is it?—Oh, damn, I have a class to teach in twenty minutes. Lab rules: You'll be here bright and early every day. I arrive at six a.m.; I'll expect you no later than seven. You don't arrive before me, and you don't stay after. If I decide that you're reliable, I'll start allowing you to remain in the lab while I'm teaching, but you'll have a period of evaluation before that happens, and of course the lab's sensors will monitor everything you do. That's not meant as a threat, just clarity—I'd rather you aren't surprised by the level of observation you have here."

It was nothing but surprising, but Claire didn't really mind; she accepted the need for security. She wasn't sure how to read Dr. Anderson, though, and she thought her new mentor felt the same about her. *Well, at least she gave me a knife,* Claire thought. That said something . . . but what, exactly, Claire wasn't quite sure.

Dr. Anderson had already dismissed her, clearly, because she was shuffling through a stack of papers and ignoring Claire's tentative good-bye wave, so Claire headed back to the door. There was a second badge station, and she used it to unlock her way out into the hallway. Disorientation set in for a few seconds, because there were few signs and the clean white tile looked the same in any direction, but she finally figured out how they'd come in, and badged out for a second time before returning to normal college surroundings. It felt weird, coming from that high-tech world to one where people her age were laughing, throwing footballs on the lawn, and flirting as if it were the most important skill in the world.

Maybe the normal world isn't as normal as I expected.

That was a sobering thought.

She headed across the busy campus grounds, and the knife stuck in her backpack felt strange; she checked often to see if somehow the outline of it was visible, but of course it wasn't. It was like a sliver of her old life sticking into her new one, and she didn't know how to feel about it.

Turned out, she had reason to be happy.

Claire crossed Albany Street and headed for Chicago Pizza, because suddenly she was starving, and it was one place she'd tried before, so a little bit familiar . . . and as she got her pizza slice and soda and negotiated through the packed room for a little table at the wall, she saw someone standing on the other side of the window, looking in.

Someone she recognized.

Derrick.

Liz's stalker ex wasn't just checking out the day's pie offerings; he was staring right at her, boring his gaze in hard as a drill. The shock made Claire's heart kick up hard, and she instinctively pushed back from the table and reached down for the pack leaning against her knee—survival instincts, even though Derrick wasn't doing anything but looking at her.

It was something in his eyes. Something just . . . wrong.

There was no chair on the other side of her tiny table, but someone got up and left, and Derrick pushed in the door as that student pushed out. He grabbed the chair along the way and dragged it noisily over to Claire's table, where he sat, put his elbows on the table, and said, "Hey, Claire. How was your day?"

She was *not* up for small talk. Something she'd learned from Shane: there was a time for distracting chatter, and a time for shutting up and watching, and this was definitely a guy she could not afford to play games with. It was *his* game, *his* rules. She couldn't win it. "You need to leave me alone, Derrick," she said, and she didn't try to hold her voice down, either. The restaurant was packed with people, and some of them looked over—not alarmed, just curious onlookers. "Walk away right now."

"I'm not doing anything, Claire, c'mon. I just want to be friends. Liz is special to me; I ought to get to know the people she likes, right?"

"Liz doesn't want to see you. I don't want to see you." Claire stood up suddenly, and the sound of her chair going over backward was very loud. Conversational buzz around them stopped. "You need to leave, right now."

"Or?" Derrick didn't seem alarmed at all. "You'll call the cops and tell them I was politely making conversation?"

Claire didn't even think about what she was going to do. If she had, she probably would have second-guessed it.

She picked up her full soda and flung it right in his face.

He gasped, jumped out of his chair, and stood there dripping and furious. Ice chunks glittered in his hair, and his shirt was stained and soaked.

Someone nearby started a slow clap. Others joined in.

Derrick's menace was no longer simmering beneath the surface. He stared at Claire as if he intended to bite chunks out of her, and the small table between them didn't seem like much, if any, protection. Neither did the people around them, who might cheer a gutsy move but would run from a fight.

She'd never missed having Shane at her back so much.

Derrick took in a deep breath, twitched all over, and forced out a smile that was all teeth. "All these people are witnesses. I never raised a hand to her, okay? *She's* the one who assaulted *me*." He raised both hands, brushed the ice out of his hair, and backed away from the table, and Claire. "Damn, girl, back off the caffeine. I'm out." He sounded like a regular guy now, bemused by her reaction, and the clapping faded off. "Sorry if I scared you, I didn't mean to." It sounded sincere. All of a sudden, the tide of popular sentiment was turning around them.

"Yes, you did," Claire said flatly. "You know it and I know it. But you don't scare me, Derrick. I've—" *killed scarier things than you,* she almost said, but that would sound way wrong in this place, this time. "I've known plenty of guys worse than you. I'm still standing."

"Chick's crazy," he said, to no one in particular—just a pronouncement, and it seemed like some of the others agreed with him. Some didn't. One girl was frowning at Derrick, clearly alarmed; at least a couple of guys were not on his side, either. One of them—a big enough fellow—stood up.

"Maybe just go, man," he said.

"Why not her?" Derrick shot back.

The guy shrugged. "Well, she's got pizza. You don't."

It was a mild, but valid, point, and right then, one of the employees—probably the manager, Claire thought—came out from behind the counter and fixed Derrick, then Claire, with quelling looks. "Whatever's going on, it stops here," he said. "Or I call the cops."

"No problem," Derrick said. He was still holding up his hands. "I'm going, man."

He did, backing through the door, but as he walked past the plate glass window where Claire had first seen him, he sent her a quick, sideways look that was so malignant it might have caused cancer.

She was shaking all over, she realized—the aftermath of the adrenaline flood. She put her chair back upright and asked at the counter for some paper towels. The soda had mostly landed on the floor around Derrick's chair, and she cleaned it up without complaint, and quietly apologized to those around her. They shrugged it off.

The pizza tasted like dust and cardboard, delicious as it probably was, and she ate fast, with her eyes fixed on that plate glass window.

Dreading the moment when she would have to step outside.

"Hey." Claire flinched, but it was the boy who'd stood up to Derrick at the end; he'd walked up to her side, but she hadn't noticed, because she'd been so intent on the window. "You worried about him?"

She laughed shakily. "A little, yeah."

"There's a back door," he said. "It lets out on an alley but it's only a quick run to the street. If he's watching the front, you can duck him for now. But if you want my opinion, call the cops. There's something not right about him."

"I know," she said. "Believe me, I know." She stuck out her hand, and he shook it. "Thanks. I'm Claire, by the way."

"Grant," he said. "Take care."

He didn't offer to walk her home, but she wouldn't have accepted, anyway; right now, the knife in her bag was the only thing she felt inclined to put her trust in.

The back door supposedly had an alarm, but it was propped open, probably to let in the breeze and compensate for the fierce heat coming out of the pizza ovens. Claire slipped through without anyone stopping her, and took a second to look over the alley beyond. It was deserted, and there was no place for Derrick to hide himself.

She ran for the side street, turned left, and headed straight home.

Even though she spent the whole walk looking over her shoulder, she didn't see any sign of Derrick. Maybe he'd gone home to wash the sticky mess out of his hair, change clothes, and plot how to make her pay.

Not really all that comforting, in the end.

Claire's moving boxes arrived an hour later at her apartment, courtesy of a small delivery truck; there weren't many, and she signed for them as they were carried up to her room and piled in the very little space that remained. She obeyed Dr. Anderson's instructions and opened the carton that contained her Morganville-invented device . . . which looked a lot like some steampunked ray gun, only a whole lot clumsier. It was there. As far as she could tell, it was intact.

Liz wasn't home. Claire locked up after the movers and went back upstairs to stack boxes in order of priority unpacking. She texted Dr. Anderson to tell her the device was safe, and Anderson quickly got back to her to order her to wait at home. Apparently, she was sending reinforcements.

Claire spent the time waiting by checking the windows for any signs of tampering. Nothing. All was secure, or as secure as it could be. She was unpacking winter clothing from the last box when she finally got a phone call to her cell—not from Dr. Anderson, but from a number she didn't recognize.

"Hello?"

"Hi, Claire. You don't know me, but don't hang up. Irene Anderson asked me to drop in and take you to her lab. My name is Jesse." She sounded calm and relaxed, and had a slightly exotic accent, something that vaguely reminded her of the Deep South, but it was well concealed. "My friend Pete and I will be there around six."

"That's late," Claire said, surprised. "I thought she wanted me to get it to her as soon as possible."

"Day jobs, they do throw a crimp in your social life," Jesse said, and chuckled. It was a warm rumble of a sound, and despite her current on-alert-for-trouble attitude, she found herself liking the other girl for it. "Coming as fast as we can. Oh, and she said you might be a little trigger-happy, so please, don't shoot. We come in peace, and I'd rather not go in pieces."

"I promise to ask questions first," she said. Jesse laughed again, and hung up.

And she did ask questions. She called Dr. Anderson, who confirmed straightaway that Jesse and Pete were known to her. Claire hadn't really doubted it, but she was still worried about Derrick; it seemed unlikely *he* knew about Dr. Anderson and the escort she'd ordered up, but just now, paranoia was an advantage.

She spent the spare few hours studying, surfing the net, and wondering—worrying—about where Shane was, and what he was doing. She'd had an e-mail, she saw—not a video this time, just plain text, telling her that he had a new phone number, and giving it to her. She memorized it and put it into her phone and logged it in her computer in her private phone list—her usual triple backup plan—and was considering calling him (just to be sure the number was right, of course).

Just as she hovered her finger over his name in the address book, though, she heard a loud knock on the door. Her gaze jerked up. It was—surprisingly—six o'clock, and they were right on time.

She still checked the peephole before she began clicking back the locks. Not Derrick, for sure; a boy and girl, both a little older than she was. The girl was the one who drew the attention first, because she was tall, well built, and had fiery red hair that fell in shining waves almost to her waist. She was also—like Eve—Goth style, with lots of black eyeliner, pale makeup, and unnaturally colored lips. Skulls and leather featured heavily in her outfit.

Claire eased the door open just a bit and said, "Jesse and Pete?"

Jesse smiled and slid a thumb toward her short, easily over-looked friend. He was built like a bulldog, but he had a pleasant face, and he gave her a weary smile and wave. "Pete. I'm Jesse," the redhead said. "So. We're taking you to Dr. Anderson, right? Let's get going. Got places to be, yo."

"Let me get my bag," Claire said. "Come in."

Pete and Jesse shook their heads, almost in unison. "Got to keep an eye on the car," Pete said. "This neighborhood, we'll get ticketed if we don't stay right here."

"Oh." Claire hadn't thought of that; there was a car sitting down at the curb, shiny and dark blue. It had tinting and what looked like death metal decals—Jesse's ride, probably. "I just need to lock this door, that's all." Because she had a horror now of leaving it open, even though she didn't *think* Jesse and Pete would let Derrick slip inside while she was gone.

"I'll go in, and Jesse can stay out here and guard the car," Pete offered. "Is this thing you've got heavy?"

"A little," Claire said. "It's not bad."

Jesse patted Pete's shoulder. "Let my man here carry it; he loves showing off his muscles for the ladies."

"Don't be sexist. I flex for guys, too."

"Yeah, but not with so much *style*." Jesse winked. "Go on, you. I'll tackle the meter maid if necessary."

Claire led Pete upstairs, pointed out the box, and Pete very happily (and super easily) picked it up and got it down the long flights without a problem. "So, you're just moving in, right?" he said. "New student?"

"Does it show?"

"Not as much as most. I don't see a lot of kitten posters and boy bands on the walls up there."

Claire almost laughed. "Not my style. Though if you know of any place I can get a sparkly unicorn poster . . ."

"Ask Jesse," he said, and stood aside as she opened up the door. "She's the sparkly unicorn fancier."

He said it loudly enough that Claire figured it was bait for Jesse to respond, and the redhead probably normally would have done it, but she was standing very still, facing away. This time of year, and with the height of the buildings, the sky was a dusky blue, well into twilight, and Claire couldn't see much farther than the other side of the street, so she couldn't figure out what had attracted Jesse's undivided attention.

Then a streetlight flickered on, shedding a cold pale light over concrete, a fireplug at the corner, some trash bags . . . and a man standing on the sidewalk, leaning against a wall, watching them.

"Friend of yours?" Jesse asked. She sounded calm and relaxed, still, but her body language said something different.

Claire couldn't see his face, but the size looked right. "It's probably Derrick. My roommate's ex. He's a stalker."

"Want us to go have a little chat?" Jesse asked, and Claire realized with a start that she was serious about it. "Pete?"

"Always up for a little heart-to-heart chat," he said, "but Anderson was pretty firm about this thing being a priority. So maybe we leave it for later, okay?"

Jesse hadn't moved; Derrick had her attention fixed as if she'd been glued down in one direction. She finally sighed and turned her head to give Pete a disappointed look. "You take all the fun out of life, you know that?" Pete shrugged, as if he lived with disappointment, and carried the box down the stairs to the car. Jesse stayed put, still attentive toward Derrick's silent, still presence across the street, as Claire locked and rechecked the door. "Do you have an alarm in there?"

"No," Claire said. "I told Liz we need to get one, but she doesn't think we can afford it."

"Better broke than dead," Jesse said. "I can smell the crazy on that man from here. I have a nose for it." In the dim light, a passing car's lights hit Jesse full in the face, and lit her up like a billboard. Her blue eyes were very, very bright, and for a second Claire had a Morganville déjà vu . . . but this was the real world, and Jesse was just a badass. Like Pete.

Maybe that was enough.

FIVE

SHANE

꜒

I was up to my elbows in hot water.

I don't mean that figuratively. It was actual hot water, with suds, and I was washing bar glasses. My second full day in Cambridge, and I had a job—crappy as it was—at a place called Florey's Bar & Grill, although the only thing I'd seen them grill so far had been some burgers and hot wings. It was the kind of place that offered up a food menu small enough to fit on a business card, and a nine-page drinks list.

So even though my official title was dishwasher, I was washing glasses. Every once in a while, there was a plate for variety. Maybe a fork. Not much else.

Like all industrial kitchens everywhere, it was humid, hot, and a little nasty; the building was old and had probably seen various owners shilling drinks for at least a hundred years. The plumbing probably hadn't been significantly upgraded in all that time. Hell, it probably had rats older than me, and maybe bigger, too. When I was done with the glasses—if that ever happened—I'd be expected to mop and scrub the place out.

A kitchen is run like an army; in fact, they call it a brigade system. The chef de cuisine ("Yes, chef!") is the general; his second-in-command is the sous chef; and then there are *chefs des parties*, who are responsible for individual workstations. Somewhere way down at the bottom of that organizational chart is something called a *plongeur*—as in, dishwasher. That's what I was doing. In a major restaurant there would be a bunch more positions, but all we had in this mini-brigade was the chef, ("Yes, chef!") Roger, who had been in the navy and swore like a sailor, too, and then Bridget, who was his second and did everything else other than swear.

Yes, I knew the system. This was, obviously, not my first dishwashing gig.

Amazing thing was, what little they cooked was pretty great. I'd been hired to fetch, carry, and clean, and since I had a valid state-issued ID, they were overjoyed (and surprised). Technically I couldn't drink in a place like this, but I got free meals to make up for it. And Bridget was a cute, motherly type. I'd already made friends with the bouncer, Pete, a short, muscular type who casually mentioned that he powerlifted with an eye to making the Olympic team someday. Damn.

What worried me, though, was the bartender. Her name was Jesse, and she was a stunning knockout redhead in tight leather. I'm usually all in favor of that, from a purely scenic standpoint, but there was something about her that set off alarms—Morganville-type alarms. I'd convinced myself that I was being paranoid, but I found myself still wondering about her over the course of the two days I'd been working at Florey's. Pete was one of those laconic types who didn't say much about other people, but he'd finally given up that Jesse had drifted into town a few years back and was one hell of a good bartender; she knew how to cut people off when they had too much, and get them out the door without trouble, which in his opinion was ninety percent of a good bartender's job.

In other words, he didn't much like to exert himself. I approved of this. A bouncer's worth isn't how much he flexes his muscles, but how rarely he has to. It was the security guys who are always looking for a fight that cause trouble.

This is why I did not get hired to be a bouncer. I knew better than to apply.

I filled up the dishwasher—a big, industrial thing—again, and started it, and took care of the overflow, then did some cleanup and trash-taking-out before it was time for my dinner break. The sky outside was sliding toward twilight, and I stood out in the alley for a little while enjoying the cool air, so unlike Morganville's dry desert wind, before the smell of garbage drove me back inside. Roger was swearing about something I didn't bother to register, since it wasn't glasses, plates, utensils, pots, pans, or cleaning; Bridget was chopping celery, knife flying in a blur, but she spared me a wink and a grin as I signed out for dinner, took off my kitchen apron, and hung it up.

I went looking for Pete.

The bar was already starting to fill, even this early, with after-work happy-hour people; the day bartender was still on duty. Jesse didn't come on until seven, and it was still a quarter to six. Pete usually started his day early, with dinner, so I figured I'd sit down with him . . . but I spotted him on the other side of the doorway, heading into the street. I followed, intending to tap him on the shoulder and ask if he was free, but then I saw he was heading for a car that pulled smoothly in at the curb. The passenger door opened, and I saw Jesse leaning over, all stark contrasts of black and white except for the fiery red sheen of her hair . . .

. . . *And her eyes.*

I stopped dead in the doorway, staring, as Pete slid into the front seat, slammed the door, and they drove off.

Had I really seen that flash of red in her eyes? Or had I just seen a reflection from the dashboard, maybe? Was I hallucinating Morganville all over the place? Maybe. Yeah, probably. Not every hot girl in pale trendy makeup could be a genuine vampire.

But maybe, just maybe, one could hide in plain sight.

Fun facts: She worked nights, never showing up until after the sun went down. She drove a car with windows tinted as dark as non-Morganville laws would allow. She went for the powder-faced Goth look, always.

She never had a problem handling drunks.

Add all that to the Goth look, and you came up with . . .

C'mon, I told myself. *Really? You move out of the one town that has a heavy population of vampires, and you think you're going to run into one halfway across the country?*

Some people are just lucky like that. Also, I hadn't gotten this job for no good reason . . . I'd followed Claire's new professor lady here, where she ate lunch and had pleasant chats with Jesse *and* Pete. I'd done it purely to find out what Dr. Anderson was like; anybody who had the Amelie Seal of Approval was automatically someone I felt I should check out carefully, and by extension, I'd been checking out Jesse and Pete, then. Hence, the dishwashing gig.

And now, Jesse, with the flashing red in her eyes. So it wasn't so much coincidence as deliberate investigation on my part. I wanted Claire to be safe, and I wanted to be absolutely certain she wasn't walking unsuspecting into a lion's den.

Now, I wasn't so sure.

I'd used the savings I had left after securing my very grungy little room above the bar to buy a beat-up motorcycle, and I wasted no time getting on it and following Jesse's modified vampmobile. Claire would hate that I was doing this; she'd think I was interfering. Which I was. But only behind the scenes. I didn't intend for her to even know I was in town; it was enough to be close, if she needed me. Or if she said she wanted to see me. I wasn't going to pull some romantic movie stunt and show up uninvited on her doorstep. She needed space; I was giving it.

But Jesse was making me very, very nervous.

I got even more jumpy when Jesse's car pulled up at the curb of a row house that I'd driven past once before and memorized everything about. I'd resisted driving past again, mainly because I knew that it would drive me crazy to be that close and not stop. Now I kept moving, past Jesse and around the block, where I stopped and dismounted. I took up a vantage point at the corner, where I could see what was going on.

Jesse and Pete went up the steps to Claire's row house, knocked, and after a while and some discussion at the door, Pete went inside. I didn't know if it was Liz, Claire's housemate, letting them in, or whether Claire was doing it. Jesse stayed outside, which was a relief.

In the idle time before the next thing happened, I saw Jesse fix on someone standing across the street from her—much closer than I was. Couldn't tell a lot about him except that he was big, and didn't seem bothered by Jesse's stare. I knew from experience how off-putting a vampire's attention could be, and it was a little surprising he didn't take the hint.

Then, the door opened again, and Claire and Pete stepped out. As Claire locked up, I drank in the sight of her like water in the desert. . . . Damn, she looked good. Still the same girl who'd kissed me a few days ago. She hadn't changed at all—but then, had I really expected her to, in such a short time?

Pete had a bulky-looking box in his thick arms, and he carried it down to Jesse's car. *Don't get in,* I thought, watching Claire. *Danger. C'mon. I know you have better instincts than that.*

But she got in the car, and it pulled out, heading for parts unknown. I mounted the motorcycle and took off after them, hanging back enough in traffic to be sure I wasn't remarkable. Plenty of students cruising around on similar rides, so I didn't stand out.

Sure enough, the drive ended up at the building where Dr. Anderson worked and where Claire did her studies. A dead end—ha—because I damn sure couldn't go strolling in, or I'd definitely risk coming face-to-face with Claire and have an uncomfortable conversation about what I was doing there, exactly. It would start with *I was worried about you* and end with her (probably rightly) saying *I told you I needed to do this on my own.*

I considered for a bit, then decided to head back to the bar. I could still grab a decent dinner before it was back to the regular kind of hot water.

For no damn good reason, I took the way back that led past Claire's row house, and as I slowed down, I saw a guy trying to open the door. I say "trying" because he clearly wasn't having any luck. He had what might have been a key in his hand, but I didn't think so. He was also bigger than I was, and I didn't think he should have any business jimmying my girlfriend's door, so I pulled in, jumped off the bike, stood on the bottom step to block his path, and said, "Hey, something I can do for you there, buddy?"

He whipped around, and I saw the fury and fear mixed together before it all smoothed into a bland, but still somehow unpleasant, mask. "What's your problem?" he barked at me, and flexed his shoulders to show me his muscle-guns were loaded. I remained unimpressed. "Just having some trouble with my key. Had a break-in last week, had to change the locks. This one sticks."

One thing about liars, they can never resist the opportunity to take it just a step too far. If he'd just left it at the first part about the key, it might have been believable, but he just kept talking, and that proved he was making it up.

Plus, of course, he didn't live there. Obviously, that gave it away.

"Let me take a look," I said, and came up one step.

"Back off." He put the thing that was not a key in his pocket quickly, and upped the ante by coming *down* two steps, letting me know he was ready to charge. Again: not impressed. "None of your business, punk, just keep walking."

I had a number of really awesome choices in front of me. First, I could take another step up, and smash this guy's face with my fist, which sounded great; second, I could take another step up, let him punch at me, duck, and *then* smash his face with my fist. Or— and the less awesome choice—I could avoid causing a scene and possible police incident, back off, and pay attention to this douche bag from now on to see what he was up to.

I went with the less awesome option. Claire actually had changed me, turned out—she'd made me think a little bit about the consequences, so I wasn't in attack mode all the time. I didn't necessarily love it, but I saw the wisdom of it, and I nodded to the big guy, stepped down out of his way, and moved to the side. "Sorry," I said, not very sincerely. "Just trying to help, man."

"Fuck off," he snapped, and charged past me. He didn't have to slam his shoulder into mine, but he did, and for a second I considered teaching him the wisdom of taking the high road, but I let it go. The slight discomfort was enough to make me feel righteous and all as I watched him walk down the block and around the corner. I had the weird feeling that he hadn't gone far, so I got on my bike, made a show of roaring away around the corner, and then coasted to a quiet stop so I could take a look.

Sure enough, the guy went back. He didn't try the door again, but he went across the street and took up a leaning-against-a-wall post. Looked like he could do it all night.

Looked like he had, before, which bothered me. He had to be the lurker I'd seen when Jesse and Pete had arrived.

What in the hell was going on? Was it related to Jesse being a vampire? Dr. Anderson? Something else?

I didn't want to leave, but after watching him for about ten minutes, I got on the bike and raced back to Florey's. It was that, or lose my job, and for now, I needed the paycheck.

Before I left, I pulled out my cell phone and reported an attempted break-in to the cops, just to make sure the dickhead got well and truly harassed. Emphasis on *ass*.

Man, the real world sucked. And it sucked even more that I actually missed Morganville.

SIX

J esse and Pete walked Claire up to the building, through the regular nonsecured hallways, and then, as they approached the secured hallway and Claire dug the pass out of her pocket, she hesitated. "Um, maybe you'd better give me the box," she said. "I don't think you can go in without an ID card..." Her voice trailed off, because Pete balanced the box one-handed as if it was filled with nothing but packing peanuts, pulled a pass out of his pocket, and looped the cord over his neck. Jesse had one, too. "Oh. Never mind."

Jesse winked at her as she slid the pass through the card reader. "Don't sweat it," she said. "We're officially unofficial. Like you, only without the crushing tuition burden."

"I'm on scholarship," Claire offered.

"So I heard," Jesse said. "Friends in low places, and all that. Again, like us. Come on, let's go see the wizard."

Claire wasn't sure if she was referring to *The Princess Bride* or— more likely—*The Wizard of Oz*; she supposed that in the latter case she'd be Dorothy, and that made Jesse the . . . Scarecrow? Not with those curves. Likewise, Pete seemed a bad choice for Cowardly Lion. He looked cuddly, but he worked as a bouncer, which seemed like the opposite of cuddly.

Jesse and Pete seemed utterly out of place here . . . Jesse for her Goth pallor and blazing hair, and Pete for his muscular frame. Here in Scienceland, people tended to be less attention-getting, and the lab coats they passed gave them second looks of either admiration or fear, or maybe both. Jesse seemed to know it, from the smile on her face and the spring in her step; Pete shuffled along with the box, and didn't seem to notice or care how people saw him.

Claire wondered what made the two of them friends. Maybe nothing, except a mutual liking for Dr. Anderson.

They already knew the one-at-a-time-through-the-lab-door protocol, and Claire ended up going last in line, though Pete tried to politely wait for the honor. Once she was in, Claire followed him to the back of the lab, where Dr. Anderson had cleared off a worktable, and as she arrived, Anderson had already folded back the wings of the box lid and was reaching in to lift out the device.

No . . . in Anderson's competent, strong hands, as she cradled its weight, it definitely looked like a weapon, not a device. A futuristic ray gun sort of weapon, sure, but if you spotted a character in a film carrying it, you'd know what it was, instantly.

Something to hurt people.

Claire swallowed. She'd been so into the details of what she was doing that she hadn't really *looked* at it, just looked, in a long time . . . and even though others had held it, she'd been assessing the weight, the balance, the structure.

Dr. Anderson made it look dangerous. She handled it competently, carefully, and then set it down on a soft foam layer she'd put on the table next to the box. Then she looked up, met Claire's eyes, and said, "Have you checked it out? Any damage?"

"No damage I can see," Claire said. "It still powers up."

"Excellent." Dr. Anderson took a deep breath and nodded. "Right. Thanks, Jesse, Pete . . . I think we've got it from here. I know you need to get to work. Thanks for helping us out."

"You were right to be worried," Jesse said. "Someone's watching her house. Big guy."

"That's Derrick," Claire offered. "My housemate's ex. It's a personal thing. I don't think he's got any interest in what I do."

"Maybe not, but it's worrying nevertheless," Dr. Anderson said. "Someone could be using him as a stalking horse. He could even be passing his surveillance details along to a third party."

Claire hadn't thought of that; she did wonder how Derrick could afford to follow Liz here, and apparently spend all his time hanging out on the sidewalk. Didn't he work? Surely he wasn't wealthy enough to be that maliciously idle. It was a great question, she realized; it was something that wouldn't have occurred to her in Morganville, but out here in the real world, it could be significant.

"I'll check him out," Jesse offered. "I didn't like his vibe, Irene. Freaky. Not that standing around outside the house with two young women in it isn't creepy on its own, of course." She smiled a little, and Dr. Anderson smiled back, and Claire was struck by how . . . comfortable it seemed. As if they'd known each other a long time. There was also a little bit of challenge in it, too. That was a complicated friendship.

"Want me to take the box away, Doc?" Pete asked. It was the first thing he'd said, and Dr. Anderson's gaze broke off from Jesse's and landed on him. "I mean, unless you want it for something. I can use it at the bar. We use 'em to put the recycling in."

"Commendable," Dr. Anderson said, and when she smiled at him, it didn't have half the wattage, though it was friendly enough. "By all means, unless Claire's got some need for it . . ."

"I've got boxes stacked to the ceiling," she said, and shook her head. "Take it."

Pete grabbed it off the table with a little too much force, and packing peanuts exploded into the air in a spontaneous snowfall. Jesse laughed and grabbed at them as they fell, and then they were all scooping up the featherlight foam chunks, chasing them around the floor since the slightest breath could move them, and generally laughing like fools as they did. It was weirdly relaxing, and by the time the mess was back in the box, and the box in Pete's big hands, Claire felt breathless and more at ease than she'd been in days. Shared laughter did that, even when you didn't really know the people you were sharing it with.

"We should go," Pete finally said, and nodded to Dr. Anderson. "Irene. See you at the bar sometime?"

"Soon," Anderson agreed. She nodded back to Pete, then to Jesse. For Jesse, she added a wink. "Both of you, take care. I don't know why, but my instincts tell me we're going to be up against it pretty soon. And I always listen to my instincts."

"Hell yeah." Jesse winked at her, smiled at Claire, and strode out of the lab, all long legs and swinging long hair. Pete waited for the door to cycle and followed, and in the sudden silence, the place felt very empty, quiet, and sterile.

Although a lone packing peanut had escaped to roll around on the floor, which made Claire feel a little bubbly giggle inside. She kept it down, though, because Dr. Anderson's smile disappeared, and she was all business as she peered at Claire's device.

"What do you call this thing?" Dr. Anderson asked her, and gently touched some of the oddly angled gauges and gears.

"The Vampire Leveling Adjustment Device," Claire said. "VLAD, for short. Well, that was what I was considering calling it, anyway."

"VLAD," Anderson repeated, and smiled. "Really."

"My boyfriend liked it."

"Your boyfriend has a questionable sense of humor."

"He'd be the first to agree with you about that," Claire said. She'd rolled her eyes when Shane had popped out with that name, off the cuff, but now she thought it was spectacularly appropriate. VLAD. She could totally see it.

So could Dr. Anderson, it seemed, because she slowly raised an eyebrow and drew a manicured fingernail along the barrel. "VLAD," she said again. "Yes. I think it seems like the right thing, after all. So. Break it down for me, Claire. How exactly does this work?"

"I'm not sure it does. I mean, it does *something*, but not necessarily what I want it to do, yet. The goal is to be able to tune in to a specific vampire broadcast emotion—like hunger—and cancel it out. Make the vampire *not* hungry. Theoretically, it could stop an attack, or at least drastically slow it down and lessen the intensity." She swallowed hard, because she had Anderson's full and unwavering attention now. "In theory, it should also be able to cancel out the specific projections that vampires can do to make other people obey them on command, wipe out memories, et cetera. It levels the playing field. That's why I called it VLAD."

"You think that it would stop them from attacking someone."

"Or at least slow them down—at the very least, it would throw them off balance. And it's possible that it would seriously disable them."

"Permanently?"

"I don't know about that. Probably temporary?"

"What trials have you run?"

"Not many," Claire admitted. "I used it on Myrnin kind of accidentally, but he didn't give me a lot of feedback about it. I think it disturbed him, though. Right now, I'm just calibrating the device to try to locate the specific wavelengths where vampire powers resonate. If I can pin that down, the theory is that I can then create a counter-wave to cancel them."

"So when a vampire projects fear at his prey—which is one of their key hunting abilities—it would nullify that."

"Well, it wouldn't stop you from being afraid. I mean, vampires are scary all on their own. But they have a way of pushing you from fear into panic."

"And their mental abilities—to conceal themselves, to cloud memories, to compel people to do things . . ."

Not every vampire had any of those abilities, and as far as Claire had been able to tell, none of the vampires, not even the very strongest like Amelie, had all of them in equal measure. But she nodded. "Theoretically, it should work," she said. "But there's a power problem to solve, and right now VLAD is way too heavy and bulky. Some of that is Myrnin's attempt to help me. He likes—gears."

"Always has," Anderson agreed, with a smile that was almost fond. "First things first—we deconstruct, we test each piece of it, design more streamlined versions . . . and we construct a simulation to run in the array to show us exactly what the response is. Once we do that, we test it on a live subject, but not before."

"On a vampire? For that, we'd have to go back to Morganville."

"Not at all," Anderson said. "This thing, if it works, is far too dangerous to be in Morganville, or anywhere that Amelie can get to it. In fact, there's a strong possibility that—" She paused, because a soft musical tone sounded in the lab, and she swiveled to face a computer monitor set in the wall behind them, concealed from easy view by a half wall. On the monitor, striding down the hallway, was a tight knot of four people, all dressed identically—no, not really, but all in dark suits that seemed identical at first glance. Three men and a woman. Her suit had a skirt, and midheel shoes, and she lacked a tie, but that was really the only way the four of them differed.

"Claire, take VLAD," Anderson said. She kept watching the monitor for a few more seconds, then nodded as if she'd confirmed her suspicions. "Come on."

Claire scooped up the heavy weight and hustled after Dr. Anderson as she moved around lab tables to a blank white wall . . . and then pressed her hand to an almost invisible panel that was set in it, white on white. It lit up with a shimmering silver glow, and a panel slid open.

There were shelves behind it. Most were crowded with labeled boxes and bottles, but there was a large empty shelf in the bottom, and Claire quickly knelt and slid VLAD into the space. As she pulled back, Anderson pressed her hand on the locking mechanism again, and the door slid shut with barely a whisper.

"Say nothing," Anderson said. "If they ask you a direct question, just tell them you don't know anything about the research, you just arrived. It's true. Whatever you do, don't lie to them, but tell them as little as you can possibly get away with."

"But—who are they?"

"Let's hope you never need to know. I sincerely don't want to involve you in things above your pay grade."

That was all there was time for, because the outer door slid open, and the first of the four stepped through. They obviously knew the protocol, too. The tallest man came through first, and nodded to Anderson as he stepped aside. He had cool, assessing brown eyes that flicked over Claire briefly before focusing back on the professor.

The other three came in quick succession, each nodding and politely waiting until the last had joined them. The last was a mid-sized man in a pale blue shirt and bright blue tie—just a shade more unconventional than the others in the group. He walked forward, extending his hand to Dr. Anderson.

"Irene," he said, and smiled. "Good to see you again."

"You, too, Charles. To what do I owe this visit?"

"Just a spot check, the usual stuff." He shrugged. "You understand how it goes. Protocol."

"I know that having four people assigned is a little heavy for a spot check," she said. "Isn't that something you only need one agent for?"

"For you, Dr. Anderson, the royal treatment," he said. "How are the biologics coming along?"

"Fine," she said, and flicked a glance at Claire. "Let's discuss this in private."

"Just a minute," said the dark-suited woman, stepping forward. "Your name is"—she made a show of checking her phone—"Claire Danvers, correct?"

"She's my lab assistant," Dr. Anderson said. "What's the point?"

"Well, we're doing background checks," the agent said. "I'll need to schedule an in-depth interview."

"An interview? What for?" Claire asked.

"For security reasons," said the main guy. "That's all you need to know. Is she read in on your projects?"

"No, she just arrived," Dr. Anderson said. She turned toward Claire. "I do some work for these people. They tend to be just a little bit paranoid, I'm afraid, even though what we're working on is pretty mundane. Nothing to worry about." She sent a smile toward the other woman. "Look at her, she's eighteen. You seriously think she could be a spy?"

"I think kids younger than eighteen have done amazing and terrible things," the woman said. "Miss Danvers, I'll be in touch for your interview. Until then, she has no access to anything related to your projects with us. Understood?"

"Completely understood," Anderson said. She nodded to Claire. "You'd best be on your way, Claire. This doesn't concern you."

"Okay," Claire said, and hesitated for a second. There was a very weird feeling in the air, in the way these four official types were facing off with her professor. "Are you sure you don't need me to call anyone, or . . . ?"

The woman looked irritated. "Who do you think you're going to call? Beat it before I find a security reason to make you stay."

Dr. Anderson gave her a look that Claire interpreted as *go ahead*, and Claire collected her backpack and headed for the door to badge out. As she did, she turned back and said, "Oh, Dr. Anderson, should I let your next appointment know you'll be delayed?"

"Yes," Anderson said, without any hesitation at all. "Just call Dr. Florey and let him know."

"I will," she said.

Dr. Florey. Jesse and Pete had said they worked at Florey's Bar and Grill. And of course, Jack Florey himself was an entirely imaginary person, the mascot of Fifth East. So there was definitely a message in that.

The door opened, and Claire exited before any of the agents could ask her anything else. She walked quickly down the hall, expecting to hear fast footsteps behind her; she half expected her badge to fail at the next security station, but it flashed green as she swiped it, and she escaped into the academic side of the building.

She had a million questions firing off in her mind, but until she found Dr. Anderson alone and able to answer them, there wasn't much point in considering them. Still, the fact that Anderson was apparently neck-deep in spy science was . . . well, chilling. More chilling than the vampire stuff, since Claire was accustomed now to thinking of it as normal.

Claire ducked into one of the student lounge areas, found a worn-out, battered couch that didn't have anyone currently napping on it, and took out her phone to look up the number for Florey's. She found it on the Internet, called, and asked for Jesse.

The roar on the other end of the phone indicated it was definitely happy hour. "She's busy," said the man who'd answered; he had to shout to be heard over the noise. "Call back later."

"Wait—I—"

No good. The phone went dead. She called back, and it rang a long time, but no one picked up. Not too surprising. She supposed that they probably couldn't hear it over the shouting. Must have been some kind of sporting event on TV, from the cheering.

Just call Dr. Florey and let him know, Anderson had said. There wasn't any doubt in Claire's mind that she meant Jesse and Pete.

Well, if they wouldn't answer the phone, there was only one thing to do:

Go there.

Claire had never been to Florey's—she wasn't old enough to legally drink, and exploring dark places full of ominous strangers after dark . . . well, in Morganville, that would have made her survival-deficient. Here, she supposed, it just made her more socially inept, but she was okay with that. She hadn't felt any urge to explore the local party places favored by students, and Liz wasn't the going-out-to-party type, either. Given the stalking, she was way too paranoid for that.

That didn't mean Claire didn't know where the bars were, though; it was just part of the landscape, like the textbook stores and bubble tea shops and Laundromats. Alcohol was an essential student service, she guessed. At least for some.

She didn't dare take time to walk, so she flagged down a cab and paid the fare to Florey's; once she got there, though, she was more than a little taken aback, because the place was *packed*. There was a football game on TV, and through the open door she could see that the small space inside was packed with drinking, cheering people. She couldn't even glimpse the bar, much less see if Jesse was working behind it.

There was a guy sitting on a three-legged stool outside of the single wide door. It wasn't Pete, but he was obviously an official bouncer; he gave Claire a blank, assessing look as she walked up, and said, "ID." That was all, no hello how are you. Not the chatty type.

She quickly took her wallet out and showed him her identification, and he glanced at it and nodded. "Drinking age is twenty-one," he said. "In case you're a foreign student. No, we don't care if it's sixteen in your home country. Five bucks cover."

He held out his hand.

"I just need to go in and talk to somebody."

"Really? Never heard that one before, cutie. Five bucks or get out of line." Because there were people queued up behind her now, she realized; they were all older than she was. Claire fumbled in her wallet, pulled out a five-dollar bill, and passed it over, and he reached down and grabbed a bright neon-green armband out of a box, and snugged it tight on her wrist. "Water, soft drinks, tea, coffee. Got it?"

"Yes," she said.

"Go on with you."

"I—I'm looking for Pete. Or Jesse."

That got her an entirely different look, one of surprise; the bouncer leaned forward a little and studied her again. "Not a good time," he said. "It's busy in there. Jesse's up to her neck in bottle caps and booze, and Pete needs to keep an eye on everything in- side. He doesn't need distracting."

"I have a message for him," Claire said. It sounded as if Pete would be easier to get to than Jesse, anyway. "Where do I find him?"

"Beats me. Good luck. Next!"

She had no real option but to push forward into the crowded room, where she was instantly lost in the roar of conversation, clinking bottles and glasses, the sharp smell of spilled beer and sweat and old wood. The glare of the TV screens washed over her, and turned everyone in the darkened room odd colors, with twisted and distorted faces. If she knew anyone here, she probably wouldn't recognize them. Bodies crowded hot against her and surged forward as a runner sprinted forward on the TV; the roar that washed over her was deafening.

I'm never going to find them, she thought in despair, and then she caught sight of Jesse's red hair on the far side of the bar, which was on the far side of the room. It was just a flash, but definitely her— not just the hair, but the pale skin and the self-assured smile.

Finding Pete in this mob looked like a lost cause, but at least Jesse was stationary. Claire swam against the tide, heading for the bar, and then ran into a solid knot of young men and women all waiting three or four deep for their turn. Claire felt suffocated; she was too short and too thin to make her own space against a horde of people who were either drinking, impatient to be drinking, or drunk.

"Hey," a voice next to her said, and Claire saw a tall young man standing close by, leaning in. "You need to order something? Let me be your hero."

"If you want to be my hero, tell the redheaded bartender that Claire needs to see her out back," Claire said. "Please?"

He grinned. He was a good-looking guy, cocky and confident of his ability to get anything he wanted. "As long as you promise to have a drink with me later."

"I'm not your type," she said, and gave him a mysterious smile. He raised his eyebrows, looked over the sea of heads and focused on Jesse, then back on Claire.

"Oh," he said. "Right. Sorry. Well, what kind of hero would I be if I didn't help out with a hot bartender hookup? Gotcha covered. You sure I can't bring you back a drink or anything?"

"I'm sure," Claire said. She'd been to enough parties in Morganville to know that she shouldn't let strangers get her drinks, ever. "Thanks."

"Brian," he said. "Brian Taylor. Of the Boston Taylors." He said that last in a funny drawling accent, and—as much as possible, in the crush—gave her an old-fashioned from-the-waist bow. He didn't do it very well, when measured up against Myrnin and his old-school elegance, but she gave him points for effort. "And you are . . . ?"

"Claire Danvers, of the nobody in particular," she said. "Thanks, Brian. I appreciate it."

"No worries. Go on. I'll have her meet you out there."

He pressed forward toward the bar, and Claire let the current of people sweep her back the other way. Something bad must have happened on the screen, because there was a collective groan, followed by violent shouting and gesturing, and she had to duck to avoid getting either a beer in the face, or an elbow in the head.

In the process of ducking, she caught sight of someone in a long white apron coming through the double doors behind the bar, carrying a gigantic tray full of—she assumed—freshly washed bar glasses. And for a second she froze, because everything about that split-second glance, *everything*, told her she knew him.

It was a flash, nothing more, and the guy carrying the tray was moving fast to deliver the glasses, but she could have sworn, however irrationally, that . . .

That it was *Shane.*

But of course it wasn't. In the next few seconds she stood on tiptoe and tried to get another look, but there were too many people in the way, and besides, Shane was in Morganville. It was a tall guy, broad shoulders, brown hair. There were probably hundreds of thousands of guys fitting that description in Cambridge and Boston. She was missing him so badly that she was projecting his face onto others who just fit some template.

God, she missed him. Suddenly she felt short of breath, flushed, frightened by the intensity of her reaction; she wasn't even sure *what* she was feeling, really. Sadness, and longing, and a need that just cut the strength out of her.

The tide carried her right, left, finally back to the center, and she was within striking distance of the door, finally. She had to wiggle her way between incoming patrons, some of whom were high-fiving their buddies, and finally gained the free air on the other side.

The bouncer looked at her, checked his watch, and said, "Had a good time?"

"Fantastic," she said. "Thanks."

He gave her a wolfish grin, and went back to checking IDs.

Claire made sure he wasn't watching before she turned the corner and headed through the narrow, not very pleasant little walkway between Florey's and its east-side neighboring building; it was deserted, but it felt ancient and oppressive, and the bricks looked as if they were probably at least as old as the Civil War, if not older. Cambridge, and Boston, had an impressive amount of history that she was only just starting to appreciate.

She wasn't so trusting that she just assumed Brian Taylor (of the Boston Taylors) was willing to help her out of the goodness of his heart, so she loitered in the angle at the edge of that narrow walkway and the wider alley, where the back door of Florey's was, next to a big industrial Dumpster that stank even from here of old booze and rotting food. Nobody was there. She waited, and waited, and checked her watch: fifteen minutes, and still no sign of Jesse.

Maybe Brian had blown the whole thing off. Or maybe Jesse just didn't care.

It was another fifteen minutes, and Claire was preparing to try her luck with the bouncer again, when finally, the back door banged open, and Jesse stepped outside. She stretched, all sinuous curves and long legs and arms, and then pulled out a pack of cigarettes, shook one out, and put it in her mouth as she flicked a portable lighter.

"That's a bad habit," Claire said, stepping out. Jesse took a deep drag, let out a cloud of smoke, and smiled.

"I know," she said. "So. What was so urgent I have to spend my precious break time on it? Please don't tell me it's that guy watching your house. I don't have the time right now."

"Dr. Anderson got a visit from some government types while I was still there," Claire said. "She wanted you to know about it."

"Huh." Jesse frowned and took another long pull on the cigarette, held the smoke, and then let it slowly trickle out in a gray fog. "Anything particular they seemed to be looking for? Did they ask what she was working on?"

"What do *you* work with her on? Because, no offense, a bartender doesn't seem to be the world's most likely team-up with a physics professor."

"Hey, I have depth," Jesse said. "We have things in common."

"Yeah, I get it, you're friends, but why would she call *you* about a visit from the CIA, or whatever they are? She also didn't specifically ask for you. She told me to call Dr. Florey. Which means you, or Pete. Right?"

Jesse took her time answering. She took one last drag and stubbed out the cigarette on the brick and finally said, "It means one of us, yeah. Look, this is really none of your business, Claire, you get that, right? So why are you in it?"

"Because I work with Dr. Anderson, and if there's one thing I've learned about working for scary scientists, it's that you'd better stay aware of exactly what they're into if you want to avoid troubles of your own," Claire shot back. "I'm not saying I'm doing it out of general altruism. It's selfish."

That earned her a glance that was, at least partially, admiring. "Okay, then. Consider your ass covered. Now. Tell me *exactly* what she said. Word for word. Can you do that?"

"She said, *Call Dr. Florey and let him know.* That was all."

"It's a general heads-up," Jesse said. "Not run-for-cover DEF-CON Four phrasing. So we're still good. I'll break Pete loose to go over and make sure she's okay."

"I thought you'd go."

"It's easier for Pete to cut out than it is me. People notice when I'm gone. Speaking of"—Jesse checked her watch—"time to water the stampede again. God, I hate game nights, except that my tip jar runneth over."

Claire nodded. "Okay. Is there anything you want me to do?"

"Go home," Jesse said, and winked at her. "Unless the hot boy you had giving me the message is waiting for you. In that case, hop on that. He was polite."

"He was just doing me a favor," Claire said, and felt her cheeks growing a little warm. "I'm going home."

"Your loss. Watch your back," Jesse said. "If Anderson's got eyes on her, you probably will, too, not that they really expect to see anything. You're an eighteen-year-old from Podunk, Texas, after all. They don't know you're secretly a badass."

"Am I?" Claire asked. Jesse didn't know anything about her—or at least, she'd assumed that to be true.

"Oh, yeah," Jesse said, and smiled off into the darkness. "You couldn't possibly have survived Myrnin if you weren't."

With that stunning comment, she went back inside, and the back door slammed shut behind her. Claire stared after her, thoughts tumbling around in chaos, but what finally stuck was *she knows about Myrnin. And Morganville.*

Just who *was* she, anyway?

It was a mystery Claire knew she was going to have to solve . . . but not tonight. It was dark, and the alley was creepy, and she suddenly wanted, very badly, to retreat to the safety of their little row house, lock the doors, and call Shane.

She needed to hear his voice.

Feeling safe, as it turned out, wasn't in the cards for her, because when she got home there was an official-looking card stuck to the front door, and when Claire pulled it off she saw that it was from the police department. The note with it said that there had been an attempted break-in reported by a passerby, and to double-check all interior spaces and locks to ensure that no one had entered.

Fabulous.

Derrick wasn't at his usual post, which was nice, because the note made Claire feel even more paranoid, and she rushed in, locked the door, and yelled for Liz. Useless, because of course Liz wasn't home; she would have gotten the note if she had been. It was still and dark inside, and Claire methodically made the rounds, checked all the windows, and finally ended up in her top-floor room with the door shut and all the lights burning brightly. She made an effort to unpack a few more boxes (she was rapidly running out of space for what she'd brought) and finally called it quits, fired up her laptop, and tried to reach Shane on Skype. No answer. After she'd tried his phone and gotten the same nonresponse, she instead tried Eve.

And Eve answered so quickly it was as if she'd been sitting

there waiting. Her image came on the screen, face turned pale blue by the computer screen's reflected glow, and the sight of her was enough to make Claire feel a rush of tears. "Hey," Claire managed to choke out. "Thought I'd check in and see how it was going."

"Claire Bear!" Eve bounced up and down in her chair, twisted around, and yelled, "Michael! Get your undead ass in here, guess who's calling?"

"I don't have to guess, and you don't have to yell," Michael said. Claire hadn't seen him approach, but all of a sudden he was there, leaning over Eve's shoulder to give her a light, sweet kiss. "Hey, Claire, how's your new place? Are you settling in?"

"Not so much, and it's—" She couldn't think how to describe it, so she picked up the computer and panned it around. "It's like that."

"Yow," Eve said. "Who picked that paint, a drunk color-blind frat boy? Because a drunk color-blind sorority girl would have better sense."

"I know." Claire sighed. "This whole thing . . . it's—a lot to take in. I started meeting with my new professor. I like her, I guess. But it looks like it's going to be complicated."

"Oh, we are *so* not going to waste time talking about dusty professors and boring classes, unless they're sexy, sexy classes. Let's get to the important info. Do you hate it enough to come running back here to us yet? And yes, I'm actually kind of hoping that will happen. Sorry, but we miss you loads, Claire." Eve, always quick to cry, had a glimmer of tears in her eyes. "It's not the same around here with you gone."

"She's right," Michael said. He would have probably gone on, but Eve put her hand up in front of his mouth.

"Sorry, just need to clarify . . . what was that you said?"

"That you were right."

"Ah. I thought you said that. Just wanted to be sure. Although I think you left out the word *always*, there, and I know you meant to add it in," Eve said. "Just trying to be helpful."

He managed to hold back his sigh, but only just, and leaned forward into the camera. "Hey," he said, "could you please tell my lady here that she doesn't have to harass me *all* the time?"

"Sorry, I do have to. It's part of the marriage vows. Didn't you read the fine print? To have and to harass."

"Honey, I hate to break it to you, but you need glasses."

Eve smacked him, which meant exactly nothing to a vampire; he did her the courtesy of making it seem like he actually noticed. When she tried it again, he caught her hand, held it, and kissed it. Well, that was hotly romantic, and Claire felt the temperature notch up a couple of degrees between them. "Um, you guys, get a room."

"Got one," Eve said, and smiled so serenely she looked like the Mona Lisa. "Got several, and trust me, we're working on breaking them alllllllll in . . ."

Claire put her hands over her ears. "La la la, can't hear you!" Then she took her hands down and said, "Wait a second, *my* bedroom?"

"Couldn't exactly use Shane's, could we? It smells like sweat socks and Mentos in there. Besides, if he found out about it, there would be a whole lot more strange conversations around the dinner table than anybody really needs." Eve waved it away. "Okay, enough about our luscious sex life, about which you don't want to hear anyway. Amelie invited us to be on the new Morganville City Council. Takes the place of the old vampire-themed one, and it has to be more than fifty percent humans. I guess they figured including me and Michael would send a message about how seriously she was taking this whole new let's-be-nice-to-each-other thing."

"So how's that going?"

"So far? Pretty well. Since she came out with her new plans, everybody's been quiet. The vamps don't love it, but so far they're playing by the rules even if they're gritting their teeth while they do it."

"And Captain Obvious?"

"Silent so far. I get the sense that he's giving this the chance to work out." Michael automatically referred to Captain Obvious as *he*, even though the latest incarnation of the pro-human resistance leader was, in fact, female. And their friend. "Let's hope everybody can keep it together this time."

"Let's hope," Claire said. "And like Shane always says, pray all you want, but keep the shotguns loaded."

It was, in fact, a favorite saying of Shane's, and they all smiled at it . . . but then Michael's and Eve's smiles faded and they exchanged a look.

A look Claire didn't like. "What?" she asked. Neither of them answered. "Where's Shane?"

"Working," Michael said, before Eve could answer. "Sorry. He's a little hard to get hold of right now or I'd link him in. He misses you, though."

"Yeah, I can tell, he's been really texting me all the time."

Eve's eyes got round. "Really?"

"No."

"Well, in his defense, his hands *are* really big," Eve said. "He's never been that good at it."

"I hope you're just talking about texting," Michael said.

"Well, you can hope," Eve said calmly, and Michael choked back a laugh. Eve sobered then, and said, "Seriously, Michael's right. Shane doesn't do anything but miss you. All the time. But he promised you he wouldn't bug you, and he isn't. He's just . . . giving you space. Takes a lot of strength." Michael put a hand on her shoulder, and she looked up at him and smiled. "If it was Michael telling me to wait, I couldn't do it. I'm just not that strong. Or that patient."

"You forgave Shane awfully fast," Claire said. "Both of you."

Michael shrugged. "I lied to him, and he's hardwired to trust me, from all the time we've spent together growing up. So I don't blame him for believing me. I hear I was pretty convincing." He looked grim about that, and she knew it still hurt like a raw open wound inside him. He'd been controlled by another vampire, made to push away those who loved him, like Eve and Shane and Claire. He'd done it in one bold move, just by kissing Claire and telling them all he'd been doing it for a while.

They'd believed him. For a while.

But they hadn't believed Claire.

"I still owe you," he told her quietly. "Believe me, I haven't forgotten."

"Better not," she said, but she smiled as she said it. "I'm not still mad, Michael."

"I know. But it doesn't matter whether you are, or aren't. I still owe you."

She left it at that, because he wasn't going to yield, and moved the conversation on to other things. Eve had been invited to join an exclusive Morganville club of the wealthiest ladies in town, all of whom were snobs; she'd turned it down (although she had considered joining just to cause them grief). Then she'd accepted an invite from the vampires to join some kind of tea association. "I figure that if the living dead have any kind of blue-haired old ladies, it would be the tea association," Eve said. "They're too polite to be rude to me to my face. So, that'll be fun. I'll just pretend not to understand when they're all subtle about their dissing."

"And she's going to be on her best behavior," Michael said. Eve mouthed silently, *not likely*, and Claire covered her smile with her hand. "Listen, I know it's late, so you get to bed. Anything you want me to tell Shane . . . ?"

"Are you really going to tell him all the sexy romantic things I want to say?"

"Not hardly."

"Then just tell him to call me when he can," she said. "Or text. If he can get his big fingers on the tiny little keys."

She needed a hug, but she settled for extravagant air kisses from Eve, and a movie-star fond smile from Michael, and then she logged off to face the empty, cold house that had less personality than a broom closet in what she still thought of as home: the Glass House.

Still not sleepy, Claire unpacked some posters, unrolled them, and pinned them up on the walls. One was a gift from her parents, a poster of Hawkeye from the *Avengers* movie, because they knew she thought he was cute, and she wanted that bow and arrow, badly. A couple of her favorite band posters. Another movie one-sheet, this one from *The Hunger Games*. Katniss was cool, and again, she coveted the bow and arrows. Definitely of use in her normal life. Well, life before MIT . . .

She froze in the act of pushing the thumbtacks in on that one, because she heard the downstairs door rattle. Then, a knock.

Claire slipped down the steps, careful to walk on the edges

near the banister to avoid creaks, and risked a quick peek out through the peephole. She expected loathsome Derrick, but what she saw surprised her—a group of people, boys and girls, talking among themselves.

And in the front of the group was Nick, who'd walked her home.

She unlocked and swung the door open. "Hey, Nick," she said. "Guys."

Most of them smiled at her. A few were too deep in their own things to bother. Nick's smile was especially bright.

"Hi, Claire. Look, I'm sorry to bother you, but we were on our way to crack some books at the coffee shop. You like coffee? And books? I figure you would, since you enrolled here, and it's kind of a prerequisite."

"That's his idea of logic flow," one of the girls said—a cute African-American girl, wearing a knitted cap with earflaps and dangling yarn balls. She rolled her eyes. "No wonder he needs to crack books, because he sucks at critical path. I'm Kass, by the way."

"Hi, Kass. Um, thanks, Nick, that's really nice of you, but I—I'm waiting for my housemate. We've got dinner on tonight. Maybe some other time?"

"There's a party later, is what Nick the Quick is failing to mention," one of the other boys said. He was a weedy kid about Shane's age, very self-assured and hipster-chic with his tight, too-small buttoned sweater, jeans with the hems turned up, and porkpie hat he'd probably stolen from the character on *Breaking Bad*. "So you should blow off dinner and come with." He had his arm around a plump blond girl who had pink streaks in her hair and matching cat-eye glasses, and a retro cotton-candy-pink dress. "Right, Sarah?"

"Right!" she agreed, and grinned. "We might get tattoos, too. I was thinking about a dragon."

"Tattoos," Claire said, and pretended to think it over. "Well . . . that sounds fun, but honest, I have to stay home. You guys have a good time. And Nick—" *Never going to happen,* she wanted to say, but she couldn't, in front of his friends. Which was probably why he'd brought them, to be honest. "I'll see you later, okay?"

"Okay," he said. "One more time: study, books, party, tattoos. Sold?"

"No," she said. "But thanks. Have a good time."

"Oh, we will," the other boy said, and kissed Sarah, who giggled. "Your loss, Tex—what's her name again?"

"Claire," Nick said, still watching her. "Her name is Claire."

"Right. Well, Mine's Robert, but everybody calls me Drag. Don't ask."

"I won't," she said, and stepped back over the threshold. "Good night. Be safe, you guys."

"You, too!" It was a chorus, and the group wandered off with their backpacks and enthusiasm, and for a moment, she badly wanted to change her mind and join them. Just be part of something again, and not stuck here in the dark.

But she closed and locked the door, and went back upstairs instead.

No Liz. Claire did her e-mail, called her parents, and finally changed into her pajamas. She was worried enough by that time to call Liz's cell, and got an answer, finally.

Liz was drunk. Epically. From the sound of it, she was either at a bar, or a very noisy party. Claire couldn't get much out of her except that she wasn't planning on coming home soon, and yes, she'd take a cab.

"Everybody's having fun but me," Claire muttered, and threw her cell onto the nightstand in annoyance as she wrapped the covers tight. She turned the lights off, and tossed and turned, unable to sleep for the unfamiliar creaks and pops of the old house.

She slid out of bed and padded downstairs to the kitchen without turning on the lights, opened the fridge, and pulled out the carton of milk to pour herself a glass. She'd just put the milk back and shut the door when she heard the sound of the front door opening, and almost said, *How drunk are you, anyway,* but something stopped her.

Something subliminal that she didn't realize until a full ten seconds later: she hadn't heard a car, or Liz stumbling up the steps, which she assumed Liz would be doing.

This was utterly quiet.

Claire grabbed her milk glass and backed away into the narrow pantry closet, where she crouched down, bathed in the aroma of old spices; there were some huge packs of toilet paper and paper towels in here, bought from some big-box outlet store, and she quickly moved them in front of her, just in case. She hadn't shut the pantry door completely, so she knew she'd see when the lights came on . . .

But the lights didn't come on. Instead, she saw the glow of a flashlight sweep across the kitchen, and then the pantry door whipped open and the flashlight bore straight in. She ducked behind the wall of paper towels, and after a heart-stopping second, the flashlight moved away, and the pantry door swung shut.

It was all done so *quietly.*

Claire waited until she heard the stairs creaking, and then moved the paper wall out of the way to move to the doorway. She couldn't see much, but she thought the kitchen was empty. Whoever it was had gone upstairs; she heard footsteps overhead, so they'd gone into Liz's room.

Derrick?

The thought made her heart race, and she slid a butcher knife out of the block, just in case. Shane had taught her the right way to knife fight, but that didn't mean the idea didn't terrify her; if Derrick got his hands on her, she was done. He was too big, and too crazy.

Stay away, Liz. Just stay where you are.

Claire picked up the kitchen phone and got a blessedly clear dial tone. She dialed 911 with shaking fingers, and whispered the information to the operator that she was hiding in the kitchen with a knife, and there was someone in the house. The operator sounded unimpressed, but professional about it, and promised the police were on the way, and to hide until they arrived but keep the phone on.

Which Claire intended to do, but then she heard a man's voice from upstairs, and static, like there would be on a walkie-talkie. She edged to the kitchen door, looking up at the stairs, and saw a black-clothed man walk out of her room, and another come out of Liz's. She ducked back inside and flattened against the kitchen wall, but it didn't seem like either of them had spotted her.

One of them was talking. "—Nothing. Nobody home, and we didn't find anything. Looks like a normal college girl to me, sir. She's got *Hunger Games* on the wall and textbooks and clothes, not a lot else here. Bed was unmade but she's not here, we looked. Went through all the boxes, nothing . . . No, sir, I'm sure. She's probably out with friends."

He was talking about *her*. And this wasn't Derrick, not even if Derrick had brought a friend. This sounded calm and professional. The two men came down the steps and went out the front door without pausing, and closed it quietly behind them.

Then they *locked it.*

Claire rushed to the peephole and stared out. In the glow of the streetlights, she saw two completely normal-looking guys in dark shirts and pants heading down the steps. Athletic, mid-twenties to early thirties. Short haircuts. They could have been Jehovah's Witnesses or CIA, she had no idea.

But either way, they were able to enter and leave the house without leaving a mark.

Dr. Anderson had been right to move the device to safekeeping, because Claire was almost sure that whoever these guys were, they were looking for evidence that the little student from Morganville was something else again.

And she knew, somehow, that it would mean a lot of trouble if they found out the truth.

The phone was still on, and the operator's voice buzzing like a bee. Claire held it up to her ear and said, "Sorry, false alarm—it was my roommate. We're okay here."

There was more to it, because the operator was worried Claire was under duress, and the police still showed up to check, but Claire assured them it was all okay.

It wasn't though.

It really wasn't.

And then Liz came home, too drunk to make it up the steps on her own, and vomited all over the bathroom, and Claire had to clean it up and put her to bed and deal with the pitiful hangover that came later . . . but all the time, what she was really thinking was, *who's after me? Why?*

And, from time to time, *why hasn't Shane called?*

SEVEN

SHANE

)

Claire saw me.

For a split second, all I could think was *there she is,* and I froze, because I'd wanted so badly to catch another glimpse of her . . . and then reality set in, because she was across the room from me, in Florey's, and she was staring right at me.

I didn't think about what I was going to do, I just did it: I moved, fast, and blocked her view with a bunch of noisy, clamoring patrons bellied up to the bar. Then I dumped the load of glasses on the ledge where the bartenders could easily grab them, and yelled in Jesse's ear, "My girlfriend Claire is in the bar. Don't let on that I'm here, okay? I'm not supposed to be in Cambridge!"

She sent me a wide-eyed, disbelieving glance, but she hardly had time to argue; she was popping the top on a beer with one hand (without a bottle opener, she had some kind of crazy thumb technique that was much faster) and mixing a rum and Coke with the other. The two other servers behind the bar were equally busy. They'd go through the load of glasses I'd delivered in about an hour, and I already had two industrial-sized dishwashers running and was doing the overflow by hand. It was definitely the busiest day Florey's had seen since I'd arrived.

I grabbed the tub with the dirty glasses in it, hoisted it on my left shoulder, and used it to mask myself as I headed back into the kitchen. My arm—the one that had been bitten and healed up— twinged when I did that, but there was nothing wrong with it that a little exercise wouldn't cure. It still burned, from time to time. And yeah, it worried me. I'd been bitten by a devil dog, after all. There could be side effects. But I wasn't running a fever, or feeling sick, or anything like that, and I knew that going to a traditional doctor wasn't going to reveal anything.

The last thing I wanted to be was at the mercy of the vampires, even their resident doc, who was a pretty good guy as bloodsuckers went. I shuddered at the thought.

Once I made it to the back, I dumped the bin on the counter and drew fresh hot water, and tried not to think about what the hell *Claire*, of all people, was doing at a bar on game night. She must have been with someone. Who? Friends, maybe. Yeah, it had to be friends. This wasn't her kind of scene, and I knew that. She wasn't just here on her own, and she wasn't here to make new drunk friends, either.

Then why did every bone in my body demand I walk out, take off the apron, grab her, and march her out of there? She wasn't in any danger, except of being trampled in the crowd. Nobody would hurt her. Pete ran a tight ship, and anybody who got out of line answered to him. Nobody was eager to do that.

Why was she here?

She couldn't be looking for me. She couldn't.

I washed up ten glasses, then dried my hands, took out my new phone, dialed, and propped the thing up on the counter away from the dishwater, on speaker. It took three rings, but Michael finally answered. "Hey," I said. "No time to talk, but did you tell Claire where I was?"

"What? No, man. You made me promise. I won't tell her. That's your business."

"Eve? Would Eve tell her?"

"No. She wants to, but she won't."

"Crap. Well, Claire's here."

"Here, where?"

"In the bar. Where I'm working. Oh, and living in the room upstairs. The job kinda comes with room and board. So it isn't like I can permanently duck her if she catches on."

"Did you talk to her?"

"Hell no, I didn't talk to her! I'm washing dishes in the back!" That, and I was scared she'd hate me for following her. Scared she'd think I'd broken my promise, although I really hadn't—I was keeping away. Just . . . within reach, if she needed me. "Look, just—I don't know if she saw me or not, but if she asks to talk to me, just tell her I'm at work. It won't be a lie."

"You're sliding over the line from best friend to friend who asks me to cover up for him," Michael said. "Just flashing the warning sign, man. Asking somebody to lie to your girlfriend is never a good step in a relationship."

"I know. I just—look, I'm going to tell her, but I want her to have the time she wants, that's all. I'm trying to stay out of her way—" I was interrupted by a yell from the bar area; they were out of beer mugs, again. I yelled back that they were coming, and sure enough, Luis, the other dishwasher, picked up the slack and took them out. "Look, I've gotta go. We good?"

"We're good," Michael agreed. "Watch your back."

"I hear ya. My worst problem right now is dishpan hands."

"I'll send you some lotion and nail polish. Want me to buy you a mani-pedi, too?"

"Mother—" He hung up on me before I could get the rest of it out, which was probably for the best. I shook my head and scrubbed glasses—damn, I hated lipstick, at least in this context—for another twenty minutes or so before Jesse suddenly tapped me on the shoulder. I jumped and almost dropped a martini glass, which would have come out of my not-so-awesome pay, but she caught it on the way down. She had great reflexes.

Too great.

"Your girlfriend is Claire Danvers?" she asked me, and set the martini glass in the clean tray.

"Yeah. Is she still here?"

"No, I never saw her in there, but I got a message she'd be waiting in the back. Do you want to talk to her?"

Yes. I wanted to talk to her so badly it made my stomach churn. "No," I said. "Just don't tell her I'm here, okay? It's complicated." Dammit, my arm twinged again, and the muscles burned and contracted. I rubbed it, frowning, and wondered if I'd been overworking the recovery just a little.

"Copy that, friend. All right, she asked for me, so I'm going. Keep up the good work." She winked at me, and yeah, she was hotter than just about any girl who'd ever winked at me, at least in a theoretical sense. But I'd had plenty of experience around hot vampire chicks, and it had never ended well for me. So I sent back a noncommittal nod, and tried not to watch her ass as she headed for the door. I was the only one managing to resist, looked like. She drew male attention the way pitcher plants draw bugs . . . and the outcome would be the same.

You could drown in that honey.

Jesse was gone her full fifteen for her break, and when she came back in she gave me a quick thumbs-up. "She's okay," she told me. "Heading home. So, although you haven't said so, I'm guessing you're also from her hometown."

I nodded without committing to anything; I didn't know if Jesse actually knew where Claire was from, after all. But she must have, because she glanced around the kitchen to be sure Luis was neck-deep in his own work before turning back to me with her eyes flaring a brief, bloody red. Her lips parted just enough to show me the tips of her fangs, sliding smoothly down, sharp enough to pierce steel.

In response, I showed her my left wrist, which was covered by a thick silver chain bracelet. It looked like fashion, but it was also a weapon, and a good one. Then I pulled down the neck of my T-shirt to show her the matching necklace.

She laughed softly, and the glow and fangs were immediately banished. "I'm just messing with you," she said, and gave me a quirky, in-on-the-joke smile. "You're a cool one, Shane."

"As long as I don't have to be a cold one."

"I knew I liked you. You've got"—she licked her lips, not at all suggestively. Okay, maybe a little. Or a lot—"spice."

"It's my body spray; it's real manly. Don't take it as an invitation. I've got nothing for you, Jesse."

"Don't sell yourself short, handsome. But in any case, you're not my preferred flavor of snack. And I'm not one of those who go in uninvited, if you take my meaning."

"I get it. You like to think you're a *nice* vampire."

The smile vanished, and what was left in its place was just . . . dangerous. "Let's not call each other names. Someone might get hurt. What are you doing here? Hunting? Because if that's your thing, we can work it out somewhere else. I have to earn a living here."

"Just pulling down a paycheck, same as you," I said. "Look, I really didn't expect to run into any vam— very nice ladies such as yourself in a city like this. My understanding was they were all concentrated back home, where the Founder kept an eye on them."

"She does love to keep us close," Jesse agreed. "I left town thirty years ago, and I did some traveling—finding others and bringing them home. When Professor Anderson came here, I was assigned by the Founder to watch over her."

"Or just watch her?"

She shrugged. "They're not mutually exclusive, as it turns out."

That was uncomfortably close to what I was doing with Claire, so I decided to let that part go. "You're assigned here, then. Officially."

"Yes." She cut her gaze around one more time, and checked her watch. "And because you understand the score, we never had this conversation, or I'll have to get in contact back home and ask what they want me to do about you and your adorably blabby mouth. Clear?"

"Clear," I said. "If I find out you're hunting here, though, I'm not going to be happy."

"Well, wouldn't want that, now, would we?"

"No, we wouldn't," I said, "since I'm Frank Collins's boy."

That caused her to pause and reassess me, carefully. Then the smile came back, tempered a little. "I met your father once, when he was about your age. I liked him," she said. "He was always direct. And I see you're just like him."

"No," I said. "I'm not. But enough that you know where I'm coming from, and I don't deal in bullshit. If anything happens to Claire because of you, this will be a real different conversation."

"I have no interest in seeing anything happen to her," Jesse said. "I like the world out here the way it is. I've got no nostalgia for pitchforks and torches, and so I have a willing mate to provide for my needs, and if I get peckish for a little different fare, there are always people willing to make a donation. You just have to know where to go, and when to stop."

It sounded good, but I was still wary. She was suitably wary of me, too; I saw it in her last look at me as she went through the door to the bar area. Well, that was out in the open, at least. Now I would have to watch my back around her, and Pete, too, if Pete was in on Jesse's secret. I had to assume he was.

Then one of the other bartenders bawled out that he was running low on shot glasses, and I had to get back to work.

The glamorous life.

Closing time was when all the patrons went home, or staggered out the door, anyway, but it wasn't the end of shift for the rest of us. The battle-weary troops in the kitchen cleaned up there, then bused tables and loaded the rest of the glasses into the dishwashers before heading out. The bartenders tallied their registers, deposited the take with the manager, and counted out their tips, yawning and bleary-eyed. Pete and his other two bouncers helped with the trash pickup and general straightening, and by the time we were done it was after three in the morning, the streets were cold and empty, and I took out the trash to the Dumpster before heading upstairs to bed. Hated the accommodations, but damn, the commute was great.

The mattress was cold and lumpy, and the whole place (and me) smelled like industrial soap and beer, an uneasy and toxic mixture. Mick, the manager of Florey's, let me know that if a brew went missing out of the cooler from time to time, well, that was probably just breakage, but if it got too extensive he'd have to start checking.

The beer I took upstairs was the first one I'd snagged. It was a dark brew, imported, and it tasted much better than the rough, cheap whiz that Michael and I had started out drinking back in Morganville when we were stealing it from my dad's fridge. When my dad had a fridge. And a house. And a family.

I'm living just like my dad, I thought, and took a swig of the beer. It burned a little going down—hoppy and malty and dark, like my mood. *I've got nothing but a backpack and some stashed weapons and a bad attitude. And I keep running into vampires. Must be the Collins luck.*

That brought up way too many things I'd bolted down over the last few years. *The Collins luck.* Yeah, we were a lucky tribe, all right. My sister burned with the house. My mother died in a bathtub of blood, maybe at the hands of the vamps, maybe not. My dad had gotten turned into a vampire, plugged into a computer, and died back in Morganville, or at least I hoped he had. You never could tell, with those bastards.

I had no family left. Well, except for Michael and Eve, who had adopted me and all my traumas . . . and Claire, who I'd thought was going to be my home, forever. Only she had made it really clear that home had boundaries, and I'd crossed them, and now I was outside looking in. It hurt. It hurt really deeply, in a self-pitying, angry kind of way. I knew I was guilty, and it was my own damn fault, but that didn't stop some little-boy part of me from blaming her for freezing me out. She was supposed to forgive me, right? *The way your mom forgave your dad when he hit her? Is that what you want?* God, I hated that damn voice of reason, the one that kept the selfish little angry boy in check most of the time.

I took another pull from the beer, and another, and before too long all the walls I'd built so carefully around my pain were mud, soft and flowing and sticky. I remembered seeing Claire for the first time, fragile and wounded and needy. I remembered the first time I'd kissed her, and the trembling intensity of it. I remembered the first, breathless, anxious time in bed with her, the beautiful imperfection of it, terror and lust and joy all mixed together. I remembered a thousand wonderful things, and then all the bad things invaded right after them, because when the wall comes down it's too late to try to build it again.

Pandora's box was open.

The bottle was empty. I went to the cooler and got a six-pack, and worked my way through that while trying to forget about my dad's furious disappointment with me, his abuse, his willingness to sacrifice me for the cause ... and then once I'd pushed that back, all the times that I'd been at the mercy of a pair of fangs, and helpless. Too many times, in Morganville.

And then, I brooded about the draug.

They were the worst, the draug—creatures in the water, creatures that were worse than the vampires and more alien than anything I could really imagine. They didn't have feelings, except cold hunger, and they'd had me for a long time in their tanks. Feeding on me. Trapping me in dreams, and nightmares, until I wasn't sure I could tell the difference between the two anymore.

By the time I'd managed to work through *that* trauma, I was out of beer, and stumbling drunk, and I felt . . . empty. Just empty. No more anger, no more fear . . . just a vast vacuum that needed filling with something other than all the fury I'd held inside, and finally released.

I needed Claire. *Needed her.*

And so I clumsily unlocked Florey's, reset the alarm as I left, and weaved along the silent sidewalks heading for her apartment. I didn't think ahead to what I was going to say to her. I guess in my beer-soaked mind it would all just magically work out, and she'd be so happy to see me she'd forget about everything else. Because everybody loves having the drunken self-pitying boyfriend banging on their door at, Jesus, four thirty in the morning. At the time, hey, it seemed like a fabulous idea.

I never got there.

See, I forgot all the lessons that had been drilled into my head in Morganville: First, never get stumbling drunk, because you never know when you're going to need your wits and reflexes about you. Second, see the first rule.

And third, never ever do it after dark.

For some reason, I thought that Morganville was the equivalent of *Dead Space* Level Twelve, and having survived that, I didn't rate the nerdy, vampire-free streets of Cambridge at more than a Level Two.

Turns out that it wasn't vampires I had to worry about. It was just a gang of guys who'd finished off the night badly and was looking for somebody to blame, and I was staggering down the wrong damn street. There were six of them, and approximately one quarter of me, and those weren't good odds in any game.

In real life, you don't get a reset, and you don't get extra lives, and I got the crap pounded out of mine. I don't really know how it happened; I saw them coming, whooping and hollering and high-fiving, and then they went quiet when they saw me and I guess they didn't like the T-shirt I had on, or maybe they thought I was some rich, stupid kid out for a stroll, but after the first punch it was all just a blur because there wasn't any way to fight six guys at once. It was more a matter of going down, curling up, and trying to survive it while being dimly aware that the beer wasn't making it any less painful, and that one of them had a really high, shrill, ragged voice as he yelled *faggot* in my ear and kicked me in the liver.

And then I heard the ring of metal on concrete, and I went cold, because one of them had found a piece of rebar lying around, and I knew with sudden certainty that these guys were going to kill me right here on this stupid sidewalk, for *nothing*, without even the reason of knowing my name or hating my politics. They were just going to kill me because they needed to kill something, and I was handy.

At least zombies would have had a reason.

I would have been dead if Team Vampire hadn't swooped in and saved my drunken ass.

I didn't see a lot of it, given that I had a pretty good concussion and blood in my eyes, but I saw pale skin, a killer smile, whipping hair that flared red in the streetlight, and curves that would be fairly impossible to forget. Jesse had come to my rescue, and so had Pete; my fireplug of a friend had taken the rebar and was strategically applying it to arms and legs with dispassionate calm. There was a lot of screaming, and within seconds, *seconds*, it was all over and there were seven guys on the concrete.

Then Jesse helped me stand up, and there were six.

"Don't worry, they're not dead," she said, and gave me a merciless appraisal. "You look like shit, Collins."

"Thanks," I mumbled. I didn't mean for the compliment. "Well, that walk sucked."

She laughed as I spat out a mouthful of blood, and if she thought I was wasting food, at least she didn't say so. Pete brought the rebar along with us, and we went to a car parked about a block down. It was a long walk. I passed the time by wondering (probably aloud) why Pete had brought along his iron stick. I know it was probably aloud because he finally said, "Fingerprints," as he tossed it in the trunk of the car and helped Jesse pile me into the back. "You're drunk."

"You're perceptive," I said, and slid sideways until my already-sore head collided with window glass. "Ow." That wasn't adequate to the situation, but I didn't think it was manly to cry like a little girl. I pulled myself into a leaning position and breathed deeply, trying not to think of how the world was spinning. "It was only a six-pack."

"Of?"

"Russian imperial stout."

"Oh, honey," Jesse said from the driver's seat, clearly amused. "The Russians have nothing to do most of the winter but drink as a hobby. You really should work up to that stuff. Take it from me, I was around when Gregory Rasputin was still the man to beat in a drinking game. You're going to regret that."

"He's going to regret it a lot more," Pete said. He was poking and prodding me, a fact I realized late, and when I ineffectively slapped at him to stop, I missed and smacked myself in something that was already bruised. Not sure what. "Might have to take him to the ER. He could have internal bleeding."

Jesse cocked her head and glanced back at me, and I saw that red glow in her eyes again. Weirdly, it seemed comforting right now. Homey, even. "He might have, but he doesn't," she said. "I could tell if he did. Oh, he's got plenty of hemorrhages, but they're not life-threatening. And he's no stranger to cuts and bruises. Watch his head, though. I saw them get in a good shot at least twice."

"He'll have a hell of a headache from the contrecoup, but doesn't look like anything too bad. Might want to get an X-ray, though."

I was starting off my time in Cambridge pretty much the same way I had my return to Morganville: with hospital visits. "What the hell," I sighed. "I haven't had a good X-ray in a long time. Could be fun." Because unlike most drunken tough guys, I'd seen enough to know that head injuries were nothing to fool around with. You could look and feel fine for a day, then drop dead of the swelling and exploding veins.

"I think you're confusing X-rays with something from a porn movie," Jesse said, "but sure. One ER visit, coming up. I hope that whatever you had going with those guys was worth all the trouble. What did they do, kick a puppy, insult your mother . . . ?"

"Nothing," I said. "I didn't do anything. They just wanted to hurt someone, and I was there."

After a moment of silence, she said, "Yes, I know how that can happen." She sounded grim, like she personally knew it, and hey, she probably did. She might have even been on the receiving end, but you could never assume that kind of thing with vampires. "Why were you wandering around in the dark, Shane? I'm assuming that coming from Morganville you know better."

"I thought it'd be safer here."

Pete laughed. He had an odd kind of laugh, one that hitched in the middle. "You don't get out much, Shane. That's kind of cute. Take a walk in a genocide zone and tell me humans can't be worse than bloodsuckers. We're hardwired to be bastards, take it from somebody who did volunteer work in the Congo."

Thing is, I already knew that perfectly well, because I knew what Amelie, the Founder of Morganville, was afraid of. She was most afraid of us. Humans. And our tendency to kill whatever we feared and/or hated.

Our ability to target things that were different.

I wasn't any better, I thought. I'd hated vampires most of my life, and I still didn't feel totally comfortable around them, even if Jesse had just joyously kicked some ass to save me.

Hardwired. Pete was probably right about that.

They got me into the somewhat deserted ER, and it took only about four hours (some kind of record, I was assured) to get me into X-ray and find out that yes, I still had a functioning, if lightly bruised, brain, and that nothing important was busted in the rest of me. By that time, the beer's comfortable cushion had evaporated, and with the cold light of dawn coming, Jesse had taken off and left me to Pete. He didn't seem especially upset about losing his beauty sleep; maybe he was used to staying up until dawn, given the bar job and his clear alliance with Jesse, which seemed to be more about business than pleasure. Jesse had left him the car and gone her way on foot; she must have had some bolt-hole put away nearby, because she seemed pretty casual about the sunrise. Unless she was pretty old, she'd still be susceptible to the burns delivered by the daylight . . . and even if she *was* old, she wouldn't enjoy being out in it.

Once I'd paid the bill (which ate up all my free cash, plus a loan from Pete, silently offered) I collapsed back in the car and let him drive me back to Florey's. We passed Claire's row house along the way, and I remembered the foggy, ill-formed plan to stagger up to her door and let her forgive me and drag me upstairs to bed. Wow. That had not been smart. It was almost good I'd wandered into a beating instead. At least I'd preserved my self-respect.

Because now, sober, I knew exactly how it would have played out. Claire would have been kind and pitying, and given me aspirin and a blanket and pillow, and I'd have slept it off on some direly uncomfortable couch with her upstairs and unattainable. And then I'd have had the awkward awakening, the explanations, the apologies, and . . . what?

I was afraid that there would be nothing, afterward.

"What were you guys doing?" I asked Pete, as he pulled to a stop in front of Florey's. "How did you find me?"

"Didn't," he said tersely. "We were looking for those jackasses. They'd already beaten up a gay guy two blocks down. Cops don't always get on this stuff quick in our neighborhood, so we do. It's kind of a hobby."

I paused in the act of opening the door and looked at him with what were probably cartoon-wide eyes. "Wait a second," I said. "So, you're best friends with a hot vampire chick who likes leather."

"Yeah."

"And together, you fight crime?" I couldn't help it. I cracked up.

"Everybody needs a hobby, man," Pete said. "Now go inside, because you're going to start throwing up soon and I don't want it on my floorboards."

Dammit.

He was right about that, too.

EIGHT

Claire started to call Professor Anderson to tell her about her nighttime visitors, but she realized that it was probably a very bad idea . . . if the government really was involved, they had the power and the ability to monitor cell communication as easily as breathing. In fact, her conversation with Michael and Eve, even encrypted on the Morganville system, was probably vulnerable in some way, though she imagined that Amelie's paranoia was a pretty decent firewall against such things. Some things needed to be said in person, though. In a secured environment.

So even though she slept remarkably little and felt hungover from the lack of sleep, Claire got up early and jogged to the lab. It was very quiet at that hour—just after dawn, really—and she passed a few students sleepily heading to early sessions. The hallways of the secured area were deserted and silent. Claire quickly badged into Anderson's area, and found the professor already there, sitting at the desk in the corner, typing away. Anderson turned around, frowning, when she heard the warning chime of the security door, and her eyes widened when she saw Claire.

"Is everything all right?" she asked, and got up to come closer. "You look pale."

"Long night," Claire said, and took a deep breath. "Can I talk here?"

"Give me your cell phone." Claire handed it over, and Anderson took it over to the computer. She linked it on with a cable and did some key-clicking, and handed it back about a minute later. "I've installed an app to block anybody trying to snoop. They'll get playback of innocuous conversation instead, so they won't be able to tell there's anything wrong. Now you can talk freely."

"My house was searched last night by two men. I think they thought I'd gone out, like my roommate. Professor—they didn't break in. They let themselves in, like they had keys."

"Did you get a look at them?"

Claire nodded. Anderson sat down in her computer chair and brought up a screen. More mouse movement and key clicks, and suddenly Claire was looking at a photo album of surveillance photos . . . not the grainy kind, either. These were sharp and clear as high-res stills. "See anyone you recognize?"

Claire pointed over her professor's shoulder at one of the men pictured there. "He was one of them, for sure. I'm not sure about the other; I just got a quick look. Could have been one of the others, but I'm really not sure at all. Who are they?"

"Well, they're not from the people I work with directly, but there are plenty of players on the board. Best to be careful. Do you have an alarm system?"

"No, I told my housemate we need to get one."

"Convince her. It wouldn't hurt for you to learn to use that knife I gave you, either."

"I know how to use it," Claire said, pretty calmly she thought, given that suddenly she was hip-deep in government agencies and foreign spies when she'd thought all that she was getting into were vampire politics. "Professor—are you sure that we're not in over our heads, somehow? Is this related to VLAD?"

"I have no way of knowing what it's related to," Anderson said, which was just logical, Claire guessed. "I am under contract to several government and privately funded groups; any one of them could have decided that you should be carefully checked out. Let's not read too much into it, shall we?"

"They came *into my house!*"

"And left you and your possessions unharmed. Let's not call in an air strike quite yet." Anderson gave her a warm, comforting smile. "Now, I'm glad you're here early. There are some things about VLAD that still puzzle me, and I'd like to go over them before our test today."

"Test?" Claire had a blinding moment of panic; nobody had warned her there was a test coming.

"Not for you," her professor said, laughing, because the panic must have been visible. "We're testing VLAD on a live subject at noon."

"By subject, do you mean—"

"Vampire, yes, that's exactly what I mean."

"There are vampires *here?*"

"Not in the school per se, no. But close by. Because, of course, Amelie doesn't trust anyone to leave Morganville without a little oversight, especially someone who's been so deeply into Myrnin's confidence. Luckily, I'm a friend of my particular minder, and she's agreed to keep the secret—for now. I'd rather not involve her, but we do need a live subject, and she's the only one I have at hand."

"But—I thought you were scared of Amelie finding out about VLAD!"

"I was. But the fact is, she's going to find out. It's more important for us to make quick, efficient progress than to go carefully. Myrnin would take my side, and yours; I think he'll be able to contain her paranoia, at least for a while. And so while this will be a risk, it's probably one we have to take. Now. Let's go over the questions."

Dr. Anderson brought VLAD out from the secured area, and Claire answered about an hour's worth of detailed questions on the internal workings. Some of the questions startled her, led her off on tangents that started discussions about better ways to channel and concentrate the energy being generated. It was . . . well, exciting. Problem solving was always thrilling for Claire, and clearly it was for Anderson, too.

Finally, her professor nodded and stowed VLAD away, and Claire got ready to do something even more exciting.

She was disappointed.

"Sometimes, being my assistant isn't going to be action-packed," Anderson said, and pointed to a huge bin full of paper. "Shred all that, then take the pieces to the incinerator at the end of the hall for burning. I like to be thorough."

"What is all this?"

"Old projects," her professor said. "Don't read it. Just shred and burn, or your eyes will melt." She said it so matter-of-factly that Claire had a moment's hesitation, before the other woman laughed. "Don't worry. I haven't perfected that eye-melting technology quite yet. Shredder's over there."

That commenced a vividly exciting morning of sitting in a chair feeding paper into a machine that spit out shreds, and putting the shreds into a giant plastic bag when the bin was full. It took a full three hours to go through the stack of paper, and Claire quickly learned that shredded paper might be more volumetric than the flat kind, but it wasn't really that much lighter in total weight. She struggled with the bag down the hall, located the incinerator room, and dumped the paper down the chute before she pushed the big red button to fire up the oven.

She couldn't help but think that it was awfully convenient, having a thing like this so close to the lab. Or to labs that did all sorts of mysterious, biological things. She imagined grisly scenarios in which mistakes had gone down this chute, and shivered.

When she turned around, empty bag in hand, Jesse was standing in the incinerator room watching her. The sudden appearance of the woman made Claire's hackles rise on the back of her neck, and at the same time she felt an uncomfortable flush on her skin. Something about Jesse invited contradictory impulses, seemed like. She looked just as calm and composed as she had the night before, though she wasn't wearing leather just now; she'd changed into a loose black shirt, jeans, and heavy boots that Eve would have swooned over, considering all the buckles. Her red hair was twisted back in a loose, sloppy bun and fixed with a pair of chopsticks.

"Hey," Jesse said. "Irene sent me to find out if you were done. Looks like you are."

Claire rattled the bag. "Looks like."

Jesse was sizing her up in an odd sort of way, she thought, and as the two of them walked back toward the lab through the clean white hall, Claire finally said, "Do I have a big ink stain on my face, or . . . ?"

"No," Jesse said, and smiled slowly. "I was just thinking that there's more to you than meets the eye, that's all. You inspire a certain reckless passion in others, did you know that?"

"*I* do? In who?"

Jesse didn't answer that. She badged through into Anderson's lab, and Claire had to wait to follow; by the time she was inside, Jesse was at the table with the professor, and the device—VLAD—was laid out on a lab table on top of a foam cushion. "Doesn't look like much," Jesse said. "You're sure, Irene?"

"No, of course I'm not sure, or I wouldn't have asked you here," Anderson said, a touch impatiently. "And I don't like doing it, either; I don't really know what the outcome's going to be. But we need to have a baseline, and like it or not, you're the only game I have in town."

"Only game in . . ." Claire repeated, and felt the truth hit home with a vengeance. She fixed her gaze solidly on Jesse. "You're a vampire?"

"The kid's sharp," Jesse said. "Yes, sweetie, I'm a card-carrying member of the undead. Remember how I didn't come into your house, but Pete did, to get the box? I thought that would tip you off, being a Morganville kid and all, but you didn't seem to suspect anything."

"I would have, if we'd been back home, but I didn't expect to find . . . one of you here."

"Mistakes like that get you killed," Jesse said. "There aren't a lot of us out in the wild, sure, but there are still a few, and most of them aren't as nice as I am." She flashed Claire a grin that wouldn't have been out of place on Eve's face. "Relax. I don't bite."

"Oh, she does," Anderson said. "Just not unless she's invited to."

"Well, you should know," Jesse purred, and laughed when Dr. Anderson's cheeks turned pink.

"All right, now that you've made your point, sit over there, Jesse. What's going to happen is that I'm going to point this weapon at you and press the trigger, and you should report to me exactly what it feels like. It shouldn't hurt you."

"Shouldn't?" Jesse's eyebrows climbed higher. "Not sure I like the variable in that statement. Claire, you tried this on any other vampires before?"

"Myrnin," Claire said.

"Did it hurt him?"

"I don't think so."

"Well, I'm not Myrnin, and I'm not so willing to hop on the crazy train, but all right. Just for you, Reenie."

Anderson rolled her eyes. "God, *please* don't call me that name. Just go sit in the chair. I promise, it'll be a very brief exposure."

Jesse crossed the room to the plain aluminum chair that sat against the wall, put her hand on it, and said, "Here?"

"Yes, please."

Jesse sat down, crossed her legs, and folded her hands in her lap like a church lady, which she was most certainly not. "Ready, aim, fire."

"Not funny," Anderson said softly, but she raised VLAD, sighted, and pulled the trigger.

Nothing came out of the gun—no rays or smoke or visible

sign of any kind—but Jesse sat up very straight, eyes opening wide. Anderson immediately let go of the trigger and replaced VLAD on the foam pad. "Are you all right?" she asked, and took a step forward. "Jesse?"

"Stop," Jesse said, and held her hand out. She looked ... odd, and her face was utterly expressionless. "Irene, stop right there, please."

Dr. Anderson did, looking *very* worried, until Jesse finally dropped her hand back to her lap and relaxed. "That was ... interesting."

"Apparently," Dr. Anderson said, and smiled, though it was clearly a troubled sort of smile. "What just happened to you?"

"I'm not really quite sure. I can tell you that when I sat down, I was feeling a little nervous about what was about to happen, and I was also feeling a little"—Jesse cut her glance toward Claire for a second, and probably amended what she was going to say—"a little amused, I suppose. And all of a sudden I was both those things, still, but ramped up to eleven. It was ... disconcerting, because those are not two emotions that go very well together. You understand?"

"It amplifies," Claire said. They both focused on her. "The way I set it up to start with, whatever the vampire feels, it's amplified by the device. I think it kind of works on humans, too. But more on vampires, obviously."

"Well, if your question was, Did it work? It works." Jesse started to stand up, and—incredibly—suddenly faltered and braced herself against the wall. "Whoa. It also makes you wicked dizzy, in case you didn't know that."

"I didn't," Claire confessed. "Are you okay?"

"Fine. Just have to shake it off." Jesse pushed away from the wall and smiled at Dr. Anderson. "I'm not a wilting flower, unless that gets me extraspecial treats."

"It might," Dr. Anderson said. "I'm sorry. I shouldn't have asked you to do that, but I needed to know if this was something that had potential, or just another empty promise."

"Oh, it's got potential all right," Jesse said. "If I'd been hungry and that thing had hit me, I'd have gone for your veins, and you'd have had to stop me any way you could. So be warned. It's not a toy, and it might make an angry vampire *damn* angry."

"The idea is to reverse those emotions," Claire offered. "To make an angry vampire less angry, a hungry one less hungry . . . and like you said, it's disconcerting. I suppose it could be used kind of like a vampire stun gun, I guess."

"You're looking for something nonlethal to use to defend yourself," Jesse said. "Well, that's not a bad goal, and it's not a bad start. I suppose I'd be okay with testing it for you when you take it to the next step. But just remember: I'm not the usual vampire, either. I've got a pretty good grip on myself. The next one you run into might not be quite so in control."

"Jesse—I'm not ready to report to Amelie about this thing. Myrnin kept it from her for a reason when Claire was working on it; I'm quite sure she'd have shut it down if she'd known. I'd really like to proceed with this line of inquiry, but I'm afraid that she would object. So can we agree to keep it quiet, for now? Please?"

Jesse was silent for a long, long moment, frowning. She crossed her arms and paced a bit, and then finally bit her lip and nodded. "For a while," she said. "But you know I can't keep it from her for long. And if she asks me a direct question about it, I can't lie."

"I know," Anderson said. "You've always made it quite clear where your real loyalty lies."

There was something strange in her smile, something almost a little angry, and she and Jesse locked stares for a moment that stretched on too long for comfort.

Then Jesse smiled, too. "You know, this is super fun, but I actually have to go sling some drinks tonight, and I need to get ready. Being this gorgeous ain't easy, you know."

"So you tell me," Anderson said. "Go on, and stay out of the sun."

"Nag. I'm wearing the super sunblock—don't you worry." Jesse stuck her tongue out, just like a three-year-old would do, and Claire had to laugh. There was something oddly childlike about her, considering she was also capable of turning cold at a moment's notice, like any vampire. She was certainly old or she wouldn't be so nonchalant about roaming around during the day, and she wasn't even wearing the thick layers of protective coats and hats that most vampires preferred. "You two don't get up to anything funny around here. I'm done bailing people out of trouble for the next couple of days. It's been busy."

"Yeah? Who'd you bail out today?"

For no apparent reason, Jesse smiled, and made a locking motion at her lips. "Can't say," she said, "but he was real, real cute. Maybe I'll tell you the story later."

"You'd better."

Jesse waggled her fingertips and swiped her badge to get out of the lab, and it felt like half the light had left the room, somehow. She was . . . intense, Claire thought. And really, kind of cool.

Dr. Anderson certainly thought so; she stared at the door for a full ten seconds after Jesse was gone, then snapped out of it and cleared her throat, put on her glasses, and walked back to stare down at VLAD. "Right," she said. "We have some work to do. First step is that we disassemble, label, and scan every part of this so that we can make a virtual model. I want to be able to prototype this on the 3-D printer next time."

"The—what?"

"The 3-D printer," the professor repeated, and pointed to a big, strange-looking thing in the far corner of the lab. "It takes a solid block of paper, plastic, or metal and repeats a design. With good enough specs, you can print anything. The guys down the hall are working on 3-D printing of human organs. You remember the replicators on *Star Trek* that could make anything you wanted, from a roast beef sandwich to a phaser? We're working on it. And actually, we've made a daunting amount of progress."

That was . . . new. Claire thought about Myrnin, clinging to his antique microscopes and time-tested tools, and wondered what he'd think about all this. He'd probably feel it was too far from nature and the cycles of the moon and sun; that's what he always said about things that he didn't quite grasp. For all his brilliance, and he *was* brilliant, he just couldn't shake off the bonds of his background in alchemy.

Maybe he'd change his mind if she brought back a new, shiny, 3-D printed, *working* copy of VLAD. It might solve the weight problems, too, if they could machine it out of some very light-weight materials. Maybe, with enough imagination, they'd even be able to model a vampire brain and print an artificial one to fit in-side Myrnin's computer, eliminating the need for anyone to die for science ever again in Morganville.

Well, she could dream, anyway.

Dr. Anderson was putting out a wide selection of tools for the

disassembly, and pointed Claire toward a rolling 3-D scanning device; her job, as each piece was disassembled from VLAD, was to
tag it with a number and description, scan it individually, and put
it in a bin. Dr. Anderson was very careful; when she got to the little vials of bubbling liquid—Myrnin's addition, along with all the
whirling gears—she kept the liquid as well, though she siphoned
off a bit for testing. Bit by bit, the device came apart into its component pieces, and the lab began to smell like hot solder and cool-
ing metal.

By the time it was done, Claire yawned, stretched, and glanced
up at the clock. It was already five o'clock. She hadn't intended to
stay so long, but there was still more to be done; the scanner had to
download into the mainframe, so that Dr. Anderson could begin
to work with the component pieces in wireframe form.

"You should go," Dr. Anderson said, and yawned. "Sorry. I got
up early, and I know it's been another long day for you. I can handle reassembly tonight."

"Want me to put the parts away?" The bin was full now, and just
as heavy as the whole device had been. Dr. Anderson nodded, and
Claire carried it back to the concealed panel, which was still open.
She slid the bin inside, on Anderson's instruction, pressed her hand
to the panel on the side. It lit up red, and the door slid shut.

"I programmed it for your palm print," Anderson said. "You can
open and close it on your own now. But only if there's no one else in
the room but me. If someone tries to force you to open it, it'll simply
stay closed, so you just tell them you don't have authorization. Without authorization, you wouldn't be of any use to them."

She'd thought ahead, Claire thought, and it was a little chilling
that she'd thought as far as someone holding a gun to Claire's head
and forcing her to try to open the hiding place.

But that was someone from Morganville for you—always thinking of the worst-case scenario.

Claire said good night, and started for home.

She was walking down the street from the Mudd Building, dodging excited groups of students who were apparently headed to the Biopolymer Lab, when her phone rang—no, it hadn't, actually, because she had a voice mail, not a call. Dodgy reception in the lab, she guessed.

The call was from Liz, as were the three text messages. All were alerting her, with cheery good humor, that Liz had invited someone to dinner, and to please come home on time, before six.

Claire checked her watch. She just had time to make it.

Elizabeth met Claire at the door, which swung open before she'd even reached for the doorknob. She was wearing a fancy dress, nice shoes, earrings, a glittering necklace, and she even had on lipstick.

Claire blinked. "I thought we were just having somebody over for dinner."

Liz dragged her inside and closed the door. She leaned closer to whisper, "We are, but put on something nice. I want to impress him, okay? It's important!"

"Um . . . okay." Claire wasn't sure why *she* had to dress up to impress Elizabeth's date, but she was willing to meet her halfway for the sake of good roommate karma. Up the stairs, and into her room. She dumped her backpack on the still-unmade bed and sorted through her limited clothing choices, settling on a fitted white shirt and some black pants. Plain, but nice. Adding one of the necklaces Eve had given her—a Day of the Dead skull, enameled in all kinds of bright colors—jazzed it up a little. Claire fluffed her hair in the mirror and decided that she wasn't going to resort to makeup; after all, it was Liz's date, not hers.

When she made her way downstairs, she heard Elizabeth laughing, and she opened the door to the kitchen and saw her in an actual apron over her fancy dress, stirring a pot. A man was sitting at the small kitchen table—not a college boy at all, a man of about forty, probably, with little gray threads at his temples and sparkling blue eyes in a suntanned face. Even sitting down, he seemed tall. He was wearing a denim work shirt with the collar open, and a sports coat, and he had a little smile on his face that Claire somehow didn't really like.

She'd rarely taken an instant dislike to anyone, but . . . she might have to make an exception, she decided.

"Claire, this is Patrick," Elizabeth said. Which caught her by surprise. Somehow, Claire had thought that she'd introduce the man as her father, which he was certainly old enough to be. Or an uncle, or something. But just plain Patrick? "Dr. Patrick Davis, I mean. He's one of my professors."

"Really?" Claire raised her eyebrows and carefully nodded to him. "Which class?"

"Biology," Patrick said. "Elizabeth's a very bright student. I hope you don't mind that she invited me over for a meal."

Claire avoided answering that by joining Liz at the stove. "What are you making?"

"Chicken and stuffing, peas, and carrots," her housemate said. Her smile looked excited, but it trembled a bit in the corners. "Sound okay?"

"Delicious. What can I do?"

"The bread? Just put it to warm in the oven."

Claire did that, and fetched herself a glass of Coke from the fridge. She didn't ask Dr. Davis if he wanted anything, because as she was putting ice in the glass she caught him staring at Liz in a way that was not very professorial. More predatory.

Oh, God. Seriously? *Gross.*

"Funny," Claire said, "but I don't think I ever invited any of my professors home for dinner. Not even the ones I liked."

Liz gave her a pleading look. "Well, that's too bad. You haven't had the fantastic teachers I have, I guess," she said. "Patrick is great."

"I'm sure." Claire sipped her Coke for a minute, thinking about it, and then said, "You know what, I think I really should be studying, and—"

"Oh, no, please, don't let my presence drive you away," Patrick said. He sounded earnest and kind, and he even had a hint of a gentle Irish accent, which threw her off her wary game. "Liz assures me that she doesn't cook very often; I want you to share in the bounty. I'd very much like to talk; Liz tells me you're doing quite interesting work."

"I—excuse me?" Claire paused in the act of picking up the bread tray to turn to look at him. Liz kept her gaze fixed steadily on the pot she was stirring, as if she hadn't heard a thing. "What interesting work?"

"Well, I hear you're enrolled in an individual study program at MIT. I don't think there's been more than a handful of people who could claim that in the entire history of the university. Tell me, how did that come about?"

Claire forced herself to move—to set the stove dial, open the door, shove the tray inside on the rack. But she knew she looked awkward and nervous. *Very* awkward. Her brain was scrambling to keep up with the changing scenery. She'd pegged Dr. Davis as one of *those* teachers . . . the ones who used their jobs to pick off the easy prey, like Liz, who craved acceptance and protection. She was sure he was on a quest to seduce her housemate, if he hadn't already.

So this seemed like a very sharp left turn, at best. And in a worrying direction.

He was clearly waiting for her answer, so she said, "I'm actually just here temporarily. It's sort of a special project. I'm working with one of the professors. They do those kinds of visiting student projects all the time. Maybe you heard about the boy from Africa who powered his village's technology from found objects . . ."

"Oh, yes, I know all about the public relations projects," he said. "But I think what you're doing is a great deal more . . . interesting. Isn't that right?"

Claire jerked and knocked a lid from the counter; it fell to the floor and rang like a bell, and it provided a nice sonic distraction from what she was sure was going to be a very telling silence. She fumbled for the pot lid, and Liz bent down at the same time, and in the confusion Claire whispered, urgently, "What the hell does he want?"

"What? Nothing!" Liz snatched the pot lid from her hands and rinsed it off in the sink before slamming it down on the pot she'd been watching. "If I'd known you'd be so judgmental I wouldn't have asked you in!"

"You didn't *ask*," Claire hissed back. "Whatever."

"Everything all right, ladies?" Dr. Davis asked, and Liz turned, took a deep breath, dried her hands on the apron, and smiled like a plastic mannequin as she carried the pot over to the table and set it down.

"Just fine, Patrick," she said. When Claire gave her a look, she got defensive. "He told me to call him that. I know it seems strange to call a professor by his first name, but——"

"But I do like to be informal," he broke in. He rose from the table and took the pot holders from Liz to move the chicken breasts to the table, and then the peas. "Please, let me help. Be seated, ladies. May I get you another drink, Liz?"

"Oh, just water," Liz said. As he busied himself at the sink with glasses and ice, Liz grabbed Claire's shoulder in an iron-hard grip. "Do *not* screw this up for me. I need a good grade, and I like him!"

"And he likes you," Claire whispered back. "Probably a little too much, don't you think? He came to *dinner*? Who does that?"

Liz's eyes turned furious, and she squeezed tighter. Deliberately pinching flesh. Claire bit back a wince. "Like I said, don't screw this up," she said. "I deserve something good for a change. I've had enough bad things in my life."

Maybe she did deserve a good time, but Claire was one hundred percent convinced that this wasn't it. Dr. Davis was pleasant and casual, but he was also oily and manipulative, and he creeped her out. And what was that dig about her personal study program? What did he know?

Maybe a lot. Maybe too much. Claire felt as if she was playing a deadly game without knowing the rules or the players. It made her long for the straightforward violence of home.

"Now then," Patrick said, and deposited the cold glass of water in front of Liz, patted her shoulder, and walked over to his own chair in a triangle between the two of them. "What were we talking about? Ah, yes——"

"The chicken looks delicious," Claire said. "How did you cook it?" That elicited a nervous flood of cooking info from Liz;

Rachael Ray would have been proud, because Liz seemed to have memorized the entire recipe, start to finish, and it had a lot of steps. Same for the stuffing. Dr. Davis's smile grew fixed and grim, but he waited out the tidal surge of information. His gaze mostly held on Liz, but Claire felt it when he shifted to her.

She didn't like it.

The business of serving out the chicken and vegetables took most of the time, and then when Dr. Davis tried to reframe his question, Claire jumped up to get the bread from the oven and passed that around, too. Liz nervously chattered on, clearly scared to death that Dr. Davis would think he wasn't wanted (and he wasn't, on Claire's part), which had the nice side effect of blocking his attempts at boxing Claire into conversation again.

For a while, he gave up, preferring to trade idle chatter with Elizabeth—none of it invited or required any participation from Claire, so she ate dinner with single-minded focus. The chicken really *was* good. She really needed to learn how to make that.

By the time her plate was empty, the other two at the table were only half finished, and Claire drained the rest of her Coke and rose to take her plate to the sink. "Thanks, Liz," she said. "I really have to go study."

"Oh," Liz said. "Really? Well, if you have to." It was the token protest, with an undercurrent of *please go away and leave us alone now.* Which was a relief, and Claire headed for the kitchen door.

She didn't quite get there before Dr. Davis said, "I understand that you're studying with Dr. Irene Anderson. She has quite the reputation as—let's say, an eccentric, even at MIT. How do you find working with her?"

It would have been rude to keep on walking, but she opened

the door and stood in the threshold as she answered. "Fine. Look, I really have to—"

"I'm very intrigued by Dr. Anderson's research."

"You know her?"

"Quite well, actually. She has a great interest in cryptobiology—projecting the abilities and vulnerabilities of imaginary creatures. Such as, say, werewolves, zombies, vampires. We debate the subject often. It's a lively discussion topic. What would you say the primary vulnerability is for a vampire, say?"

Claire smiled thinly back at him. "Sorry, I hadn't really thought about it. I don't have time for that kind of thing. I have way too many real-world things to worry about right now." She intended it as a total shutdown and dismissal, but he didn't take the hint. Of course.

"Well, hypothetically—you're a very smart young lady, Claire. Hypothetically, do you think that vampires could be controlled and put to good use as, say, soldiers? Or secret agents? I suppose they'd be great at all sorts of dangerous occupations that humans would hesitate to do. Provided one could totally ensure their compliance."

"I suppose." She *really* didn't like where this was going. "Liz, thanks for dinner."

"It was lovely to meet you," Dr. Davis said. "Miss Danvers."

"Sure," she said flatly, and let the door swing shut behind her.

She went up the stairs to her room and locked the door, put on her headphones, and tried to block out the world. If he came knocking, she'd ignore him. And she'd damn sure be telling Dr. Anderson about this. And maybe Amelie, too.

An hour later, she stripped off her headphones, yawned, and

pressed her ear to the door to see if the coast was clear to go to the bathroom. It was. The kitchen was silent, and the bathroom was empty. After her visit, though, she heard sounds coming from Liz's room on the second floor, and she went up the stairs, fast.

Dr. Davis was definitely taking advantage of more than just the chicken dinner. And from the sound of it, Liz was enjoying every minute of it.

Ugh.

Claire put the headphones back on and turned the music way up, just to be sure she didn't hear any part of that. It didn't really help. And it made her fidgety, angry, worried, frustrated . . . in all kinds of ways, actually.

Shane hadn't called. Why hadn't he called? She checked her phone, and yes, the battery was still good. Everything was fine.

She angrily stripped the headphones off and, driven by a mix of emotions she really didn't want to examine too closely, selected his number and pressed CALL.

And this time, he answered. "Claire?"

He sounded . . . he sounded close. And out of breath. As if she might be able to reach out and touch him, just . . . collapse in his arms and let all this go away for a while. Make everything right again. And she wanted it, wanted it so so much. So much that for a long, shaky moment she couldn't even make her voice work right.

"Claire . . . ?" His voice was softer now, almost a whisper. "God, please talk to me."

"I'm here," she whispered back. Somehow she didn't want to raise the level of her voice; it sounded intimate this way. Close. Personal. "I called you. You didn't answer."

"I know. I'm sorry. Please—it doesn't mean that I don't care, I just—" He moved, and she heard his breath catch. And she heard that his voice wasn't quite right, either. "I just couldn't call you back."

She sat up straighter, because all her alarm bells were ringing now. "Shane, are you all right? What happened? Are you hurt?" Because he was. She could hear it, especially when he tried to laugh.

"I'm fine."

"You're not, don't even try to tell me that. What happened?"

"Got my ass kicked," he said. "It's not exactly breaking news. Except oddly enough it had nothing to do with vampires, can you believe it? Well, it did, because a vampire saved me from getting stomped to death. So there's that. It's a fun story. I'll tell it to you sometime."

She wanted to cry, it hurt her so much not to be with him. To not take care of him when he needed her. "You don't sound good. How badly are you hurt?"

"Cuts, bruises, a pretty nice concussion that rang my bell. Nothing broken, which is a miracle. I've had worse. Hell, Claire, *you've* had worse. Don't worry, I'm all right. I really am." His voice lowered again, into that low purring whisper. "Are you? Okay?"

"Yeah," she whispered back. "I miss you. I miss Eve and Michael. I miss home. Is that bad? It's probably bad. You're going to think I'm whining like a little kid."

"No. I——" She had the weird feeling that he was about to confess something, too, but then . . . then he sighed. "I think you're amazing. And I think it's good that you're doing this. It's your dream, Claire. I wouldn't want to stand in your way."

"Do you think you did? You didn't. *I* was standing in my way. And . . . I'm not so sure that this is my dream after all. It's turning out to be . . . kind of a nightmare." A particularly loud moan came up through the floorboards, and Claire buried her head under her pillow with the phone cradled close to her ear. "I really hate living with Elizabeth. And she's getting it on with a skanky professor right now."

"Right now?"

"One floor down. It's gross. I can't even tell you how gross it is. There are no words."

"Okay, then listen to my voice," he said. She closed her eyes, and fell into the sound of his breathing. "You don't have to listen to anything else, just talk to me. Tell me what's going on in your life."

"I'm just—" Her voice choked, and she told herself very firmly that she would not, absolutely would not cry. She cleared her throat. "My professor and I are working on the thing I brought. You know? But it's not like it was back home. I feel as if I can't really trust anyone here. I don't know if anyone has my back. There's Liz, but she's turned out to be a total flake; honestly, I don't even know if I like her at all anymore—I mean, I feel for her, she's had a rough time of it and all, but we're nothing alike, Shane. Nothing. My professor—I don't even know. I don't know if I can trust her or not. Sometimes I know I can, and then . . ."

"So, really, no different from your last job, right?"

She laughed a little, but it felt wretched. "And I don't really know anybody, and the people I do know, the people I want to fit in with—I just don't, and I can't. What's worse is . . . I don't matter here, Shane. I feel like I just don't matter. Stupid, right?"

"No," he said. He sounded so gentle it broke her heart. "It's how most people feel most of the time, Claire. You've grown up being special, and this is how most people live their lives . . . alone. On their own. Unnoticed. And they get used to that feeling. It's just new for you."

"Yeah," she whispered. "I'm sorry, I shouldn't complain. That's really selfish and I don't mean it that way; I don't. . . ."

"Shhh." The breathy sound he made gave her chills, and she curled up tight under the covers, imagining the warmth of him next to her, imagining his hands sliding down her arms. Comforting and sweet and tender, and safe. So safe. It was hard to think he was so very far away when she needed him so much. And he needed her. She could feel it coming out of the phone like a fever heat. "Don't do that. You're the least selfish person I've ever met, Claire. You teach me every day how to be a little bit better. And I miss you, you know that? I can't stand not seeing you, not touching you. . . ." His voice was soft, and it was shaking, and she felt shivers now in deep, secret places. "I love everything about you. Did I tell you that before? Everything."

She managed, somehow, a fragile little laugh. "You've had a concussion for sure."

"No, I mean it. Claire, I—look, my life is one long series of screwups and bad decisions, and I know that. I own that. But you . . . I just want you to be happy. And it cuts me when you're not."

"I'm happy with you," she whispered, very very quietly. "And I love you. Leaving Morganville wasn't about you; you know that. It was about me. And maybe I'm finding out that all these dreams I had . . . maybe they're not really what I want after all."

"Yeah?" She heard the smile in his voice this time. "So what do you really want? A storybook life in Vampireville, with your life on the line every day and a half?"

"I'm considering it."

"Good," Shane said. "That's good. So . . . are you saying you're pulling up stakes? Coming back?"

God, she was tempted. So tempted. "I—look, you know how I

am, don't you? I don't like quitting. I don't like running away. And I'm not sure it's a good time to leave Liz here alone."

"I thought you didn't like her."

"Well . . . I don't, but it's still pretty cruel of me to run off and leave her with a giant rent payment when she's got a stalker after her."

"Stalker?" His voice sharpened. "Tell me."

"No. Because you'll just come charging to the rescue."

"Claire—"

"No. It's fine. We can handle it." She managed to sound firm, and after a long silence, he sighed, and she took that as surrender. "Tell me about your day," she said. "Not the getting beat up part. What you did. Normal stuff. I want to know."

"I've got a job," he said. "I know, what are the odds, right? It's okay. Hard work, but I'm not afraid of that. Long hours, low pay, but nobody's coming after me with a knife or a gun or fangs so far, so it's a step way up. Also, I don't have to clean out sewer blockages. Remember that job? That was fun."

"You lasted thirty minutes."

"Which was twenty-nine minutes more than it deserved. So, what's your favorite thing about Cambridge?"

"The people," Claire said. "They're quirky. I like them. MIT's full of awesome nerdy people and I feel at home with them. It's just . . . everything else. I feel like I'm some kind of fugitive here, like I'm hiding from something. Maybe myself."

"See, I thought you were going to say your favorite thing was the beans. Don't they make baked beans in Boston? Who doesn't like those?"

"And pizza. They make good pizza."

"Now we're talking. You know how I love a good pizza."

"You should come up here."

He hesitated for a long, long moment, and said, "Do you mean that?"

"I don't know." She curled tighter into a ball; suddenly, the room felt cold, and she pulled the covers around her. "If you did, I don't know what that would mean. I couldn't let you stay in the apartment; Liz would freak out. Again."

"This is the same Liz currently banging her professor downstairs?"

"Okay, fair point. But I'd be at the lab all day, and you'd be—"

"Out of place," he finished for her. "Excess. Yeah, I get it. You don't need me hanging around and making things awkward, with my non-MIT-ness."

"No, no, I didn't mean—"

"Claire, it's all right. You wanted space, I'm giving it to you. When you're ready for me to come there, I'll be on your doorstep faster than you can imagine. But not until you're ready. I promised you that, and I'm keeping the promise."

"Okay." She took in a slow breath and let it out. "Is Michael looking after you? Making sure you don't have any kind of brain hemorrhage or something?"

"Oh, I have people watching me like hawks. I can't even get up to pee without an escort. It's super fun."

"Good. I'm glad they're taking care of you. Please take care of yourself, too. I wish—I wish I could be there."

"Wish you could, too. Want to make it up to me?"

"Yes."

"What are you wearing?"

She smiled in the darkness of her little pillow cave. "Footie pajamas and a chastity belt."

"You know that's not playing by the script, right?"

"I thought you said you loved everything about me."

"Not the chastity belt. Listen, I'd better—"

"Yeah," she said. "Yeah, I know. Get some rest. Heal. Shane—I love you."

"I love you, too," he said. "Watch your back."

He hung up first, but it didn't really matter by then; she felt he was so close to her that he might as well have been right there in the room.

She carefully took the pillow off her head and listened.

Blessed silence. Maybe Professor McCreepy had already departed, but if he hadn't, at least the gymnastics were over.

She fell asleep with the phone in her hand, held close to her heart.

Elizabeth didn't come out of her room the next morning when Claire knocked; she got a muffled, tearful "go away" through the door, and Claire shook her head. Yeah, she'd seen that coming. Professor Douche Bag had almost certainly had his way and told Liz not to call him again; he'd have plenty of other college-age girls to charm. Claire had met a few older professors like him, and they had made her feel more than a little ill. It might not be illegal, but it felt badly wrong.

And it might have been nothing but coincidence, how he'd landed on the subject of vampires, but it still creeped her out.

"Can I get you anything?" Claire asked. "Liz, are you going to be okay?"

"I'm fine," Liz said, and burst into more wet tears. So, the only injury was probably to her heart, and her ego. "I'm sorry. I should have known better, shouldn't I?"

"Everybody makes mistakes," Claire said. "You won't make that one again."

"No." Liz made a strangled gulping sound and blew her nose. "I'm never *looking* at another man again. Ugh. They're all evil. Evil!"

Claire knew some who weren't, but this wasn't the moment to disagree. It was the required Friend Solidarity moment. "All evil," she agreed. "Can't trust them. Look, are you sure you're okay? You're sure he didn't hurt you or anything?"

"He *ripped my heart out!*" Liz cried, and more blubbering ensued, and Claire assumed that meant a no, at least in the physical assault sense. "You go on. I'll be fine."

Liz said that last in a theatrical, heroic whisper. Claire rolled her eyes, because she knew that her role was to insist on staying, make her some breakfast, dry her tears, listen to the story of the Great Failed Romance over and over again, get her chocolate, and not say anything that wasn't in total agreement. She'd done it with Liz before, in high school, and she just couldn't face it. Not today. Not missing Shane the way she did.

So she took Liz at her word and said, "Okay, then, I'll see you tonight! Are you going to class?"

"No!" Liz wailed.

Claire escaped while she could.

She was halfway toward campus when her cell phone gave a chime, and she checked the message. It simply said, *don't come in 2day.* Not Professor Anderson's phone, weirdly enough; it was some unknown and blocked number. Probably, Claire realized, Jesse's . . . which maybe wouldn't be associated with Professor Anderson, and therefore not monitored. More intrigue. It made her head hurt.

Well, on the plus side, she had a free day, since Anderson had demanded she devote all her credit hours to independent study. Not a bad thing, really. But no way was she going to stay penned up in the house with Liz, either. She knew how that day would go, and she really wasn't up for rewatching *The Notebook* and getting sugar-blitzed on ice cream.

Instead, she spent a completely stress-free afternoon of wandering the campus, buying coffee, hanging out at the cafeteria, and surfing the net . . . and running into Nick.

He was sitting by himself, studying, and as she walked past him with her mocha she didn't think he'd seen her . . . until he looked up and smiled.

She stopped. It wasn't a decision, exactly, more of an instinct she couldn't control. He had a very sweet, and slightly unhinged, smile. Like Myrnin's actually. "Hey," she said. "What's up?"

"The opposite of down is the dumbest possible answer I can come up with," Nick said. "Or, you know, nothing. Which would also be true." He kicked out the chair across from him. "Need a seat?"

She hesitated, as if she was committing to something, even if it was just sharing a table. "Sure," she finally said, and settled. She didn't relax, though. Nick nodded, and kept his expression completely neutral—she supposed he was afraid he might scare her off. Which was true. If he'd done anything else, she might have just picked up her mocha and bolted. "Are you studying?"

"Trying," he said. "But funnily enough, all I can think about is pizza. You ever have days like that? Pizza days?"

"Pizza days, ice-cream days, hamburger days . . . Why don't we ever crave things that are good for us?"

"Nobody sane has broccoli days. That's crazy talk."

They chatted for a while, awkwardly but calmly, and then a third person arrived to break the tension, and her friendly banter made things seem okay. Before too long, two more people arrived, and it was a group, and the group was just . . . fun.

Before she realized it, they'd ordered pizza (for Pizza Day) and had debated the merits of nerd favorite films, and discussed what kind of roof and tunnel hacks were being planned for the semester in their various dorms, and a ton of other things that just made her feel . . . at home.

Until the phone rang.

She didn't even really pay attention to the caller ID, she just answered it, still laughing over something that the black-haired girl Jacqui had said, and then had to block her ear from Simon laughing about it to say, "Hello?"

"Claire?" It was Eve, and she sounded stressed. "Hey, uh, sorry to bother you, but I'm just giving you a quick heads-up. . . ."

"About?"

"Um, things are kind of a little bit crazy here right now. So, apparently Myrnin sort of disappeared? And he might possibly be heading toward you. Just so you know."

Claire sat up straight, then picked up her backpack and took the phone away from the still-laughing table full of people to a quieter corner. "What happened?"

"All I know is that Myrnin got pissed off and left, and Amelie's not in a real good mood. She's scary when she's angry. So, she wants Michael to go after and make sure Myrnin comes home fast, and safe. And of course be sure that he doesn't do something crazy enough to make the wrong people pay attention. And I guess I'm going with Michael? Because why not. You have any guest beds?"

"I've got floor space," Claire said. She felt a completely conflicting mixture of elation and terror . . . Myrnin, on his own, wandering in the world? And why was he heading toward *her*? But it meant she'd see Michael and Eve again, and that could only be a good thing. "When are you coming?"

"Uh, we're actually in the car right now. It's a road trip, because, y'know, vampires don't do really well with the flying, surprisingly. I guess it's the fear of people opening up the window shades and all the frying and screaming. Plus, it seems like a lot of them have a fear of heights." Claire heard Michael's indistinct voice in the background, and Eve added, "Not him, though. He says."

"Tell him I said hi."

"He's blowing you a kiss. Okay, actually, he isn't, but he ought to, so I'm saying he did. But the point is, we'll be there in a couple of days, since Michael says he doesn't plan to sleep. If Myrnin pokes his crazy head up before then, call me and try to keep him, you know, stable."

"Is he *un*stable?"

"I don't know, how can I tell? You're the crazy whisperer!"

She had a point. Claire couldn't help but smile about that. "So, Shane's coming with you?"

There was a long moment of silence on the other end. Too long. And then Eve said, "He—he's working, sweetie. I'm sorry, it's just going to be us. . . . Um, Michael, honey, is that a cop car? . . . Oh shit. Okay, gotta go, love you, bye!"

Before Claire could say anything else, Eve was gone into the wireless void.

Working? Shane was working, and he wasn't coming with them? That didn't make any sense. He'd have blown off any job to get a ride out of town with his two best friends. Especially if they were heading toward her.

It was upsetting. And worrying.

Claire put her phone away and hitched her backpack to her shoulder. She cast a wistful look back at the table. They were all talking animatedly, unaware she'd even stepped away. It had been kind of a false friendship, she thought; she'd felt like she was one of them, but really, she wasn't. They wouldn't miss her.

Nick did. He was watching her, and he raised his eyebrows and mouthed, *You okay?*

She nodded and pointed a thumb toward the exit. *Gotta go.*

He looked as if he might get up, but then Jacqui said something to him, and he answered her, still watching Claire, and settled back down in his chair.

She walked away. That was a good thing, she was thinking; it was a good thing that he didn't feel like he had to follow her. She wasn't interested.

Dammit, she missed Shane. Why wasn't he coming?

What was it they weren't telling her?

The next couple of days passed in a blur, because Claire kept trying to get Michael or Eve or Shane on the phone, and none of them answered. It was like they were ducking her. She didn't even have work to keep her occupied; Dr. Anderson called her to tell her, in a calm but firm way, that she needed some time alone to complete a special project, so she'd assigned Claire some online reading to catch up on. It was complicated stuff, and it was the only thing Claire could really be grateful for; she'd rarely been challenged before by a professor, but this was definitely next difficulty level. Dr. Anderson was *not* underestimating her.

Liz finally emerged from her room, and—of course—demanded a girls' night in with pizza and a romantic movie. Claire countered by suggesting *Kill Bill*, because that probably would make her feel better in the end. Liz agreed. She wasn't tearful anymore; she'd gone past shock to anger, and anger was a good thing, in Claire's opinion. Liz being angry meant she wasn't going to make a similar mistake anytime soon. It also, oddly, made her more likable. And more like the girl Claire remembered from school.

Claire went out for the pizza. Boston was ripe with excellent pizza choices, and there was one only a couple of blocks from the house; she reflexively looked around for Derrick, and spotted him in his usual spot across the street. He was sitting down on a bus stop bench, reading a book. Or pretending to. When he saw Claire, he waved.

She flipped him off. It seemed to amuse him, which was too bad; she'd been hoping to really make him angry enough to do something he could get arrested for.

She picked up the hot pie and was walking back with it when she spotted the creepy Professor Davis sitting at an outdoor café, enjoying a coffee with a girl young enough—again—to be his daughter. She looked captivated, too. Starry-eyed and naive, and willing to believe that Professor Davis was that missing daddy figure in her life that would solve all her problems.

Claire couldn't resist.

She changed course.

Dr. Davis and his new conquest were so into each other—or at least, she was breathlessly into him, and he was enjoying it—that it took at least a full minute for either of them to notice Claire when she paused at their table. Dr. Davis even pushed his coffee cup toward her, as if she were the waiter, before looking up in annoyance, then confusion, and then—gratifyingly—worry. He straightened up in his chair, and she smiled at him.

What would Eve do?

It was easy enough to channel her best friend's talent for snarky destruction.

"You're not returning my calls, Patrick," Claire said, in her best injured, pouting voice. "I thought you were going to come by to talk about our problems."

"Claire," he said, which was an obvious and rookie mistake; it meant he knew who she was, and she saw the chagrin settle over his face as he realized it. He turned toward the girl he was with, no doubt to protest his innocence.

Claire didn't give him the chance. "I ran into your wife at the mall and she says she is *not* going to give you a divorce, so what am I supposed to do about the babies? Just you wait. I'm going to make sure you step up and be a good father to our twins! You promised!"

She didn't wait to see the results of the bomb she'd thrown; she just held her head high and walked on with the pizza and didn't look back. She didn't have to. The scrape of the girl's wrought-iron chair legs on pavement, and Patrick's injured, wounded protests were as good as any picture. It might not matter, and probably wouldn't; she'd torpedoed one date, but he'd have another one tomorrow, or the next day.

Still. It felt good to have a little payback for Liz.

Claire was humming under her breath as she jogged up the steps, reaching for her keys . . . but she stopped dead when she saw that the door was already open. Not just open . . . left open by inches, and swinging gently in the breeze.

"Liz?" Claire stepped inside, heart pounding, and dumped the pizza box on the floor as she turned on the overhead light in the entry hall. The cheap yellow bulb flooded it with harsh light, but what it told Claire was that nobody had broken in here . . . instead, all the locks had been neatly clicked back, including the dead bolt. Liz had opened the door. "Liz!"

She burst into the kitchen, but there was nothing strange there. Liz must have washed the dishes, because they were sitting neatly in the drain board, and the counters had been cleaned.

Claire ran up the steps, but she slowed as she approached the landing to Liz's room. The bedroom door was open, and the square of darkness seemed oppressive and scary to her. She reached around the facing of the door, found the light switch, and flipped it on.

Liz's unmade bed. Clothes strewn on the chair in the corner. Makeup toppled randomly on top of the dressing table. An electric candle burning on the nightstand.

And on the floor a foot inside the door, blood, still fresh. It wasn't just a drop. It was splashes and smears, indistinct shapes printed into the stains. Blood on the wall next to the light switch, too.

Claire stepped over it carefully and checked under the bed, then the closet. There was no sign of her friend. She backed out onto the landing, took her cell phone out with shaking hands, and forced herself to look around with fresh eyes. There were smears

of blood out here, too—not as many, but now that she was looking for them, she saw where Liz had been taken out of the room.
They disappeared in a few feet, as if she'd been wrapped in something, or picked up and carried.

Claire raced upstairs and checked her own room, just to be
sure, but it seemed undisturbed. While she was doing that, she
dialed the number that had sent her the text message earlier in
the day.

"Holla," said a warm, smoky voice on the other end. There was
a rustle of cloth, and then the lazy tone went away as Jesse said,
"Claire?"

"Somebody took my roommate," Claire said. "Was it you?"

"I— What?"

"You're a vampire. *Did you take her?*"

"Hell no, I didn't take her." Jesse's voice had gone tight now,
and Claire could almost picture her standing up and pacing in
that fluid, predatory way vampires had. "What do you mean,
someone took her?"

"I mean she's gone, the door's hanging open, and I think there's
blood in her room," Claire said. She was starting to shake now, a
delayed reaction that meant it was hard to hold on to the phone.
She gripped it tighter. "I'm calling the police."

"Dammit. No, don't do that, not yet. Stay there." There was a
murmured voice off the phone, and Claire suddenly realized that
Jesse might have a visitor, a personal kind of visitor. "Tell me exactly what happened, Claire."

"I went out for a pizza. My roommate was here by herself, as
far as I know, but when I came back the door was open and there's
blood in her room. She was hurt. And she's not here."

"Is there a sign of a break-in?"

"No," Claire said. "It was unlocked, and—" In a flash, she remembered the black-clothed men entering the house the other night. Unlocking the doors. "Oh, God. Did Dr. Anderson tell you about the men who broke in the other night?"

"Yes. Claire, is there any possibility they might have mistaken your roommate for you?"

She honestly hadn't thought about it until Jesse said it, but her stomach knotted up, and she let out a trembling breath. "Maybe."

"Okay. Here's the deal: Stay right where you are. Don't touch anything, don't shut the door, don't try to solve the mystery yourself. I need to see it just as it is. I'm three minutes out. I'll alert Irene."

She hung up, and Claire hesitated a few seconds before sitting down on the steps. She shivered. The house felt cold and empty, and she hated leaving the front door open like that; she half expected to see the creepy face of Derrick, Liz's stalker, peering in.

No Derrick, though. That was strange. Wasn't he almost always hanging around waiting for Liz to come and go? And he'd been up on the steps before, Claire had seen him. *Could* this be Derrick, finally working up his courage to hurt Liz? But would she have ever let him in? Claire's instincts said no, but maybe there had been some kind of faked emergency, or Derrick had used some other way to gain entrance. . . . Claire's mind was whirling, and her finger hovered over the emergency call button on her phone while the seconds crawled by with torturous intensity. *If she's more than three minutes, I'll call the cops,* she promised herself. And what if it really had been Jesse, after all? And Jesse was just coming by to clean up the mess and make Claire herself disappear, too?

She was on the verge of pressing the 911 button when suddenly, there was a shape standing in the doorway. Not coming in—just waiting. *Oh, God,* Claire thought in alarm, and bolted to her feet . . . and then realized it was Jesse. She had on a hoodie, which she'd pulled up over her head, and a baseball cap under the hood that shaded her pale face, and she had her hands in her pockets; it was a normal look for a town like this, nothing that would get a second glance. A lot less obvious a sun-cover than the extravagant leather coats and big hats that Morganville vampires seemed to favor.

A second later, though Jesse didn't speak, Claire realized what she was waiting for, and said, "Come in."

Jesse didn't reply, just stepped into the entry hall. She glided with the eerie, silent speed that Claire was accustomed to, but never okay with, and she pushed the hood back, took off the hat, and looked around the entry hall with methodical calm. Her eyes—a muddy, dim red now—swept over Claire, but didn't pause. She made a fast walking circuit of the limited area, then crossed to the stairs and knelt down to put her face close to one of the stairs. Then she came up a few stairs and did it again. Jesse worked her way quickly up to the second-floor landing, examined the blood there, and then went into Liz's room.

It was all accomplished in eerie silence. Jesse didn't speak to Claire, or acknowledge her in any way, until she finally stepped out of her friend's room and looked up the stairs at her. The expression on the vampire woman's face was blank—blank enough that Claire wasn't sure if she ought to wait, or run.

Then Jesse said the thing that Claire least expected to hear. "It isn't your roommate's blood."

"What? But—it has to be!" Unless Liz had fought back, maybe

cut one of the intruders . . . she supposed that could happen, but the idea of Liz actually scoring a hit was pretty far out there. "Can you tell whose it is?"

"Not easily. If I'd already tasted that blood, I'd know it, but from what's smeared around in here, I'd have to say that it's a male in his late twenties who drinks too much Red Bull." Jesse shrugged when Claire stared silently at her. "It has a certain smell to it. So does coffee and strong liquor. But I can definitely tell you that it wasn't a girl your age who was hurt here. You said the door was open. Maybe she fought with someone, hurt him, and ran for it. That would explain the open door, if he took off in pursuit."

"Can you—can you track them?"

"Not them. Just him. And only if he keeps bleeding. What the hell? We can give it a try, I guess." Jesse pushed her cap back on and flipped up the black hood. "Come on. We've got as good a chance of solving this as the police right now, and I don't really want the cops involved in anything if it traces back to me, or to Irene."

"But—what if Liz—"

"Trust me," Jesse said.

Claire hated it when vampires said that, and she was just about to say so, when someone else darkened the doorway at the bottom of the stairs. Tall, broadly built, and she instantly thought *Derrick*, and felt a surge of fury.

It wasn't Derrick.

Shane was standing there on the doorstep, staring up at her. His face was set and pale, and his whole body said that he was braced for a painful impact, but he just nodded to her and said, "So, I've got no doubt that we're going to talk about this later, and that will be hard, but for right now, you're going to need my help."

Jesse frowned at him. "Shane?"

Claire somehow descended a whole flight of stairs without even realizing she'd done it. All of a sudden she was on the landing outside of Liz's door, and her hand was hurting from the strength with which she was clutching the railing. Her knees were trembling, but the rest of her felt . . . numb. "Wait," she said. *"You know him?"*

"Yeah, of course I do. He's the dishwasher at Florey's."

Claire's mouth opened and closed, but she couldn't sort out the whirl of words flying around in her mind. *I wasn't wrong. I did see him there.*

That meant that Shane had been here for days. Maybe longer.

Long enough that he'd lied to her about it, and so had Michael. So had Eve.

"Oh, we're going to talk," she said then, and the chill in her voice surprised her. "But for right now, you'd better tell me what you think you know about this."

"Outside," Shane said. "We need to get moving. Now."

"Why?" Jesse asked.

"Because the people who took Claire's friend might come back."

NINE

SHANE

)

Of all the ways I wanted to come face-to-face with Claire again...this wasn't the one I would have preferred. I knew that there was a slim chance we might accidentally meet, but this wasn't any accident; I was showing up on purpose on her doorstep, and there was no way to pretend that I hadn't been here, hadn't been interfering in her life, hadn't been keeping eyes on her.

Because I was about to confess all that.

Jesse's anti-sun disguise was pretty good; once her oversized sunglasses were on and her hands were in her pockets, most of her pale skin was protected from accidental sun exposure. It helped that today was cloudy and a little rainy. Claire locked the house's front door and followed Jesse into the street, where I was waiting for them under a tree (that was polite of me, I thought; look at me, being all vampire-sensitive). I nodded to both of them and led the way at a brisk walk a couple of blocks, then turned the corner. There was a café there with an awning. I sat down at one of the fragile-looking tables, and Claire and Jesse took seats on the other side of me. Jesse didn't look pleased.

Claire—actually, I was too scared to look at her directly to tell *what* she might be feeling. She hadn't jumped into my arms and declared her eternal love, so I was going to assume that I was in trouble. Big trouble.

Didn't matter right now, given the situation.

Jesse's gaze flicked from me to Claire, then back again, and I saw her making the connections. "Shane, just to be sure I've got all this right: you followed her from Morganville, but didn't tell her about it. And you, Claire, you didn't know he was here."

"That's right," Claire said. I didn't say anything, but then again, I didn't have to; just being here was silent agreement. "I didn't know he was coming."

"That's on me. I didn't want you to know."

I could tell that she checked herself right then, and because I knew her, I also knew that she was thinking that our personal relationship issues weren't the worst thing happening today. "Then tell me what happened today."

"Okay, here's the truth," I said. "I pass by the house every once in a while—it's kind of on the way to work, okay? And last time I was by here, I saw this big guy trying to jimmy your front door. I warned him off and asked the cops to step up patrols."

"The attempted break-in card," Claire said. "Was it Derrick who was trying to break in?"

I nodded. "He said he lived there. Obviously, a liar."

"He's her stalker."

"Well, that fits. He had the vibe."

"So it was Derrick who went in to get her."

"No," I said, and leaned forward to lower my voice. "It was four guys in a very slick military maneuver—one in a delivery van with a sliding door that blocked the view of the front, and three who went inside. They had master keys, because they opened it up fast and went in quietly. Then, about a minute later, they came out with a girl with a black hood over her face—like some kind of CIA rendition from the movies. She wasn't protesting too much; I think she was too scared. I was going to move, because I honestly thought it might be you, Claire, until I saw her getting into the van; she didn't move like you, and she was as tall as Eve, so I thought it must be your friend. One of the men went back inside, and then all of a sudden, Derrick showed up. I don't think he knew what was going on—he was across the street in his usual spot, holding up the lamppost. All he knew was that the door was open, so he bolted inside; he didn't even know they'd taken the girl out."

"Liz," Claire said softly. "Her name is Liz."

"I know. Sorry. I would have done something, except I'm not in the best shape right now."

She paused, biting her lip, studying my face. "God, Shane. You weren't kidding, were you? You really got beat up."

I had, and I felt it. The aches and pains were bad enough, but half my face was throbbing, and I knew the bruising was going to darken into a spectacular tie-dye pattern. Plus, my damn arm hurt as if I'd cracked a bone, though I knew I hadn't, or at least the X-rays hadn't showed it. The skin itched something crazy, as if I'd fallen into a bunch of poison ivy. Not too likely, even if we were Ivy League–adjacent.

I really didn't want to look at Claire directly, because despite the apparent concern in her words, her voice had a fragile, hard tone I didn't like. I don't know what would have been worse, seeing pity from her, or seeing . . . something else. Instead, I stared at a discolored spot on the table and scraped at it with my thumbnail as I continued my story. "Derrick and the other guy came stumbling out less than a minute later, and Derrick looked hurt. They tossed him in the van, too, and took off."

"Do you know where they took them?"

"Not a clue," I said, "but I got a picture of the van and the plate, plus at least one of the guys." I dug out my phone and passed it to Jesse, who navigated the menus with an impressive amount of ease, considering she was an ancient bloodsucker; I'd already worked out that she had to be pretty old, because she wasn't particularly worried about the sun. Even with the hoodie and hat, most vampires would have been scared, but Jesse seemed cool and calm and not the least bit flammable. "Maybe you've got some contacts who can use that?"

"Likely," Jesse said. "All right, Claire, you obviously can't go back home. Whether this was some separate event related to your friend—and I'm going to have her background and family checked—or whether this had to do with you and your work with Dr. Anderson, it's not safe for you there, and it's our fault you stayed as long as you did in a difficult situation. When you reported the first event to Irene, I should have insisted you get out of that house immediately, but she was convinced that they were only looking for the device, and since it had been moved . . ."

"Wait," I said. "What *event* are we talking about?" Because it seemed to me that I'd missed something important. Something Claire should have told me.

It was probably wrong for me to be upset about that, considering how much I'd kept from her, though. Didn't stop me.

When she didn't immediately start talking, though, Jesse spilled it for her. "Two spy types let themselves into the house the other night," she said. "While Claire was there. She hid, and they searched the place. Nobody got hurt."

I felt my jaw go tight, and I tried really hard not to clench my teeth too much. "Until now, you mean. Unless you don't count humans getting abducted as *hurt*."

"Down, boy. I'm not your enemy. Claire called me to help." Jesse flashed a brief, biting smile at me. "After she asked me if I had gone munchies on her friend, of course. But that's a sensible and sane question, for someone who's lived where you've lived. I would have asked it, too, in your shoes. Relax." She moved her fingers on his phone's keypad, lightning fast, and then handed it back. "I've forwarded the pictures on to a friend who can do the footwork. Quick thinking, getting the shot. And not rushing in. You'd have ended up taken just like Derrick, I think. No offense, but it's likely these are men trained in quick, quiet abduction. It's not like fighting vampires."

"Nothing here is like fighting vampires," I said. "It's more like fighting smoke. I think I liked it when I had an actual enemy to face."

"Oh, don't worry, you have some. We just haven't seen them yet," Jesse said. "But we will. And when we do . . ." She showed fang, just a flash; anybody who happened to catch a glimpse would have doubted their sanity, especially since the teeth disappeared in a flash. "When we do, we'll settle this Morganville style."

"What'll we do about Liz, and Derrick?" Claire asked. "They don't have anything to do with this, if it's about me and Professor Anderson and vampires. They're just caught in the middle."

"You know what generally happens to people in the middle, Claire?" Jesse asked, as she got to her feet. "Cross fire." She speared me with a long look, and I threw it right back at her. "Shane, get her someplace safe. I'm holding *you* responsible. I have your phone number now, and I'll be in touch when I have something. Until then, lay low."

"What about the police?" Claire asked. "Shouldn't I call them?"

"Call them if you like," Jesse said, "but when you do, they're going to ask you to explain why you dumped a fresh pizza on the floor inside the house, found blood in your housemate's room, and didn't call 911 immediately. They'll match the store receipt to your route and the time you were seen entering the house. And the first person they'll detain is *you*. You had the keys. There was no forced entry. And in the police's experience, generally the person who lives in the house is the first person to suspect."

It was all pretty damn logical. Brutally logical. Claire swallowed hard and nodded. "No police then."

"Smart girl."

I watched Jesse as she walked away, hood up, hands in her pockets. She didn't even hurry. Yeah, that was some scary confidence, considering she was essentially vulnerable out here, alone. "Sorry," I said. Not to Jesse, but to Claire. I was still trying not to look her in the eye. "I'd rather talk about all this someplace safer. Can we go?"

"I'd rather talk about it here," she said, "because at least if I'm here, I can order coffee, and I probably won't scream in frustration out loud. Think of it as a public buffer zone."

Oh, great. I winced, but I asked the question. "So, do you feel like screaming? Specifically, at me?"

"A little bit," she said. "But God, this doesn't matter right now, does it? What about Liz? What's going to happen to her? I mean, even Derrick doesn't deserve . . . Jesse didn't mean it about cross fire, did she?"

"I don't know," I said. "Claire, this is *not* a good place to stay. Jesse said to keep you safe, and in my opinion an open table on the sidewalk isn't exactly the textbook definition of secure. . . ."

"Do you have an apartment?"

"I've got a room at Florey's. It's not spacious. Or clean. But it's cheap, and the work's solid. It'll do until things settle down, if you're, ah, not too picky."

"Well, it couldn't be much worse than where I was living," Claire sighed. "All my stuff is back there, though. All my clothes, anyway. I've got my computer and books, and that's what's important. Hey . . . did you know Jesse was . . ." Claire gave the universal Morganville sign for teeth in the neck, and I smiled, just a little. Carefully. Not just because it hurt like a son of a bitch.

"Hey, it's me," I said. "I can spot 'em a mile away." I only wished that was true; it would have avoided so many problems over the years. My dad was the one with the nose for the Nosferatu . . . not me. "Pete's human, by the way. In case you were wondering. He cut himself on a bottle the other day, and I helped him dress the wound. Didn't heal immediately."

Claire nodded, because it was a good piece of proof, at that, because vampires couldn't control the speed at which they healed, not without putting something on the wound that held it open or continued to burn, like silver. "Is Jesse the only one you've spotted?"

"Yeah, so far. Though it's pretty rare to find one on her own out here, isn't it? Vampires like safety in numbers, because they're so rare, especially these days. If she feels confident enough to be out here on her own, I'm pretty sure she's somebody we don't want to cross." I shifted, because my arm was hurting again, bone-deep throbs as if I'd just slammed it hard into a brick wall. *And* it itched like mad. I clenched and released my fist, and then shook it out, hoping that it'd get better. It didn't.

"What's wrong?" Claire asked. She still sounded distant, and a little unwilling to ask, but she *was* asking. Which was encouraging.

"Well, when you get a major-league ass-kicking from a bunch of guys, even if they generally suck at it, you do feel it later," I said. "No big thing. I'll live." Yes, I was trying to be a tough guy. I didn't feel like it, right at that moment; I wanted to curl up against her, feel those wonderful soft hands touching my face and tracing lightly over the hurts. She always, always made it better. There was something so healing in being with her; it felt like standing in the sunlight when I'd spent my whole life in the dark.

But the best I could feel from her right now was . . . shade.

We sat in silence for a long, painful moment, and then a waiter came up and asked us if we wanted anything, in that annoyed voice that waiters develop in college towns when they figure you're only marginally good for the check in the first place, and tips are out of the question. I tried to order a plain coffee, Claire tried to order a mocha, we talked over each other, and we both looked up at the same moment, and . . .

. . . And we stopped, just staring at each other. Because all of a sudden it was real. The moment was real, and there was no avoiding it anymore. The waiter's annoyed sighs finally sparked me to say, flatly, "Beat it," and he did, muttering under his breath the whole time. I didn't care. I didn't care if Jesse descended on us, fangs out, and the entire zombie horde from *Dead Rising* suddenly started shambling through the restaurant. They could wait.

Claire said, "I really thought you were back in Morganville. You got Michael and Eve to lie to me."

"I just asked them not to volunteer where I was, that's all. I know it was the wrong thing to do, but sometimes—sometimes it doesn't matter. Right, wrong, it's just the thing you have to do. And I had to see you. I had to know you were okay. I'll apologize for basically hovering, but I can't be sorry for being worried about you. I didn't crash your door and demand to see you. I just . . . stayed close."

"Watching me from a distance," she said. "You didn't trust me enough to let go."

I felt a surge of panic, followed by a confused bolt of realization. Was she right? Was it a trust thing, and not a worry thing? How did it look from her side . . . like I'd been following her, spying on her, judging her? Yeah, it probably did look that way, horribly enough. It wasn't what I'd been doing, or at least I didn't think it was.

I leaned forward, elbows on the table, and I held her gaze as I said, "Claire, I don't want to let you go. But that has nothing to do with not trusting you. I trust you with my life. Always have."

I didn't keep talking, because that pretty much said everything I meant to say. She blinked slowly, thinking about it, and then sighed, shook her head, and said, "You're an idiot, but I know you mean that. And you're not angry. I know that, too. You just . . ."

"Wanted you," I said. "Needed you. That's why I'm here. Maybe it's a bad thing, I don't know; if you look me in the eyes and tell me to go back to Morganville, I'll go. I won't like it, but—"

She suddenly sat straight up, eyes growing wide, as if someone had jabbed a pin in her, and she lunged forward and caught hold of my hands. I was surprised, but not too surprised to wrap mine around hers. Touching her stilled some voice inside me I hadn't even known was screaming.

"Michael and Eve," she said. "Did they call you?"

"Not for a couple of days . . . Wait." I checked the phone's call log, and there it was, a missed call from Eve. No voice mail. "What's happening?"

"Even if you went back there, you'd end up here again," she said. "Michael and Eve are on their way. Amelie sent them after Myrnin."

"*Myrnin* is coming here? By himself?" I admit it, that gave me a surge of tired frustration so strong I wanted to stake him myself. "What the hell is he doing?"

"I've got no idea, and neither did Eve, but they're following. They're supposed to get him to come home."

"I am *not* driving back home in a car with Bipolar Man," I said, and I meant it. "Seriously. I've got weapons."

She hadn't let go of my hands, after the rush subsided, and I thought that was a good sign. I tried to think what I was going to do if she tried to pull away and sit back. Let her go, I guessed, even though my instinct was to try to hold on.

But she didn't pull back this time.

"You screwed up," she told me. "I can't believe you stalked me like this."

"If I'd been stalking you, I'd have been bumming cigarettes from Derrick across the street," I pointed out. "I was working independently in the same town, not calling and not talking to you. If you want to call that stalking, I have to ask for an on-the-field review of the play by the ref."

"Too bad for you that relationships don't have referees."

"You're right, that does suck. I could use a slow-motion replay right now."

"You're an idiot," Claire said, and I went cold inside, and very still. Here it was, the moment I'd been trying so hard to avoid thinking about, when Claire wised up, realized that I wasn't the smart guy with prospects she needed to be with . . . but then she smiled, just a little, and the ice freezing my lungs and heart started to thaw. "You're an idiot, but I know why you came. You're conditioned to think that everything is a threat, and you were afraid that I was going to be in trouble here on my own. You were trying to save me. But Shane, *I don't always need saving.* Understand?"

"Oh yeah," I said. "You've saved me plenty of times. I got the point. But nobody from Morganville ought to be out there alone. It isn't safe, and you know it."

"Nothing's safe," Claire told me then, with the conviction of someone a lot older. "Nobody's ever safe. But that doesn't mean you don't respect what I want, Shane."

"I'm sorry I let you down," I said. "But I couldn't stay there while you were here. Not without making sure you'd be okay. Like you said, Morganville conditioning. If you want me to go, I'll go. Just tell me. Right now."

I'd startled her, and worried her, and forced her to stop analyzing, and she blinked slowly and said, "I don't want you to go. I missed you, Shane. I missed you so much."

Her voice broke on the last word, and I saw the shimmer of tears in her eyes. Tension unwound from a coil inside me, and I wanted to put my arms around her and hold her . . . but then the waiter appeared near our table again and pointedly cleared his throat, and I resisted the urge to throw a sharp, illegal elbow into his midsection.

"We're going," I told him, and stood up without letting go of

Claire's hand. I pulled her to her feet. "Come on. I'll make you coffee at Florey's."

We made it only half a block before I couldn't stand it anymore. I stopped, pressed her against the brick side of a building, and leaned in. I managed to stop myself just short of kissing her, and said, "Is this okay?"

"Shut up," Claire said, and grabbed me by the collar to pull me in.

It was like falling into summer . . . warm and sweet and hot. I'd needed to touch her, and I had; I'd needed to kiss her, and the damp, soft feel of her warm mouth did all kinds of things to me. Sweet relief, and desperate tension, all at the same time. It went on for a while, lips and tongues meeting and merging, and I was the one who stepped away first, because *damn*, I'd forgotten the power of that between us. How she made me feel. How I made *her* feel. My sweet little Claire's lips had gone red and flushed, and her cheeks were pink, and her eyes very bright. She looked drunk with pleasure and delight, and I imagined how she would look in the morning light, the way I loved to see her best.

I squeezed her hand and said, "I need to get you home. Right now."

She nodded and slipped her arm through mine, and we walked quickly the short distance to Florey's.

When we turned the corner, though, there was a police car sitting in front, light bar flashing, and the manager Mick was in the door talking to two cops and looking very serious. I pulled Claire to a halt, and saw Mick spot me.

He gave me a slow tilt of the head to the side. *Get out of here.* I picked up the signal and backed Claire up. "Change of plans," I said. "Florey's is out. Do you have someplace else we can go?"

"Not really—what's going on?"

"Not a clue, but whatever it is, remember that I'm from Morganville."

She didn't get it for a second, and then she looked sharply at me. "Oh God, Shane, did you bring *weapons*?"

"Only my favorites," I said. "But they're kinda illegal."

She shook her head and tugged at my hand. "Come on."

TEN

Claire wasn't sure that the police were *actually* after Shane, but if they were, staying in plain view was a bad idea. She bought (over his protests) an MIT hoodie for Shane from one of the souvenir shops, and he put it on with an annoyed sigh. She pulled the hood up for him. "Just trust me," she said. "You really need to lay low. These police aren't going to be the kind that you can call off with a plea to the Founder; they're serious stuff. And don't forget, my own place is a crime scene. If they've connected me to you and found your weapons, it looks even worse."

"Okay," he said, "I can see your point. So where are we going to go? Got any friends who don't mind hiding wanted fugitives? Because it usually takes a little longer than a few days to make those."

Shane had a point, and she didn't really have an answer, but it didn't really matter. Shane had already pulled out his phone and checked something. He scrolled and hit keys, and put the phone to his ear.

"Who are you calling?" she asked.

"Pete," he said. "Look, the guy hangs out with a vampire chick and is some kind of midnight vigilante. He probably isn't too judgmental when it comes to hiding other people's secrets."

"You think he knows about Jesse?"

"Yeah, I'm sure he does. Hold on . . ." Shane turned partially away from her, focusing on the new voice in his ear. "Hey, man, it's Shane—yeah, I know about the cops. Speaking of that, I need someplace to get out of sight. You got any suggestions?" He listened for a few seconds, then made a scribbling gesture to Claire, and she dug out a pen and paper and handed it over. Shane wrote something down and handed it back to her. It was an address. "Got it. I owe you, Pete. Big-time."

He hung up and dropped the phone in his hoodie's pocket. Claire held up the address. "Where's he sending us?"

"His place," Shane said. "It's not far." He offered her his elbow, and she threaded her arm through the crook, and they set off toward the south, down the tree-lined street. Funny how it felt so *familiar,* too . . . just another street in another town, but the two of them were together, and that made it home. Even knowing what she did—Liz missing, the police after Shane—she felt oddly peaceful now. Whatever was coming, they'd be facing it together.

Shane winced and let go of her to rub at his arm beneath the hoodie's sleeve. "It's nothing," he said before she could ask. "Itches like crazy, and it burns. I've never been allergic to anything, but maybe that's what it is. Maybe I'm just allergic to hot, smart college girls."

"Ha, ha," she said, and reclaimed his other arm. "Maybe you're allergic to being in trouble all the time."

"Nah, I'm completely inoculated against that one. It's in the genes." Shane checked his piece of paper, then his phone's map, and nodded up the street. "One block up, then right. His place will be on the left."

There was no sign of police presence, at least, as they made the final turn and spotted the address on the note. It was a squatty brick building dwarfed by the taller, more elegant row houses on either side, and to Claire's eyes it looked more like a storage shed than a home. The front door was a faded green, plain wood, no design. She didn't see any windows on this side of it.

"Is he here?" she asked.

"No, but he told me how to get in." Shane walked up, counted bricks, and pulled one out. Behind it, he found the key, and used it to open the door. "After you."

"No, seriously, you go first. I hardly know this guy. What if he's working with the people who took Liz?"

"Pete?" Shane shook his head, evidently finding the whole thought funny, though Claire felt it had been a pretty reasonable caution. "Never happen. But okay. I'll protect you."

She hit him in the shoulder. "I don't *need* you to protect me."

"Then why am I going first?"

"So you can take the first punch while I throw the second?"

"So I'm bait? Ouch. You've been in Morganville *way* too long, girl." But he was grinning when he said it, and he went in first, alert and ready for anything. She came in behind him and shut the door—always cut off the ability of an enemy to sneak up behind you, if you can—and locked it. "Pete? Anybody here?" He shook his head at the continued silence. "He said he doesn't have any roommates. I think we're good."

They came down a short, narrow hall into one largish room that served as the entire house. It had been fixed up with some kind of portable dividers on wheels into a sleeping area with a neatly made bed (Pete, Claire thought, was a much better house-keeper than Shane ever had been), a clean little kitchenette with a two-person table, and a small living area with a couch and TV. Not much else, except books. Pete had stunning amounts of them, lining every inch of the walls in custom-built cases. Shane whis-tled when he looked around, and shook his head. "Okay, I thought I knew Pete, but I would have pegged him for a magazine guy, at best," he said. "And only *Sports Illustrated*, at that. Think he's read all these?"

"I would have," Claire said. She wasn't very often jealous, but somehow, this little, neat, clean place seemed perfect to her. The only thing that had its own separate walls was the bathroom, tucked into a corner—it held a toilet, sink, counter, tiled floor, and corner shower. She peeked in, feeling like an intruder and, at the same time, a tourist in somebody else's life. She liked it. Pete looked like an orderly, calm, interesting kind of guy.

"I'm going to have to give him shit for all this," Shane said, as he wandered around. "He lives alone and makes his bed? Who does that?"

"People who like things neat?"

"It's not natural." Shane turned as she walked toward him. The light from the windows on the sides of the house caught his face, and she winced a little at the sight of the bruises—they were get-ting spectacular now, but probably didn't hurt nearly as much as before. He looked a little tired, she thought, and although he was trying not to show it, a little worried, too. He knew how alone they were here, away from home. And how vulnerable. Plus, he'd be missing his weapons, most likely.

"So," he said. "Here we are."

"Yes. Here we are." She didn't give him anything more than that, and he continued to watch her warily, as if he was no longer sure what she was thinking. She took a step closer, and then another one, until she had to look up into his face. His brown eyes were half closed, and she knew that look . . . sharp with longing. "Claire—we're both in the same place, but . . . are we together?"

It was a brave question. A lot of people wouldn't have asked it, Claire thought; it would have been easier to just assume things, pretend, gloss it over. But that wasn't Shane. And he didn't flinch when she said, "I want to be. Do you?"

"I can safely say that there is nothing I want more in my life," he said. "Problem is, you have to want it, too. Both magnets have to attract."

"Opposite poles," she agreed, and took that last step forward, until she was pressed against him. His arms slowly went around her . . . not like they had on the street, full of confidence and strength, but testing her. Seeing what she was going to do. "We could talk all day about magnetism and poles and the Pauli exclusion principle and spin glass effect, or I could just do something about it."

She rose up on tiptoes and kissed him. The second their lips met, she felt his tense muscles go slack, and she could almost feel the relief that washed through him. And the laugh that vibrated against her lips from his. "I love it when you talk dirty physics," he said, and then the tension was back in his muscles, but it was the good kind, and he picked her up and collapsed backward to Pete's neatly made bed, which bounced and creaked in protest. Claire let out a surprised burst of laughter, too, and straddled him to lean over and kiss him again, deeply, sweetly, with a core of heat that never failed to scorch but didn't burn. It wasn't that she'd forgotten how amazing this was, but that her body had deliberately hidden the memory from her to protect her from the longing, and now all those nerve endings were awake, remembering, and craving it again. His big hands held her shoulders, then slid up to caress her face in warmth, and as she unzipped his hoodie and pulled his T-shirt up, he shivered and arched against her. He let out a sigh as her own hands moved over his abdomen and up to his chest. His skin felt amazing—soft and warm as satin against her palms.

He hooked a finger on the collar of her shirt, just about where the buttons started, and as she sat up, he said, "Mind if I help you with this? Because I think I need to see what you're wearing under there."

She smiled and moved his hand away, and unbuttoned the first button. "There," she said. "How's that?"

"I think I need at least—how many buttons do you have? Six more."

She nipped gently at his full lower lip. "Only if you take off the shirt."

He sat up as if he'd been jolted with a cattle prod, and the hoodie and T-shirt came off so fast she was afraid he'd pull a muscle. Oh God, he was lovely; even with the bruises, which made her ache inside, he was so incredibly *gorgeous*. It made her breath catch in her throat. So did the luminous light in his eyes as he settled back down on the pillows.

"Your turn," he said, and put his hands behind his head. "Six buttons."

"Five?"

"Only if you don't want to keep that last one on the shirt."

She smiled, and started unbuttoning. One at a time, slowly, watching the fire intensify in his eyes, feeling his body tensing under hers even as he tried to look utterly relaxed.

The cool air kissed her shoulders as she slipped off the blouse. "Pretty," he said. His voice sounded different now, low and rough as a cat's tongue. "I guess I have to see if that bra has a matching set of panties."

It did.

Neither of them stayed on very long, though.

Lying there, drowsy and warm in Shane's arms, Claire couldn't imagine how she'd walked away from him. From this. She'd had lots of frank discussions with the more worldly Eve about sex, about what could be good and bad about it. The worse, Eve had always said, was when the guy was all about getting his own thrills and treated the girl like a posable doll. Sure sign of a going-nowhere relationship.

Shane wasn't like that, not at all. It was a collaboration, and a partnership, and he left her feeling joyous and sated and utterly, utterly calm. They had plenty to worry about, but not here. Not between them. She made a sleepy, happy sound and pressed herself closer to him; his arms were around her waist, and he made a solid, hot blanket that pressed against her back. Sometime during the afternoon they'd managed to pull the covers up over them, which was good, because their clothes were somewhere scattered on the floor in entirely random order.

Shane kissed the back of her neck, drawing a delighted shiver. "I missed you," he whispered.

She giggled a little. "I could tell. That first time was a little bit fast."

He groaned. "You're killing me."

"Only a little. The second was much better."

He licked her ear, which made her let out a little shriek of protest, and she twisted around to face him. He propped up on one elbow, looking down at her. His hair was a mess, and she pushed it out of his eyes. "I love you."

"I know." He took her hand in his, and kissed the palm; his lips felt warm and damp and soft on her skin. "And I let you down. I know that. I'm not saying I won't make mistakes; I will. But I promise that I won't make that particular one again."

"Fair enough," she said. "I make plenty of mistakes, too, you know."

"You mean, besides getting involved with me?"

She shook her head and kissed him. It was a drowsy, lazy kiss this time, full of honey and joy. "I wish it could be like this. Just . . . this. All the time."

"Life doesn't work that way. You know that."

"What if it did?"

"We'd be living in a cardboard box and starving to death?"

"Wow, you really know how to take the sexy away, don't you?"

"It's a gift." Shane's fingers stroked down her back, then up, in a mesmerizingly random pattern. "We should probably get up and make some dinner. Plus, I guess we should wash the sheets before Pete comes back. Seems like good manners."

"I'm amazed you even thought of it."

"I'm on my best behavior."

"Mmm, I could easily argue with that. Oh . . ." She caught her breath, suddenly, because he tried to prove her right. He kissed her

shoulder, then her neck, then her mouth, and then the lazy peace
turned intense again, for a while. This time, though, they were
truly exhausted, and it took at least another half an hour of sleepily murmuring to each other before Claire finally managed to convince him to get up, dress, and help her strip the sheets and
pillowcases from the bed. Pete had one of those tiny little washer/
dryer combo units tucked in the corner, and she put everything in
with detergent, then showered and left her hair wet as Shane
squeezed in after she stepped out. There wasn't room for two,
which was probably good, considering how sore her muscles already felt. A good kind of sore, but still.

They were both dressed, if just barely, when the door rattled,
the lock turned, and Pete stepped inside. He flipped the dead
bolt behind him, and stopped dead at the end of the hall. Claire
and Shane were sitting innocently on the couch; she was reading
one of Pete's books, a science fiction classic by Isaac Asimov
she'd been meaning to find, and Shane was flipping channels on
the TV.

Pete said, "Why are the sheets off my bed?"

"Just trying to help you out, do a little housework," Shane said
blandly. "Hey, man. Thanks for letting us stay for a while."

"If by *a while* you mean *until dawn*, then yeah, cheers," Pete said.
"You've got serious heat on you, man. I'm not just talking about
the cops. Scary suit-wearing types, you know the ones, Claire.
You've seen them before. They were looking for you, and they
came looking for Shane, too. Whatever you're in, you're in deep.
About my bed, did you two—?"

"Look at it this way, we did laundry," Shane said. "If it was the
couch . . ."

"This is why I hate houseguests," Pete said. "So. Pizza okay?"

They both nodded. Claire said, "I'm sorry about the bed, Pete. Thanks."

"I'm just messing with you. Hell, that's the most fun that bed's had in ages. If you're about to ask if I've heard from Jesse, no, I haven't. She never showed for her shift, which bugged the crap out of Mick, believe me; he was already stressed enough about you and your big bag of fun illegal weapons you were keeping on his property, Shane. Why the hell didn't you tell me about that?"

"What would you have done?"

"Told Mick."

"That's why I didn't tell you. Look, man, it's not that I'm some nutcase with a gun collection; everything I have in there goes toward keeping me and Claire safe from what you already know is out there."

Pete wasn't stupid, and his eyes narrowed and turned flinty-dark as he reached for the telephone. "Jesse's not the problem here."

"Jesse's a vampire. Whether or not she's trouble, she's proof that there could be others out here who aren't so well behaved. You hang out with her . . . You know how dangerous she can be, right?"

"She's one of the least dangerous people I know, because she does exactly what she means to do, every time. She's never lost control of herself, not even once. Can't say that for a lot of humans." He held up a finger to pause the conversation, and ordered a pizza delivery. He didn't ask what they wanted, which Claire thought was probably fair enough; they'd abused his hospitality a bit, though he probably hadn't expected anything else. Once he'd hung up, he went right back to the subject at hand. "I swear to God, if your troubles drag her out into any kind of real trouble, the ass-kicking you got last night will be a love tap, and I will use your skull for a hockey puck."

Shane considered that for a second in silence. Claire could tell he took Pete seriously, despite the differences in their height. Whatever fighting skills Pete had, clearly Shane had seen them and respected them. "Understood," he said. "But I don't think any of it's Claire's fault. It seems like Jesse's in deep with this Dr. Anderson, and the government piece is coming from there. Cops, I've got no idea. I didn't break any laws."

"She did," Pete said, and nodded toward Claire. "They're saying you might have killed your roommate. And that Shane helped you. And by the way, your weapons stash doesn't make you look any less guilty of that."

"I didn't kill *anybody*," Claire said. "Liz was abducted. Shane saw them. And Jesse's trying to trace the van. Look, Shane's got pictures."

Shane pulled them up on the phone and held them out, and Pete looked them over. He seemed accepting of that, at least; he handed it back without comment except a nod. Then he went into the kitchenette and got out paper plates. "Beer?" he asked them. "I'm not going to card you. That's the day job."

"I'll have one," Shane said, just as Claire said no; it wasn't that she was some kind of antialcohol crusader, she just didn't like beer, overall. Pete brought her a Coke instead, and then he settled in the small armchair off to the side of the couch. They all watched the TV flicker on in silence, a cold substitute for a fire, and finally Shane said, "So, I guess you two already know each other, but Pete, this is Claire, my—"

"Fiancée," Claire said. She wasn't sure why she felt compelled to say it now, of all times and places, but she was. Shane turned his head and stared at her, and the surprise (and pleasure) in his face made her smile. "Hey, you asked me, remember? And I said yes? Months ago. I just thought it might be time to get on with saying it."

"Fiancée," Shane repeated. "As in, I'm going to marry her."

"Yeah?" Pete asked. "Congrats. When?"

"We haven't talked about that yet," Claire said. "Soon?"

"Soon," Shane agreed. Their fingers twined together, and he moved closer to her on the couch. "Of course, it could be a jailhouse romance if we're not careful. And that would suck. We already did that a whole bunch, early on. Me in a cell, you outside . . ."

"Well, for variety, maybe it'd be me in the cell this time, and *you* out there figuring out how to get me free. Although I'm just afraid that you might do something crazy to make that happen."

"It might involve illegal activity, yeah," Shane said. "I wouldn't even mind ending up in jail with you, but they'd probably separate us. And that wouldn't be what I had in mind. I guess our only option is to stay out of the cage, then."

"I think it's a goal," she agreed. "Did you hear anything at all from Jesse, Pete?"

"I got a text, she said she was following a lead. That was it. I'm hoping she'll end up here soon . . . she usually just drops in without notice. Vampires aren't real respecters of personal privacy, seems like."

The washer dinged to let them know the cycle was done, and Claire quickly rose and took care of loading the wet sheets into the dryer. It seemed like the least she could do. Pete and Shane didn't chat. It wasn't like Shane and Michael, who had an easy, almost unconscious connection that neither of them really had to think about much; Shane had to read Pete, try to figure out what he really meant and felt. Maybe that connection would develop, over time, but for now, Pete just seemed a little guarded, a little wary.

Maybe that was just his default setting.

There was a knock on the front door, and Pete headed for it. Shane got up, too, frowning. "That was too quick for pizza," he said. Pete nodded without pausing; he had a baseball bat hidden in the shadows near the doorway, and he grabbed the length of wood on his way. Then he checked the peephole.

"Is it the police?" Claire asked. She felt a little short of breath, suddenly, because if it was, there didn't seem to be an easy way out of this place. Defensible, but limited retreat. And they couldn't fight their way out, not against regular human police. It would be wrong on every level, even if they weren't guilty.

"No," Pete said. There was an odd tension in his voice, and he stepped back from the door, opened it, and said, "Get in, quick."

It happened fast—one second he was standing alone on the doorstep, and the next . . . the next, there were three people crowding the hallway with him. Two supporting a limp, maybe unconscious third.

As Pete slammed and locked the door, Claire bolted forward. So did Shane.

And Eve let out a strangled little sound that was half glad cry, half sob.

She and Jesse were supporting the deadweight of a very pale, very still Michael Glass.

With a wooden stake in his heart.

"Christ, is that guy dead?" Pete blurted out, when he saw the stake. Shane ignored him, grabbed Michael's weight by the shoulders, and helped Jesse carry him over to the couch. Eve followed, and Claire hugged her hard when she paused to try to catch her breath. She was shaking all over.

"He's okay," Claire said, and rubbed her back. "Eve, it's okay. It'll be okay. . . ."

"Pull it out," Shane snapped at Jesse, who had crouched down beside the couch to stare at the stake in Michael's chest. "Hurry up, he's too young, it could really hurt him."

"Stop! Don't touch it. It's spring-loaded," Jesse said, and pointed to a symbol burned into the side of the wood. "I know this mark. It's a Daylight Foundation inventory sign. It's got a silver payload built in. If you try to remove it, it'll flood his heart with silver. It'll kill him."

Shane had reached out for the stake, but now he pulled back, eyes narrowed and simmering with fury. "Who the *fuck* is the Daylight Foundation?"

"Trust me, nobody you need to screw around with," Jesse said. "There's a method for disarming this thing, but we need to be very careful. I've got some experience. Let me handle it."

"What the hell happened out there?" Shane demanded. No one answered him, not even Eve; she was staring down at Michael, her face ashen. Claire held on to her, because it seemed that, after having made the single-minded effort to get Michael to safety, Eve had completely lost all strength to keep herself upright. She wasn't crying. She wasn't doing anything, except . . . waiting, with a kind of fatal, desperate patience. The ruby wedding ring flashed and trembled on her clenched left hand. "Claire. *Claire.* Go check the door, make sure nobody's coming after them."

She didn't want to leave Eve, but he was right; it was important. Pete seemed rooted to the spot, staring at the completely unexpected second vampire in his living room; he seemed to be re-thinking his whole life strategy, in that single moment.

"Go," Eve whispered. "I'm okay." She stood on her own, some-how, and Claire squeezed her arm and rushed to the door to look through the peephole.

There was a streetlight conveniently situated outside that cast a harsh glow over the sidewalk, which seemed deserted except for Jesse's car, parked across the street. The peephole didn't offer much of a glimpse off to the sides, but Claire was pretty certain that ev-erything was clear. She turned back and gave a thumbs-up sign to Shane, who nodded and looked down at Michael again with tense, desperately still silence.

Then the door behind Claire's back vibrated under a sudden, very strong volley of knocking. *Too* strong. Claire yelped and whipped around to stare out the peephole again, and saw a pallid face under a shock of wildly windblown black hair. No human being was nat-urally that pale.

She unlocked it and said, "Get in, quick!" because it was Myrnin . . . and behind him, Oliver.

The two vampires entered in a rush of displaced air, and Oliver quickly shut and locked the door again. He leaned against it, seem-ing tired—weirdly—and Claire had a chance to think, *Why is Oli-ver here?* Because even though he'd been exiled from Morganville by Amelie, she didn't think he had any reason to be poking around this part of the country. Oliver looked ragged, too—and dressed down, in worn blue jeans grimy with oil, a faded, loose T-shirt with some kind of wolf design on it, and his long, salt-and-pepper curly hair worn in a loose, sloppy ponytail in back. It didn't seem to have had a wash recently. Neither did he.

And Myrnin . . . well, at least he wasn't dressed any worse than he usually was, but he seemed *very* pale, and not any cleaner than Oliver. They'd both been traveling hard, she guessed, although vampires didn't really smell bad, unless they came in contact with things that did. From the general miasma around the two of them, they'd been around rotting garbage for a while.

Myrnin stared at her for a long few seconds, then scraped his disorderly hair back from his face, and said, "They don't have you, then. But do they have *it*?"

"It? What does that mean?" Claire asked. He didn't answer her. He just hugged her, suddenly and violently, and before she could even make a surprised sound he was gone. It was like being hugged by a snowman, only less . . . moist. And more unpleasantly fragrant.

Oliver said, "We went to see Irene Anderson. Myrnin has a good relationship with her, even now. However, she was . . . unhelpful. She had no idea where you had gone, only that you had taken the device with you from her laboratory."

"I—wait, what? I didn't take anything!"

"Oh," Myrnin said, and turned back toward her from where he stood next to Eve. "Oh, that is such very, very bad news. Because if you didn't, someone did. Someone with laboratory access, since I personally reviewed the records."

Myrnin sounded . . . sane. Despite the tangled hair, the dirty homeless-style clothes, the smell of garbage and the whiff of things much worse. He looked taut, worried, and paranoid, but *not* crazy.

So, things were very, very bad, then. Claire sometimes thought of him as only recreationally crazy; when things were life-and-death, her boss (and friend) seemed to make a concerted effort to view things with icy precision. He paid for it later, but she'd never been less than grateful to him for making the effort.

"You're saying someone broke into Dr. Anderson's lab and took VLAD."

His eyebrows rose. "VLAD?"

"The—the device. Vampire Leveling Adjustment Device." She realized, belatedly, that Oliver, who was decidedly *not* in her inner circle of people she trusted, was listening, but he refrained from comment. His attention was fixed on Michael, as if he actually cared.

Which, knowing Oliver, he actually might, though he'd no doubt deny it.

She was almost sure Myrnin would glower at her for naming her pet project after a famous vampire—Vlad Tepes, commonly thought to be the historical inspiration for Count Dracula—but he only shook his head in impatience. "We must go, and quickly. We can't stay here," Myrnin said. "Oliver and I are being hunted."

"By who?"

"Whom, my dear girl, *whom*. Grammar really has descended to the lowest—"

"Myrnin!"

"I have no idea." His tone was flat, and there were dangerous embers of red in his eyes. "When I do, there will be reckoning for Michael."

"He took a blow meant for me," Oliver said. "Stupid. I could likely have avoided it if he'd given me the chance."

That made Eve spin around and level him with a white-hot glare. "Likely? *Likely?* You asshole, he *saved your life!*"

Normally, having a human use that tone with him would have made Oliver snarl, show fangs, and "teach her a lesson" . . . but he did none of that. He only looked away, and Eve glared a moment more before kneeling down at Michael's side and taking his limp, pallid hand in hers.

"He feels cold," she told Jesse. "Please, if you're going to do something—"

"I'm thinking," Jesse snapped. "Just *quiet*, all of you. I've only seen this twice before."

"What happened?" Shane asked. "The other two times?"

She didn't answer, which meant, Claire thought with a cold shiver, that the vampires who'd had those stakes in their hearts likely hadn't survived.

Jesse finally said, "Right. There's no safe way to disarm it. Oliver, I need you."

He didn't move until she turned her head, frowning at him, and then moved to Michael's side. "Yes?"

"You're faster and stronger than I am," Jesse said. She didn't say it as a compliment, just a simple statement of fact. "I need you to pull that stake out, straight and as fast as you can. I will put my hand over the wound in case the silver triggers; I may be able to stop it from entering his bloodstream."

"At the cost of your hand," he pointed out.

"No other choice," Jesse said. "I'm old enough. I can survive. Daylighters haven't killed me yet."

Claire held her breath as Oliver nodded, reached down, and took hold of the stake. He locked his gaze with Jesse's, and she counted down. *Three, two, one.*

On *one*, Oliver moved in a blur, faster than the human eye could catch, and Jesse's hand slapped in place, covering the still-open wound as the wooden stake pulled free. Or at least, that was what Claire presumed happened, because she didn't actually *see* it, only Jesse's hand on Michael's chest, and the stake moving at bullet speed to hit and shatter on the far brick wall.

It splattered liquid silver all over the wall.

Jesse didn't move, though she made a sound—a small one, in the back of her throat. And then Claire realized why.

Her hand was covered in silver. Dripping with it. And she couldn't move until Michael's wound healed, or he'd be poisoned, and at his young age, likely die quickly.

Her hand was burning. Sizzling. Claire clapped her hand over her mouth to hold in the nausea as she saw skin erode and tendons working beneath, and *still* Jesse sat very still, unmoving, pale as a marble statue.

"I think it's closed," Jesse finally whispered, and just . . . collapsed. Oliver moved, but—surprisingly, Claire thought—Myrnin was already there, grabbing her as she fell backward and easing her to the colorful area rug beneath.

Eve threw herself forward and frantically checked Michael's pale chest for any sign of damage. "He's okay," she said. "Michael? *Michael!*"

He opened his blue eyes, blinked, and said, "Eve?" His voice was shockingly faint, but he was alive.

Myrnin fumbled in the pockets of his oversized coat—there were a lot of pockets, some flapping loose—and brought out a small stoppered vial of powder. He supported Jesse's head and shoulders on his knees as he pulled the cork with his teeth and emptied the powder over her burning hand.

She cried out and arched up into the air, and he held on to her as she writhed and fought. "Easy, dear lady, easy, it will stop; the pain will stop. It will halt the silver and heal your wound, though the scars may take some time—easy, Lady Gray, be easy . . ."

Lady Gray? He knew Jesse—well, of course, he would, wouldn't he? Because she'd been sent by Amelie from Morganville in the first place. Still. Claire blinked, because she'd never seen Myrnin act quite so . . . gentle. Or so formal. And Jesse let out a long, trembling breath and smiled up at him. Whatever he'd given her had worked. The damage was still pretty serious, but from the smile, and the way its wattage increased second by second, the pain was subsiding. Myrnin put his hand on her cheek in a small, comforting caress—something Claire couldn't remember him doing before. Not quite that way.

"Well," Jesse said, with a lilt in her voice that hadn't been there before. "It's a rare sweet day that brings you out of your cave, little spider."

"And a rarer one that sees you brought low, Lady Gray. A brave act. Very brave."

"Foolish, if the boy doesn't make it," she said. "Oh, bother it, leave my hand alone. The silver's still burning, but it'll pass. I'm too old for it to do much more damage."

"You don't look a day over a thousand," Myrnin said. My God, Claire thought. Was he actually *flirting*? Well, if he was, she couldn't really blame him. Jesse was . . . kind of a stunner.

Michael was trying to sit up on the sofa, something Shane and Eve were trying to prevent; Claire joined them, and when it became clear that "no" was not a viable option, she helped prop him upright. "Hey," she said to him, "weren't you supposed to *stop* trouble, and not be so much in the middle of it?"

"Best laid plans," Michael said, and coughed. It had an alarmingly wet sound. Eve grabbed a handful of tissues from a box on the coffee table, and when he stopped coughing and took them away from his mouth, they were soaked in fresh, red blood. But he seemed to be feeling better. "I think that might have been about as close as I could have come to dead."

"Just about," Shane agreed. "You ever heard of someone putting a silver injector inside a stake before?"

"Never," Michael said, "but it seems like a damn great idea, except when it's in my chest."

"Yeah, that's kind of what I was thinking." Shane squeezed his shoulder and crouched down to eye level. "You good, bro?"

"I'm good. And it's good to see you've kept up the tradition of getting the holy shit beat out of you, even when you're in a nice, civilized place."

"It was *not* my fault."

Michael just shook his head. He still looked very pale, and his eyes were red-rimmed. He was holding Eve's hand, and he tugged on it, bringing her down to whisper in her ear. She nodded and turned to Pete—who was still standing exactly where he'd been, looking utterly overtaken by what had crashed in on them. As well he might, Claire thought. He'd been worried about sexed-up sheets, and suddenly there were wounded vampires and a big splash of silver dripping down his brick wall. Even for someone who'd known Jesse, this sudden onslaught of the undead might be a little tough to handle.

"Excuse me," Eve said to him. "Do you have any, ah, plasma? In bags?"

Pete gave her a blank look, and finally just turned around and walked to the armchair. He sat down, put his head in his hands, and checked out of the current reality.

"Guess that's a no," Eve said. "All right. Sorry, you guys, but he needs to feed, and I'm going to volunteer a vein. So if you're squeamish, turn around."

Claire did, not so much because she was faint at the sight of blood, but because it seemed uncomfortably intimate to her. Shane turned, too, and took a look around the room. Oliver was examining the remains of the wooden stake, though he was being very careful not to touch any of the remaining silver leaking out of it. Myrnin and Jesse seemed to be very cozy. "Well," Shane said, "at least we're not alone on the run anymore. Apparently, the cops may be the least of our worries right now." He put his arm around her waist and pulled her closer, and she willingly went. "You all right?"

"Fine," she said, and shivered. "That was sudden. And intense."

"I think Pete's having a migraine. And I'm not sure the silver's coming out of his rug, either."

Jesse had climbed to her feet before he'd finished the sentence, and she walked to the small bathroom and came back in a moment with a thick roll of gauze bandage. She carried it to Myrnin and held it out with her eyebrows raised. "Do you mind?" she asked him.

He bowed a little, took the gauze, and held her hand steady as he wrapped the bandages. He was good at it, Claire realized; he'd definitely had lots of practice at treating injuries, and for this one, it didn't matter whether it was a vampire or human. The bandages were all the same. He ripped one end of the gauze in two, wrapped it snugly, and tied it off; that, Claire was sure, came from experience in eras where such things as sticky tape had yet to be invented. Once he was done, he smoothed the bandages down, and his hand lingered on hers.

Jesse gave him a slow, bright smile, and Myrnin's pale cheeks reddened, just a touch. He let go. "All better," he said. "My lady."

"My lord," she said, and did a pretty fair curtsy, considering she was wearing blue jeans and a low-cut black knit shirt. Her dark red braid swung forward over her shoulder in a thick rope, and as she looked up through her eyelashes at him, Claire thought that Jesse had probably practiced the art of flirting for at least a few hundred years. Poor Myrnin.

He was definitely outclassed, and *way* out of practice, because he cleared his throat and turned his back on her—not the most graceful end to that conversation—and said, "Claire. With me."

She automatically moved to follow him as he headed for the kitchen, but Shane didn't let go of her; his strong grip pulled her to a halt, and Claire looked up at him, frowning.

"I'll be okay," she said. What she saw in his face was not jealousy, or worry, or anything like that; it was caution, pure and simple. This was all wildly strange, today. She understood exactly how he felt, wanting to slow it down and make things a little more understandable. "Let me talk to him and see if I can make sense of any of this."

"You're talking to Myrnin," Shane said. "I think that might be a little too much to ask." But he let her go, and she followed her friend, her boss, and her headache into the little kitchen area. She glanced over at Michael and Eve as she did so; he'd finished drinking from Eve's wrist, and was using the leftover gauze from Jesse to put a neat bandage around the small wound. The look in his eyes as he watched Eve's face was vulnerable, grateful, and more than a little heartbreaking.

Anybody who believed vampires couldn't feel things like living people did had never met Michael Glass.

They got as far from the others as it was possible to be, within the walls of Pete's small apartment, and Claire tried to put at least a few feet between her and Myrnin. Ugh. Where had he been hanging out, the city dump? But it was clear that hygiene wasn't his biggest issue at the moment, from the fiery intensity of his gaze on her. "You and Irene," Myrnin began. "What have you done?"

Claire was taken aback, because she hadn't expected him to accuse her like that. "Nothing!" she said, and crossed her arms over her chest. She knew it looked defensive, and she didn't care. "*You're* the one who told me to work with her, Myrnin, so don't blame me if something's gone wrong in all this. *I* just wanted to come to college!"

"And it's working out so well!" he said. "I trusted Irene implicitly. She has been my agent here in the world for some time, and she has helped conceal our true nature from those who come looking."

"Like the government?"

Myrnin didn't answer that. He couldn't stand still, and now he stopped moving uneasily from one foot to the other to move toward the counter and restlessly open and close the drawers. Claire caught a glimpse of random junk in one, forks and spoons in another. He wasn't looking for anything, he just needed to fidget. "Irene has always had ties to the federal government," he said. "But that never concerned us directly, until recently."

"Just tell me *what happened!* What made you leave Morganville and come all the way out here in the first place? I know Oliver was already on the road—did you run into him, or did he find you?"

"That is a great many questions in a row. Oh, look, he has peanut butter. Do you like peanut butter?"

"*Myrnin!*"

"But it's crunchy . . ." She stared at him with inarticulate frustration, and he put the jar back in the pantry and closed the door. There were some rubber bands dangling from the knob, so he picked a couple off and began playing with them. That was good.

It would be less distracting, for both of them. "I left Morganville because I intercepted a communication that claimed to be able to prove, without any doubt, the existence of vampires in the world."

"Oh, God, Myrnin, did you find this on the Internet? Because you can't believe everything that's on there."

"I know that! And no, I did *not* believe it. Not at first. But this was no excitable fan of films posting to his friends; it was a doctor, who was preparing a scholarly paper. It was a Google alert, by the way." He seemed ridiculously pleased that he had figured out how to set one. "He was located in Boston. I felt there had to be some reason that such a revelation would be located so close to Irene, and I phoned her. She did not answer."

"People do that sometimes. It doesn't mean—"

"I sent you here, Claire. I sent you to Irene, for safety. And I was afraid . . . I was afraid that she might have betrayed us. Perhaps even accidentally. If word of vampires was out, and taken seriously, then it would only be a matter of time before word of Morganville would be circulated as well. We control these kinds of events; we must, or be wiped from the earth. Normally Oliver would have dispatched agents to see to it, but Oliver was, ah, indisposed. . . ."

"Exiled, you mean."

"Yes, yes, but I couldn't wait for Amelie to decide who best was ready to deal with this crisis. I know Irene, and I had a good sense of where to locate Oliver. I thought the two of us together could easily handle things."

"And how did that go?"

He snapped one of the rubber bands in a convulsive movement, and dropped it to the floor. The second one was tougher, but he was pulling on it way too hard. "Not . . . very well," he admitted. "I still haven't been able to locate this doctor that Google found so easily. The human world is much more confusing than I recall. And Oliver was not terribly cooperative. Then Amelie tried to re-call me to Morganville. It's all been very stressful."

Claire sighed and resisted the almost impossibly attractive im-pulse to shake him. "Tell me what happened *today*."

He blinked at her and restlessly snapped the rubber band around his wrist. "Oliver and I attempted to track down this doc-tor at his offices, but he was not there. Oliver got into a dispute with someone who called us homeless bums and attempted to spit upon us. I managed to prevent him from doing anything too fool-ish, but it wasn't a very good few moments for our tormentor, I'm afraid. And then we went to the doctor's home, but again, he wasn't there. I was somewhat at a loss how to proceed. I'm not generally used to putting out so much effort." He went to the faucet and turned the taps on and off. Claire had a faint hope that he might use the opportunity to wash up, but evidently it didn't occur to him. "Michael found us just as we were trying to see Irene; we were again barred entrance to the university because of our clothing and general dishevelment, and he promised to help us get a motel room where we could wash. Eve said she would secure us new things to wear."

That would have been interesting. Claire would have paid money to see what Eve would have bought for Oliver, much less Myrnin. It would have, at the very least, been crazy amazing.

"I'm guessing things didn't get that far," Claire said, "since you're still stinky and wearing rags."

Myrnin looked down at himself and sighed. "My apologies. Life can be harsh. Yes, we were followed as we left the university by men in some sort of large vehicle. When we stopped at the mo-tel and obtained our room key, we were attacked without warning.

Michael managed to put himself in the way when the one with the stake came for Oliver, who was busy fighting another; we did not immediately know that the stake was anything but wood. But Oliver had seen something like it before, and stopped me before I tried to pull it out. I remembered that Lady Gray was here, watching over Irene, and I begged her help. And she brought us here."

"And did they follow you?"

"No." Myrnin seemed very certain of it, and Claire wondered why for a moment, until she knew. They wouldn't have left anybody behind capable of following. "But we didn't think it wise to wait for the police to arrive. Jesse thought this would be the safest place. I did not expect to find *you* here."

"It's been an eventful morning for us, too," Claire said. "My friend's been abducted, and the police think Shane and I might have had something to do with it."

"Really? Did you?"

"No! Why would I?"

Myrnin shrugged. "I don't know, but it had to be asked. This friend of yours, does she have any knowledge of vampires?"

"Not a bit. She doesn't believe in them. Not even in that 'maybe it's real' way that a lot of college kids seem to have."

"Hmmm. Then her vanishing might have nothing to do with us, and therefore, it's of no concern."

"Excuse me? *No concern?* She's my friend!"

That seemed to surprise Myrnin, who frowned at her and stopped stretching the rubber band as if she'd captured his full attention, at least for a moment. "We stand in danger, Claire. Very real danger. Irene says that your device has disappeared from her lab; someone with real credibility in the world intends to produce evidence of vampirism, perhaps including actual captured specimens.

These are things that we can't allow, for our own health and survival. We must locate these people, stop them, and erase all knowledge of this event; when these things happen, they are cancers, and must be cut out. You understand?"

"I understand that there's more going on here than just what you're into," she said. "Dr. Anderson's been dealing with some scary spy people, who have—probably not coincidentally—been in my house when they thought I wasn't there, looking for something that might have been VLAD. And then my friend gets taken by men in a van? Sounds to me as if they've gone to the next level. Maybe it's connected to your doctor's publication plans."

"If it is, if there is governmental involvement in all this, it's grave, Claire, grave indeed."

"So not like a cancer, then."

"No, still very much like one. But I will need a much larger scalpel." She hoped he didn't mean it literally; with Myrnin, you could never exactly be certain. "None of that matters just now. We must leave this place, and find Irene. She is exactly the thing that our enemies, if enemies they intend to be, will need—a human with deep knowledge of all things vampire. One with ties to the community, and credibility. We can take no chance that she falls into the wrong hands."

Myrnin's logic was often fuzzy, but this time it seemed right on the mark. Dr. Anderson *was* vulnerable; if so many pieces were moving on the board, she needed to be made safe before anything else happened. *Before Liz's rescue,* part of Claire mourned, but she knew she couldn't help Liz, not immediately.

It occurred to her, then, to ask Myrnin the all-important question. "What's the name of the doctor? The one who has the proof about vampires?"

"A Dr. Patrick Davis," he said. "I doubt you'd know anything of him."

"Well," Claire said, "you'd be wrong about that."

And she began to see how all the disparate pieces of this fit together, to make a not-at-all-pretty picture.

Oliver moved toward them, and gave Myrnin an impatient frown. "If you're done gossiping with your little friend, we need to leave this place," Oliver said. "Now. Apparently that idiot boy Shane's gotten himself in trouble with the police. They'll surely track him sooner or later, as they're not the complete fools one might wish."

"Perhaps we should leave Shane behind, then," Myrnin said casually. "It *would* simplify our troubles considerably."

"No!" Claire said sharply. "Leave him, and you leave me. And I don't think Eve and Michael will be too happy with that, either. You're welcome to take it up with them."

Myrnin looked as if he might be inclined to try, but Oliver shut him down decisively. "We leave no one behind. And Shane knows as much, if not more, about Morganville than anyone else; we don't dare leave him behind. He'd be a gold mine of information."

"He'd never talk," Claire said.

"Everyone talks," Oliver said. "The question is, do they tell the truth when they do? I don't trust the boy's lineage. There are glimmers of his father in him, still, and I'm not certain he wouldn't glory a little in bringing Morganville down, once and for all, in his family's memory. So he comes with us, and there's no more on the subject."

All of a sudden—and Claire had to confess to herself that she'd forgotten all about him—Pete stood up. It was such a sudden move that it drew all their attention to him. He looked pale, tense, and grim, and he said, "Jesse, I know I said I was down with all this vampire crazy shit, but this is next level. What am I supposed to do, just . . . roll with it?"

"Yes," Jesse said. She sounded gentle about it, but firm. "I'm sorry, Pete, but you do. I don't want to see you hurt."

"You think you could hurt me?"

"I think I wouldn't have to," she said. "And again, I'm sorry. Come with us. Staying here means that we leave you vulnerable to the people hunting us, and you've already seen the lengths to which they will go. Claire's friend, and the attempt on Michael's life . . . Their questions to you will not be gentle. If you come along, I will look after you."

Pete grinned, all of a sudden. It was a bleak sort of amusement, but at least it had some kind of relationship to humor. "Not used to getting that from a girl, you know."

"I'm not a girl," Jesse said, and canted one eyebrow high. "Am I?"

"Hardly," Myrnin said. He seemed embarrassed, in the next instant, and strode decisively for the front door. "Onward."

Claire paused next to Eve and Michael, and exchanged a quick, warm hug with Eve, and one with Michael, too. "Are you feeling okay?" she asked him. Michael gave her a nod. "Good enough to keep up?"

"I'm fine," he said, which was probably as much of an overstatement as the kind of thing Shane was prone to say. "Shane, dude, who kicked your ass for you?"

"Your grandma," Shane said. "Come on."

Claire had actually forgotten all about her cell phone until it rang—and then she panicked, because if the police were on the lookout for her, a cell phone was as good as a neon sign saying HERE I AM. COME ARREST ME. She grabbed for it and checked the screen, and then answered when the number registered as unknown. "Hello?"

Any hope it might be a wrong number vanished when she heard the fast, terrified breathing on the other end. "Claire?" It was a bare whisper, but it was Liz's voice. "Claire, are you there?" Her friend's voice was thready and shaky, and she was clearly afraid of being overheard.

"Liz? Liz, I'm here! Where are you?" Claire plugged her free ear as Shane started asking her something, and turned away from all of them to concentrate on listening. "Liz, can you hear me?"

"You have to get me, please, Claire, please come get me . . ." Liz's voice was quietly desperate, and full of fear. "They took me out of the house. Derrick tried to stop them, but—"

"Was Derrick with them?"

"No, no, he saw it and he tried to stop them, but they took him away and they put me in the dark with—with something that—I feel weak, I'm so dizzy, please, you have to come and get me . . ." She started to cry, and Claire's heart went out to her. There was something so little-girl desperate in it that it ached.

"I will," Claire promised. "Tell me where you are, honey."

"I—" Liz drew in a sharp, hard breath, and for a long second she was silent. When her voice came back, it was even softer, and the words rushed faster. "I got the phone from one of the guys who came to check on me, but they'll miss it; they'll know . . . I'm in the tunnels, the steam tunnels, under the library storage annex. . . . Oh, God, they're coming. . . ." That last was said in a breathless whisper, and then Claire heard a sharp cry, and a clatter, and the phone went dead on Liz's end.

When she turned, all of them were looking at her. Shane, Eve, and Pete: the humans. Oliver, Myrnin, Michael, and Jesse: the vampires. Waiting to hear her news.

She said, "Library storage annex tunnels. Now. My friend's in real trouble."

"Have you considered the possibility that it could be a very deliberate trap?"

"Yes," Claire said. She opened up the back of her phone and took out the SIM card, which she held up. "If they allowed her the phone to call me, they'll be tracking this. I need to get it as far away from us as possible."

"One moment," Myrnin said, and then the door was open and he was gone. They all looked at each other, waiting, and in another moment he was back again. Holding a very pissed-off pigeon. Claire was afraid what he intended to do with the poor thing, but he handed the bird to Eve to hold—she did it at arm's length, grimacing—and he retrieved the gauze that he'd used to wrap Jesse's hand and used the last of it to wrap the SIM card in a snug little packet, which he then tied around the pigeon's scaly leg. "One does learn something from years of communicating by flying birds." He retrieved the pigeon and disappeared outside again, then came back in with a self-satisfied smile as he dusted his hands on his pants. Ewww, pigeon crap. "She'll take it miles to get away from me."

"You do have that effect upon people, too," Oliver said. "Wash your hands."

Myrnin gave him a narrow look, but Claire mouthed *please*, and he went to do it after all.

Then, without any more discussion, they headed out.

For the tunnels.

The MIT tunnel system was byzantine, and legendary; students used the wider ones for shelter and travel during the harsh Massachusetts winter, and the roof and tunnel hackers regularly explored and mapped in them. But even so, there were always new areas to be found—some long forgotten and sealed, like the famous bricked-up showers, or the tomb of the forgotten ladder. Claire checked the online maps through Michael's borrowed phone, but didn't find any sign of a tunnel beneath the library storage annex, which was at the far edge of campus . . . and that didn't mean there weren't any. Just that they had been cut off from the others.

In short, an ideal place to hide someone, because in her brief visits to the steam tunnels, Claire had quickly learned that they were *noisy*. A few random shouts wouldn't be drawing any particular attention, even if there was anyone around to hear.

"Bother this nonsense," Oliver said, as they stood outside the darkened building; it was late, and little enough was stirring outside. "False caution breeds failure. Come." He headed straight for the doorway, which Claire was *least* inclined to do, but there really wasn't much of a choice—follow, or don't, and Oliver had the gravity trail of a born leader.

Jesse, however, had the brain of a tactician, and she pulled Pete and Michael and Shane aside. "Back door," she said. "Claire, you, me and your strange friend—"

"Eve," they both said, simultaneously, and Eve held out her fist for a bump. "Or, you could call me Eve the Great, Mistress of All She Surveys. But Eve for short."

Jesse smiled at that, a real smile, lively eyes crinkling. "Very pleased to meet you, Mistress Eve. Ah, you'd be the one who married the vampire, then?"

"Am I that famous?"

"Famous enough, among the undead. We're terrible old gossips. Also, we're terrible gamblers, so it might not surprise you to hear the odds against you making it to an anniversary are not fantastically good. I hope that doesn't bother you."

"Not much," Eve said, "although it will unless I can put down a bet myself. I'd like to make a little money on my own survival for a change."

"I believe I might just like you, girl."

"You too, Red. You don't seem to suck fangs as much as some of the others I have to hang around with. Honestly, why are so many young-looking vampires such blue-haired old biddies inside, anyway?"

"Because vampires are born of being selfish, and we only get worse over the years," Jesse said. "It leads to a dreadful conservatism."

"Um—Jesse, about these Daylighters you were talking about earlier . . ." Claire said.

"A deep and weighty subject we have no time for right now," Jesse said. "And I hope that they are not behind this. But suffice to say that they are a group who believes in the existence of vampires, and believes that we are better off dead. Something they have been quite expert at accomplishing over the past few years."

"Look, this is interesting, but before we have a pajama party and braid our hair, maybe we should, y'know, show the boys how this gets done?" Eve suggested.

"Excellent idea." Jesse reached into her leather jacket, and came out with an astonishingly intimidating knife—about six inches, with a wicked curve to it. It had a distinctively gleaming edge to it that seemed sharp enough to shave titanium . . . and it looked very familiar. Claire had one just like it in her backpack. Jesse held it in her unbandaged left hand. "After you, ladies."

"Do *you* have any impressive weapons?" Eve whispered to Claire, as they headed after Oliver.

"Yep," she said, and grinned. Eve looked crestfallen.

"Well, I can throw a mean comeback, so there's that. I will *crush* them on wit."

Oliver was all business at the door, where he opened up the building simply by smashing in the thick glass door with a single punch. Not subtle, but effective enough, and although alarms probably went off somewhere, Claire didn't hear a sound inside in response to the intrusion. Oliver stepped inside, and she followed, shoes grinding raw on the broken pieces. "Look for some kind of mechanical closet," she said. "It might not be marked. Listen for the sound of air handlers, compressors, that kind of thing."

"This way," Oliver said, and struck off down the hall in a confident, loose-limbed stride. He found a set of stairs going down, and took them; at the end of the concrete landing lay an unmarked set of double doors, painted a dull beige. There wasn't a handle, only an inset keyhole. He frowned at it for a few seconds, then—once again—took the most direct method of dealing with the problem. He punched the door. His fist went entirely through the thin metal, and he took hold of the jagged opening and yanked. Something broke, probably the lock, and the doors sagged open.

All the punching was, Claire realized, not without some cost to him; his hand was bloody, and the knuckles looked misshapen. He winced a little and pressed down on some of the knuckles until bones snapped back into place, then wiped the cuts clean on his filthy clothes. They'd already closed up. He met Claire's wide-eyed stare for a moment, and gave her a sinister little smile. "Well?" he asked. "It's your friend we're after. Perhaps you should get on with it."

"Don't mind him," Jesse said. "He's always been a mean, narrow man. I really don't know what anyone sees in him."

"Quiet. You were only queen for nine days. And you only survived your own execution by Amelie's intervention, or you'd not be here berating me. Beheading is final for humans *and* vampires."

That, Claire thought, was the beginning of an interesting story that didn't seem to match with Jesse's vibrant modern outlook, but there wasn't time to ask questions.

"Shouldn't we wait for the others?" Claire asked.

"Do you want your friend alive?" Oliver asked, which settled the question, pretty much. Pete, Shane, and Michael would have to catch up.

The mechanical room was dark and cool, but Eve had handily brought along some small LED flashlights, which she and Claire used to good effect as the vampires went ahead through the dark. The noise from the air handlers, which had been soft outside, rose to a dull roar as they edged past rows of color-coded pipes and metal conduits; after a brief, burning brush with the uninsulated curve of one of the pipes, Claire got a lot more careful. There were plenty of sharp edges, too. It would be a dangerous place to have a fight—too many things you could bang into, and burn flesh on. Clumsiness would be just as deadly as an opponent.

But no opponents presented themselves. It was just pipes and conduits, control panels, softly glowing indicators and lights, and not much else. It wasn't even dusty. Claire did spot a rat staring at them in surprise (and probably outrage) from the top of one cluster of conduits; it ran off as soon as she looked at it, probably to spread the word among the Kingdom of Rats that probably existed down here ... and her chattering brain was momentarily distracted by the image of a King Rat sitting on a throne, with a giant crown, surrounded by a bunch of other rats all secretly plotting to kill him and take his place. Because if she'd learned anything from being in Morganville, it was that a ruler could never, ever relax.

Oliver suddenly paused, and so did Jesse, who'd moved up next to him; her pale, slender hand came up in a clenched fist, in a gesture that Claire knew from hanging out with Shane meant *stop right now and hold*. She and Eve paused and stood ready for anything, and after a moment Jesse nodded to Oliver and pointed to her own chest, then off to the right. He nodded back. She flitted away into the shadows.

Oliver turned and pointed to Claire, then gestured imperatively for her to go ahead of him.

As bait?

It didn't seem like the moment to have an argument, since everything was being done in such silence. Claire edged out ahead of him with her LED light pointed down toward her feet; it served only to make the darkness around her seem more dense and choking. She narrowly avoided a dangerous eye-level collision with a protruding metal corner, ducked, and crept forward. The ceiling was getting lower, it seemed, and she could hear a faint squeaking sound that she assumed were more rats sounding an alarm.

Claire swept the light forward, trying to see where she was going, and ... and there was Derrick.

Derrick was dead. Drained white. And there were huge, unreal puncture marks in his neck, and ragged skin around them. One single drop of red had trailed down his neck and dripped on the concrete underneath, and his eyes were open, wide and surprised. They'd gone dull and filmed with gray—dried out from exposure to the air.

Claire gasped and jumped backward. She couldn't help it; coming up on a dead man here, in the creepy zone, was something that woke instincts she couldn't control no matter how hard she tried. She almost banged her head on the sharp metal corner she'd avoided, but Oliver's outstretched hand stopped her cold. "Quiet," he whispered, and his voice was about as sharp and uncaring as the metal. "He's been dead for hours, beyond anyone's help. There's something in here with us."

"Some*thing*?"

"Yes. It doesn't smell like a vampire, though it moves like one." That sounded . . . ominous. Claire paused to unzip her backpack and take out the sharp, shiny knife that Dr. Anderson had given her. She wished she had something more long-range, like Shane's flamethrower, but she stopped the thought almost immediately; Shane had always told her, *you fight with what you've got, not what you want to have.* "There's a door beyond the body. Go open it. We may need to move through quickly."

Again, she was bait—warm, pulsing bait that anything even remotely like a vampire would find tastily attractive. And she knew that he meant her to be just exactly that, but at the same time, it was a decent strategic move. Jesse was somewhere in the shadows with her own killer knife; Oliver was a deadly force even without a weapon. And Eve, somewhere beyond him, was more than capable of helping out, even unarmed. It wasn't just her wit that could be deadly.

Claire stepped carefully over Derrick's body—and didn't *that* give her a nightmare flash from every horror movie, ever—and moved toward the single, small door that was set low in the wall. It was too small to go through standing up. She put the flashlight in her teeth and pulled the door handle, and it protested—not locked, just a tight fit. Her second yank got it free, and it swung open with surprising silence. She'd expected an appropriately eerie creak, at the very least, but someone had—ominously—oiled it to ensure it didn't make noise.

And then something hit her, hard and stunningly without warning, from the left, and the flashlight spun away.

Claire didn't even have a chance to cry out; her breath was driven out of her in a soundless burst an instant before her vocal cords responded, and then she was flat on her back with her head ringing from impact with a metal pipe, and she couldn't understand what had happened, and there was *something* leaning over her, something pale and naked and awful with eyes like a cesspool on fire, and she felt the cold dribble of its saliva on her throat. It was only an instant, but it was a snapshot of a nightmare: a distorted mirror of a human being, with a hugely exaggerated jaw open far too wide with vampire fangs wider and longer than she'd ever seen extended and ready to cut. The nose was smashed and shrunken like a bat's, the ears shriveled little clumps at the sides of the head, and if the thing had ever had hair, it was long gone. Impossible to say if it was male or female; Claire couldn't even imagine thinking of it that way.

And then it was lunging for her throat.

She reacted instinctively, shoving the knife deep into its chest. That helped—it kept it away from her throat. But it was still snapping at her, not dying nearly fast enough. She shut her eyes convul-

sively, and that was good, because she didn't see what happened
next, though she inferred it later. Instead of the icy bite on her
neck, she felt a sudden chilly splatter of liquid flood over her that
smelled rancid, like raw meat left in the fridge for months on end.
The weight on her convulsed and fell away, and Claire balled up in
a protected fetal curve toward the wall, retching.

The thing's head bumped against her hip and rolled away. De-
capitated, by Jesse's extremely sharp knife. "Claire. *Claire!*" Jesse's
calm, cool voice, and her hand on Claire's shoulder. "Up. We need
to go, quickly."

It was almost impossible to shake that horrible event off that
easily, but Claire somehow managed . . . she accepted Jesse's help in
standing and retched again, emptily, at the stench of the dead
thing that had tried to kill her. It was a vampire, she guessed, but
not any kind of vamp she knew about. Even Myrnin's lab mistakes—and he'd made more than a few of them—weren't quite
that disgusting. It was like some kind of a bastardized DNA
merger of bat, human, and spider. She tried not to look at it too
closely as Jesse hustled her back to the now-open small door. Thankfully, Jesse didn't ask her to go first; the vampire woman, even
taller, easily bent and moved fluidly through the narrow opening.
Claire followed her, scrambling on hands and knees in the claus-
trophobic concrete space. No conduits in here, at least. Claire realized she'd dropped her flashlight in preference to keeping hold of
her knife, but even as she did, Eve moved in behind her and flipped
hers on to light the way. "You okay?" Eve mumbled—and when
Claire glanced back, she realized Eve was holding the flashlight in
her mouth, the better to crawl forward.

"No," Claire said, and coughed again. She couldn't risk throw-

ing up in here, that would be disgusting for everyone, but the
stench . . . Eve was coughing, too. It wasn't just her. The vampires
seemed immune, and she briefly, violently hated them for it. "I will
be, though."

The tiny tunnel seemed unnaturally long, but that was probably just Claire's nightmarish shock taking hold; she felt weirdly
unsteady, and her whole body felt the aftereffects. It would hurt
later, she assumed, but just now, she mostly felt numb and clumsy.
She also knew that there were things in this tunnel she would later
regret touching; she could feel tiny bones crunching under the
press of her hands and knees, for instance. But right now, she really
didn't care.

The world narrowed to that dark, concrete tunnel, and the rapidly disappearing form of Jesse ahead of her—*how did she crawl so
fast?*—and then, suddenly, it opened up again, into a big, echoing
room. Claire heard the harsh scritch of glass embedded in the bottom of her sneakers when she slid out and stood, and for a moment
she was blind until Eve crawled out after her, and directed her
flashlight around.

"Wild," Eve said, and wiped her mouth with one forearm.
"Yuck. Drool. What the hell is this?"

This, it looked like, was someone's hack project, long abandoned . . . in the grand tradition of MIT, someone had discovered
this place, and started tiling the big room, which had probably
started as some kind of storage area. The mosaic started in the
middle of the room in swirls of black misty white, and spun out in
a dizzying pattern toward the edges. Claire couldn't decide if it
was meant to be hypnotic, or a representation of a black hole, but
it made her feel as if she was standing on stars. It was unfinished

toward the corners, and the tools and pieces of cut tiles were untidily stacked next to the large bulk of an ancient bunch of pipes that burst out of the wall like a frozen iron octopus.

Handcuffed to the pipes was Liz. Unlike Derrick, she was still alive, but she looked pale and terrified, and there was an open wound on her throat—not as bad as Derrick's, but it was still trickling blood, and there was a lot spread around her. She was shivering and only half-conscious. Eve rushed over to her and clamped a hand over the wound, and Jesse used her knife to cut a piece from her shirt to use as a bandage.

"Can you break these?" Eve asked, and pointed at the cuffs. Jesse nodded and snapped the metal apart without too much of an effort; whoever had put them on hadn't taken the precaution of coating them with silver, which was lucky. "Okay, let's get her up."

Claire took Liz's other side, and working together she and Eve managed to lift the third girl up. Jesse could have helped, but at this point, Claire preferred to have her free and ready to fight.

Because there was no way this was so easy.

Sure enough, there was a heavy, metallic sound from behind them, and as Eve turned the flash that way, Claire saw that a solid grating had come down over the doorway to the narrow little tunnel out—a heavy barrier, coated with a nice, shiny coating of silver. Jesse and Oliver wouldn't be moving that one, not easily, anyway. And Jesse was already at a disadvantage, since her burned hand couldn't have healed so quickly.

"Stay with her," Claire said to Eve, and took the flashlight to look around the rest of the room. It was pretty bare: concrete walls, the explosion of piping where they'd found Liz, and some concrete cubicles off to one side. Nothing they could use. "Maybe the other guys can get to us and help us out of here."

"Assuming that the bad guys aren't already on them," Jesse said. "And since I doubt all of this was run remotely, I can almost guarantee you they've got troubles of their own. We need to get out on our own."

"Bugger this," Oliver growled, and stripped off his shirt. He wrapped it tightly around his hands and moved to the silver grate, took hold, and tried to force it upward. As he did, though, a jet of liquid silver activated, and sprayed over him.

His bare chest took the brunt of the attack, and he spun away with a cry; in the glare of Claire's flash, his chest looked bone white, then spotted with red flares and blisters as the silver ate into him. It wasn't fatal, but it had to be really painful. He scrubbed the shirt over his skin to get the liquid off before more damage was done, but it seemed pretty obvious that the booby trap wasn't done yet; another try would only douse him further, unless they could find a way to block the nozzle set somewhere above. Claire angled the light up and found the canister and jet, and traced the activation circuit.

She pulled the wire out from the dull mud that had been smeared over it to conceal it, and quickly cut it in two with her knife. "Safe," she said.

"Again, then," Oliver said. His chest looked scarred, and from the red glimmer in his eyes it still hurt incredibly badly, but he stepped up, wrapped his hands, and took hold again of the silver-coated grate.

It groaned, and strained, and shook, but it didn't move. He was forced to back off and let his stinging hands recover.

Claire stared at the grate, then used her flashlight to get up close. It had come down on tracks. Was there some kind of release? There had to be, probably on the other side where it couldn't be seen. Somebody had come in here to work; they wouldn't want to risk being sealed in with no way out.

"Eve," she said. "I need something stiff, but flexible. Do you have anything that can—" Before Claire finished the sentence, Eve was holding something out to her—the leather collar she'd been wearing around her throat, studded with silver. Basic anti-vamp defense stuff. Claire dashed over to get it and came back to the grate. *If I designed this, where would I put the trigger?* She imagined it as a design in her head, then spun it around. Right. Back of the track, where it would be hidden from view, but reachable. Not *easily* reachable, because that would defeat the whole purpose. But Claire took hold of the collar—which was perfect, really—and carefully ran it down one side of the track.

One of the studs caught on something—just a slight break in the friction, but enough to tell her where the release could be. Claire reversed her hold on the collar and used the buckle this time. It took six tries before the silver hooked on, but she got a firm contact, and yanked straight down.

Something clicked.

Claire took hold of the bars and tried to raise them. They slid up an inch, then two, before her trembling muscles gave up the fight. She felt something pull in her back, and winced.

"Here," Oliver growled, and bumped her aside. "Leave it to those with the power to manage it, for God's sake." His hands were burned—she could see the lurid red streaks vivid in the glow of the flash—but he used his shirt again as a cushion and grabbed on. One strong heave, shoulders bunching and a surprising number of muscles flexing under the paper-white skin, and the grate shrieked slowly upward. It got to the top, and there was a second click. He let go. It held in place, concealed with just the sharp tips of it sticking down. If she hadn't known it was there, she wouldn't have known to look.

Oliver fell back, chest heaving as he pulled in breath after un-needed breath; the burns had gone all the way up to his shoulders, and the bright red flesh looked unhealthy and extremely tender. But Oliver was *old*. Why was it so hard on him? Amelie could han-dle the stuff, after all. Then again, Jesse had been badly burned, too. Was it just that some vamps were less sensitive to it than oth-ers? Or maybe even something in the lineage—Bishop's bloodline being more resistant. Interesting problem, and part of her brain chewed away on it even as she asked him, "What can I do?"

"Go away," he snapped, and shut his eyes. His face was taut with effort, and Claire backed off. Most vampires with silver burns had to have blood, quickly. She didn't necessarily want to be Oli-ver's portable life support unit.

Jesse moved forward with her arm around the still-almost-limp Elizabeth. "Come on," she said. "You can collapse later, but for now move your ass, Oliver. Help will be on the other side, if our friends aren't in bigger trouble than we are. Claire, you go first. I'll take care of your friend. But we can't stay here. You don't build a trap unless the hunter comes to take his prize, sooner or later."

Claire dived into the narrow, concrete tunnel. Her knees and elbows and palms were already abraded from the earlier journey, and this time it hurt like hell. She, or all of them, had shed little slivers of door glass along the way, and she could feel the shards stabbing into her skin. One big exercise in pain, and exhaustion, and claustrophobia, and she was *very* glad to see the metal of the door at the end.

Wait.

We didn't close that, she thought, and put the flashlight in her mouth so she could lean forward and throw her weight against it. Nothing. Not even a budge. No handle to turn on this side, and even if there was, Claire thought that it might have been nearly impossible to get the right amount of leverage at the awkward, bent-over angle she had to use. She remembered it had been tough to open before.

Staying where she was didn't seem like much of an option. Neither was backing up; behind her, Jesse was somehow managing to balance Liz's head and shoulders and crawl backward, dragging the girl with her; Eve must have been trying to support Liz's legs.

Which, from the length of the tunnel, would have left Oliver either in the other room, or dangerously close to those silver spikes on the gate.

Claire lunged forward and slammed her shoulder into the door—once, twice, three times . . . and it suddenly gave, spilling her out into the other room. She rolled through a pool of congealing, rotten blood, and the nausea welled up again as she spotted the severed head of the bat-thing, and Derrick's body . . . and then a brilliant beam of light swept over her, blinding her, and she heard Shane say, "Claire!" in a breathless tone that made her shiver from the bottom of her soul. Next thing she knew, she was swept up in his arms, and lost in a strong, enveloping hug. "God, the blood—"

"Not mine," she said. "And it smells disgusting."

"I wasn't going to mention it," he said, and laughed a little, holding her close. "I'm guessing it came courtesy of that thing there?"

"Yeah. Whatever it is."

"Nasty. Did you kill it?"

"That would have been awesome, but Jesse did the honors . . ." Claire's voice faded as she pulled back, and she glanced back at the tunnel. Jesse was out, and Myrnin was helping her pull Liz free. Michael, standing ready, grabbed Eve's reaching, flailing hand and yanked her out, too, and straight into his arms.

Nobody hugged Oliver. Not surprising. Although Michael did frown at the sight of him. "What the hell happened to *you?*"

"What does it seem?" Oliver growled, as he settled his shirt back on over his silver-abraded arms. It must have hurt. "Someone built a very nice rattrap with the girl as its cheese. And although it pains me to admit it, without Claire's cleverness we might have been stuck there."

"Bad news, then, because we might be stuck here, too," Pete said. He was farther back—covering their asses, Claire guessed. "We've got company, folks. And I'm a little short on firepower up in here. Jesse?"

"Coming," she said. She still sounded unruffled, a total contrast to the tension everyone else seemed to feel; it was as if none of this bothered her a bit.

And Myrnin seemed quite taken with that, Claire thought; she'd never seen him look at anyone with quite that much admiration. It surprised her that it made her feel a little . . . what was that? *Jealous?* Couldn't be.

"What've we got?" Shane asked. He stepped forward, too, because if there was any kind of a fight, Shane Collins had to be on the front lines of it; Claire rolled her eyes and pulled him back. "What? It was just a question!"

"Looks like six guys out there," Pete said. "Six I could spot, anyway. All armed. The four of you might be bulletproof, but I'm not in the mood to try dodging semiauto rounds today. Any ideas?"

"It's the only way out," Claire said. "At least, that I know of. Eve, you take that wall, look for something we didn't see before. I'll go this way."

But it was actually Shane who found the exit—a rusted iron grate just big enough for a person to fit through, set in the floor in the corner next to an equally rusty water main. Flood control, Claire guessed; it must go directly into a runoff tunnel. Well, that was a good thing. Runoff tunnels generally spilled out somewhere, and if they didn't, there would be other ways out. Maintenance crews regularly came down to clean out brush and debris that collected in them.

As Jesse pried up the grate—too heavy for anyone else except Oliver, and his hands were pretty much shot for the moment— Pete called back to them with a new, tense note in his voice. "Okay, they heard that. They're on their way, I can hear them talking. Look, they're probably going to spray and pray, unless they've got some kind of anti-vamp devices."

"Spray and pray?" Claire asked Shane, who shrugged and mimed firing an automatic weapon in a circle. "Oh. Not good."

"Nope." He bent and added his muscles to Jesse's. Between the two of them, they managed to get it up and over, and it fell with a heavy, loud boom on the other side. "Okay, Jesse, you first."

"No," she said. "I'll stay. Michael, you go, make sure the way is clear. I'll help Eve down."

He didn't protest; Michael jumped down, and Claire had no idea how far down it was, but it sounded like a long drop. No way any of them could make it without vampire help, or risk broken bones at the least. It'd be pretty dumb to die of a broken neck, after all this trouble.

"Ready," Michael's voice echoed up. Jesse braced herself over the hole and held out her hands to Eve. Who hesitated.

"Maybe there's some other way," she said.

"Maybe you'd like to see if you're bullet resistant," Jesse said. "But I believe your husband won't let you fall."

"Yeah, but I don't know about you," Eve said. She sighed and held out her hands. "Fine. If I die, I'm coming back to haunt you."

"That'll be fun." Jesse took Eve's weight easily, even with her silver-wounded hand, and lowered her down, then released. Eve's surprised cry echoed back up, followed by a breathless laugh.

"All good," she called up. "Nice catch, handsome."

"Anything for you," Michael said. They may even have kissed. "Ready, who's next?"

"Claire," Shane said, and Myrnin nodded. She didn't like it, but nobody looked like they were going to take no for an answer this time. She held out her hands, and Jesse took hold, winked at her and gave her a reassuring smile, and swung her out over nothing. Claire had a dizzying moment of terror, because even though she knew intellectually that Michael was down below her in the dark, ready to catch her, it didn't much matter. Humans feared the dark, and they feared falling into it, and *wow*, it was scary.

Before Jesse could let go, Pete yelled, "Down!" and Claire felt herself being swung away from the hole, thrown toward cover, and a lot of things happened all at once. A deafening, ear-shredding burst of gunfire in the enclosed space. Bright flashes. Yelling and screaming. Bodies moving against the bursts of light.

The only thing Claire could do was curl up and try to make herself small.

Shane fell on top of her, driving her breath away, but he wasn't hurt, just shielding her from the chaos; she could feel the hot press of his breath against her neck. "Are you hit?" he yelled, and she said no, but she wasn't sure he could hear her.

A sudden, ominous silence fell. The smell of burned metal and gunpowder was choking, and Claire coughed a little, even as she tried not to draw attention. *Stay small, stay safe,* her instincts were telling her. *Don't move.*

And then Shane moved, rolling away and up to his feet, because Pete was shouting and tossing him something that Claire recognized seconds later as a large gun. Some kind of assault rifle, she guessed. Shane held it as though he'd fired something like it before—and he probably had, knowing his dad's paramilitary training—and fell in beside Pete. "Call out!" he yelled. "Let me know you're okay!"

"Fine," Claire heard Oliver say. Then Jesse, in a clipped, tight way, affirming that she and Liz were both fine. Pete was all right. Claire said the same.

But Myrnin didn't answer.

Claire found him lying still on the ground, eyes shut, and she thought she might have actually screamed; he was lying like Derrick, pale and still and bloodied, and the blood that was on his face dripped to the concrete.

Then he opened his eyes and said, in a small, annoyed voice, "Ouch. I haven't had that happen in *ages.* I still don't favor it." And a bullet literally pushed its way out of his forehead.

Claire fell to her knees. She watched the bullet tumble off the slope of his skin and hit the concrete in slow motion; it left a little splashed trail of blood as it went, until it made a loop and rolled to a stop against a wall. She *saw* it, but she didn't exactly believe it . . .

she'd seen vampires heal, but she'd never actually thought about bullets, and where they might have gone.

But they had to go somewhere, and that somewhere was *out*.

"Glad it was you and not me," Shane said, and offered Myrnin a hand up. "Any brain damage?"

"Since the bullet actually passed through his brain, then yes, idiot boy, there's certainly brain damage," Oliver said. And sure enough, as Myrnin tried to rise, his left side didn't function properly, and he stumbled and pitched into a drunken fall on the floor. Oliver sighed in annoyance and helped him rise, again, and this time held on as Myrnin staggered. One foot didn't seem to be responding. "It will pass. And his brain's the least fragile thing about him, in any case."

"You say the nicest things," Myrnin said. He was slurring his words, and he threw an arm around Oliver's neck. "Marry me."

"Exactly what part of the brain did that bullet hit?" Shane asked, hovering on the edge of manic laughter.

Oliver sighed. "He means *carry* me. And no. I won't."

Claire shook herself out of the strange fugue she seemed to be in, got up, and went to Pete, who was at the doorway. There were two dead men there. Both were wearing suits, and there were gold pins on their lapels—some kind of horizon, and a stylized sun rising over it. Pete was kneeling down with his eyes on the entrance while patting down the corpses—at least, Claire assumed they were corpses. They weren't moving, and there was a hell of a lot of blood. Or, in vampire terms, wasted dinner. She supposed she ought to feel shocked about it, but these same two men had been intent on killing her, and Shane, and if Myrnin hadn't been a vampire he'd have been lying just as dead.

She couldn't work up much emotion at the moment.

"Anything?" she asked. Pete shook his head.

"No ID," he said. "But I don't think it matters right now. Two down, and four more still out there. Those aren't bad odds, but the problem is that they have us exactly where they need us—we make any attempt to break out through the door, and they can just pick us off."

"Not the vamps," she said.

"They're not stupid. They know how to place a head shot; they did it on your friend back there. The vampires can't get to them before a bullet in the brain takes them down, at least temporarily."

"But we're not *going* out through the door—are we?"

"No. But somebody has to stay and make sure they stay out until we're clear." Pete gave her a brief, funny smile, and she was struck all of a sudden by how oddly cute he was. "Odds are it isn't going to be one of the vampires. They like to leave humans for that kind of time-buying exercise."

"Not true," Jesse said. Claire didn't know where she'd come from, but suddenly she was there, standing next to Pete. It was gratifying that Pete evidently hadn't seen her coming either; he flinched the way Claire knew she had about a thousand times, out of sheer surprise. He sent Jesse an exasperated look. She recognized that, too. "I'll take the last train out, Pete. You go and help get everyone else to safety."

"Jesse—"

"Just go," she said. "And give me the gun. I can shoot, you know. I learned when firearms were still as simple as powder and shot, and I've certainly survived far worse people than these." She sounded utterly sure of it, as calm as if she was discussing a simple stroll in the park. If she took strolls with an assault rifle. She turned to face the door, and raised the gun and placed four quick, competent shots. "There. That'll give them something to think about for a bit."

Pete pushed Claire back toward the hole, where Shane was urgently gesturing; Myrnin was already gone, dropped down for Michael to catch, she assumed. Oliver was lowering Elizabeth down. "Careful with this one," he called to Michael. "Don't want her bleeding out. We might need her later." That sounded . . . less than altruistic, although Claire hoped Liz didn't catch the reference.

She didn't seem to. She was so woozy she didn't even scream as she was dropped, or as she was caught.

And then it was between Shane and Claire. "You first," he said.

"Why?"

Shane and Pete exchanged looks. "Seriously?" Pete asked.

"Yeah, she's like that." Shane turned to her. "Because you're my girlfriend, and I'm not going until you're safe. How's that?"

"Good enough," she said, and then Oliver was holding her and dangling her like tasty bait over the abyss . . .

. . . And she was falling.

She somehow managed not to scream, though every instinct told her to; it seemed to take forever, but then she was landing in a strong pair of arms that cushioned her, expertly adjusted her weight, and settled her on her feet as neatly as if she'd just floated to a graceful stop. "Shane!" Michael said. "Jump!"

"I hate this," Shane said. When Oliver tried to reach for him, he held out his hand in a direct refusal. "Ready?"

"Ready," Michael said.

Shane jumped. Michael caught him, and tossed him onto his feet as neatly as if it was a regular acrobatic act. *Cirque du Soleil, only with vampires,* Claire thought. Then again, how could anyone be sure those bouncy people *weren't* vampires already?

Pete wasn't that self-sufficient; he took advantage of Oliver's reach to lower him down, and seemed grateful to be on the stone floor of the runoff tunnel once he was safely landed. It was mostly dry, Claire realized; a thin, dark trickle of moisture ran down the center, but it had been parched recently in Cambridge, unseasonably so. At least they didn't have to worry about keeping their heads above water.

Oliver jumped, and Michael stepped aside to give Oliver space to land; as with all vamps, he did it gracefully and effortlessly.

Above, Jesse's gun suddenly let loose with a murderous volley of shots, all growing louder and louder. And it was covered up by a much louder, more sustained roar of returning fire. "She's coming," Oliver said from where he was still supporting Myrnin, who was giving them a lopsided, loony grin. "Be ready!"

Even with the warning, they weren't, and Michael had to scramble to get out of the way as Jesse dropped suddenly down the hole, red braid twisting and waving in the air as she plummeted. She was out of breath, the tip of the assault rifle's barrel was hot and smoking, and she was smiling as if she was having the best possible day of her life as she landed like she had shock absorbers for legs, rising smoothly back up to an unruffled, relaxed stand. "Time to go, children," she said. "Now."

"This way," Oliver said, and strode off in his chosen direction. There wasn't much to do but follow. He dragged the still-reeling Myrnin with him. Jesse let them all go first; she stood staring up at the hole, ready to shoot any face that appeared overhead, but it seemed as if for the moment, their opponents were either baffled, or cautious, or both.

She was right behind Claire as they ran down the tunnel. No

way could they run vampire speed, burdened by humans, but Jesse seemed to have practice in regulating her speed to an easy cruise; she didn't overtake Claire even when Claire had to slow down to avoid the dimly seen debris that littered the runoff tunnel. The bones of a large dog tried to trip her up once, and Jesse's pale, strong left hand grabbed her arm to steady her. "Careful," Jesse said. She sounded amused. "Wouldn't want you to break a leg when you're almost safe."

Claire knew there was no assuming safety until they were far, far away from here, and she started to say it—and then it was obvious, because the trap sprang shut.

Claire didn't really notice the dark offshoot tunnel as they approached it; the glow of streetlights at the end was much too alluring. It was only when a group of figures stepped out of it, into her path, forcing her to skid to a halt. There were three of them facing her—two armed men, and one standing still in the center who didn't fit the template she'd become used to seeing.

A man, but carrying something different. Bulky.

Jesse hardly paused at all. "Trap!" she yelled, a sudden and shocking sound that echoed from the tunnel's concrete like thunder. At the same time, she pushed Claire out of the way, up against the far wall, to get her out of the line of fire.

As Jesse brought up her assault rifle, utterly unconcerned with being outnumbered, the figure in the middle raised that bulky, clumsy thing he was holding, aimed, and fired. Or at least that was what Claire assumed happened—there was no light, no sound, nothing but a shiver that went through Claire's nerves as if she'd stood close to lightning.

And Jesse gasped, *dropped her weapon*, and staggered backward, hands clapping to her head as if she'd been stunned. She let out a sharp, agonized cry, and suddenly dropped down into a crouch—a fear position, a child's futile attempt to hide from her tormentors.

She was sobbing.

And it hit home to Claire with a white-hot surge of rage what was going on. That was VLAD. *Her* VLAD, being used on her friend.

But it works, some ice-cold part of her said. *The field test is successful.* She told that part of her to shut up and die, and lunged off the wall, trying to get to the man holding her creation and pointing it at Jesse.

It was Dr. Davis, and he looked elated. In fact, he was grinning in triumph.

Claire yelled in inarticulate fury, and lunged toward him. She saw one of the armed men standing next to Dr. Davis turning toward her, and the barrel of his gun swung with him . . .

. . . And then Michael was in the way, grabbing the gun and slamming it up with stunning force into the man's face. Her would-be shooter dropped like a sack of mud . . . but then Dr. Davis hit Michael point blank in the back with a shot from VLAD, and Claire, rushing at him, saw Michael's face go alabaster white, his blue eyes terrifyingly wide as he pitched to his knees.

Like Jesse, he curled into a protective ball, shivering. Unlike Jesse, he was making a hoarse, faint, screaming sound.

Myrnin was lurching toward Dr. Davis, and he—through accident or design, fell before he could be shot. Behind him, though, came Shane. He'd picked up a thick, splintered length of tree branch, and he stepped up and swung it like he was planning a home run with the second gunman. Score. That one fell, too, as unconscious as the one Michael had clocked.

Dr. Davis focused not on Shane but on Oliver, the last vampire standing. Claire leaped over Michael's curled-on-its-side body and put all her strength into a shove on Dr. Davis's shoulder as she landed.

It was just enough that he missed. But Dr. Davis wasn't done, not by a long shot; he yelled, slammed an elbow back into her ribs, and simultaneously with the eruption of white-hot pain, Claire heard Shane yell, too.

Only Shane's cry was a warning. "Reinforcements!" he said, and grabbed Claire's arm on the fly to shove her toward the exit. "Just *go*, get the hell out of here!"

Pete, Liz, and Eve were already gone, though if Claire knew Eve at all, she knew that Pete would have his hands full trying to stop her from plunging back in to defend Michael. There were more men pouring out of the tunnel, and Michael and Jesse and Myrnin were down, and Oliver was *leaving* . . .

"Get Myrnin!" Shane yelled. He paused to grab Michael's arm and pull him up. It was like pulling a sack of wet noodles—wet noodles that weakly resisted the help. "Claire, move!" There were too many coming, and Shane knew it. He'd already made one command decision . . . Jesse knelt helpless and out of it farther down the tunnel, and Shane knew they couldn't reach her and get out in time. Claire realized with horror that he'd already written Jesse off. He was saving what he could.

But he was right. She had to save one of them, and it had to be Myrnin.

Claire helped him up, and although he was clumsy, he kept himself moving as they ran/stumbled for the end of the runoff tunnel where Oliver had already gone. She looked behind her. Shane had dragged Michael's weight into a fireman's carry, and was moving as fast as he could, face contorted with effort. Michael was as limp as a corpse.

Claire saw men with guns forming up behind him, and knew with heart-stopping certainty that she was about to see Shane die. If they wanted Michael, which she thought they did, then it wouldn't mean much to them to shoot them both. Shane wouldn't make it. Michael would.

She screamed in horror, because she could *see* it, as inevitable as a train crash—the roar of the guns, the blood, Shane going down in a lifeless heap.

But it didn't happen.

"Hold fire!" Dr. Davis said sharply. "Let them go. We've got what we need."

They needed only one vampire, then. It didn't matter which one.

And as Shane reached her and passed her, Claire realized with a sick and heavy heart that they were going to totally abandon Jesse.

ELEVEN

Two blocks away, and a lot of turns and back alleys later, their little group re-formed again. It was a deserted open-area warehouse that hadn't been used in years, from the dusty smell of it. Oliver peeled back the broken fence, punched open the padlocked door, and hustled them all inside.

As soon as Shane eased Michael down to a sitting position, he crouched down to look at his best friend. Michael was silently weeping, face concealed behind his shaking hands. He was a *mess*, and Claire swallowed hard when she saw how badly VLAD had affected him. Whatever adjustments Dr. Anderson had made to it when she'd reassembled it, she'd ramped it up to eleven.

Shane put his hand on Michael's shoulder, squeezed gently, and then bolted to his feet with his fists clenched as he advanced on Oliver. "What the *actual hell*, man? You left Jesse behind! You left *us* behind!" He didn't stop. He got right up in Oliver's face and shoved him. It was like shoving a stone wall, and it was Shane who got pushed back a step. That didn't make him calm down. If anything, Shane's face grew a deeper shade of red. "You son of a bitch, you *ran!*"

"Yes," Oliver said coldly. "I did. That is a tactic called retreat, perhaps you've not heard of it. When the odds are against you and victory is impossible, strategic retreat in order to regroup is the favored option. And you, stupid boy, are what we used to call cannon fodder. Of *course* I left you."

"Yeah, you know what, Sun Tzu, running's also called cowardice. You think you're so much better than humans, but you know what? We don't abandon our friends, we *go back*. Asshole."

Oliver ignored him, which was an impressive accomplishment, since Shane was angry, in his face, and well within punching distance. He focused instead on Claire. "The device," he said. "That was yours. The one that disappeared from Anderson's lab." He shoved Shane out of his way as if he were a buzzing, annoying fly, and strode toward Claire. "Did you give it to him? Did you know what he would do with it? *Do you know what you've done?*" Shane tried to get in his way, again, but Oliver wasn't having any. He slammed Shane back with one hand, grabbed Claire, and towed her to where Michael was huddled against the wall, with Eve holding him in her arms. "Look at him. *Look!* Do you know what you've done to him? How long it could last? Do you have any idea what kind of destruction you've unleashed against us? It's the death of us, do you understand? *The death of us!*"

It wasn't Shane this time, but Myrnin who stepped in. He was obviously feeling better; he seemed steady enough as he took hold of Oliver's shoulder, and unlike Shane's merely human effort, Myrnin's wiry, deceptive vampire strength forced the other man around toward him. "Don't yell at her," he said, and for all his occasional goofiness and erratic behavior, in this moment he was utterly steady. "If you want to vent your spleen, face me. I allowed her to build and test it. I allowed her to remove it from my custody. I sent her to Irene. All of this is my fault, not hers. And if you lay another hand on her, I will rip it off." That last bit was delivered with such dead-level seriousness that Claire got a chill. "Stop portioning the blame and begin solving the problem, Oliver. Done is done, and dead is dead, but Jesse is still alive, and so is Michael. We must reclaim the device, reverse these effects, control the damage that this *vampire expert* whom none of us foresaw has wrought. *That* is the plan. Now, it is up to you to produce the strategy, *my lord.*"

Oliver snarled, and his fangs came down; his eyes glowed an unholy shade of red, and for a moment Claire really, genuinely thought he was going to rip into Myrnin with everything he had . . . but he stopped. He stopped and stood quietly for a moment, eyes closed, before he said, "You may well be insane, but you're not wrong. Those are the goals we should focus on. Very well. First, we need blood. And being that we are very far from friendly territory, or withdrawals from our own blood bank, I would suggest you coach our humans as to how they can best help us. Michael especially will need blood, if he is fighting this . . . influence. And you look weak as a kitten."

"Do I?" Myrnin asked, and smiled slowly. It had a sharp edge of lunacy to it. He made a purring sound low in his throat. "Do try to pet me, then. You can report back how sharp my claws might be, once your throat grows back."

"Fool."

"Narrow roundhead."

"You thieving, insolent Taffy—"

"Enough!" Claire shouted, sharply enough they all looked up. "We're not fighting each other. Myrnin just said it, and you agreed: we get Jesse back. We get VLAD. We stop Dr. Davis. Yes?"

Oliver unwillingly nodded. Myrnin smiled.

And Eve said, from where she sat holding tightly to Michael's shaking body, "And we help Michael. We help him, Claire."

"Yes," Claire said softly. "We help him. I'm so sorry. I never meant—"

Eve's dark eyes fixed on her, red from crying. "I don't want to hear it," she said. "Science doesn't fix everything. Sometimes, it just screws everything up, okay? He wouldn't have hurt you. He'd *never* have hurt you. Why does it have to be him?" Michael was reacting to Eve's anger and distress, rocking back and forth now, and Eve held on, rubbing his back, soothing him like a restless child. "Shh, it's okay, honey. I'm here. I'm here with you. It's all going to be okay."

Her stare dared Claire to make that happen. Now.

Liz was basically unconscious, still; she'd lost a lot of blood, and Claire thought that her coping mechanism was to just try to sleep until everything set itself right. Not a bad plan, really, but it didn't help anyone else deal with the issues. She also wasn't fit to donate any blood, which left her, Shane, Pete, and Eve. Eve, however, had already devoted blood to Michael, and he was going to need more; Claire knew that would be her responsibility. It ought to be, because she was the reason Michael was so badly hurt.

She felt the guilt of it bubbling in her stomach, like acid.

There was trouble among the potential donors, because Pete wasn't having any of *that*. "Hell no," he said, from where he sat with Liz. His voice was tight and utterly firm. "No vampire's getting a fucking drop out of me. Especially not *these* vamps. They left Jesse behind. She trusted you, and you let her down."

"Pete—" Claire began, but Shane put a hand on her arm, silencing her.

"Look, man, I don't exactly like it either," Shane said. "But if we want to get her back at all, we're going to need their help. Did you see what Davis had on his side? That had to be ten guys, all armed. Sure, we might have put down some, but I have the feeling he can get more. He's got outside resources, something we need to shut down fast and hard, for everybody's protection, *including* Jesse's. It isn't just that they've got her. It's what they're planning to do with her that's the problem."

That got to him, Claire saw; Pete flinched a little, and finally nodded. "Fine," he said. "I'll put up with this shit for a while longer. But I'm telling you, man, the day hasn't come yet that I'll let a vampire bite me. Never going to happen."

"You've never—what about Jesse?"

"Jesse's not like that. She doesn't go around biting people. She has a code."

"And it's never failed?"

Pete evaded Shane's eyes for a second. "Almost never. Anyway. Never with me."

"You like her, right? You trust her? You want to save her?"

"Of course I do!"

"Then this is the best way," Shane said. "And trust me, I never, ever thought I'd be arguing to let a vampire bite somebody, but honestly, we need this. She needs it, and we all need it to give us the edge, because we don't know what we're dealing with. Pete, you're a tough guy—hell, I'm not so bad either. But we don't come with shades and secret spy crap and semiauto weapons, either. So let's not give away the only advantage we have, all right?"

It was a good argument, and Pete unwillingly, finally, nodded. Shane gave him a good-for-you kind of nod in return, and they tapped fists. Then Shane walked straight over to Myrnin, looked him in the eye, and said, "Here." And offered him his arm, skinning up his sleeve to show the veins. "Doesn't mean we're going steady."

Myrnin stared at him a few seconds, then glanced at Claire; she could see the confusion in him, and the wish to trade Shane for her, but she held still and didn't make the offer. Mostly, she had to admit, because she was curious to see how it worked—how the antipathy between her boyfriend and her boss/friend played out in this really oddly intimate exchange.

And Myrnin wasn't in any position to be choosy; he was still weak and shaky, and the hot red embers in his eyes were flickering faster than before. So he took hold of Shane's arm and, without any visible change of expression, extended his fangs and bit, hitting the vein with effortless ease.

Shane winced and closed his eyes as Myrnin's mouth closed over his skin, and she could see the cell-deep urge to pull away boiling up in him. Somehow, he controlled it, though he looked like it took everything he had to stay patiently still. Myrnin, for his part, was polite enough to stop after less than thirty seconds, and even put pressure on the wound to stop the bleeding before stepping back. Not a drop had escaped him, and his masklike expression never shifted at all. "Thank you," he said, with perfect courtesy—or at least, it would have been courteous if you didn't know how he usually said such things. Like his face, his tone was perfectly blank.

Shane, on the other hand, was so easy to read he was practically a flashing neon sign. And what it spelled out wasn't good, but he nodded in return. Bare politeness minimum, and they both took giant steps back to put space between them.

Guys.

Claire shook her head, went to Oliver, and presented her wrist.

He gave her a long, narrow look and said, "No, thank you."

"I'm not good enough for you?"

"Don't be a git, blood is blood. But I'm not presently in quite that much need. Don't worry, I'm sure there will be a further catastrophic disaster for which we will be woefully unprepared, if our luck holds."

"Damn, Oliver, that is some industrial-strength sarcasm," Shane said. "I'm surprised. I thought you were saving it for something special, like the Apocalypse, or at least teatime."

"I can easily avoid teatime. It's a perk of being vampire. No one has asked me to tea in a very long time."

Myrnin held up his hand. "I did."

"And we won't ever discuss that again," Oliver said. "Feeling better?"

"Pish, I only lost part of my brain. It wasn't even the most important part." Clearly, Myrnin did *not* want to say anything the least complimentary about Shane, or his blood. "Yes. I'm restored. Now, let's go rescue Lady Gray."

"Your inability to comprehend the vaguest notion of priorities has always astounded me," Oliver said. "We attempted a frontal assault last time, as you recall. This time, we shall send a scout to examine the situation, instead of stumbling onward like drunken fools into a cathouse."

Wow. Oliver really *was* busting out the weapons-grade sarcasm. Which meant, Claire thought, that he was also seriously rattled by events—and maybe by Jesse's capture, since he didn't seem to despise her nearly as much as he did most other people. "I'll go," Claire said.

"No, you won't," Shane said, "since I'm the logical choice to be doing the scouting. Not afraid of the dark, able to shoot pretty much any kind of weapon, can punch a vampire in the face, have training in scoping out the enemy . . . and also, I have a pulse, which means I'm not really valuable to the bad guys like one of you vamps might be. So I'll go."

Eve held up a hand. "You forgot the downsides. Can't see in the dark, aren't as bullet-resistant as a vampire, can't punch as hard—"

"Hey, I thought you were on my side!"

Eve shrugged. "I'd rather you not die." She looked down at Michael again, and the implication felt like a dagger in Claire's guts. She hadn't, after all, objected to *Claire's* going. Michael stirred a little, and made a soft, protesting sound, and Eve hugged him tighter. "Hush, honey, it's okay, it's okay, nobody's going to die. You're all right."

It broke Claire's heart to see that. It *was* her fault, and Eve was right to be angry . . . Claire hated herself for bringing this whole situation together. She wished she'd never even thought of the stupid damned device.

But it works, the cold science-y part of her brain noted. *He's out of the fight. What if you had it, and pointed it at a vampire attacking you? Any gun can be used in a wrong way, but if you use it the right way it saves lives. . . .*

She didn't want to hear it, not while she was staring down the barrel of the consequences.

"I want to go," Claire said. "Please." She must have sounded as wretched as she felt. "I need to go."

They both looked at Oliver, who was definitely the one in charge just now; he'd been a general long ago, and he still had the ruthless clarity of one. "Shane goes," he said. "He's expendable, in the great scheme of things, and presents less of a temptation to our enemies."

"*Expendable* was not the word I was looking to hear to boost my morale, but whatever. Good call." Shane was already moving to pick up weapons, including a knife that Myrnin silently produced from within his battered waistcoat and handed over.

"Wait," Oliver said. "I've not finished. Claire also should go."

"Wait a second—" Shane said, but it was Claire's turn to nod. She moved in and snagged the knife from him. "Look, if they want anybody, they'd want Claire. She can tell them all about how the device works, right? Doesn't make any sense to send her in there! I don't agree about the expendable thing, but at least I don't have a lot in my brains for them to pick over."

"They already know too much—enough to use the device, anyway," Claire said, and tested the weight of the knife. It felt heavy and cold in her hand, but it would do. No silver edge on it, which made sense for a vampire's personal weapon; it would do just as good a job against human enemies, though. "And they won't get me. But I'm not going to let them get you either, Shane. We watch each other's backs, Morganville style."

He didn't like it, but he flashed her a quick, unwilling smile. "You can take the girl out of town, but you can't take the town out of the girl," he said. "Outstanding. Let's do it."

Claire lowered her voice and shot a glance toward the other human still with them, who was leaning against the wall of the warehouse, head down. "What about Pete? Should we take him?"

"Not sure Pete could handle it, honestly. He's a good guy but he's a little out of his depth. Being a bouncer never really required a whole lot of stealth. Kind of the opposite, actually."

She hugged Shane then, and he hugged her back, and then they spun away to collect other things—a flashlight from Eve, and last, Claire got a clip of bullets from Pete. Pete, she couldn't help but notice, hadn't volunteered to mount up. Hadn't even tried. Shane was right—being a bouncer, even in a reasonably tough bar, wasn't any kind of prep for the kind of industrial-strength risk-taking that was a typical Morganville afternoon.

And then they were on their way. Liz slept on, curled at Pete's feet; Michael and Eve stayed huddled together. Myrnin waved forlornly, and Oliver . . . Oliver looked regal, like a king bidding farewell to troops he never expected to see again.

"I hate that son of a bitch," Shane said, and smiled and waved back.

"I heard that," Oliver said, just loudly enough to be heard.

And then they were out, jogging down the alley. Claire said, "He's sending us as bait, isn't he?"

"Yeah," Shane said. "Really, *scouting*? He's not even trying to hide it this time. I think we're the diversion. Fine. Let's get to diverting."

Night was starting to give way to the faint and distant suggestion of morning, but the alleyway was still drowning in oddly shaped shadows. Claire used the flashlight carefully, just quick presses to show them the obstacles, and then Shane led the way through. He had her hold up a couple of times, either out of too much caution or because there really still were minions chasing them . . . and instead of going back to the runoff tunnels—they had no chance of jumping up the way they'd come down, anyway—he took them the long way around, through mostly deserted streets. When a police car cruised by, headlights splashing over them, Shane casually put an arm around her, and she snuggled into him. It also concealed the weapons they were carrying.

The police moved on.

They arrived back at the front entrance to the Library Annex, and Claire had expected that the cops would be all over it—after all, Oliver had shattered the front door getting in. But instead, a neat plywood replacement had already been installed, the glass swept away, and there was no sign the police had been there at all.

"Your buddies don't want company," Shane said. "Which confirms why there wasn't any alarm. They'd just kidnapped somebody, and the last thing they wanted was the police busting in on them. Plus, there's that weird bat-thing and Dead Derrick to explain." He tried the door—locked, of course. "Hang on a second."

"Do you need the flashlight?"

"Don't need light to pick locks," he said cheerfully. She didn't know how he did it, but about thirty long seconds later, he gave a satisfied sigh, and she heard the padlock that secured the broken doors click open. "New personal best. Okay, inside, but go carefully. Enemy territory."

Inside, the building was silent, just as it had been before; she moved past the offices and storage areas to the door of the mechanical closet, which was tightly closed again.

And a voice—Dr. Davis's voice—said, "Nothing to find down there, kids. If you're looking for your friend, she's in good hands."

He was standing at the dogleg end of the hall, flanked by two men with weapons. And yes, the weapons were aimed straight at Claire and Shane, which didn't surprise her, but did give her heart a little kick start of fear.

Dr. Davis was holding VLAD. He'd been expecting a vampire rescue. She and Shane, alone, were likely a surprise.

Shane kept his hands down at his sides. "Can't we talk about this?"

"I don't see why not, but the fact is, your redheaded friend isn't going anywhere. Where are the other vampires? The males?"

"Males," Shane repeated. "I'm guessing you refer to Jesse as *the female.*"

"Well, yes, clinically; they're very far from human, you know, though they can certainly simulate it easily enough when they wish. Do you have any concept of what you're involved in, either of you? How dangerous it is to trust these creatures? You can't. They will kill you."

"You're the ones with guns," Claire pointed out. "And you're the one who killed Derrick."

"Derrick was none of your concern, and certainly wasn't mine," Davis said. "I don't suppose taking the two of you as hostages will gain me anything from the immortals. They don't have any regard for humans."

"Sure they do," Shane said. "They regard us as walking meal deals. But don't worry, they especially wouldn't come running to rescue me. My dad was a genuine vampire killer."

"Really?" That got Davis's full attention. "I always suspected that there would be such a thing, with its own lore and skills . . . Stoker's novel hinted as much. I assume the business was not passed down. You don't seem terribly motivated."

Shane gave him a humorless grin. "Oh, I don't know. I have my days."

"You came after Liz to get to me," Claire said. "Didn't you?"

"I like redundancy in all that I do," he said, and rested a proprietary hand on VLAD. "You developed an object we badly needed in order to keep any captives we managed to secure in line. The immortals are very dangerous, as I'm sure you already know. So, I suppose the answer to your question is yes. Liz was a means to an end, the end being your acquisition for our project."

"By immortals, you mean vampires."

"It's the common word for them, but the important thing about them from a biological standpoint is that their tissues simply don't age. They are—petrified, in a sense. And yet also alive. There are a few other organisms capable of this kind of extraordinary behavior but—"

"Not really here for the biology lesson, professor," Shane said, interrupting what was sure to be a Myrnin-worthy gush of information. Claire was a little disappointed, actually. "We want Jesse released. Now. And that thing you're holding doesn't belong to you, so we'd like it back, too."

Dr. Davis and his two minions actually exchanged amused glances before he said, "You're playing well out of your league, boy. Please don't bluff. It's just embarrassing."

"He's not bluffing, professor," Claire said. "Really."

Shane shook his head. "Ah, come on, don't call him professor, he's got no right to that. He's a scumbag who gets college girls to bang him for grades. Right, Claire?"

"Definitely. By the way, Liz cried all night. In case you were interested, *professor*."

"Here's a tip," Shane said. "If you leave a girl crying, you're probably not doing your Don Juan routine right, asshole."

Dr. Davis said nothing, but his expression compressed into an angry mask, and his eyes bored holes into the two of them. His grip tightened on VLAD.

And that was exactly the moment that the two men standing next to him just . . . vanished. Not literally, in a dramatic puff of smoke, but more of a now-you-see-them, now-you-don't blur of motion. Davis didn't even notice for a few seconds, and by then it was too late; Oliver was there, teeth bared, facing him.

Davis's startled cry and stumbling backward retreat was almost fun to see. Almost . . . and then Myrnin was behind him, shoving him forward into Oliver's embrace. Oliver spun the man around, and Myrnin stripped the device from Davis's hands.

Then Myrnin froze, looking at Claire with a blank, odd expression, and said, "Did you build another one already? Because this most assuredly is not the working model."

And that was the moment when Dr. Irene Anderson stepped out from the closed doorway behind them, aimed with the VLAD weapon that *she* was holding, and shot Oliver with it.

The effect was immediate, and drastic. Oliver flung Dr. Davis away from him, cried out, clapped his hands to his head, and sank down against the wall, shaking. *Weeping.* He got to his hands and knees, tried to rise, and she shot him again, and this time . . . this time Oliver didn't get up.

Claire, openmouthed, stared at her professor, and didn't know what to do. What to say. *Maybe she misunderstood, maybe . . .*

She hadn't.

Dr. Anderson turned toward her, and the look in her eyes was flat, cool, and very scary. "That's three of them out of commission," she said. "But I know Oliver didn't come here alone. Where is Myrnin?"

Claire involuntarily glanced aside at the place Dr. Davis had been standing, but the area behind him was vacant now. Myrnin was nowhere to be seen. "You played me," she said. "You played me all along. You agreed to take me on as a student not because Myrnin asked you, but because you found out I had something you could use. Something your crazy friends wanted. He trusted you, but you—"

"I got the hell out of Morganville, Claire, just as you did, so please don't pretend that there is some higher moral ground on which you're standing. The vampires used me just as they used you; they found a young, impressionable, and bright girl and fed her to the monster. You and I survived that. Not everyone did."

Everything Dr. Anderson was saying was true, but—but it didn't describe Myrnin, not really. It wasn't his fault. He tried, tried hard, to be a good person, a *real* person, not just a soulless monster sucking blood out of people.

But when he failed, he failed spectacularly, like a doomed meteor plunging to Earth.

Claire suddenly realized that a shadow off to the side, about six feet away from Shane, wasn't empty anymore. Myrnin had managed to make his way there. He didn't have the weapon anymore; his hands were empty, and he stood very quietly, utterly immobile. Waiting for a chance to strike.

But any second, Dr. Anderson might notice him. So Claire kept talking. "That doesn't give you the right to—"

"To do what?" the woman snapped, eyes blazing. She took a step forward, then another, and Shane instinctively shoved Claire back as he got in the way. It also put Anderson closer to Myrnin, and Claire expected him to lunge for her . . . but he didn't. He was waiting for her guard to drop completely. "To do exactly what you were planning to do—develop a weapon that would allow humans the chance to really defend themselves from a vampire attack? To create a nonlethal solution to the problem you *know* exists? Because you are the one who put us in this position, Claire. *You* solved the problem of the disease that was destroying them; *you* helped them defeat the only enemies that they feared. You put the top predators back on top, and you were right to think we needed a way to stop them." Dr. Anderson touched VLAD's casing with a light, almost reverent hand. "I'm just the one who pointed it at them first."

All that sounded right, but at the same time, wrong, all wrong, but Anderson's passion robbed Claire of the ability to argue . . . until Shane did it for them.

"Bullshit," he said, with a strange, tight little smile. "Man, you sound just like my father. He was really good at this, too; good at justifying all the lying, stealing, beating, and killing he needed to do. Oh, it's all for a higher cause, kid. Don't you sweat the details. We're fighting monsters; we have to get our hands dirty. But *you* used Claire to get the weapon here, and then you used her to get Myrnin coming to the rescue when he heard there was trouble. Then you used Liz, because you knew Claire would come for her, and we'd all help. You weren't picky about who got hurt. Still aren't. So don't preach at us like you're some kind of saint. You're just another sinner."

Claire nodded. "You could have taken Myrnin when you talked to him about the missing gun—which was never missing in the first place. But you waited."

"Of course I waited. I wanted them all. We need to have as

large a sample size as possible to conduct our tests, document results, and present it all to the agency that Dr. Davis and I work for.
And no, Claire, it is *not* the government that I'm working with.
Sorry to disappoint you. But those who employ me are well funded
and they do have the best interests of humanity at heart." Dr. Anderson's eyes turned colder, and she aimed the device straight at
Shane's chest. "I know Myrnin is here, somewhere. You probably
have a good idea how to find him; you seem to have him on a leash.
This won't kill your boyfriend, but it'll damage him for hours,
maybe days. Maybe even permanently. I've set it on its highest intensity. Want to see what it does to a human? I imagine it won't be
too pretty."

She had reinforcements coming. Dr. Davis was missing, and
he'd be coming back with plenty of help. Oliver was helpless. So
was Jesse, somewhere, and Michael and Eve wouldn't have anywhere to go that was safe, either. They'd had strength in numbers,
but that strength was gone, all gone. Shane couldn't take her before Anderson took the shot, and Claire was sick with horror at
the thought that something she'd built, something she'd intended
to be a positive thing, could do so much damage to those she loved.

She shut her eyes for a long second, and then opened them and
said, "You don't have to do that. Maybe you're right after all. I've
seen how much harm vampires can do. I've seen how much death
there's been. I'm not naive, Dr. Anderson; I designed that thing for
a reason."

"Then *help me*," Anderson said. "Don't make me hurt you or
Shane. Tell me what I need to know."

It was the moment of truth, and Claire didn't hesitate. She
pointed at the corner where Myrnin was hidden in shadow. "He's
right there. I'm sorry, Myrnin. I'm sorry!"

That last part came out in a wail, because he was moving out fast, but not fast enough.

Irene Anderson was quick on the trigger, and VLAD's blast caught him no more than three feet from his hiding place. Claire watched, feeling suddenly cold and numbed, as Myrnin cried out, pitched forward to the floor, rolled on his side, and stared up at her with a tormented, dark expression. Not angry. Just . . . disappointed.

"I'm sorry," she whispered, as Anderson shot him again, and all that was Myrnin just . . . vanished out of those eyes.

TWELVE

SHANE

☾

Whatever I expected, it wasn't this. It wasn't Claire selling out *Myrnin*, of all people. Oliver maybe; we both had enough cause to do that. But without any kind of warning, without so much as a hesitation, she'd given him up, knowing that Anderson was going to shoot.

I can't say I wouldn't have done the same, but I never claimed to like the guy so much. We had a cheerful sort of loathing going on; he'd save my life out of sheer duty, and I'd do the same for him, but neither of us would shed any tears over a tragic accident.

But Claire . . . I knew she had this *thing* with Myrnin. Not love, maybe; not in the sense of the romantic kind of love, anyway. But whatever her feelings were, they ran deep, and so did her loyalty.

For her to stick it to him like that . . . it shook me. It made me wonder in that instant, if I really knew her at all.

I'd been thinking we could still salvage all this—let Myrnin take Anderson, grab Oliver, get the hell out before Dr. Davis's armed cavalry returned. But Claire . . . Claire changed all that. Claire gave up—she gave up on the whole idea of winning. And I never saw it coming.

From the frozen shock on Myrnin's face when she'd pointed him out, it wasn't what he'd expected from her, either.

I didn't love the guy, but I winced and looked away when Anderson kept shooting him. No visible wounds, no bleeding, but the agony was obvious. She was hurting him, and from the cruel, wet light in her eyes, she liked hurting him a whole hell of a lot. I wondered what kind of crush *she'd* harbored on Myrnin all these years, only to see Claire take her place in the lab, and maybe in the vampire's affection.

I tried to step in, but Anderson swung around on me, ready to fire, and I was forced to come to a halt with my hands up. "Yeah, right, okay," I said, and I kept my voice quiet and calm. "Lady, he's down already; he's down. You can quit now. He's no threat to you."

Dr. Anderson stopped firing then, and she got a look on her face like she was sickened by what she'd done—but only for a second. And then it was gone, replaced by that righteous glow I remembered so well in my father. He was all about the cause, and he'd sacrificed everything and everybody for it. Including me, of course.

I wondered what, and who, she'd sacrificed along the way, if this was her cause now. The crazy thing was that Myrnin had still trusted her—had trusted her the same way he did Claire. He'd never suspected that she'd turned on him.

And now Claire had just stuck the knife in, too. Not a good day for Team Vampire.

I didn't try to go see if Myrnin was okay; it was pretty obvious he wasn't—just like Oliver, who was rocking and moaning in the corner. And Michael, whom we'd left trembling in Eve's arms like a scared little kid. I've staked vampires, don't get me wrong; I'm no wilting flower when it comes to doing what needs to be done, when it needs doing.

But what Anderson had done, and was doing . . . it was cruel.

Claire was chalk-white, and her eyes were huge; I was afraid she might just fall down, too, as the enormity of what she'd done hit her, but instead, she lifted her chin and met my stare without flinching. Like she was trying to tell me something. I had no idea what, but maybe, just maybe, Claire had some sort of a plan.

It made more sense than thinking she'd suddenly developed a talent for two-faced betrayal.

Trust her, something in me said. *No matter what it looks like. No matter what she says or does, or what anybody else says or does. For God's sake, trust her.* Because that was the lesson I'd learned so hard over the past few weeks. When everything went crazy, when nothing made sense . . . Claire made sense. I just had to trust even when I couldn't see.

I brushed the back of her hand with mine in a silent caress, and tried to make her understand that I was about to play along. I hope she got the message, because after that, the first thing I did was shove her backward. "The hell, Claire? He was our only shot at getting out of this! What the hell were you thinking?"

She stumbled, looked stunned, and for a second I thought she'd totally missed my attempted reassurance—but then I knew she hadn't. I couldn't even pinpoint *how* I knew . . . but she and I were in sync, again, and we understood each other. "He wasn't our only shot, and we weren't getting out of it," she said. "And don't you push me, Shane. Don't you *ever* do that again."

"Or you'll what? Get your buddy there to vamp-tase me?" Anderson was watching us closely, and I made sure I put as much bitterness into it as I might have once felt. "You stabbed Myrnin in the back, Claire. I thought you actually liked him."

"More than I like you," she shot back. "I *left* you, Shane. I left Morganville. I left Myrnin. I came to make a new life and try to be somebody else, and you all *followed me!* Why am I the bad guy all of a sudden? She's not hurting them, she's just . . . she's just disabling them. Like you said. A Taser, only for vampires."

"Look at them. *Look!* You're sure that it doesn't have lasting effects?" I asked her. "You're sure that Michael's going to get up and laugh it off? Yeah, and even if it is temporary, I'm sure Oliver's going to take it totally well when he quits crying like a little girl. You just made damn sure they *all* kill us really, really dead, you understand that? If you wanted to go to war with Amelie, you've done it. She's never going to let this stand."

"Amelie will never know," Dr. Anderson said. "Oliver was in exile. She sent Michael to chase down her wayward missing pet madman. If all of them disappear along the way, well. Accidents happen even to vampires. And no one can possibly swear they were ever even here."

"Except Liz, and Pete, and Claire, and Eve, and me," I said. "So I guess we'll have to take a fertilizer nap in your rose garden, right? Oh, wait, you're the *good guy.* Sorry, I was confused for a second."

"I can assure you that the four vampires won't be killed. They're invaluable lab specimens, so long as we can keep them docile, which this weapon does very well," Dr. Anderson said. "And I think I can persuade the rest of you that it's in your best interests to keep silent. Liz is a young, impressionable girl. You, Shane—well, if you won't be convinced, I'm sure I can talk Liz into blaming her abduction on you. You'll spend half your life in prison."

"You don't have to do that," Claire said. "He won't say anything. Shane—listen to me. If we all stick together, if we tell the same story, we can be safe. For the first time in our lives, *safe*. Amelie won't come here, it's too much of a risk. We can stay here, live our lives not afraid of them for a change. We can be happy."

"And, of course, if you decide your principles are more important, I'm sure we can still fall back on Option One," Dr. Anderson said. "I admit, it's not my first choice. I dislike hurting humans. My goal is to make a world where vampires can be contained, constructively managed for their own safety and for ours. If you agree with that, I think we can all get along just fine."

"You going to make Eve agree with that, too? With letting Michael be some kind of—of lab rat?" I demanded. "Shit, Claire, you know it's never going to happen. Maybe you can convince me about the rest of them, but not Michael. He's our friend. He's my *brother*."

"I don't really need four subjects," Dr. Anderson said then, ready to make the concession at just the right time. My dad would have been proud. "Three will do. Michael can be kept safe, but unharmed. Does that answer your concerns?"

What had happened, in the moments since Claire had given up Myrnin, was pretty amazing, because we'd gone from being on the deadly end of the deal to negotiating for favors, and I didn't think Dr. Anderson had even realized she was being played as thoroughly and masterfully as she'd once played Claire. It was impressive. And a little scary. That funky weapon wasn't pointed at me anymore, even vaguely; it was aimed down at the ground.

That didn't mean it couldn't come right back up again, if I did something stupid, but by focusing my anger on Claire, I'd won some breathing space from the real target. I'd put Claire and Anderson on the same side, and now they were just working out details.

I just hoped Claire wasn't buying into what I was selling. I couldn't really tell now. She still looked pallid, shocked, and fragile, and I wanted to take her in my arms so bad it hurt. . . . But that wasn't what would help either of us right now.

"You'll have to sell it to Eve, not me," I said. "But you back off Michael and I might be able to live with the rest of it. Maybe."

"There's no maybe, Shane. Maybe earns you prison. So I suggest you think hard about your next answer, yes?"

I let the moment drag out, and then finally nodded. I was trying not to look at Myrnin, because he was curled in a fetal ball on the floor, whispering to himself, and if I'd ever thought he'd looked crazy before, well, I'd been wrong. He looked wrecked now, and I wasn't sure any of those pieces were going back together again. Myrnin had been breakable, and now he looked shattered.

Claire had a dull, hard look in her eyes, one I recognized; she was trying to keep everything inside, to just get through to the next moment without feeling the pain. I knew that look because I'd just about invented it.

"So what do you want me to say?" I asked, and looked at her directly. "Claire, tell me what you want me to say. You know I'll do anything for you. I always have."

She pulled in a sharp, shaking breath, and said, "Just say you'll back me up when I have to talk to Amelie. Tell her you never saw any of them, or any of . . . this. Tell her that as far as you know, everything's normal here."

"What about Jesse? Amelie sent her to watch your boss, here. She's going to be suspicious when Jesse goes missing, too."

"Jesse will be handled," Anderson said. "She has pressure points, and I know how to apply them. She'll do what I tell her when it counts, and she's got little love for Amelie anyway."

I knew all of a sudden exactly what that pressure point was . . . Myrnin. Jesse had a special little sparkle when she talked to him; she was fine with Oliver, but *extra* fine with Count Crackula. Dr. Anderson would keep Jesse in line by threatening more damage to Myrnin. And it was all okay, because hell, they were just vamps, right? Didn't matter if they got hurt. Lab rats.

I could feel the ghost of my dad nodding in agreement with that, and it made me feel sick, deep down. "Thought you and Jesse had some kind of friendship going," I said.

"We did, once," Dr. Anderson said. "And you of all people should understand that you can't rely on a vampire for sentimentality. They just don't have the wiring in their heads to really feel the way we do. It's counterfeit, a mask they wear to drew their prey in and keep them close. They're predators, pure and simple. They're just extremely good at it."

There were sounds in the hallway, and I heard some kind of vehicles pulling up in the parking lot. The fun was over now; Claire had made her play, I'd supported it, and now . . . now we'd see if Dr. Anderson really believed us.

Patrick "Douche Bag" Davis appeared in the doorway. "We've got secured vehicles outside," he said. "We can manacle the vampires with silver—they won't go anywhere. What about these two? Are they prisoners?"

I felt the weight of Anderson's stare on me. I was hanging over the fire pit, for sure; she wasn't kidding about getting Liz to blab that I was the one who'd kidnapped her, and that put me in federal prison, doing long time. I was used to Morganville's jail cells, but this was something else.

"I need a show of good faith," Dr. Anderson said. "So, you're going to show us where you left your friends Michael and Eve. We need to retrieve Pete and Liz, as well. For their own safety."

That phrase made me grind my teeth, but I tried not to let it show. "Sure," I said. "I'll take you there."

"Of course you will," she said. "Because if you don't, I'll find them anyway, and I promise you, the outcome won't be quite so nice. I want Claire's cooperation and support, and she's clearly willing to offer it. But I don't need yours, Shane. You can go missing just as easily as the vampires, and there are a surprising number of John Does who die in Boston every year. You could be one of them, donating your body to the medical school. Are we clear?"

So clear I could practically see the shine on it. I nodded without bothering to say anything, and when Patrick Davis gestured to me, I followed. Before I got in the blacked-out van, though, I turned around. Dr. Anderson was behind me, with Claire next to her.

"Just one thing," I said to Anderson. "I owe Dr. Davis something."

She probably knew what was coming, because she didn't make a move, and I didn't wait for permission. Sometimes, it's just better to ask for an apology.

I punched him in the face, and damn, it felt seriously good, all the way down my arm and into my guts. Just a little violence, to let off the steam from the boiling pot.

"That's from Liz," I said. "Asshole."

Dr. Anderson laughed. Davis went down hard, cradling his

probably broken nose, and someone made a joke about nosebleeds and vampires, and I didn't listen because I swung into the passenger seat, buckled in, and rested my head against the glass. For a second or two, the red haze refused to clear. That's the danger of letting the beast off the chain for a bit; sometimes, he just doesn't want to come back. But by the time the driver was strapped in and the door had slammed shut, I was my old, cheery self again, and I gave him a smart-assed thumbs-up.

"You're damn lucky one of us didn't put a bullet in you," he told me.

"I live a charmed life," I agreed. "Head out of the lot and turn left. I'll give you directions."

Claire and Dr. Anderson hadn't gotten in the van with us. I turned my head and watched the two of them standing there with another set of guys in suits, and I hoped like hell that I was doing the right thing, because if I wasn't, if somehow I had gotten all this wrong . . .

Then we were all going to suffer for it.

The warehouse looked as deserted as ever. I made the driver park a block down, just in case Michael had recovered enough to give some kind of warning; I ended up at the head of a column of four guys, including the driver. He was a bland, blank sort of guy, but then you put a dark suit on most men and they start blending together. He was African-American, but that didn't make him any different from the others, except the usual height and weight and jacket-size variations.

"So what's your deal?" I asked him, as we moved down the alley toward the warehouse. "You work for some kind of company?"

"Yeah, kid, I'm a vice president at Van Helsing Incorporated."

"Ha, very funny, yeah, I've read *Dracula*, surprise." Jackass. "What I mean is, are you some kind of true believer or just hired on?"

"You asking if I've lost people to the vampires? Because yeah. We all have. So shut your mouth and do your job. Let us do ours."

That answered my question pretty well, actually. True believers. Not great news, considering that I had a lot of experience with those kinds of people. Much better to be dealing with hired guys who didn't have an emotional stake in what was happening.

"I'm Shane," I said. Step one, try to form a bond. Any hostage negotiator will tell you that's important to stay alive.

"Don't care what your mommy and daddy called you," he said. "Now shut up and show us where you left them."

So much for bonding. I followed instructions, and reached the warehouse's bent siding where we'd crawled in. I pointed to it and indicated he ought to let me go in first. He nodded. I didn't take that as any kind of promise he'd wait, though. He might give me a minute, or he might just come in yelling, guns at the ready.

I ducked inside, and immediately was on the business end of a nice, sharp piece of broken bottle at my throat. "Whoa, whoa, whoa, girl, I'm on your side," I told Eve. She let out a gasp and stepped back, dropping the glass, and then lunged at me to wrap her arms around me. She smelled like tears and desperation.

"Oh, God, thank you. I was so scared—Shane, he's not getting better; we need to get him out of here. We have to—" Her voice faded out as she pushed back from me. I hadn't said anything, but I guessed my body language had clued her in that something was off. "Where's Claire?"

"Trust me," I said. It was all I had time for, so I said it fast. "Trust me whatever happens. Okay?"

"Okay," she said, but her voice shook, and from what I could see of her face, she looked terrified. "Shane——"

And then the driver edged into the room, nailed her in place with a sudden flare of a flashlight, and as she tried to block out the beam, he stepped aside to let the others inside. "Freeze! Down on your knees!" he yelled, and then it was all over in seconds. Liz was awake but scared out of her mind, and she screamed and tried to hide in a corner; Pete threw a couple of punches, but it was half-hearted, and he went facedown on the dirty concrete in under ten seconds.

Eve, pinned under the driver's hand, stared at me with coal-black, burning eyes, and said absolutely nothing.

Trust me, I mouthed, and hoped she could read it. If she'd had the broken bottle in that moment, I was pretty sure I'd have been leaking all over the floor, especially when two of the four men went to Michael, grabbed him, and dragged him away.

He wasn't better. Not even a little bit better. And it scared me to see him shaking and whimpering like that, as if every demon in the world had crammed itself into his head at once.

It scared me a little more to see the black promise in Eve's eyes as they handcuffed her and pushed her out after him. Then I watched them load up Pete and Liz, too.

The driver came back over to me and nodded. "Not bad," he said. "You might have some promise after all. If you hate vampires, we can use you. We can always use good men."

"I don't think you understand what that word actually means," I said, and walked on my own back to the van. On the way there, I discovered a sudden and urgent need to throw my guts up next to the Dumpster. It smelled like rancid Chinese food, but I was pretty sure that wasn't why I felt so bad.

Betrayal had a bitter, horrible taste all its own, and no matter how much I rinsed my mouth out with bottled water from the van, I couldn't get rid of it.

I wondered if Claire was tasting it, too. If I was feeling *this*, what could she be suffering? Because she was the one who felt things too deeply, cared too much.

I hoped she wasn't just as wrecked as Myrnin, when all this was said and done.

The drive that came after that was surprisingly long, and the sun was already coming up when we arrived . . . at some kind of a farm, from what I could see of the landscape. We'd made it out of the city and into the country, although there were plenty of little one-Starbucks towns. On the east coast, "in the country" wasn't the same as it was in West Texas, where you could drive for two hundred miles and hardly glimpse a ruined shack, much less a town square.

The last town I'd been able to spot with any kind of signs had been Meldon, and since I didn't want to pull out a map and try to figure out our location, I just filed it all away for later.

Not much to learn from my new friends; they continued to be blank slates, and they weren't chatty. Eve was, but what she was saying was vicious and I was trying not to hear any of it. Boiled down, it meant she blamed me. Guess that wasn't too surprising. Better me than Claire, anyway. After a while she ran out of ways to tell me I was an evil, backstabbing traitor and she wished she'd never met me. But I was afraid of the silence even more, as it turned out, because it had a kind of dense, hot gravity to it.

And it hurt. Bad. I might tease Eve, maybe too much, but I loved her like a sister; I thought she was brilliant and funny and sharp as my best knife. Thinking that she hated me, even if she re-considered later . . . yeah, it cut pretty deep.

When the van finally rolled to a stop, I got the hell out of it, fast, hoping to just walk away, but they weren't going to make it that easy. The driver came around the hood and shoved me back toward the van. "You're in charge of the mouthy one," he said. "Shut her up or I'll do it for you, and you won't like how I do it."

I felt sick, but there wasn't a lot I could do about it. I just nodded, grabbed Eve by the arm, and pulled her out of the van. She kicked and screamed, and I yanked her close enough that the dawn light got her full in the face and made her blink.

"Let me go, you asshole!" she said, and shoved at me with her bound hands. "Swear to God if you touch me again I'll chew your fingers off!"

"Eve, chill it. I told you to trust me, didn't I?" I kept it low, almost a whisper, but I yanked her arm extra hard so that the driver, who was watching closely, witnessed the pain that burned across her face. "I'm trying to keep you alive, you and me and Michael and Claire and everybody else. So just—dial it down. Hate me all you want; in fact, that helps. But just do it at a lower volume, would you? Or he'll hurt you."

She glared at me, but I saw her nod, just a little. Not that she was on board with the whole trusting thing; I could see from the fire in her eyes that she wasn't. She was just giving me some rope, the better to choke me with later. Hanging, she would have said, was too good for me.

"If anything happens to him, or to Claire, I'll skin you and use your hide for a throw rug," she said.

The place smelled like a working farm; there was a drifting stench of fertilizer coming off the fields, and I could hear the low mooing of cows somewhere out in the distance, hidden by thick layers of mist. I hoped they weren't vampire cows. I didn't want to get eaten by a steak. There was a large two-story farmhouse with an old-fashioned wraparound porch on it, complete with white-painted rocking chairs and little ceramic statues of ducks on the steps leading up to it. Adorkable, as Eve would have said if she was in a better mood. In the mist I could see the dim outlines of a barn of some kind. Could have been red, it was hard to tell.

"Inside," the driver ordered me, and I hustled Eve up the steps and into the house.

It was like time had stopped in the eighties, with all the pastel fabrics and ruffles and white wood. If this was Douche Bag Davis's house, his wife had definitely decorated it. Then she'd probably divorced him, and he hadn't bothered to change it up; the layers of dust on those balloony curtain tops and on the decorations scattered around proved me right.

We didn't have much time to admire the decor. There was a kitchen off to the right, with the divine possibility of all kinds of sharp objects and explodable chemicals, but the driver was right behind us with his gun. Pete was behind him, but he had Liz over his shoulder, and it looked to me like all the fight was out of him. Behind him came another, unburdened guy, and two more dragged Michael, who was still convulsed into a shuddering ball.

Beyond the front room with its dusty ceramic ducks and floral wallpaper, though, things changed. The next room had been renovated with a steel door, and a vinyl floor, white walls, embedded fluorescent fixtures above. A lab. I knew what they looked like, though I wasn't one to spend a lot of time in chem classes. This one had a variety of cages up against the wall, from ones small enough to hold rats up to big ones that could have safely contained a tiger.

They put Michael in that one.

"No, relax, it's okay," I said, as Eve tried to pull free of me. I kept my voice low and gentle, because I could feel the desperation in her now, and knew she was on the verge of breaking. "He's safe. Nothing's going to happen to him. I'm more worried about us."

"Us?" She frowned at me, still distracted; I got that. If it had been Claire in the cage, I couldn't have concentrated, either. "What do they need us for?"

"They don't," I said. "Which is why I'm worried."

The driver, right on cue, turned to the four of us—me, Eve, Pete, and the limp form of Liz—and said, "In there." He emphasized it with a flick of the gun toward another doorway. Steel. With a prominent lock on it.

"Hey," I said, and held up my hands. "I'm on your side, remember?"

He laughed. "Yeah, kid, sure you are. Inside. Don't worry, you're not in any danger. We need you, to keep your smart little girlfriend in line."

"Wait," Eve said. I thought she was going to go ballistic again, but she stared the guy down, calmly, and when he nodded, continued, "Could we maybe have a bathroom break first? Because I personally need to pee like mad."

He looked irritated, but it wasn't like bad guys didn't understand the need to pee. Everybody got that. Not everybody cared, though, and I held my breath a second hoping he wouldn't just toss a bucket into the room or something, but then he nodded, reluctantly. "Go with him," he said, and pointed to one of the other guys who'd been holding Michael. "Door stays open."

"Are you *kidding*?" Eve's voice rose, and she put her hands on her hips. "What are you, some kind of perv? You get off on watching teenage girls—"

He flinched. "Fine. But you have one minute, and if you're not done, the door opens hard." He jerked his head, and his boy took Eve off, out the other door. "Anybody else got a shy bladder?"

Pete and I shook our heads. I raised my hand. "But I wouldn't say no to the bathroom, either."

"Me, too," Pete said. "In case this is a long stay in jail."

"Count on it," the driver said. "All right. When the girl comes back, you go next." He pointed to Pete. "You go last, Shane."

"Why me?"

"Because I dislike you the most."

Ditto, I thought, and smiled at him. He smiled back. I was thinking about how I was going to take the gun away from him, and he was probably thinking about how hard he was going to shoot me when I tried it.

Diplomacy.

Out of the corner of my eye I saw Michael, in the cage, raise his head. Funny. In my peripheral vision, his eyes were burning red. I remembered what Myrnin had said about Michael needing blood to fight whatever this force was acting on him . . . and no matter how strong that cage looked, it wasn't good enough to contain Michael, or any of the vamps, if they really wanted out.

Turns out I was wrong about that. Michael took hold of the bars—moving quietly—and started to bend them. They didn't go far. He kept trying, but whatever the cage was made of, it was definitely proof against vampire muscles. Not silver, because it didn't burn him. It was just . . . stronger.

He let go and, as one of the guards glanced his way, collapsed back into a shrinking, shiver ball of misery.

Nice, I thought. At least we had one ace in the hole, even if it was locked up. Sooner or later, they'd underestimate him, and let him loose.

And then the joker would definitely be wild.

Eve returned from the bathroom, and Pete left; she leaned against the wall and folded her arms, staring defiantly at our driver. He walked over to check Liz, slumped against the wall. I'd already done it. Her breathing was good, but I didn't like the chalky pallor of her skin. Whatever they'd given her to put her out when they'd abducted her, it had really taken her down. I supposed we were lucky they hadn't given us the same tranquilizers . . . yet.

"I've been thinking about it," Eve said.

"About what?" I asked, still watching the driver.

"I think you're still an asshole." And she turned and slapped me. Hard enough to leave a mark. I blinked and caught her hand on the second attempt, and felt her other hand, disguised by all the drama, shove something into the pocket of my jeans. I didn't look down, just straight into her face.

"Well," I said, "I think I get your point." I shoved her backward, and the driver got to his feet, frowned, and opened up the steel door. He shoved Eve inside, then me, and dragged Liz in as well.

"If you want to go at each other, do it in there," he said. "But I'm not sending in any bandages. You want to fight, you can just bleed freely."

"He's not worth the effort of a punch," Eve said. She turned her back and walked away, arms folded again.

Pete arrived and was shoved inside, and the door boomed shut. I didn't get a bathroom trip, probably to punish me for being myself.

The room, upon inspection, was a plain concrete box, no windows, nothing. There was a faintly antiseptic smell, as if it had been used for storage of medical supplies, but there was nothing left but us, and a small hand-sized drain in the center of the floor. My dad had already said that a human body could fit through any size of hole large enough to accommodate the head; it was just a matter of dislocating enough bones. Yeah, he was fun that way.

But this hole wasn't even big enough for my clenched fist, never mind my skull. So that was out. Fortunately.

I checked the door and the ceiling and the corners. I didn't see any cameras watching us, but I didn't think I could rely on privacy; tech had gotten way too good for that. We'd been spied on once by someone we'd thought of—wrongly—as a friend, and I wasn't about to spill my plans, such as they were, to Douche Bag Davis and his friends.

I was scared for Claire. Heart-stoppingly scared. She was all alone, surrounded by wolves who could take her down at any time, and the only thing she had to use was her guts, and her wits.

Fully armed, then. But it still scared me.

I put my hands in my pants pockets and slouched, like any street-corner punk. Give me a backward cap and saggies and a sports jersey, and I'd have nailed the whole look. But it wasn't just attitude. It gave me the chance to figure out what Eve had managed to shove down my pants—a thing that I wasn't going to tell Claire about, incidentally.

It was a piece of rusted metal, probably some kind of flange to hold the sink drain in. About four inches long, jagged on the end. As weapons went, it was jailhouse-nasty. Pretty much perfect, actually. Too bad I hadn't gotten a bathroom trip; there must have been plenty of other opportunities in there for fun mayhem-makers. You could kill somebody with a bar of soap, if you tried hard enough.

"So," Eve murmured, head down so any cameras wouldn't see her talking. "What's our play, then?"

"Still hating me?" I talked to my shoes, too, and kept it quiet, in case there were microphones as well as cameras.

"It'll take a little bit longer for the burn to go away, yeah. Why? Am I hurting your little tender feelings?"

Yes, I thought, but I said, "Bitch, please. You know I ain't got no feelings."

"About that plan?"

"Yeah, about that," I said. "Looks like you're going to have to kill me."

"Goody."

THIRTEEN

What have I done?

It kept running through Claire's mind at breakneck speed, over and over ... that moment when Anderson had pulled the trigger, and the Myrnin she knew had just disappeared. What was left was a crying, shaking wreck of a man who didn't even seem to be a vampire, just a shattered relic of a human being. If she'd passed him in a doorway, she would have assumed he was a homeless, mentally disturbed wreck.

Which, technically, she guessed he was. And she'd done it to him.

Claire had rarely felt so alone. She'd thought coming across the country to MIT was a new start; she'd thought she was here to learn, to grow, to change. But instead, it had been a scam from the start. Anderson had never intended to teach her a thing. She'd just wanted VLAD, and Claire was the means to the end.

Speaking of VLAD, Dr. Anderson had been hard at work on it, apparently, and she'd taken it from concept to harsh execution while Claire had been thinking they were going back to basics. All that she'd been doing, she understood now, had just been busywork, so Dr. Anderson could perfect what she'd already done.

And test it.

"Can I see it?" Claire asked Dr. Anderson, who was still holding VLAD; she'd added a much-needed support strap to it, but it was probably starting to feel really, really heavy. "I just want to understand what you did. I was thinking of adding a modulator to it, but—"

"Don't even think about it," Anderson said. She adjusted the heavy weight a little, which meant that she was starting to feel the strain, just as Claire had hoped. "And we're not going to talk about the tech."

"But I—I thought you wanted me to help you—"

Anderson gave her a brief, cool, impersonal smile. "Don't try it. You may have given Myrnin up, but that doesn't mean I trust you with the toys yet, Claire. That, you have to earn. I believe you as far as I can throw your boyfriend right now. And he's a pretty solid-looking guy."

She looked tired, Claire thought, and a bit shaky herself. She was watching Professor Davis, who was trying to get some kind of blood sample from Myrnin; he was having a time of it, not because Myrnin was fighting him, but because he couldn't hold still. Finally, it took three armed men to pin Myrnin down flat, and he made a sound halfway between a wail and a sob that tore Claire right down to her soul. *I did this. I did all of this.*

She swallowed hard. "So what now?" she asked. Her voice had gone harder, and she couldn't seem to soften it. "You've got Myrnin, and Oliver, and Jesse, and Michael. You've got Shane and Eve. What else do you want?"

"I want data," Dr. Anderson said. "You're a scientist, Claire. You realize what a rare opportunity this is, I hope—we have vampires who can be tested in lab conditions. We can break down the biology, which is something Dr. Davis has been looking into for some time. We can *win*."

"I didn't know we were at war."

"Of course we're at war. And we were winning for a while; the vampires were sick when I left Morganville, and getting sicker. If you'd left it alone and let nature take its course, it would have been over by now."

"Did you make them sick?" Claire asked, horrified. Myrnin had never completely believed the idea that Amelie's vampire father Bishop had developed and spread that disease. Had it happened right in front of him?

But Dr. Anderson was shaking her head. "No. I can't claim credit for that. I just made sure that the research went nowhere on how to fight the illness. Seemed like for once, nature was favoring humans instead of vampires."

Claire shivered. She thought she'd understood Dr. Anderson; she'd thought they were alike. But they weren't, deep down. They'd both survived Morganville, but they'd come out of it completely differently.

"If you didn't think we were at war," Anderson said, "then why did you make this?" She patted VLAD's metal frame.

"I just wanted—I wanted a way for us to stop them if it came to a fight. That's all. It's supposed to be for defense."

"Well, you know what they say: the best defense is a good offense. We've been working on enhanced anti-vampire weaponry for some time. Including biological weapons."

"Dr. Davis was running experiments," Claire said. "That bat-thing that killed Derrick. That was his?"

"Yes," Anderson said. She was watching Myrnin, but not with any compassion or regret. It was all clinical, the look in her eyes. Clinical and bitterly cold. "He'd made considerable progress, but our samples were degraded. We'd had to rely on what I brought with me out of Morganville, and it wasn't much. I was working on getting Jesse to cooperate with me, but for all her friendly ways, she's smarter than that. Too bad. If she'd just done it peacefully, I wouldn't have had to take the steps I did."

"Is Jesse——?"

"Alive? Yes. Happy?" Anderson shook her head. "I didn't want to do it. But she pushed me into it. I've got a monitor on her. So far, the effects haven't worn off. I'm starting to wonder if the beam does permanent neural damage."

"*Permanent?* What did you do to VLAD? It was never supposed to be that powerful——"

"I made it work," Anderson snapped. "Your job now, if you want to stay on the right side of the fight, is to take the model that Dr. Davis was using and make it work as well. I didn't have time to complete it before this crisis erupted. Myrnin's arrival pushed us into an accelerated timeline. I think we've gotten the situation contained, but if any communications made it back to Amelie, we may have a fight on our hands, and I need at least one more working device to be safe. So you do that, and I'll make sure your boyfriend and your other friends get out of this in one piece. Clear?"

"Clear," Claire said. "Dr. Davis's gun didn't work? That was a bluff?"

Dr. Anderson shrugged. "I thought you'd recognize it, and it would slow you down so I could use the one that did."

It was good strategy. Shane would have approved.

"We're ready here," said Dr. Davis. His goons were strapping Myrnin into some kind of harness. Oliver had been taken out already, locked in a similar straitjacket. "Back to the farm?"

"As quickly as possible," Dr. Anderson said. "Nobody's scheduled to come into this building until ten, but an early arrival could compromise everything. Let's move out. We won't be coming back here."

The farm? Claire didn't know if that was some kind of shorthand code, but it didn't sound like the MIT lab, anyway. She went along with them quietly, and ended up sitting next to Myrnin. He was wrapped up like a mummy in the thick canvas jacket, and his head lolled forward so his dark hair cascaded down in waves to veil his face.

"I'm sorry," she whispered to him. "I'm so sorry." She could feel the animal shuddering of his body, wave after wave of what was either pain, or terror, or both. "I never meant for this to happen, Myrnin, I swear. I just—I just didn't see it."

He turned his head toward her. She saw a red flash from his eyes from behind the curtain of his hair, and felt a brief pulse of something from him—hunger, anger, blind rage. Then he sighed, slipped to one side, and rested against the metal wall of the van. Chains clinked as he shifted. They hadn't taken any chances, she saw; the chains were coated with silver, and so were the manacles around his wrists and ankles. It was burning him.

Oliver, across from her, was in a similar state, but he wasn't trembling quite so badly. Maybe he'd just had more practice at handling fear and pain, or maybe he hadn't gotten quite as bad a dose of VLAD's medicine. But he didn't look by any stretch good, either.

Last of all, they loaded Jesse.

She looked awful. Her red hair was tangled into a dry net; her lips were dry and pale and crusted, and her eyes were glowing a pained, painful red. She looked alien and strange and pitiful, all at once, and she, too, was wearing the padded jacket and chains, and they locked her down next to Oliver. She didn't seem to see Claire, or if she did, to comprehend any of what was going on. And she looked *dangerous.*

But the sight of her seemed to somehow make Myrnin a little better. He stopped shaking quite so much, and sat up straight again. So maybe there was something still inside there, after all.

Claire hoped so. The alternative was way too awful to consider.

It was a long, silent ride. Dr. Davis was up front with Dr. Anderson, and Claire's only company, besides the out-of-it vampires, were the three armed guards crowded inside. None of them were talkative. She wasn't even sure they *blinked.* She had plenty of time to observe them, in the dim interior lights—there were no windows back here, which was probably lucky for the vamps. Three men of about the same age, thirties to forties; the oldest had some gray in his hair, but not much. All fit. All wearing what seemed like similar dark suits. Claire was no expert, but they didn't look expensive—more like . . . uniforms.

And they were all wearing a pin on their lapels. A rising sun pin.

This looked less and less like the government, and more and

more like something private that Dr. Anderson had gotten herself in deep with. Private, but well funded. *The Daylight Foundation.* The people Jesse had been so worried about.

Somehow, that was even less comforting than the idea the government knew about the vampires.

"So," Claire said to the man sitting next to her. "Are you, ah, from Boston?"

He didn't say anything. He didn't even look at her. He did look at his watch, though, and adjusted the grip on his gun. He seemed calm enough, but she wasn't going to get anything out of him. Or any of them. Shane might have; he liked to be provocative and confrontational, but it was a tactic that Claire knew she wasn't good at.

So after a few more lame attempts at conversation failed, she waited.

It seemed to take forever, but they finally bumped off the smooth main road onto something that seemed a lot rougher, and then finally pulled to a stop crunching on gravel. The daylight that streamed in when the door slid open made the vampires flinch and squeeze their eyes shut, but they were all old enough to bear a little sun without injury. Still, Claire ached for them as their skin began to steam in the merciless glare. Oliver's broke out into little tongues of flame before they unlocked him, and they hustled him out quickly.

Claire climbed out, and was immediately grabbed by the man who'd been sitting beside her. "Hey!" she protested, but that got her nowhere. So she looked around instead as he pulled her onward.

Farm hadn't been code. It was an actual farm, and there was an actual barn and a square two-story farmhouse with a porch. She hoped for the farmhouse, but instead they headed her off to the big, dark red barn.

She expected hay and horse stalls, but inside, the structure had been turned into a lab, a nice one that had a thick concrete floor, clean-room walls, steel tables and cabinets and bright overhead lighting. It was full of equipment, too. Some of it Claire recognized, but a lot was new to her. Dr. Davis took charge of the three vampires and had them led over to the right side of the large open space, where he had them manacled to large steel staples in the floor. All three promptly collapsed into protective crouches.

"This way," her guard said, and dragged her left, after Irene Anderson.

That part of the lab was a replica of what Dr. Anderson had at MIT, with a few changes, one of the most vivid being that two tables were neatly laid out with parts and schematics. Claire recognized one of them as being the constituent parts of VLAD; the second table, though, was different.

That was the pieces of the mod, Claire realized. This would tell her exactly what Dr. Anderson had done to make her device into an offensive weapon. Claire picked up the plans and studied them, took each part and looked it over. She was still examining things when Dr. Anderson thumped down the heavy weight of VLAD on the table . . . not the working one, she realized. That was still slung across Anderson's chest.

This was the prototype model that hadn't yet been upgraded.

"I'm pretty sure you can figure this out," Anderson said. "The plans are right there. You wanted to be my lab assistant. Do your job. Any funny business, and I promise you, your boyfriend will suffer for it. Got it?"

Claire nodded. She focused on the plans first. Anderson was

right—it was a straightforward enough job, but a lot of it required her to disassemble the base model, and reassemble it in the new configuration. She studied the schematics, and examined each piece that she was to add into the machine. *That* was an amplifier, capable of boosting the signal at least a hundred times beyond what she'd originally planned. *That* piece, snapping on underneath, was an inverter that changed the signal from something that enhanced to something that canceled—which was what she had originally intended, to be able to remove a vampire's desire to attack instead of having to fight in the first place. These were the modifications she'd have made in the course of her studies . . . something that would have made VLAD a mostly benign defensive weapon.

But the last piece was the most sinister. It was a complex combination of several different pieces, but from what Claire could puzzle out, it was designed to trigger a *different* set of emotions. Fear, obviously—overwhelming, paralyzing terror. It also seemed to have some other component. From what Claire had seen of its effects, it must have sensitized nerves and created a strong pain reaction. Like a Taser, only more intense, and very long lasting.

"What are you doing?"

She jumped. Irene Anderson was staring at her, cold suspicion in her gaze.

"I'm sorry," Claire said. "I just wanted to be sure I understood what I was doing first. I didn't want to make any mistakes."

"Don't," Anderson said flatly. "You've got an hour. Move it."

Claire took a deep breath, put the nonworking VLAD in the center of the worktable, consulted the plans one last time, and began the work.

She built the thing, piece by piece. The tools were all right there, everything precise and perfectly laid out for her. Anderson was watching her, and she made sure that she did nothing, absolutely nothing, that would draw any suspicion.

Not even Dr. Anderson could keep her focus completely on her forever. Claire felt when it started to wander; it was like pressure coming off of her, and she had to work hard to not give any kind of physical signal that she knew something had changed.

Just do the work. Do the work.

By the time she was down to the last of it, Anderson's focus had mostly moved on, though she remained close. And when Myrnin suddenly convulsed and cried out, writhing in his restraints, it drew Dr. Anderson's complete attention for a critical few seconds, just as Claire fastened the last piece of the machine on board.

She'd already identified the opportunity, when she'd been going over the plans. The last component had switches built inside. They were tiny, not meant to be manipulated without specialized tools, but she'd deliberately chosen the smallest possible screwdriver, even though it was the worst tool for the job she was apparently doing.

It fit into the tiny slots just far enough to slide the switches opposite directions.

I have no idea if I'm modding this right, she thought. But all she could do was reverse the order of the switches, and hope that it worked.

As she finished and put down the screwdriver, Dr. Anderson was right there to take control—even before she'd managed to take the weapon off its stand to hand it to her.

"Good job, and done in time, too," Anderson said. She handed it to the man who'd been Claire's shadow and guard all this time. He didn't bother with the safety strap. "It's time to see if you're reliable, Claire. If you aren't—if you decided to try to pull a clever one and sabotage me—then we're going to find out right now, and it won't go well for you. Or for your friends. This is your final exam, do you understand? Pass, and you win the lives of those you care about."

Claire met her eyes. "And what if I fail?"

"Then we have acres and acres of farmland waiting for fertilizer," Dr. Anderson said. "I'm fighting for the human race. I'm not going to flinch from whatever I have to do to save innocent lives for the future."

"Neither am I," Claire said. "You should have trusted me. I'm really tired of people not trusting me."

Shane would have recognized that tone. But Dr. Anderson missed the warning altogether.

Anderson led the way to the other half of the room, through the clear glass door that separated the two parts. The three vampires knelt where they'd been left, all still submissive. Dr. Davis had blood samples laid out on his lab tables, neatly labeled, and he was talking to a lab geek in a white coat—but one, Claire noticed, who also had the rising sun pin on his lapel. He looked up when he saw Anderson, Claire, and the guard, and nodded.

"Excellent," he said. "We've been waiting."

"You can afford to lose one, Patrick? Just in case Claire's tried to do something interesting with her project?"

"I have redundancy now," he said. "So yes. If I had to pick one, I'd say the older-looking one. He seems like the most trouble."

"Oliver?" Anderson nodded. "Very well. He's got quite the reputation as a killer. I think that seems appropriate." She turned to the guard, took the heavy weapon, and held it out to Claire. "Take it."

Claire didn't hesitate. The weight settled in her hands, throwing off her balance, but she felt better for having it. Stronger.

"Before you try using it on me," Anderson said, "please remember that my friend here has a weapon pointed at your head."

Claire glanced aside, and saw that the guard behind her had drawn his sidearm, and yes—it *was* pointed at her, steady and calm. He wouldn't hesitate, she thought.

"What do you want me to do?" she asked. But she already knew.

"I want you to shoot Oliver," Anderson said. "I want you to prove to me that I can trust you. He looks as if he is recovering faster than the others, and I want you to render him nonthreatening. Then I want you to continue shooting him. Do you understand?"

Claire swallowed hard, and looked at Oliver. He hadn't raised his head. He looked frail, and unexpectedly old and vulnerable. "Why?"

"Because I need to be certain we can kill them this way," Anderson said. "The simulations say it will work. I need to prove the theory, and document how long it takes to accomplish it. You wanted to be a scientist, Claire. This is what it takes."

Oliver looked up. It seemed to take a vast effort, from the shaking of his body, but he raised his head and met her gaze. His eyes weren't red. They were dark, and human, and afraid.

"Please," he whispered. "Please."

Claire didn't honestly know what he was asking. She didn't know what he wanted. But she knew what she had to do. It had to be done fast, and confidently, and above all, it had to be done without hesitation.

She took a deep breath, said, "I'm really sorry, but she's right. I have to do it."

And then she raised the weapon and held down the trigger.

It seemed to take forever. Oliver was caught in the beam, twitching, eyes wide, mouth open, and the chains rattled against the hasp like chattering teeth . . . and then, he collapsed. Dead weight. He fell hard, with no attempt to save himself, and hit the concrete limp and lifeless. All the color that remained had drained from his face, leaving it eerily blue-white; his eyes were open, dark, and blank. His fangs were down, his mouth half-open.

He didn't move.

"How can we tell if he's actually dead?" Davis asked. He sounded completely unaffected by the whole thing. Claire felt hot, unsteady, numbed into stillness. She couldn't look away from Oliver's eyes.

Dr. Anderson went to Oliver, knelt down, and used a silver knife from her belt to cut him. No reaction, though his skin still burned and sparked along the edges of the cut.

She stabbed him. Nothing.

"It's dead," she said. "Congratulations, Claire. It's quite a breakthrough. With a little more experimentation, we can understand everything about vampires—how to use them, how to control them properly. And it's all thanks to you."

"I know," Claire said. "So's this."

She couldn't hesitate, couldn't stop to second-guess herself. She turned the weapon on Jesse and shot her, too. Then turned the gun on Myrnin. She didn't have time to hold down the trigger quite as long before the guard started to rush her, clearly not sure whether this was a killing situation or not, and deciding to err on the side of caution.

It was enough time for her to smash VLAD against the concrete floor and destroy the delicate circuitry before he tackled her.

"No!" Anderson yelled, too late. Myrnin and Jesse were lifeless on the floor, like Oliver. "No, you fool, what did you do?"

"I ended your experiment," Claire said, as the guards shoved her down to a kneeling position. "Because you're not a scientist. You're a monster. I'm not leaving any of them at your mercy."

Anderson's face turned red with fury, and she grabbed the wreckage of the weapon off the floor. "Shoot her!" she shouted. "Shoot her, and shoot her friends, too. And bring me Michael. At least we've still got *him!*"

"Come on," the guard said, and grabbed Claire by the collar of her shirt. "Might as well die with them. That was stupid, you know. Real stupid."

Claire knew. But this time, doing something stupid was the only way she could outsmart her enemies.

Dr. Davis was kneeling down next to the bodies. "Looks like they're dead all right. In any case, they're of no use to us now. Take them out of here and get rid of the bodies. Burn them."

That was exactly right. Burning was the only way to truly be sure the vampires were dead. Davis wasn't taking any chances . . . and Claire didn't want him to take any, either. She needed the vampires to be unlocked.

The air outside of the barn was brisk and cold, and it tasted like snow was coming, even though the sun was still shining. A pretty morning. Probably the last sunrise she'd ever see.

She'd kind of given up on the crazy idea of surviving this, she realized, and that made it possible to take in a deep breath and enjoy the last few moments in the world. She'd done what she could. And maybe it would work out.

But most likely, it wouldn't. The barn seemed deathly quiet behind them. She pictured Dr. Davis's lab monkeys unchaining

Jesse, and Myrnin, and Oliver . . . and she could see it so vividly in her mind, the limp, dead way their bodies slumped to the floor.

She'd either saved them, or destroyed them. There was no middle ground.

And then she heard the yelling coming from the farmhouse where Shane and Eve and Michael were being held, and the day got just a little bit brighter, somehow. *Yes.* She wasn't the only one raising hell.

Time to raise a little more.

Her guard was distracted for a moment, and when she tripped over a rock and jolted against him, she threw him off balance. His gun weaved off target.

Claire saw it in slow motion in her mind, just the way Shane had drilled her. Against an armed opponent, you had to be decisive and fast, because any hesitation would be your last.

She whirled into his grip, throwing him further off balance, and whipping him around in a strange, stumbling dance. She got her foot between his, and then they were falling, and he instinctively let go of the gun to break his fall. She threw her weight against him as they landed, and flung out her hand to grab the gun as she rolled past it.

She almost missed it. Her fingers slipped off the grip, and she fumbled it, but retrieved it with one last, desperate effort that pulled muscles in her side as his weight continued to roll her forward. She used physics in her favor this time, wrapped her legs around him, and used their momentum to whip him hard around, slamming him on his back into the gravel as she rolled up on top of him.

She had the gun, and she aimed it right at his head.

He dropped his hands at his sides, signaling surrender. He looked young, and very scared, all of a sudden.

Claire didn't have it in her to shoot him, but she hit him with the gun, hard enough to leave him curled up and moaning.

Then she ran for the farmhouse, where all hell was still breaking loose. And all the way there, the fear sank in deeper and deeper.

What if I just killed us all?

FOURTEEN

SHANE

🌙

What got us loose was an old wrestling trick, but hey, there's a reason those guys keep making money. First, pick a fight—a loud one, loud enough to attract the attention of the guards. Next, *have* a fight, the more real, the better. (And trust me, Eve can throw a punch when she feels like it. Girl knows how to power out from the shoulder.)

Last, score yourself a bloody head wound, self-inflicted and minor, to sell the show as you flop down defeated, beaten, and—in this case—preferably looking really dead. Have your friends sell it with lots of distress and screams for help while getting their hands very bloody. Eve was maybe a little too over the top, but Pete sold the whole package—he looked grim, scared, and smeared blood around like I'd sprung an arterial leak and was pumping out the last pint.

In all probability, our new friends didn't really care, but like all employees, they would be expected to explain inventory breakage, and nobody wanted to have to say that they'd let me bleed out on the floor without some kind of due diligence.

They opened the door, came in, and I passed Pete the rusty piece of metal I'd used to cut my head open as he bent over me, hands pressed to my neck. "Come on, man, hurry up, he's losing too much blood!" he said to the two guards who entered. One came toward me, holstering his gun. The other stood at the door and kept his weapon out and ready.

Pete stood up and backed off to make room for the guard, who touched down one knee next to me. Eve was screaming and crying, and kept saying that she couldn't find a pulse, which was nicely distracting. Pete kept backing up, and put his bloody hands over his face as he did; his shoulders shook with what looked like genuine tears. I was impressed. The guy had a future career on the stage. It looked so much like real grief, and there was so much chaos going on around my limp body, that the guard who was at the door missed how close Pete was getting until it was too late.

Pete whirled around, grabbed the man's gun arm, and shoved it up as he jammed a knee up into a region that made me wince. That guard doubled over. Eve, at the same time, lunged across my body at the guard checking me out, and I came alive to wrestle him down as she pulled his gun free and rose to point it at him.

The other guard's gun went off as he and Pete struggled, but Pete put him down hard with a blow from that rusty piece of metal, and scooped up the weapon. "Get her!" he yelled, and pointed at Liz as he threw himself to one side of the doorway. I scrambled up, grabbed Liz, tossed her over my shoulder, and was immediately thrown off balance as she started to struggle.

Dammit, this was *not* the time for the girl to be waking up. "We need out of this room!" I said to Eve, who nodded and joined Pete at the door. She tapped him on the shoulder to let him know she was behind him, and he moved fast, out of the room and firing. Turned out that he was firing deliberately high, because when I followed him and Eve out, the guards were down behind overturned steel tables. There was a lot of confused shouting going on.

We ran the gauntlet before they could get organized, because there wasn't much else we *could* do. Eve broke off and ran to Michael's cage, which I wouldn't have let her do if I'd had any kind of choice in the matter, but she was thinking ahead; she'd lifted the keys from the guard we'd tackled, and as Pete kept the others' heads down, she fumbled through the selection and found the one that turned the lock.

Michael wasn't nearly as debilitated as he looked. He uncoiled himself from the ball he'd been in, crawled out, and lunged at Eve.

For a scary second, I was afraid she'd just signed her death warrant, but it was just a hug, not a full-on attack; his fangs stayed in, and the energy of rising to his feet seemed to be just about all he had, because he sagged against her almost immediately, and she had to drag/carry him toward the door. I caught a glimpse of his face over her shoulder—my boy Mikey was *back*. Not well, not by half, but that was him, looking at me through those blue eyes.

You go, bro.

It all took about ten seconds, but it seemed like half an hour to make it to the far side of the room; the guards started firing back at us within half that time, and Pete stopped aiming over their heads and started punching neat holes into the steel tables they were hiding behind. That kept them down. I almost went over backward as Liz started kicking and writhing; she was taller than

Claire, and strong, and panicked. I let her slide off as we reached the far doorway, and she nearly collapsed as she tried to take her weight on both feet. When she tried to break free of me, I yanked her closer. "I'm Claire's boyfriend!" I yelled at her. I guess the blood dripping all over my face didn't make me look any more trustworthy, because she didn't seem reassured. "Go!" I shoved her ahead of me, and she stumbled on barely functioning legs to the closed steel door.

It didn't open.

"Eve!" I yelled, and gestured for the gun she was firing. She tossed it to me and lunged for the door, trying keys with frantic haste. The semiauto pistols that Pete and I were firing each carried fifteen shots, but Pete was already down at least nine, and Eve had popped off four. It wouldn't last long if we were trying to intimidate a room full of guys with bullets and the hard-core training to use them.

None of Eve's keys worked. She grimly started over, trying them again, and I used four more of our bullet inventory. I hoped I wasn't hitting anybody, but at that moment, I wasn't really opposed to it, either.

Michael came through for us. He moved Eve out of the way, grabbed hold of the handle, and yanked, hard. It broke off, and he pushed the hardware through on the other side, reached in, and pulled back the tongue on the lock. Then he half collapsed again, and Eve had to drag him out by the arms into the hallway.

We weren't out of the fire, but at least we were off the frying pan, and I know Pete breathed a sigh of relief as we escaped. Michael yelled something I didn't catch, and then he got to his feet and charged forward—by vampire standards, it was more of a lumbering stumble than a charge, because he wasn't moving any faster than the rest of us. But he took down a guy aiming at Eve, tackled him to the floor, and his vampire instincts finally kicked in. I heard the low-in-the-throat snarl, saw the flash of fangs coming down, and felt a sudden answering burn inside. It came from my arm first; I'd almost forgotten the bite I'd gotten there before I left Morganville, but this reminded me, hard enough to make me stagger and catch myself against the wall. The pain crawled up to my shoulder, and spread like fire over the network of my bones, and I didn't know what the hell was happening to me. I sagged, coughing, and heard Pete demanding to know if I'd been hit. I shook my head.

I wasn't wounded, but I felt sick, really sick, and I knew it was Michael going vamp that had triggered it. Something was wrong with me. Very wrong. It was as if I was reacting to him.

Liz was confused and scared, and she bolted forward, trying to get free of all of us crazy people; I couldn't say I blamed her. We weren't exactly the world's most credible rescue crew ever, what with all the blood, Michael burying his fangs in a guy's throat, Eve ignoring it to scoop up his fallen weapon, and me trying to puke against the wall.

She didn't make it far.

Dr. Davis stepped out of the kitchen. He was holding a gun of his own, and he pointed it at Liz; she skidded, arms windmilling wildly as she tried to check her forward momentum. She didn't make it, and crashed against him. He grabbed her, put an arm around her neck, and hugged her to him as a human shield as Pete and Eve both focused their guns on him.

Michael finished with his dinner—I wish I could say that was a joke—and looked up at Davis, eyes glowing a shade of red that ought to exist only in horror movies. He licked his lips, but he didn't move from the crouch he was in. Somehow, that was more frightening.

And I was feeling something new now. Not better, exactly, but stronger. Faster. And with it, I felt an nearly uncontrollable need to rip Michael's head clean off his body. As if he was the only real enemy in the room.

I was pretty sure that last part was wrong.

I shook my head to try to clear it, and blood drops flew like sweat after a good workout. The cut in my head was still bleeding freely. I saw Michael sense it, *felt* him sense it, and something inside me grinned in anticipation, and roared for him to try it.

Michael didn't come at me, and somehow, I managed to stuff down that impulse to go at him. *Liz,* I reminded myself. The girl was clueless and in danger, and neither one of us needed the distraction right now of whatever weird thing was going on inside me.

"I'll kill her," Dr. Davis said, and backed toward the door; he was dragging her with him. I realized that we were in a bottleneck, and his guys would come boiling out of the clean room behind us any second; I backed up, grabbed the steel door, and muscled it shut. No way to lock it now that Michael had busted us out, but at least it would slow them down. Not for long, though. I heard them sliding metal tables out of the way.

Eve stepped forward toward Dr. Douche Bag, and she looked like an ice-cold warrior princess, if warrior princesses came armed with semiautos this season. "Go ahead," she said. "As soon as you do, you're dead."

He licked his lips, and I saw the doubt in his face. I didn't *think* Eve would pull the trigger in cold blood, but I wasn't really sure, either.

Neither was he. Standoff. It couldn't last, because his rein-

forcements were coming at speed, and ours—well. We didn't actually have any that I knew about. Our only chance was to make it
outside to the van, hope the car keys were on the ring Eve had ap-
propriated, and drive like holy hell.

That also meant leaving Claire behind, though. And while I
wouldn't shed much of a tear for the vampires with her, there was
no way I was leaving this damned farm without my girl.

I didn't have to, as it turned out.

The front door opened behind Dr. Douche Bag, and Claire
stepped inside. She looked tired, stressed, roughed up, and anxious, and her eyes skimmed over us, cataloguing the situation and
resting for a long second on mine. I couldn't tell what she was
thinking or feeling, but my God, I loved her when she took one
long step forward, pressed the gun in her hand into Dr. Davis's
back, and said, very calmly, "Let her go."

I would have probably added, *you giant bag of dicks,* but that
worked just fine. Davis looked as surprised as Wile E. Coyote sus-
pended over a canyon, and he dropped his weapon and let Liz go,
fast. Liz lurched away a step or two, then came back and grabbed
the gun, which she pointed right at the good doctor's face.

Yow. That did *not* look friendly. For a sick, breathless second, I
really thought the girl was going to do it . . . and then she backed
off, shaking.

Davis sank down to a crouch, hands up, clearly full of surrender.

"Come on," Claire said. "Come *on,* we have to go. *Right now!*"

She didn't need to issue a formal invitation. We all bolted to
follow her as she left. The farmhouse behind us was ringing with
shouts, and I heard the steel door scrape open; we didn't have
long before they had us in their crosshairs. To add more trouble,

there were three guards coming out of the barn across the gravel yard.

They were dragging three limp vampires by their feet.

I don't know why, but that sight shocked me. Myrnin, Oliver, Jesse—not just vampire-pale, but blue-white. Dead white. My God, what had *happened* in there?

The guards yelled when they saw us, dropped their cargo, and went for their weapons. We made it to the shelter of the van before they were able to draw and fire, and I slid the door back to let Michael in first—he was already burning in the sunlight—and Eve, Pete, and Liz piled in next.

Claire didn't get in. She put her back against the cold metal, breathing hard, and she seemed to feel as sick as I did. Seriously, my whole bloodstream was on fire, and if we hadn't been in a live-or-die situation, I probably would have been collapsing under the pain . . . but for now, that had to go away. Better to burn than eat bullets.

"I killed them," she told me. She sounded devastated. "I thought—I thought I was saving them. But I think I just killed them."

She was right. The three vampires lay in the sun, not moving. Oliver's skin had started to smoke a little, like mist coming off a lake. It wouldn't take long for him to blacken, and then to start to burn. The others would follow. Myrnin was old, Jesse might be even older, I wasn't sure. But in the end, they'd be ashes and bones.

It was going to kill her, knowing she was the cause of all this.

"Get in," I told her. Eve had already scrambled into the driver's seat and was trying keys from the ring; one worked, and the engine caught. "We have to go. Right now."

And we tried. We really did. I got Claire into the van, piled in after, slid the door shut, and Eve gunned it in a tight, gravel-spewing circle to head for the exit.

Another van accelerated forward to block us in.

She backed up, yelled, "Hang on," and busted through the white rail fence next to the barn, bumping and churning through the dry furrows of a field and heading at an angle for the farm road that had led us here.

We didn't get far before the van—no off-roader—bogged down. The tires spun dirt but couldn't find purchase, and as Eve rocked it back and forth, she just dug us in deeper.

Stuck.

We had a grand total of four guns, one half-empty, one almost gone, two nearly full. We had a vampire who was looking a little more himself, but still operating at about a quarter speed, at best.

We had me, who was shaking with the need to shoot his best friend and rip his dead body apart, for absolutely no logical reason that I could think of . . . and it terrified me. It was as if I was possessed.

I looked at Claire, hoping that she had some miracle up her sleeve, some genius move that would get us out of this.

But Claire looked, in that moment, like a vulnerable eighteen-year-old girl, scared and numbed and overwhelmed, and I dragged her into my arms and held her because that seemed like the only thing I *could* do, hold her. Try, in that last desperate moment, to keep her safe. Because any second now, they were going to surround this van and riddle it with enough bullets to make us look like a drug cartel piñata. They had nothing to lose. We'd proved we weren't going to be useful to them, and Dr. Anderson didn't need Claire anymore if she'd just destroyed their vampire stock of lab rats.

And Michael would live through that. Sadly.

"I killed them," she whispered to me. Her voice was shaking, and I felt hot tears wet against my skin. "Oh *God*, Shane, I killed them . . ."

I couldn't do anything but hold her. I don't know if it helped her, but it helped me push back the violent impulses inside of me that said I ought to take out the only remaining vampire among us, before it was too late.

The gunfire started, and I flinched and threw Claire to the van floor, covering her. I heard the others hitting the deck, too. I waited for the sound of metal punching in, glass breaking . . . but it didn't come.

Whatever they were firing at, *it wasn't us.*

I waited for a few more seconds, then carefully rose to a crouch. I couldn't see a thing out the front windows, because we were pointed the wrong way, but if nobody was firing at us, it was giving us a chance we couldn't waste.

I opened the van's side door. "Out! Everybody out! Run for it!"

I didn't even know where we'd go, but staying where we were wasn't an option. Being out in the sun was going to be hell for Michael, though, and I looked around for something to help him. I found a plastic tarp rolled up in a bin behind the driver's seat, and I tossed it to him; he broke the rope that held it closed and draped the thing around him like a portable tent.

"I'll go first," he said. "Watch Eve."

I nodded. With him so close to me, it was hard not to do something violent. The conflict inside was tearing me apart, but I tried not to let it show; even so, Michael gave me a weird look before he bailed out, blue tarp flapping around him like the world's most heavily waterproofed cloak. Pete and Liz followed, then Eve.

Claire and I were the last ones out.

"What are you doing?" I yelled. "Move—" Because the rest had stopped dead where they were, only a few feet from the van.

And then I saw why.

The guards were down. Well, one was still running and firing wildly, but as I watched, Jesse—Lady Gray—took a running leap that crossed at least twenty feet of space. She landed flat-footed in front of him, grabbed him by the throat, and tossed him twenty feet *back*, to Oliver, who caught him and—well, broke him. I tried not to see more of that than I had to.

Myrnin was up, too, although all I saw of him was a flicker of motion as he disappeared into the barn. Oliver finished up with the guard, nodded to Jesse, and he followed Myrnin.

She went into the farmhouse. And then there was screaming.

There was a lot of screaming.

"Jesus," Eve whispered. She crossed herself, an involuntary motion dragged up from childhood habit; what we were seeing was something that not even I had seen before: vampires let loose from all their inhibitions. The purest expression of predator.

It was bloody terrifying.

"They're—they're killing—" Claire was shaking now, and her face was blank. "They're killing everyone."

I put my arms around her and didn't say anything. I concentrated on breathing, on trying to cool the fire in my blood; it wasn't getting easier. In fact, now that the three older vamps were back in the game—and sweeping the table clean—it was actually worse. These instincts were screaming at me to do something.

Kill them. Kill them all.

I dropped the gun I was holding. I was afraid to keep holding it. I wasn't sure I could control this thing inside me too much longer.

Myrnin emerged from the barn. He was still icy pale, like a walking corpse, and he was holding two big, clumsy guns—the things that Claire had developed and used to bring down vampires. One of them was trailing wires and broken circuitry.

I thought we could use the one of those that still worked just now, because Jesse came out of the farmhouse, and she looked *unholy*. I didn't think anything could be left alive in there. There was just that vibe coming off of her—one of dark, total destruction.

Oliver came out of the barn as well. I'd seen him in relaxed moods, almost in good ones; I'd known him as a pseudo-friendly hippie coffee shop owner, and as a snarky, superior man with a violent edge.

But I didn't know this version of him. It was all vampire, all the time. A god of death.

He stood there in full sun, white as marble, staring at us with eyes red as rubies, and slowly smiled. His fangs were out, and it was incredibly creepy. He was burning, turning black in the sun. And he didn't even care.

Michael stepped forward, hidden under the tarp, and said, "Are you finished?" He didn't sound spooked, or bothered. I guessed that all this was normal to him, on some really horrible level. He understood. "Because all that's left here are friends. Understand?"

Oliver nodded.

I wasn't at all sure it was anything but a gesture, and I braced myself for the attack.

FIFTEEN

Seeing Oliver, Jesse, and Myrnin that way—reduced to their purest hunting instincts—had terrified Claire on a very deep level, but the scariest moment was at the end, when Oliver had no one left to fight.

No one but them.

For a long, long few seconds Claire was convinced he was about to take them out too . . . and then he just turned and walked away.

"Wait," Claire said. Shane tried to hush her, probably scared that attracting Oliver's attention was a very bad idea—and he was likely right about that—but she had to know. "Did you kill them all?"

"What did you expect us to do?" he snapped without turning toward her.

Claire felt numbed by it all now; she knew on some level that killing all these people had been necessary, because they'd been doing their level best to kill her friends, but . . . but she couldn't face it. She started for the barn, but Shane held her back. "No," he said. "Claire, don't. You don't need to see that."

"What about Dr. Anderson?"

"Ah," Myrnin said. "I almost forgot." He flashed back inside the barn, and when he came out, he was dragging Dr. Anderson by the collar of her lab coat.

She was alive. Bruised, battered, but *alive*. He'd put her into one of the straitjackets they'd used on him and Oliver, and strapped it too tightly for her to move, though she was trying to fight her way free. He'd also gagged her.

Good. Claire couldn't imagine anything she wanted to hear from her right now. She was overwhelmed by the conviction that if she hadn't started all this by her stupid little project, those *stupid* VLAD guns, then none of it would have had to happen.

None of those people would be dead right now.

Oliver and Jesse, meanwhile, walked out to the van that lay stranded and stuck in the field. The two of them easily picked it up and carried it back to the gravel. "We need to go," Oliver said. Dr. Anderson was screaming behind the cloth, and trying to kick at Jesse, who ignored her. "We'll take both vans. Myrnin will ride with you. Michael . . . ?"

"We'll come with you," Michael said, and Eve nodded. He turned to Shane, and something strange passed between the two of them that Claire couldn't understand. She'd thought they were good, but there was some kind of caution there, some wary distance. "See you back home?"

Shane nodded. "Be safe, man. You okay?"

"Better," Michael said. He sounded more like himself, at least; he wasn't as pallid as the other vampires, and he seemed less . . . alien, somehow. *What did I do to them?* Claire wondered. She'd had to make guesses about how to adjust VLAD's settings, and she hadn't been at all sure that it would be enough to reverse the effects of the first blasts . . . she'd been right about the reversal, but it seemed to have done something else, too. Something scarier. It was as if their essential humanity had been stripped away. Even Myrnin's. She couldn't meet his gaze; it was too strange, too . . . too frightening.

"We can't just leave all this here," Shane said. "For one thing, our DNA's all over the place."

"What do you propose?" Oliver asked.

"Well, it's a farm. There's gasoline and fertilizer."

Pete nodded, suddenly looking a lot steadier than he'd been. "I'll help you," he said. He and Shane moved to a storage building next to the barn, and began rolling out drums and equipment. It didn't take long, with vampire help, to wire up improvised bombs— something Shane had learned from his dad, Claire assumed—and set them in both the barn and farmhouse.

"What was this?" Claire asked numbly. "I—who *are* they?"

"Were," Myrnin said. "They were from the Daylight Foundation."

"But what do they want?" She was shivering now, shuddering, and she half expected Myrnin to notice, to ask if she was all right.

He didn't. There was nothing in him right now that cared.

"They want vampires dead," he said, and the slow, cruel smile on his face chilled her into ice. "The war has been coming for a while now. But they've chosen the wrong way to start it in earnest."

Shane came back with Pete, and they all climbed into the van. In this vehicle they had Liz, Pete, Claire, Shane, and Myrnin; Eve was the only human in the other van, mainly because Michael could probably protect only one of them at a time.

Myrnin was looking at Liz and Pete. "Now, what shall we do with these two?"

Claire shuddered at the lack of feeling in his words, and quickly said, "They're okay, Myrnin. They'll be fine."

"They are not Morganville," he said. "And they are not fine." He put down the weapons, and before Claire could stop him, he grabbed Liz and pulled her close. Claire and Liz both screamed, and Pete lunged forward. Shane would have, but he'd just climbed into the driver's seat. None of that mattered. Myrnin ignored Pete's attempt to pull him off, just as he ignored Claire's words that tumbled out begging him not to hurt her, and Liz's struggles to pull free.

Then Liz stopped screaming. She went entirely still in Myrnin's hands, staring into his eyes, and Claire swallowed and let go. She wanted a weapon—a silver one, preferably—but there was nothing in the van that could really hurt Myrnin.

Nothing but VLAD.

Pete had already thought of it, and he picked one of the two up—the damaged one. God only knew if it would work, but if it did, it would only make things worse. "Not that one!" Claire yelped, and scrambled over to grab the other. "Put it down!" Pete did, and Claire turned VLAD—the original version—on Myrnin. "Please. Please don't make me do this. I don't want to do this."

"Claire," Shane said softly. "Don't."

Because Myrnin's head had turned toward her, and the look he gave her was bone-chilling. It wasn't a human sort of expression. She remembered what they used to call him, in the bad old days; what his neighbor in Morganville Gramma Day still called him.

Trap-door spider. This was the old, worst version of Myrnin, and the most powerful.

"Put that down, or I'll snap her head off like a daisy and beat you with it," he said. It was almost a purr. "I'm not intending to hurt her. But I'll happily do it if you try to use *that* on me again. And I won't stop with her. Do you really want to be trapped in this van with me in a murder-crazed state?"

He sounded rational, but he wasn't, and Claire froze. She didn't dare try to shoot. He was fast, ridiculously so, and he'd move the barrel aside in these close quarters and then . . . then it would be a bloodbath.

He'd probably be sorry later. Probably.

She put the weapon down.

Myrnin turned his gaze back on Liz, who seemed terrified and mesmerized at the same time. "Now," he said, in that same warm, terrifying purr. "Let's see what it would be best for you to remember. Ah, I know. You were abducted and held here at this place. You don't know what their business was, but you believed that they dealt in drugs and slaves." He paused and frowned, then looked confused. "Do they still have slaves these days?"

"Sex slaves," Shane said. "Yeah."

"Ah. How unpleasant. Very well, they dealt in drugs and sex slaves here at this place. There was an attack by some rival force. Everyone was killed. Then the farmhouse was destroyed. You were lucky to escape with your life by hiding in the fields." He released Liz, who sank back to the floor with her back against the van's wall. "She'll remember nothing else. Don't speak to her. She won't be able to respond, for now."

Claire had no idea Myrnin could do something like this—though she supposed she should have known. He'd built a machine that could wipe out human memories. He'd have been able to do that only if he'd had the ability to do it himself, and known the techniques. But she'd never really seen him do it, full on.

He looked completely alien to her right now. *I've turned him up to eleven*, she thought, and had to choke back a terrified, completely insane laugh. This was a very bad idea, having Myrnin in a small enclosed space with four tempting pulses. He'd be hungry. He'd *have* to be hungry.

"Yes, I am, a bit," he said, and she blinked. That terribly disturbing smile grew wider. "Does it surprise you I can read your thoughts? Your own fault, Claire. You turned on parts of my brain that I'd shut down years ago. For safety. I imagine that Oliver and Jesse are having much the same issue. I do hope that Eve doesn't irritate them too much. I don't hold out much hope for poor Irene, but then, she did bring it on herself."

"Myrnin—"

He shook his head. "Leave it." Then he turned toward Pete, and riveted him in place with a stare. "Now, for you. I think it's best you were never here. I'd just leave you to burn with the rest, but you *are* Jesse's friend, after all. She wouldn't appreciate that. So here is your story: You were home, sleeping. You don't know anything about this entire affair. In fact, you drank too much. When you do make it home, that's precisely what you'll do: drink too much. I'd like this to be as accurate as possible." Pete sank down against the van's wall, next to Liz, staring straight ahead. He and Liz were both in some sort of limbo, held there by the power of Myrnin's mind. It was unsettling how powerful he was right now.

"Shane," Myrnin said, and her boyfriend turned face forward.

"If you try to mess with my head, Count Dickula, I'll rip your throat out," Shane said. There was a tense, trembling flatness to his voice that Claire didn't remember ever having heard before, but he was probably just as freaked out as she felt right now. "And don't you even *think* about touching Claire. I mean it."

"Drive," Myrnin said. He didn't seem ruffled. He didn't even, truthfully, seem to pay attention to what Shane had said. Claire hesitated, looking from him to the blank, zombified stares of Pete and Liz, and finally scrambled up to take the passenger seat of the van. She belted in just as Shane hit the gas.

"Just so you know, I didn't drive just because he made me from the power of his mind," Shane said. "I did it because the sooner I can get him out of here, the better I'm going to feel." He hesitated, and reached over to take her hand as he steered the big van over the rutted gravel road. Claire sighed in relief at the touch of his warm hand, and the feeling of safety it gave her to be in contact with him again. "Are you okay?"

She laughed. She couldn't help it, and it had a distinctly crazy edge to it that earned her an alarmed look from him. "*Okay?* No. No, we just left a whole bunch of dead people back there, Shane. *Dead people.*"

"I'm aware of that. But they were kind of trying to kill us hard and ugly. You don't really think they'd have let us get out of there alive, do you?"

"I don't know. I just—" The feelings boiled up in her again— despair, hopelessness, guilt. Anger, too. Anger at herself, and Myrnin, and Oliver, and Jesse, and . . . the world. But mostly at herself, for all the mistakes she'd made. "It's my fault." All the misery distilled down into that one, nuclear-hot three-word sentence. Toxic. And Claire covered her face with her hands, fighting back tears.

"Ah, yes, lovely. The guilt phase. Just what we needed," she heard Myrnin sigh, and heard his head bang hard against the van.

Shane didn't say anything. He just put his hand on her leg and kept it there, a gentle and constant pressure, as they drove on into the rising light of day.

They were about a mile out when the explosives went off. Claire gasped at the fireball and looked behind them; the other black van with the rest of their survivors was there, following closely. The smoke rose up into the clear morning air like a black balloon, and in another five minutes they'd gained the intersection with the interstate. Shane relaxed as they merged with traffic, heading for Boston. On the access road, sirens wailed—fire and rescue and police, heading out to the scene of the explosion.

Claire dried her tears on her sleeve and took in deep, centering breaths. "Are we going to get away with this?" she asked.

"Depends," Shane said. He was watching the rearview mirror with special intensity. "If anyone connects these vans with the farm, and the explosions, maybe not. But they're pretty generic, and if we're lucky, most of Dr. Anderson's little playmates were out there at that farm. Even if they weren't, I don't think they're going to be interested in talking to the cops about what kind of weird operation they had going—way too many questions to be answered. If we can hit it out of town and get back to Morganville, we're fine."

"Promise?" Claire asked.

"I promise," Shane said. "I promise you, we'll be all right."

It was a promise he couldn't keep, she knew that, but she loved him intensely for trying. All the differences she'd thought existed between them . . . those had fallen away, when it counted. She'd craved a normal life at MIT, but now . . . now, she had to face the fact that Morganville was never letting go of her. Even when she'd thought she was escaping for a while, it had followed her. No, it had been *waiting* for her.

And look what it had cost, this little bit of freedom. Look how many lives she'd ruined.

Claire let her eyes close. She was suddenly, overwhelmingly tired, and honestly, she had no idea how she was ever going to feel better, ever again.

She didn't have any memory of sleeping, but when she opened her eyes again, Shane was pulling the van in at the curb near Pete's apartment. It looked quiet and peaceful; no sign of police, nothing unusual. "I think we're good," Shane said. "So how does this work, exactly? You just whammy him and dump him on the sidewalk?"

"If you mean, do I complete the removal of his memories and send him inside to drink himself into an unconscious stupor, yes. Exactly," Myrnin said. He sounded a little more himself, and when Claire glanced back she saw that he was sitting slumped against the van wall, looking tired. He was kneading his forehead with the heel of his hand, as if it hurt. His color looked better, too . . . not quite so luminously white. "But first I must consult with Lady Gray."

"Jesse? Why?"

"Because he is her vassal, not mine," Myrnin said. He slid the door open, took a second to prepare himself, and then launched himself out of the van and down the sidewalk at a deliberately normal pace to the other van parked behind them. The door slid open for him, and he climbed inside.

"We could just drive off," Shane said. "Might be a good plan, actually."

"Might be," Claire agreed, "but you know they'd just track us down."

"Can't run, can't hide," he agreed. "Sucks to be us, right?"

"It never sucks if you're with me," she said, very quietly. He looked over at her, gave her a heart-melting smile.

"There are all kinds of completely inappropriate things I could say right now, but I'll be a good boy."

They were quiet for a moment, and then Shane said, "Heads up," and Claire saw in the side-view mirror that Myrnin was coming back, with Jesse. The two of them climbed in and slid the door closed, and Jesse crouched down across from Pete. She looked better, too—less feral, more in control. "Pete," she said. "It's Jesse. Can you hear me?"

"Yes," he said. That was probably the flattest tone Claire had ever heard from him. "I hear you."

"Pete, I need you to tell everyone at the bar, and everyone who comes asking, that I left town. You don't know where I went, only that I hooked up with a guy from my past." She looked at Myrnin, and smiled, briefly. "Nothing strange about it. I'm fine. I'll call you when I get settled. Understand?"

"Yes," he said. "You're leaving town. But you'll call when you get settled."

"Good," she said. She leaned forward and kissed him gently on the lips, then the forehead. "You've been a good friend, Pete. I'm so sorry you got caught up in all this, but you're not going to remember any of it in a few minutes. Just remember that I love you, all right?"

"I love you, too," he said. For a moment, the old Pete was back, and he blinked at her. "Jesse? Did you just kiss me?"

She laughed. "Only a little. Don't think it means we're engaged." She leaned forward and brushed his short-cropped hair affectionately. "Take care of yourself, Pete. Maybe I'll be back. Stranger things have happened."

"Definitely," he said, and smiled, just a little. "See you."

She sat back on her heels, and nodded at Myrnin, who leaned in and captured Pete's stare. It seemed to take more effort for him now, but Pete's expression smoothed out and took on that blankness again, and Myrnin said, "Go home, Pete. You remember what I told you to do?"

"Yes," Pete said. "Go home. Drink. Forget everything that happened today except what Jesse just said."

"Exactly so. Good-bye, Pete."

"Good-bye," Pete said, and climbed out of the van. He walked to his front door, opened it, and was inside in thirty seconds.

Myrnin slid the van door shut. "Next, we say good-bye to your friend, Claire. And we get what's needed and head home."

"What if I don't want to go?" Claire asked. She wasn't serious, but it was almost worth seeing his double take. And Shane's very anxious expression.

"You can't stay here."

"You could at least ask me what I want to do," she said. "But yes, I know staying here isn't an option. Not anymore. There're too many questions. And too much chance I could be connected to what happened out there. At the very least, Liz is going to be connected, and that means I'll be questioned as well. Plus, my boyfriend's basically a wanted felon."

"So not my fault," Shane said. He put the van in gear, and it was a short drive to the row house Claire shared with Liz. There were no signs of police, at least, though there was some kind of official seal on the door. "We're not going to want to hang around here, guys. I'm guessing my picture's been passed around, at the very least."

"It'll be fast," Claire said. She got out of the van, leading Liz by the hand, and walked her up the steps. She broke the seal on the door with her house keys, opened up, and shut the door behind them. Inside, the lights were off, and the house smelled like unwashed dishes and old wood.

Liz blinked and looked around, like a sleepwalker just coming out of a coma. "I— What happened—Claire? Claire, I— Those people, they took me...." She blinked again, and Claire saw the horror dawning in her eyes. "Oh God, I can't believe I got away. They were going to sell me!"

"I know," Claire said softly. "But you're safe now, sweetie. Derrick was one of them. He's gone now. You're going to be all right."

Liz burst into tears, and Claire managed to get her into her room, bundled her in bed, and sat with her for a few minutes until Liz fell into an exhausted, restless sleep.

Then she went upstairs.

I can leave all this, she thought. There were only a few things she really needed—memories, mostly. Things that mattered. They went into one suitcase.

She sat down and wrote a note, for Liz. And the police, because they'd be looking, too.

Liz, it said. *I'm sorry, but you were right. MIT's not for me. I'm a small-town girl at heart, and the pressure here is too intense. I miss my friends, and I miss my boyfriend, and I miss the life I had back home. So I'm going. I'll send for my things in a couple of weeks once I'm settled again. I'm sorry about the apartment, and I hope you will be okay without me. Call me soon. Your BFF— Claire.*

It wasn't much, but it sounded right, and it had the virtue of being true . . . all except the BFF part, but Liz would have expected that.

Claire left the note on the bed, grabbed her suitcase, and headed out to the van. She ducked inside, put the suitcase down, and strapped herself into the passenger seat.

"Ready?" Shane asked.

She nodded.

They drove past the MIT campus, and she got one last look at the domed beauty of the Maclaurin Buildings, flanked by the Pierce Lab and Building 2. Overnight, someone had put an old-school MTV spaceman on top of the Great Dome, complete with stiff little American flag. Someone had done another brand-new hack, a giant Transformers statue in Killian Court; a student walked up and pressed a button, and it glided from robot into car, complete with movie sound effects. The assembled crowd cheered, then dispersed to their classes.

I could have been one of them, Claire thought. She could have been a roof and tunnel hacker. She could have hung out with Nick and his crew. She could have been Jack Florey leading an orange tour. She could have done anything.

But instead, she was doing this. Heading back to Morganville.

And to her surprise—her great surprise, actually—it was all okay. *I'm not meant to be out here,* she thought. Where she went, Morganville went, and the last thing she wanted to do was bring that darkness here, into this light.

"Be safe," she whispered, to nobody in particular, as they took the next turn and headed for the freeway, and home.

———

In Ohio, they ditched the vans, selling them for cash to a scrap-yard and buying two big dinosaur SUVs. Having two, they decided, would allow four vampires and four humans to travel in relative comfort, and being able to change vehicles meant they probably wouldn't kill each other before the trip was over.

Whatever VLAD's beams had done to Oliver, Jesse, and Myrnin had mostly worn off. They looked, and sounded, more like themselves, less like cold-blooded killing machines. But Claire couldn't quite forget what they'd been, back on the farm.

She knew she'd never forget it again. What they could be.

Michael and Eve chose to travel with her and Shane for a while, with the three other vamps and Dr. Anderson in the second vehi-cle, and that should have felt normal again. Better.

But it didn't.

Maybe it was just the exhaustion, the stress, the shattering weight of guilt, but Claire felt they were all trying to figure out how to talk to her. What to say.

She had no idea what to say either. Not for a long, long time.

Eve fiddled with the stereo, seeking out alt-rock stations until all that was left was static, and finally switched it off. Shane was napping by then, and Michael driving. Claire should have been sleeping, too, but she couldn't.

"Claire?"

She opened her eyes, which had drifted closed, and saw Eve watching her from the front. "I'm awake."

"I just—look, I need to know. How much of what happened did you plan?"

"When?"

"From the time we came out from rescuing Liz from that trap. Did you even *have* a plan?"

"I—" Claire swallowed. Her throat felt suddenly dry, tight, and uncomfortable. "Not until I knew Dr. Anderson was against us. Then I had to—I had to play along. She knew too much. And she didn't need anybody except the vampires, for lab tests. She only needed me as far as she could trust me, so I—I had to make her trust me, a little."

"You turned on us," Eve said. "You made Shane turn on us, too, didn't you?"

"I'm sorry," Claire whispered. "But it was all out of control, Eve. I didn't know how else to do it."

Eve stared at her for another long, painful moment, and then reached her hand back. Claire didn't know what to do for a second; then she grabbed hold. "Don't ever do it again," Eve said. "I don't like feeling that way, okay? It's the four of us, always. Promise."

"I promise," Claire said. Tears welled up in her eyes, and she cried a little, holding Eve's hand. "I promise."

Shane wasn't asleep after all, because he sat up, put his arm around Claire, and said, "We promise."

"You'd better, jerkface," Eve said. "How's the head?"

"Taped," he said. "It's fine. Chicks dig scars. Wait, did you just call me jerkface? Are we back in grade school?"

"I love you," Eve said.

He closed his mouth, fast, because obviously that was not what he'd expected. "I, uh, okay. Love you, too. Can we stop that? It's uncomfortable."

"Jerkface."

"Much better."

In the morning, Shane became the designated driver of one of the trucks, and Jesse took command of the other. They got as far as they could, and then Oliver booked them hotel rooms that night. He, Myrnin, and Jesse each got their own accommodations; Michael and Eve, of course, shared theirs.

Oliver handed Shane and Claire each key cards. "I have no knowledge of, nor interest in, your current relationship," he said. "Use both, use one, use neither, or sleep in the van. Whatever you choose that involves me the least." Like Jesse and Myrnin, Oliver was looking absolutely exhausted. He kept Irene Anderson with him, but Myrnin had—in Shane's terms—whammied her into submission. She stayed passive, and Oliver didn't even need to tie her up.

Claire didn't want to know what Oliver intended to do with her. She still couldn't quite bring herself to care.

She paused with her suitcase at the door of her room, and looked down the hall. Shane was puzzling out his own key card, finding out which way the arrow went into the lock; he sensed her looking, and sent her a nod.

Claire nodded back, walked into her room, and set the suitcase on the bed. She stripped her clothes off—clothes she never intended to wear again—and got into the shower. The hotel's shampoo and conditioner smelled like honey and ginger, and the soap smelled like lime; she decided that she would end up smelling like someone's kitchen pantry, but at least it was better than how she'd been smelling, like sewers and blood and fear.

She put on a clean pair of jeans, a plain blue top, and walked down to Shane's room. She knocked.

He answered. He'd been in the shower, too . . . his hair was still damp, and he was wearing the hotel bathrobe.

"Hi," she said, and came in. She closed the door behind her. "I don't want to spend another night alone, if that's okay with you."

"You seriously think I might object to that."

"No," she said, and stepped in closer to take hold of the tie of his robe. "But how about this? Any objections?" She untied one loop of the knot, and hesitated. He was watching her with a strangely vulnerable intensity. "Shane?"

"I love you," he said. It came out in a rush, as if he couldn't wait to get it out. "I love you and, Jesus, you scare me. Having to give you up was the hardest thing I've ever done, Claire; I can't do it again. Please tell me—please tell me that you're coming back for good. Or at least, if you leave, let me go with you."

"You came with me this time."

"I *followed* you. I didn't come *with* you." It seemed to be important to him that she understand the difference. And she did, she really did.

"I needed to be away from Morganville," she told him then, "and I needed to be sure what it was I really wanted. Do I want what I had back there, for a little while? That normal life? It was nice, Shane, but . . . but it's not me. Not anymore. It's too late for me to live that life. But not too late for us to live our life together. If you still want—"

"Yes," he said. "Yes, I want. If you don't believe me, untie the rest of the knot."

She laughed a little, and moved into his arms. The kiss started soft, turned urgent and sweet and damp, and then he walked her back to the feathery hotel bed and stretched her out on the duvet. Everything seemed warm, and in its comfort, in his comfort, she floated.

No. In his comfort, in his warmth, in his passion, she *flew*.

And when she floated back to earth, he was still there, warm and safe, holding her.

Before she drifted off to sleep, he kissed her hand. No, the ring that he'd given her, that promise of a someday-life together.

After all the grief, all the guilt, all the horror of the night and the day . . . he was the one thing that held it back.

He was the thing that would always give her that safe, warm space that made it possible to breathe.

In the morning, they started for Morganville.

It took another two solid days of driving, day and night, with brief stops at motels for showers and naps, but finally, they rolled past the familiar, antique faded glory of the WELCOME TO MORGANVILLE billboard. And they were greeted by the flashing lights of a police car, coming toward them at high speed.

Shane pulled over, and Jesse nosed her SUV in behind him on the side of the road. Shane stretched and yawned and said, "Damn, I never actually thought I'd be happy to see this place again, but I am seriously missing my bed." Michael, behind them, leaned over the seat to slap Shane on the shoulder.

"Me, too, man," he said. "If I have to spend another day in this car wearing hats and tarps to keep the sun off, I think I'm going to need some kind of tranquilizer."

"Hey, we had fun," Eve said, and pinched his earlobe. "In the sense of next to none at all, I mean. Next time, can we at least stop at a mall? Maybe see a movie? Avoid the mass murders of our enemies, maybe?"

"Promise," Michael agreed, but it was an absent kind of

comment, and he leaned forward to peer out through the dark windows. "Is that Sheriff Moses?"

"Looks like," Shane said. He opened the SUV's door and stepped out as Hannah Moses approached. She wasn't alone, Claire realized; there were two other men with her, dressed in Morganville PD uniforms. And more police cars coming, lights flashing.

Too many for comfort.

Somehow, Claire wasn't too surprised when Hannah drew her gun. Shane slowly raised his hands.

"I'm sorry about this, Shane," she said. "But laws are laws, and I don't want you doing anything stupid. You too, Claire, Michael, Eve—all of you, out of the car. Now."

All the good feelings were gone, Claire thought, and she climbed down from the truck's cab to stand next to Shane, leaning against the fender. Michael and Eve got out, too. Wind shivered over the desert, and drew icy fingers down Claire's face. The other police car parked behind the second SUV, and more cops arrived, all pointing guns.

"What's the meaning of this?" Oliver demanded, as he got out of the second vehicle. Myrnin stepped down with him, dark eyes flashing around in restless motion, cataloguing everyone and everything. Jesse joined them, and she held Irene Anderson still as the professor tried to pull away. "There's surely no question of our right to entry!"

"Not at all," Hannah said. "But we have something we have to take care of first." She stepped up, fastened handcuffs around Shane's wrists, then Claire's, then Eve's. "I'll need that lady over there, too. Paul, put some cuffs on her and bring her over here. Michael, if you would, please stand over there." She pointed at Irene

Anderson, who was escorted over and handcuffed. Michael went to stand next to the other van.

It was weird and confusing, but there was no reason not to trust her; Hannah seemed the same as she always had. Competent, calm, professional.

It was only as they did it that Claire realized that Hannah had just separated the humans . . . from the vampires.

And then the cops stepped back, and two others stepped forward with double-loaded crossbows. It happened fast, so fast. Four quick shots, deadly accurate to the heart, and the vampires went down. Jesse first, then Myrnin, then Oliver and Michael almost in the same instant.

Eve screamed. Claire didn't. *It's wood,* she told herself. *They're staked with wood. They're not dead.* But she didn't know why this was happening, and worse, she didn't know why Hannah was doing it.

"Hannah?" Her voice sounded small and confused, and the police chief looked at her with sympathy, and no small amount of pity.

"They'll be all right," she said. "But they'll be taken to a safe place. I'm sorry, Claire. I'm sorry for everything. But it's for the best."

"Amelie's going to—"

"Amelie's not in charge," Hannah interrupted. "*We* are. For the first time, the humans have taken complete control of Morganville, with the help of the Daylight Foundation. And the vampires are being quarantined for their own protection."

"What are you doing to them?" Eve cried. She was fighting to get free, to get to Michael, but that wasn't going to happen.

"We're going to help them," Hannah said. She sounded utterly sure of what she was saying. "We're going to help them get better."

All this sounded like what Shane and Captain Obvious and so many others had been wanting for years, Claire thought. A Morganville run by humans, not by vampires.

Then why did it feel so *wrong*?

"We'll be okay," Shane said to her. It sounded like a prayer. "It's all going to be okay."

Somehow . . . Claire didn't think so.

TRACK LIST

Music gives me the road map for the story, and I hope you'll take a musical journey with me and explore these songs and artists. Please pay the musicians for their great work, too. They need your support.

"Too Close"	Alex Clare
"Let Her Go"	Passenger
"You Spin Me Round"	Dope
"The Departure"	Signs of Betrayal
"Girls in the Back"	White Rose Movement
"(I'm The One That's) Cool"	The Guild
"DLZ"	TV on the Radio
"Stronger (Piano Mix)"	Fallzone

"Animal"	Ellie Goulding
"The Way It Ends"	Landon Pigg
"Save Yourself"	June Halo
" 'Til The Casket Drops"	ZZ Ward
"Soulgate (feat. Lilith)"	The Wolf Meyer Orchestra
"Old Man"	Redlight King
"The Riddle"	Random Rab
"Unstoppable"	Pop Evil
"Top Drawer"	Man Man
"Bedroom Hymns"	Florence + The Machine
"Devils"	Say Hi
"Love Bites (So Do I)"	Halestorm
"Meyrin Fields"	Broken Bells
"Fool Notion"	The Black Sorrows
"Never Let Me Go"	Florence + The Machine
"Violet Hill"	Coldplay
"Soil to the Sun"	Cage the Elephant
"Undisclosed Desires"	Muse
"Be Somebody"	Thousand Foot Krutch
"Short Skirt/Long Jacket"	Cake
"Bang Bang Bang Bang"	Sohodolls
"Propane Nightmares"	Pendulum
"Feel Again"	OneRepublic
"Brictom"	Eluveitie
"A Sorta Fairytale"	Tori Amos
"The Bomb (Original Version)"	The New Young Pony Club
"Sticks and Stones"	The Pierces
"Watchman, What is Left of the Night?"	Greycoats
"Palaistinalied"	Qntal

"You Make the Rain Fall"	Kevin Rudolf & Flo Rida
"Jager Yoga"	CSS
"Stardog"	Adler's Appetite
"The Ghost Who Walks"	Karen Elson
"Hopelessly Stoned"	Hugo
"Sleep Alone"	Bat for Lashes
"Old Spur Line"	Legendary Shack Shakers
"I Drive Alone"	Esthero
"Trinity"	Paper Tongues
"Take Her From You"	Dev
"Try"	Pink
"Make Me Like the Moon"	Greycoats
"The Stations"	The Gutter Twins
"Idle Hands"	The Gutter Twins
"Beautiful Killer"	Madonna
"Meant"	Elizaveta